The
CODEBREAKER'S DAUGHTER

Also By Suzanne Fortin

The Dance Teacher of Paris
The Lost Dressmaker of Paris
The Girl in the Sky

The CODEBREAKER'S DAUGHTER

SUZANNE FORTIN

embla books

First published in the UK in 2025 by

embla books

An imprint of Bonnier Books UK
5th Floor, HYLO, 105 Bunhill Row,
London, EC1Y 8LZ

A CIP catalogue record for this book is available from the British Library.

ISBN: 9781471416392

Also available as an ebook and an audiobook

2

Typeset by IDSUK (Data Connection) Ltd
Printed and bound by CPI Group (UK) Ltd, Croydon, CR0 4YY

MIX
Paper | Supporting responsible forestry
FSC www.fsc.org FSC® C013604

The authorised representative in the EEA is Bonnier Books UK (Ireland) Limited.
Registered office address: Block B, The Crescent Building, Northwood, Santry, Dublin 9, D09 C6X8, Ireland
compliance@bonnierbooks.ie
www.bonnierbooks.co.uk

Chapter 1

Buckinghamshire, England, October 1942

'For ever and ever, Amen.' Hana Phillips looked up at the class of eight- and nine-year-olds before her. Their hands still together in prayer, they lifted their heads. Hana smiled at her students. 'Well done, everyone. Now if you all stand quietly and put your chairs on your tables.'

There was a scuffling and banging of the wooden chairs being pushed back across the floorboards and then plonked on the desks. It was three-thirty, and it didn't take long before the class of twenty children had completed the last task of the day.

Hana made her way through the desks to the door at the back of the village schoolroom which opened on to the cloakroom. 'File out, row by row,' shc said. 'Coats on. Don't forget your gloves and hats. It's chilly out there today.' The first row of children filed through the door. '*Mata ashita*,' said Hana to each of them in Japanese, followed by a small bow of her head. 'See you in the morning.' It always delighted her when the children returned the farewell in kind.

'*Mata ashita*, Mrs Phillips.'

Hana had been brought up bilingual in English and Japanese. Her father had been a Cambridge don, specialising in languages and, together with her parents and older brother, Hana had spent several years living in Japan, returning to England when she was seventeen. There was nothing Hana loved more than sharing her experiences of living in the country. The children were fascinated by her stories and were always full of questions about the different culture and customs.

'*Mata ashita*, George,' said Hana, as the last of the children left the cloakroom.

'*Mata ashita*, Mrs Phillips,' replied the little boy, before sprinting out of the room.

Hana closed her classroom door and turned to go back to her desk, but was surprised to see the headmaster, Mr Capper, standing there.

'Mrs Phillips, might I have a word?'

'Of course,' replied Hana, wondering what on earth he could want to talk to her about. He certainly wasn't giving the impression this was a friendly chat.

'In my office.'

Hana followed him out through the cloakroom and down the hallway to his office. Mr Capper indicated for Hana to sit while he took his position in his chair behind his desk.

Mr Capper took a deep breath. 'I'll come straight to the point,' he began. 'One of the parents has been to see me today with a complaint against you.'

Hana's heart did a little leap. Had she heard him right? 'A complaint against me? By a parent?'

'Yes. Mrs Pitman. George Pitman's mother.'

Hana tried hard not to let her reaction show on her face. Mrs Pitman was rather vocal at the best of times. It didn't take much to upset her. 'What's she complained about?'

'Speaking Japanese to the children.'

Hana raised her eyebrows. 'We only say hello and goodbye, it's just a bit of fun, really. I'm not giving them Japanese lessons.'

Mr Capper held up his hand. 'Yes. I know that,' he replied, his features softening a fraction. 'I know you spent time in the country and have a strong connection to it and are, I think it's fair to say, rather fond of the place.'

Hana gave a shrug. 'Yes. I am. Some of my happiest days were spent in Japan.'

'Quite. And there's nothing wrong with that.' Mr Capper paused as if trying to pick his words. 'But that was before we were at war with them.'

'I'm not teaching them anything political,' said Hana. 'It's about the geography, the traditions, the culture, that's all.'

Mr Capper let out a sigh and leaned forward, picking up a letter. 'This is from Mrs Pitman, she says, you talked about the schools and universities, how the Japanese have high literacy rates.'

'That's her interpretation. It's not the sort of expression I'd use with eight- and nine-year-olds,' said Hana, trying to keep her temper. 'I did say, they were educated to a high standard and had made important scientific discoveries but that it was just part of a wider conversation.'

Mr Capper put his glasses on. 'Mrs Pitman says, and I quote: "Mrs Phillips is filling the children's heads with lies and making the enemy sound civilised."'

Hana sat a little straighter in her seat. 'That's because the general population is civilised.'

'Yes, but you must see how this looks to the parents. She goes on to say that she's not the only one to express her concerns.'

'You mean express their racial stereotypes and bigotry?' Hana looked the headmaster directly in the eye as she spoke. 'I'm educating the children from experience, not from propaganda fed by the government.'

'Mrs Phillips,' said Mr Capper, rather more sternly. 'I must remind you that you're here to educate the children and not show disloyalty to the country. In another place, rather than in the safety of my office, you might be arrested for treason.'

Hana snorted at the suggestion. 'That is ridiculous.'

'In your opinion. Now, it is our duty as teachers to educate, not to influence.'

'And the irony of that statement is, that's exactly what I'm doing.'

'If you'll let me finish.' Mr Capper took his glasses off. 'To avoid further complaints and concerns from the parents, I must formally ask you to refrain from including Japan and anything to do with the country in the classroom or any interaction you have with the children. No more *kon'nichi*-whatever.'

'*Kon'nichiwa*,' corrected Hana.

'Whatever it is, no more of that. Or any other words. Is that understood?'

'So I'm being suppressed. Is that what you want me to agree to?'

'Hana,' said Mr Capper in a tone that an exasperated parent might use to a child. 'There's a war on. Japan is the enemy. We have to be very careful about what we say and do. As teachers, we are in a privileged position of influence on young minds. In the current world circumstances, that must include not aligning ourselves with the enemy in any shape or form. If you cannot give me your assurances that you will abide by my instruction, then I shall have no option but to release you from your contract. I would also need to state on what grounds.' He paused as the severity of his words sank in. 'And I'm sure you wouldn't want me to do that.'

'I feel as if I'm being blackmailed,' said Hana.

'You're a valued member of staff. The children respect you. It is not your prerogative to take advantage of their fondness for you. If you persist, then the children will lose a very good teacher and the benefit of everything else you bring to the classroom. All you have to do is not talk about Japan. Now, think very carefully before replying.'

Hana recognised when she had been backed into a corner. Other than agree to Mr Capper's instructions, the only alternative was to lose her job. And she certainly didn't want to do that. She had to force herself to reply civilly. 'In that case, I have no option, but to agree. Although, for the record, I agree under duress.'

'I'm sure you do. Now, let's put an end to this conversation and I can reassure Mrs Pitman and the other parents that they have nothing more to be concerned about.'

Hana left Mr Capper's office as serenely as possible. Underneath her calm exterior, she could feel the rage burning inside her.

The anger and injustice didn't leave her as she tidied the classroom, prepared for the next day and then walked home. In fact, the more she thought about it, the more cross she became.

If she thought she was going to get any sympathy from her husband when she arrived home at Tall Trees, however, she was mistaken.

'He does have a point,' said Gregory, after she had relayed the whole conversation to him over dinner.

'But it's a highly prejudiced response,' she said. 'Don't tell me you agree with this type of censorship.'

Gregory sighed and rested his cutlery on the side of his plate. 'It's not censorship, it's common sense.' He covered his left hand with his right, his fingers tracing the gnarled and mottled fire scarred skin. A subconscious but habitual action. When Gregory's plane had crash landed several years earlier and he had been lucky to escape the fireball with his life. The puckered and damaged skin snaked up his arm. A tapestry of textures, smooth and glossy patches interwoven with the marbled landscape of skin, covering his shoulder and spreading, almost fan-like, up one side of his neck. It was a sight Hana had only ever been allowed to see when he was in hospital. Since then, Gregory had always kept his scars covered.

'It's propaganda,' she snapped back.

'When the war is over, you'll be able to share your love for Japan and all things Japanese once again,' said Gregory, picking up his cutlery and resuming his meal.

She hated the patronising tone to his voice, but what was the point of arguing with someone who had no intention of seeing her point of view? She didn't know why she had expected anything more of him. They disagreed about so many things these days. It never used to be like this, not before his injury. So much had changed in the last two years – not just worldwide, but in the smaller microcosm of hers and Gregory's life together. Heartbreakingly, none of it for the better.

A small silence settled before Hana spoke again. 'Don't forget, it's Freddie's birthday this week,' she said. Her nephew was going to be two years old, and her parents had planned a little family party to celebrate their grandson's special day.

'Ah. Yes. About that,' said Gregory. 'I won't be able to make it now. Please send my apologies to your parents.'

'What do you mean you can't make it?' asked Hana. The party had been planned for three weeks now and she'd specifically asked Gregory to make sure he wasn't working.

'Work-related business. We have a house guest arriving at the same time,' said Gregory, cutting into his potato. 'An American army officer. He's to be billeted with us for three months.'

Hana's eyes widened. 'What? Can they just do that without asking us first?'

'They asked me, and I agreed.'

'Just like that?'

'I didn't think it was a problem.' Gregory looked up at her. 'Is it?'

'I don't know. I mean, we don't know who he is or anything about him. Why is he being billeted with us?'

'I can't really say,' replied Gregory. 'But he's going to be working up at Bletchley Park. It seems sensible that he stays with us, seeing as we have the room.'

Hana wasn't quite sure why it bothered her so much. They did have the space. Despite her and Gregory sleeping in separate rooms, there was still the guest room and the box room. The latter Hana had always envisaged as being a nursery, but they hadn't been blessed with a child before Gregory's injury, and sleeping in separate rooms wasn't conducive to conceiving.

Gregory continued. 'You probably won't see much of him. He'll be joining us for evening meals and, of course, breakfast but other than that, you won't be bothered. You'll barely know he's here.'

Hana wanted to add that in this regard, it was no different to Gregory being there. 'Well, it's clearly been settled before I even get a say in it,' she said, not quite able to bite her tongue.

'Don't be like that, Hana. It's not very gracious of you.' Gregory's tone was terse.

'Oh, don't worry, I shall be the perfect hostess. I won't embarrass you.' She pushed her plate away, her appetite lost. She got to her feet and took her plate out to the kitchen. A part of her secretly longed for Gregory to call her back and say he was sorry for not consulting her first but hoped she'd understand. In her mind, he'd say it with tenderness and sincerity, and she'd forgive him, just like they would have done before his plane had crash landed and the consequences of that. It was, of course, wishful thinking.

Once the table was cleared, Gregory thanked her for dinner, with as much affection as if she was a waitress, picked up his walking stick and left the dining room. She listened to his uneven footsteps and the tap of his stick as he limped across the hall to his study. The full use of his leg was another casualty of his aviation crash. The click of the catch as he closed the door behind him echoed in the hall.

Hana retreated to the living room and her Japanese textbooks, her usual company for the evenings, when she practised the language and transported herself back to happier, childhood days.

Chapter 2

The following morning, breakfast at Tall Trees was a solitary affair, with Gregory having left for work before Hana even woke up. It wasn't unusual these days, and given their disagreement the previous evening, it was something of a relief.

Their weeks were always much the same. Monday to Friday, Hana worked at the school, while Gregory's hours were more flexible in that he could be called in to work at any time, any day and have to stay until whatever needed doing was done. Hana didn't know a great deal about her husband's work, only that now that he couldn't fly, he worked at RAF Halton in an unknown capacity that he didn't share with her. Apparently, it was boring admin work that even if he wanted to discuss with her, the Official Secrets Act prevented him from doing.

Hana sometimes suspected that he used the Official Secrets Act as an excuse not to tell her, simply because he couldn't be bothered to have such conversations with her.

After a quick cup of tea, Hana set off for her parents' house. They lived in the same village and Hana liked to call into see them in the mornings before she went to work.

'Morning, Mum,' she said, as she stepped into the kitchen from the back door. She gave her mum a peck on the cheek. Pamela was laying the table with the help of Freddie. If you could call it help, judging by the way he was setting out the cutlery at rather odd angles and irregular spacing.

'Hello, darling. How are you?' asked Pamela, following behind her grandson, straightening the cutlery.

'I'm fine, thanks.' It was an automatic response, and not entirely genuine. Much as she was upset by Gregory's attitude last night, it really wasn't that surprising. Hana was far more bothered by the conversation she'd had with the headmaster.

'Eggs!' cried Freddie upon seeing Hana. He promptly abandoned the knives and forks on the table and ran over to his aunty.

Hana swooped him up in her arms and kissed his rosy cheek. 'Hello, darling. Let's collect the eggs, then.'

Her parents kept a couple of hens in the garden, who obliged the family every day with freshly laid eggs. A much welcome addition to the kitchen pantry in light of the food rationing.

They went out to the chicken coop and Hana opened the pen door, letting Freddie in ahead of her.

She watched as he picked up the little wicker basket inside the coop and toddled over to the nesting boxes, his little chubby hand expertly feeling around in the straw for a warm, freshly laid egg.

Hana smiled at the delighted look on his face when he triumphantly held up his treasure. She loved the way his dark brown eyes, flecked with gold, lit up with happiness. He looked so much like his father, Hana's brother, Tom.

As she watched Freddie toddle around the coop, looking for some more eggs – one for Hana, one for Mummy, one for Granny and one for Granddad – her happiness was clouded as thoughts of her brother came to the fore. It had been thirteen months since he was shot down over France after engaging with the enemy.

Hana gave a sharp intake of breath as memories of that awful day brought back all the raw pain, as if she'd heard the news only yesterday. Tom's wife, Gwen, had taken the news of her husband being missing in action badly, and had come to live with her in-laws. Gwen's own parents lived in London and had told her that Buckinghamshire was a safer option. Hana and her parents had taken Gwen and little Freddie under their wing. It was only two months ago that they learned through the British Red Cross that Tom was now a prisoner of war.

'Breakfast,' Freddie announced, looking very pleased with himself.

Hana took his hand. 'Let's go inside and give the eggs to Granny.' She guided him out of the chicken coop and back to the house.

'Oh, have you got eggs for me?' asked Pamela. She took the basket her grandson offered. 'Thank you very much. Breakfast won't be long.' She placed the basket on the worktop, before helping him up onto the little footstool at the sink. 'Wash your hands now. There's a good boy.'

Hana watched on fondly as Pamela tended to Freddie. She knew her mother treasured every moment with him. Even though Pamela never said anything outright, Hana knew she longed to have more grandchildren, but Hana couldn't see that situation changing any time soon, much to her own sadness. As always, she pushed the thought away. It was wrong to indulge in self-pity; at least she had her husband. At least, Gregory's crash landing had been on home soil down at RAF Tangmere in Sussex and no danger of him being captured by the enemy. She shuddered at the thought considering the life changing injuries he'd sustained that day.

Hana looked towards the door on to the hallway as her father, Alfred, entered. '*Ohayou, otōsan*,' she said, wishing him a good morning in Japanese. Hana couldn't remember a time when she and her father had greeted each other in anything other than Japanese.

'*Ohayou, Hana-chan*,' replied Alfred, with a warm smile.

Hana loved that he added the term of endearment after her name, it was always said with such reassuring love.

Alfred went over to Pamela and kissed her on the cheek. 'Good morning, darling.' He picked up the kitchen towel and began drying Freddie's freshly washed hands. 'And a very good morning to you, young man.' He looked over at the basket of eggs. 'Ah, breakfast. Jolly good.'

He helped Freddie down and Hana watched the two of them take their seats at the table where Pamela had left some bread to be cut to have with their eggs.

'How's Gwen? Is she up yet?' asked Hana as she washed her hands in the sink.

'She's not feeling too well today,' said Pamela.

'I'll take her up a cup of tea,' said Hana.

A few minutes later, she was knocking on the bedroom door of her sister-in-law's room.

'Come in,' called out Gwen.

Hana opened the door to a darkened room. The curtains were drawn, and the blackout blinds were certainly doing their job. 'Morning,' she said, placing the tea on the bedside table. 'Thought you might like a cuppa. I'll get those blinds down,' she said not waiting for Gwen to reply.

Hana didn't like the idea of Gwen sitting in the dark. It wasn't good for her spirits.

'Ugh. That's bright.' Gwen shielded her eyes from the shaft of sunlight that gushed through the window.

'Freddie has been out and collected the eggs already,' said Hana, ignoring the complaint. 'He's got one for you. It will be ready in a minute.'

'Is that your way of telling me I have to get up?' Gwen yanked the blanket over her head. 'I don't feel that well today.'

'I know,' said Hana. She also knew that it wasn't physically that Gwen felt unwell. 'But you still need to get up.' She sat on the edge of the bed and gently pulled the blanket from Gwen's head. 'Come on. You don't need me to tell you why you shouldn't stay in bed.' She gave a sympathetic smile.

Gwen let out a long sigh and then shuffled up into a sitting position. 'I know. It's just there are some days when it all seems too much.'

'Of course, it does,' said Hana gently. 'Some days are very hard.'

Gwen took a sip of her tea. 'How's things with you?'

She knew Gwen was referring to Gregory. There was no point pretending everything was fine. Her friendship with Gwen was based on trust and honesty. Both knew they could speak openly to each other and say things they might not want to say to anyone else.

Hana shrugged. 'He's very distracted with work at the moment.'

'Maybe try suggesting you do something together at the weekend.'

'I suppose I could try,' said Hana, even though her heart wasn't in it. 'He told me last night that we've got an American army officer being billeted with us.'

'Crikey. When is that happening?'

'This week.'

'You don't sound thrilled.'

Hana gave a shake of her head. 'Ignore me. I'm sure it will be fine.' She felt guilty laying this all on Gwen, when her sister-in-law had so much more to worry about. She wouldn't subject Gwen to her moans and groans about Mrs Pitman's letter of complaint. Hana gave her sister-in-law a hug. 'So, how are you?'

Gwen gave an unapologetic shrug. 'Same as ever.'

'Really?'

'All right, maybe not today. You know, some days, it's just hard to find something to look forward to.'

'I know,' said Hana. 'But we have to keep trying.' She got to her feet. 'See you downstairs in a minute.'

Gwen nodded. 'See you in a minute.'

As Hana reached the bottom of the stairs, she noticed *The Daily Telegraph* sitting on the doormat. She picked it up as her father appeared in the hallway.

'You beat me to it,' he said with a smile.

Hana held out the paper to him. 'Have you got time for the crossword today?' Hana and Alfred both loved *The Daily Telegraph's* cryptic crossword and the challenge of who could solve the questions first. Hana had not only inherited her father's love of language, she also had his competitive streak.

'Always have time for the crossword,' replied Alfred. When he didn't turn to go back to the kitchen, Hana was confused.

'Is everything all right, Dad?'

'Ah, now that was going to be my question to you.' He tapped the newspaper against his leg. 'Come into the living room a moment.'

Hana followed him in. There was no point denying anything was wrong. Her father knew her too well. She just hadn't realised it was so apparent that she was still troubled by events at the school.

'I'm all right, really,' she said, before her father could ask. 'I'm just annoyed, that's all.'

Alfred sat down on the sofa, patting the cushion next to him. 'And what are you annoyed at?'

'School. Mr Capper. Parents.' Hana gave a huff of frustration. 'Censorship. Ignorance. Bigots.'

'That's quite a list.'

Hana gave an abridged version of what had happened at the school yesterday evening. 'I'm just grumpy about it today,' she concluded. 'I hate being censored in this way. I said that to Gregory and he said it was common sense.'

Alfred nodded. 'With the war going on, everyone is fearful, and harnessing that fear is a powerful tool. The government want the country to be fearful, so they continue to have the backing and support of the people. But with that fear also comes ignorance. You will find it everywhere if you look for it. You have to pick your battles, my dear. You can make a stand against this parent and the school and probably lose your job, or you can continue to teach the children about tolerance and acceptance of what is different. You just have to do it in a more subtle way, that's all. Encourage them to question and to make their own informed decisions and choices. That's the best thing you can do for them right now.'

He was right, of course. She could walk away from thc children, or she could stay and educate them in more subtle ways. Hana leaned her head against her father's shoulder. 'Thanks, Dad.' He was such a wise man. She would take his advice without question. He'd always been there for her, and she never had cause to doubt his judgement on anything.

'Don't let other people's small-mindedness curtail your own broadmindedness,' said Alfred. 'Stay true to yourself. There is more than one path up the mountain.'

'Breakfast!' called Pamela from the kitchen.

'We'd better not keep the Captain waiting,' said Alfred, getting to his feet. Hana smiled at her father's nickname for her mum.

In the kitchen, Alfred took his seat at the table, placing the newspaper on his left-hand side, just as he always did. Hana went to help her mother serve the breakfast, knowing once her father had poured his cup of tea, he would be opening the paper straight to the crossword, where he would read the clues aloud.

'Here we go,' began Alfred. 'One, down. Is this town ready for a flood. Six letters.'

Hana paused for just a couple of seconds. 'Newark!' she said quickly, at the exact same time as her father.

'That was a draw,' said Pamela, the unofficial judge of the competition.

'Three down. Confused seal ate strange vegetable,' continued Alfred, once he had written in the previous answer. 'Two words, three and four letters.'

Hana repeated the clue out loud as her mind raced through the possibilities. 'Confused seal ate strange vegetable . . .'

Her father beat her to the answer. 'Sea kale.' He filled out the grid. 'Right, next one. Five letters. Second letter "a".' He looked up at Hana.

'I'm ready.' She dried her hands on the towel as her father read out the clue.

'Worker returning with energy to make sweet treat.'

There were several beats of silence. Hana called out the answer a moment before her father. 'Taffy!'

'Well done,' said Alfred, writing down the answer.

'Last one,' instructed Pamela. 'I need the bread sliced.'

Alfred nodded at Hana. 'Ready?'

'Yes.' She went around to her father's shoulder and looked over at the newspaper. 'Five letters again for this one. Ration book returned by area D.'

Alfred was already filling out the answer. 'Dozen,' he said. He looked up at Hana. 'Area. Zone. Add D. Zoned. Reworked to Dozen which is a common amount of ration allocations.'

'Ah, that's so obvious now,' sighed Hana.

'Finish that off later,' instructed Pamela.

Alfred folded the newspaper and placed it next to him, taking a moment to line it up with the edge of the table, before picking up the bread knife. 'I don't have much time this morning,' he said, as he took a moment to ensure he had placed the knife at the exact distance from the end of the loaf that he liked. 'Need to go into work early.'

Alfred had been working as an editor for a local printing firm since the outbreak of the war. Overseeing posters and leaflets, which, although he never said, Hana suspected were dropped over France and the occupying German troops. He had retired from lecturing some years ago but still maintained links and friendships with current and ex-dons at Cambridge.

'How are things at work?' asked Hana.

'Oh, you know, busy as always,' said Alfred. 'That's why I need to go in early today.'

His vague response was about par for the course. Hana suspected he had probably signed some sort of Official Secrets Act if he was editing material for the MOD, and she didn't like to press him for any more information than he was happy to divulge. 'Loose lips sink ships' and all that. She smiled to herself, wondering if her father had overseen that particular poster campaign.

A few minutes later, Hana was pleased to see Gwen had made it downstairs, looking fresh and tidy. 'Here, come and sit down,' said Hana. 'Perfect timing.' She pulled out the chair for Gwen to sit next to her.

The sound of the telephone ringing cut through the breakfast conversation. Pamela tutted at the intrusion. 'Whoever is that at this time of the morning?'

Alfred got to his feet and went out to the hall to take the call, closing the kitchen door behind him. The kitchen was quiet, as Hana, along with Pamela and Gwen, listened to Alfred answering the phone.

'Ah, hello, Bob.' Alfred's voice drifted through the closed door. 'Yes. I'm in early today . . .'

'Work,' said Pamela. 'Poor man, gets no peace. He was there all night last Friday.'

'All night?' Hana took a sip of her tea. 'He must have been shattered.'

'Certainly was. Goodness knows what was so important, but who am I to question?' Pamela let out a sigh of resignation.

Whatever Alfred was saying was indecipherable now. His voice was low, and Hana hoped it wasn't anything serious. A minute or so later, he came back into the room. He looked a little distracted but then smiled at his family. 'Sorry about that. Just work. I need to head off now.'

'But you haven't finished your eggs,' said Pamela.

'I'm sure Freddie will enjoy them.' Alfred ruffled his grandson's hair. Then, picking up the newspaper, he went back out to the hall for his jacket. 'I may be late again tonight,' he said coming back into the kitchen with his jacket now on and his coat folded over his arm. He gave the newspaper to Hana. 'Make sure you finish that,' he said. 'I need to know the answer to twenty-five across.'

'OK, Dad,' said Hana, taking the newspaper and placing it on the table.

'You'll forget it if you leave it there,' said Alfred. He picked it up and folded it again. 'I'll put it in your coat pocket.'

'You and your crossword puzzles,' said Pamela, with mock exasperation.

'All important stuff,' said Alfred with a wink. 'Keeps the brain working.' He gave Pamela a peck on the cheek. 'See you all later. Must dash so I can make the first bus.'

They did have a car, but with the rationing of petrol, Alfred preferred to take the bus to the next village, just a few miles away.

Hana got up and followed her father out to the front door, where he paused at the coat stand and put the newspaper into her pocket.

'Is everything all right?' she asked in a low voice.

'Yes. Of course.' He made a decent attempt at a smile, which wasn't totally convincing. He opened the door and stepped out onto the path.

Hana followed him out. 'Hope you have a good day,' she said, stopping at the gate. '*Sayōnara.*'

He gave her a reassuring smile. '*Sayōnara, Hana-chan.* See you this evening.' He glanced left and right, before stepping out onto the road, buttoning up his overcoat as he went.

It all happened in such a rush at that point.

Hana was aware of the sound of a car engine getting nearer. She looked up the road and saw a black Austin Ten car speeding towards the village. It took a moment for her to realise it wasn't slowing down.

She looked back at her father who was halfway across the road. He didn't appear to have heard or seen the danger. 'Dad!' she called. 'Look out!'

As Alfred turned his head, he saw the car. But it was too late.

There was a sickening thud as the vehicle struck her father, sending him flying over the bonnet and into the air, landing several feet further down the road.

Hana screamed. She covered her eyes with her hands as if she could unsee what had just happened. She looked up a second later. She wanted to see her father getting to his feet, brushing himself down and the car coming to stop, the driver profusely apologising. But she saw none of that.

Her father was sprawled across the road, unmoving.

The car hadn't stopped at all and had already disappeared out of sight.

'DAD!' Hana realised it was she who had shouted. It released her from her frozen state and she raced out of the gate towards her father.

Chapter 3

Hana had never felt so helpless as she watched the ambulance with her father and mother inside it speed off down the road.

Everything had happened in such a blur, she wasn't even sure what order it all took place. She had rushed to Alfred and found him bleeding from his head. Thank God someone from the house opposite had seen what happened and had run to fetch the village doctor.

He had been there within minutes, administering first aid. Hana wasn't sure what he did, but just his presence reassured both her and Pamela.

As always, her mother was composed and unflappable, reassuring Hana that everything was going to be all right. 'You need to phone Dad's work,' she instructed before climbing into the back of the ambulance. 'Let them know what's happened. The number is in his diary, which is in his desk. Top right-hand drawer.'

'I should come with you,' protested Hana.

'Sorry, we can't take anyone else in the ambulance,' said the driver. He closed the doors firmly so there was no way Hana could even contemplate jumping in.

'He's in good hands now,' said Doctor Peters, as the ambulance disappeared down the road. 'Pity the car didn't stop.'

'The car!' Hana suddenly remembered it now. Up until that point, all her focus had been on her father. She gazed in the direction the car had vanished and saw only the small group of villagers who had gathered to witness the commotion in the street.

'He shot off,' said Mrs Harris, the neighbour across the road who had run to fetch the doctor. 'He didn't stop.'

'That's disgraceful,' said another bystander.

'Was it a black Austen Ten?' asked the postman. 'It nearly had me off my bike as I came around the corner. It wasn't stopping for no one.'

'Come on now, Hana,' said Doctor Peters. 'Let's get you back inside. A nice, sweet cup of tea for you. Doctor's orders.'

Hana allowed herself to be shepherded back into the house, where Gwen was waiting in the kitchen with Freddie. She gave Hana a big hug, offering words of comfort. 'Try not to worry.'

'How bad is he?' asked Hana, pulling away from her sister-in-law and looking at the doctor.

Doctor Peters gave a sigh. 'Hard to say. And I really shouldn't comment until he's had a full assessment.'

'But your initial thoughts?' urged Hana. She was desperate for some sort of hope to cling onto.

The doctor gave another sigh. 'Well, any broken bones will mend,' he began. 'Any head injuries might be more serious and take far longer to recover from.'

Gwen gave a small gasp and reached over for Hana's hand.

Hana closed her eyes momentarily as images of blood seeping around her father's head, like a macabre halo, came to mind. She took several deep breaths. Now was not the time to go to pieces.

'But let's not jump ahead of ourselves,' continued the doctor. 'Wait until you hear from your mother. Now, is there anything I can do for you?'

'No. Thank you, Doctor,' said Hana, somehow managing to keep herself composed. She got up from the table. 'I'll see you out and then I'd better telephone Dad's office.'

Hana had never had to call her father at work before, but she soon found the number, exactly where her mother had said it would be. Alfred was a creature of habit and liked order in everything he did. It was strange going into his study without him being there. It was like going into the kitchen and her mother being in a different part of the house. It was peculiar how these familiarities were embedded in her subconscious and only apparent when they were missing.

She dialled the number and waited patiently for it to be answered. It rang several times before it was picked up. 'Piper Ellis Printers, how may I help you?' came the receptionist's voice.

'Hello, my name's Hana Phillips. My father, Alfred Castle, works for you. I'm afraid he's . . .' The words caught in her throat. Saying it out loud was rather more difficult than just thinking it. 'My father has been rushed to hospital. He was knocked down by a car on his way to work.'

'I'm very sorry to hear that. What hospital has Mr Castle been taken to?'

'Aylesbury General.'

'Right-o. I hope he makes a speedy recovery,' came the reply. 'I'll pass the message on. Thank you for calling.'

'Thank you. Goodbye,' said Hana. The line went dead, and she replaced the receiver into its cradle, before returning to the kitchen.

'Everything all right? Did you get through?' asked Gwen as she put Freddie into his playpen.

'I think so. I've never had to phone his work before,' said Hana. 'It was all very matter-of-fact. I just left a message with the receptionist, and that was that.'

'I expect someone will give you a call. The manager, perhaps?' suggested Gwen. 'Sit down and have the cup of tea I've made. I put a little sugar in it for you.'

'Thank you. I think I'll let Gregory know first,' said Hana. She was on edge with her nerves and the idea of sitting down was alien. She wasn't sure she'd be able to sit for very long.

Hana dialled RAF Halton. As with her father, she had never had to telephone her husband at work before, but this was an emergency.

The call was answered, and she started speaking immediately. 'Hello, it's Mrs Phillips, Flying Officer Gregory Phillips's wife. Could I speak to my husband, please?'

'One moment,' came the reply.

It seemed an age before Hana heard the voice of her husband. 'Hana? What's wrong?'

'It's Dad. He's been taken to hospital. He was hit by a car this morning,' explained Hana quickly, her voice once again cracking. 'I think I'm going to take Dad's car and drive over to the hospital. I don't know how long I'll be, so you might have to sort supper out for yourself.'

There was a pause. 'Where's your mother?'

'She's gone in the ambulance with him.'

'So your mother is with him?'

'Yes.'

'At the hospital?'

'Yes.' Goodness, how many times did she have to say it?

'I don't know if you going to the hospital is a good idea,' replied Gregory. 'I mean, you'll just be sitting around.'

Hana didn't attempt to keep the frustration from her voice. 'But Mum is there all alone. I want to be with her.'

'I don't think you should drive,' said Gregory, finally showing some compassion in his voice. 'I could try to leave early.'

'Try? Surely, they'd let you leave early for an emergency.'

'I'm sorry, but it's not as simple as that,' said Gregory.

'Nothing ever is.' A sob caught in Hana's throat. She sank down on the bottom stair – the distance between them, not just physical but emotional, seemed wider than ever.

'Don't go getting yourself all upset,' Gregory said, more tenderly. 'I'll telephone the hospital and see what they say. I'll call you back and we can take it from there. Don't you have work today?'

'Not today. I telephoned the school and explained what happened. I won't be able to concentrate, and I don't want the children to see me upset.'

'Well, try not to worry. I'll call you as soon as I can.' Gregory put the receiver down before she could even said goodbye.

Hot tears pricked her eyes. She had felt lonely in her marriage before, but right now she felt truly alone. All she wanted was some kind of warmth and comfort, some reassurance, but even that seemed too much to ask of her husband now.

She missed the old days. Gregory wasn't the same man she'd fallen in love with and married five years ago. The carefree, loving man had been replaced with someone angry and bitter that his career had been cut short and that he'd been left unable to fly and had to walk with a stick. His hands, forearms and upper part of his torso had been badly burned when his plane had come down, and he had once described himself as grotesque to look at. Nothing Hana had said would change his mind. Day by day, he had withdrawn further and further away from her.

Hana had hoped that over time, the old Gregory would return, but every day this notion slipped a little further from her grasp.

Taking the handkerchief from her pocket Hana dabbed at her eyes. It wouldn't do her any good to wallow in self-pity. She felt guilty for thinking like that about Gregory. What did she have to feel sorry about? Hadn't he reminded her often enough, her life hadn't changed. It was his that had been ruined. Yes, he'd used that word. His life ruined. Not changed but 'ruined'.

Hana went into the kitchen and sipped at the tea Gwen had made her, watching the hands of the clock drag themselves around its face as she desperately waited for some news.

An hour later, Hana still hadn't heard from either her mother or her husband. On Pamela's part, she had to assume this was good news. However, the not-knowing was agonising. She hated feeling so helpless.

The last time she had felt this way was when she had visited Gregory in hospital after his plane had come down. Hana remembered how nothing she could say or do could make anything better. She had that same sort of feeling today.

It was mid-morning when the telephone finally rang. Hana dashed into the living room and answered the call.

'Hello, darling,' came her mother's voice.

'Mum. How's Dad?'

'He's not too good, I'm afraid,' said Pamela, her voice full of anxiety, something Hana was not used to. Pamela cleared her throat. 'Broken leg. Fractured hip. They've managed to stop the bleeding from his head wound.'

'Is he conscious?'

'He's slipping in and out of consciousness. There's swelling on his brain which needs to go down before they can do anything else.'

'I'm coming over,' said Hana, not giving it a second thought. Ideally she would have preferred Gregory to be with her, but it didn't look like he was going to turn up soon. She'd just have to get herself to the hospital. 'I'll use Dad's car.' Her father had taught her to drive before she got married and it had come in very useful after Gregory's accident. Not that he liked her to drive him anywhere now. His recovery had included being able to get behind the wheel of a car. His injury to his left side hadn't stopped him driving, even if it had stopped him flying.

'Drive carefully,' instructed her mother.

She replaced the receiver just as Gwen came in from the garden after pegging out the washing. 'I need to go,' said Hana, grabbing her coat from the hook and quickly bringing her sister-in-law up to speed with her father's condition.

'Oh dear, I hope he's all right,' said Gwen, setting the washing basket down on the table. 'Take your time,' she added. 'We don't need two of you in hospital.'

Hana hopped into her father's green Riley and navigated the vehicle out of the gates of Bramble House, careful not to catch the car on either of the brick piers on her way.

Thirty minutes later, Hana pulled up outside the hospital. In her haste, she had forgotten to ask her mum what ward they were on. She hurried into the hospital and was surprised to see Pamela in the waiting area. Her mother got to her feet. It was clear she was upset.

'It's all right. I'm here now,' said Hana, giving her mother a quick hug. It wasn't often Pamela was rattled by anything. 'Where's Dad?'

Pamela sniffed and shook her head. 'They've sedated him,' she said. 'They said he needs to rest.'

Hana's own heart sank at the news. 'I came as quickly as I could. I'm so sorry. Poor Dad.'

'The Ward Sister said we could go and see him, though. Just for five minutes. The matron is on her break, so we have to be quick.'

Hana followed her mum up to the first floor and along the corridor to the ward where her father was. He was in a small room of his own. 'A private room?' said Hana in surprise.

'Apparently, his work arranged it,' said Pamela.

It seemed an odd thing for the printers to do, but Hana really wasn't bothered about that right now. All she wanted to do was to see her father.

The nurse showed them into the room. 'You can only stay for a few minutes,' she said. 'Speak nice and calmly to him. No crying. He's only mildly sedated at the moment so he can hear you, even if he can't communicate himself.'

'I have no intention of crying at my husband's bedside,' said Pamela, straightening up and pushing her shoulders back.

'Mum,' said Hana gently. She gave another smile at the nurse, this time as an apology.

Pamela sat down by one side of the bed and Hana the other. She listened as her mother spoke.

'Hello, Alfred,' began Pamela. 'I don't know if you can hear me but you're in hospital. You had an accident this morning.' Her voice broke a little but she cleared her throat and continued. 'You were knocked down by a car. You've hit your head, so you need to rest as much as possible. Hana is here to see you.'

'Hello, Dad,' said Hana, feeling a little self-conscious. She reached over and took her father's hand in hers. 'Do you know you're in a room of your own? Not on the general ward. Apparently, your work arranged it. Who'd have thought.' She looked over at her mother who gave a bemused shrug. Now that Hana thought about it properly, being put in a private room was very out of the ordinary and rather over the top for someone who simply worked at the printers. It didn't add up.

Before she could give it any more thought, though, the pressure of Alfred's fingers tightening around her own distracted her. She looked down at her hand and could see his fingers curl and uncurl. Slowly at first, but then a little faster.

'Dad?' She returned the squeeze.

'What is it?' asked Pamela.

'He's squeezing my hand.' Hana leaned in. 'Hello, Dad.'

Alfred made some sort of stifled groan, which sounded like it was lodged in his throat. His head moved from left to right and he grunted, before letting out another groan-like sound.

'It's all right, Alfred,' said Pamela, getting to her feet and gently running her hand across his forehead.

'Dad. Just relax,' said Hana. 'You're all right. You're in hospital.' She exchanged a worried glance with Pamela, before looking back at her father. He seemed even more agitated now. His head snapping from side to side, the groans louder and the hold on her hand tighter.

'I'll get the nurse,' said Pamela.

Before she'd even moved away from the bed, the door opened and the nurse appeared.

'Oh, dear,' she said, moving swiftly to the side of the bed. 'Alfred. Calm down. You need to lie still. Stop, now. Alfred.' She looked at Hana and then Pamela. 'Would you mind stepping outside?'

Hana and Pamela obliged but listened intently from the other side of the door. Fortunately, Alfred sounded like he was indeed calming down and relaxing as the nurse, firmly but with kindness, told him to settle down.

A few minutes later, she joined Hana and Pamela in the corridor. 'I'm sorry but I'm going to have to ask you to leave now. I'll make sure the doctor comes and checks in on him, but tonight, at least, I think it's best if you don't go back in. And Matron will be back soon.'

'Yes. Of course,' said Pamela. She sounded calm but the frown between her eyes betrayed her.

Hana slipped her arm into her mother's. 'Come on, Mum.' She turned to the nurse. 'Thank you for letting us see him. We'll ring in the morning to see what sort of night he's had.'

'Good idea,' said the nurse. 'Oh, I nearly forgot.' She nodded her head towards the end of the corridor. 'There's two gentlemen wishing to speak to you.'

Hana turned and saw a man in a suit, wearing an overcoat and carrying a trilby hat in his hand. The other man was dressed in uniform. An army officer, from what Hana could tell. 'Who are they?'

'They wouldn't say. Just that they were looking for you.' The nurse looked a little concerned. She spoke in a whisper. 'They were here earlier. When Mrs Castle went off to call you, they came into the room to try to speak to Mr Castle. The Ward Sister shooed them away after a few minutes.'

Before any more could be said, the gentleman with the hat stepped forward. 'Mrs Phillips?' He gave a polite nod towards Pamela. 'Mrs Castle. Might we have a word, please?'

Hana and Pamela walked down the corridor, stopping in front of them. 'How can we help?' asked Pamela.

'It's actually Mrs Phillips I'd like to speak to,' said the gentleman.

'What's this all about?' asked Pamela.

'I'm afraid I'm not at liberty to discuss that with you,' replied the gentleman. He turned to Hana. 'I'd like you to come with us, Mrs Phillips.'

'You can't just whisk my daughter away like that,' said Pamela.

'And just who are you?' asked Hana.

Before any more could be said, the nurse stepped between them. 'I'm sorry, but you really need to take this outside. I can't have any sort of disturbance on the ward.' She pushed open one of the double doors, standing against it to stop it closing. 'If you please.'

'Of course. Thank you, Sister,' said the gentleman and led the party out into the main corridor.

Hana and Pamela followed with the army officer behind them. Whatever this was all about, Hana was sure it was to do with her father and his work.

'Can someone please tell me what this is all about?' asked Hana.

'We need to discuss this with you in private,' said the officer.

The gentleman in the suit spoke. 'My name is Stuart Hopkins. I'm with the War Office.'

The officer spoke again. 'Mrs Phillips. We need to you come with us so we can talk to you in private.'

'Am I under arrest?' asked Hana.

'No. Not at all,' reassured the first gentleman. 'But I do need you to come with me.'

'What about my mother?'

Hopkins looked at Pamela. 'I can arrange transport to take you home, Mrs Castle.'

'I'm perfectly capable of getting myself home, thank you very much,' said Pamela. 'I'll take the car. But I'm not happy about leaving my daughter. Where are you taking her?'

Hopkins looked to be weighing up his answer. 'I'm afraid I can't tell you that, but you do have my assurances that your daughter is perfectly safe and will be home later today.'

'It's all right, Mum,' said Hana. She didn't know why, but she trusted this man. And she had to admit, she was intrigued as to what they wanted to speak to her about. She had come to the conclusion that it had to be about Alfred's job. That was the only possible explanation. And seeing as it was all very cloak and dagger, she had no doubt that whatever her father had been doing at work, it wasn't simply printing posters for the MOD. She gave Pamela a hug. 'You get off home. I'll call you when I'm back.'

'I don't like this,' said Pamela, begrudgingly.

'I'll be fine,' said Hana. She couldn't deny the little flutter of anticipation in her chest at what Hopkins wanted her for.

Chapter 4

They all headed out to the car park, and after one more protest from her mother, which was quickly batted away by Hana, Pamela was in her car and driving away.

Hana turned expectantly to Hopkins and his colleague.

'This way, please, Mrs Phillips.' Hopkins indicated the black Humber Super Snipe car parked nearby. He walked over to the vehicle and opened the rear passenger door for Hana, while the officer took his seat at the wheel.

She paused. 'Where exactly are we going?'

Hopkins looked like he was weighing up his answer. 'Bletchley Park,' he replied after a second.

Bletchley Park. Why didn't that surprise Hana? She knew her father's talents were wasted at the printers. She'd never been able to understand why he was working there when he would be of much more use to the MOD in other areas, especially since Japan had entered the war. It had never made sense to her that a man with her father's credentials hadn't been approached to do something more meaningful.

Given Hana's love for puzzles, she felt rather silly that it hadn't occurred to her sooner what her father was really doing.

Everyone who lived locally knew about Bletchley Park, although what actually went on there was something of a mystery. Rumours ranged from it being some sort of military mental asylum, due to the odd hours kept by staff, to it being some sort of clerical or secretarial centre, due to the numerous young women who worked there. The truth was, no one really knew.

Hana had a feeling she was about to find out.

Hopkins got in the back of the car with Hana. 'Just now you said you worked for the War Office,' said Hana. 'In what capacity?'

'British intelligence,' replied Hopkins, settling himself in his seat. 'MI5.'

'And you're my father's employer?'

'We'll get to that in due course, once we're at the Park,' said Hopkins.

Hana took this as her cue not to ask any more questions just yet, and she sat back in her seat as the car pulled away from the hospital grounds.

It was another thirty minutes before they were drawing to a halt at the gates of Bletchley Park. The guard checked the papers offered by the driver and waved them through.

Hana's gaze darted around the place at the buildings to her right, along with what looked like a maze of huts and temporary buildings. She was surprised to see so many people walking around the grounds. Some striding purposefully with serious expressions, some alone, some in small groups, while others sauntered, chatting and laughing with their companions. It was like the centre of a busy town.

There was a lake to Hana's left and as the car swept around the driveway, an imposing Victorian, gothic-looking mansion house came into view – its red-brick façade rising high into the Buckinghamshire sky. A central tower with a domed shaped roof perched above the main entrance to the house to the backdrop of tall chimneys and a slate roof.

The car came to a stop outside the main entrance of the house and Hopkins got out, instructing Hana to follow him into the building. The mansion itself seemed just as busy as the outside area. There was the gentle hum of conversations and the distinctive click-clack of typewriters.

She followed Hopkins down the main, wood-panelled hallway and then up a broad staircase to the first floor. She had to hurry to keep up with Hopkins as he strode down the carpeted corridor, nodding and acknowledging several people as he went, before showing Hana into an office, overlooking the rear of the grounds.

It was only when she heard the door close behind her, that she realised the army officer was with them still. He walked across the room, and came to stand alongside Hopkins, in front of the fireplace.

'This old building has so many draughts,' muttered Hopkins as he picked up a log from the basket and dropped it into the fire. 'Should soon warm up in here. He took a seat beside the fireplace, indicating Hana to take the opposite chair, while the army officer took something of a back seat, at a desk in the corner of the room.

There was a silence in the room. Hopkins took out a cigarette and offered one to Hana.

She shook her head. 'I don't smoke.'

'Good for you.' Hopkins lit his cigarette, took a long draw, before exhaling. The smoke drifted towards the open fireplace. 'Right, where were we?'

'I asked if you were my father's employer,' said Hana. 'I assume he's not really working as a printer.'

A small smile played on Hopkins lips. 'No. He's not. Now, what I'm about to tell you is absolutely top secret. You cannot repeat this to anyone. Not even your mother. Understand?'

The smile had disappeared, and Hopkins looked deadly serious.

'Yes. I understand,' replied Hana when she realised he was waiting for her to answer.

'Good. Now Alfred has been working for the intelligence service for some time, but his work has been highly confidential,' explained Hopkins. 'And unfortunately, now that he's had this accident, it puts us in a rather tricky position. His expert knowledge of languages, Japanese in particular, was the key to what he was doing and, to be frank, we need someone who can decipher his notes and continue his work while he is in hospital. We need someone who can pick up where he left off in deciphering Japanese transmissions.'

Hana could feel her eyes widening as she listened to what Hopkins was telling her. 'He was a codebreaker?' she said finally.

Hopkins gave a small frown. 'Yes. Some of the transmissions are in Japanese and Japanese speakers are few and far between.'

'A code breaker?' said Hana, repeating herself. She couldn't help smiling as a sense of pride welled in her chest. She knew her father must have been doing something more than proofreading posters. Oh, and he would have loved being able to use his knowledge of the Japanese language. She looked at Hopkins. 'I obviously didn't know that.'

'You weren't supposed to,' said Hopkins. 'That's the whole point of things being top secret. Besides, your father had signed the Official Secrets Act.'

'And you want me to step in for him?' Hana asked cautiously, just so there was no misunderstanding.

'We're low on manpower when it comes to the Japanese language and deciphering their messages. They need to be done quickly. We haven't got time for people to learn the language. We need people who know it already. From what I understand, that's you, and I rather think your language talents are wasted, not to mention, unappreciated by the school where you work.'

'The school?' Hana gulped at the idea that she might have been reported to MI5 for trying to educate the children about Japan.

'Don't look so worried. It's my job to know. One of the chaps working here mentioned it. Apparently, you taught his son. The parents were, shall we say, concerned.'

'Pitman,' said Hana. Honestly, that family was determined to make life difficult for her. 'When you say "mentioned", what you actually mean is reported.' She let out a big huff of indignation. 'I was only teaching the children to say simple things—' She stopped as Hopkins held up his hand.

'You don't need to explain. We wouldn't be having this conversation if we had any doubts about you. Don't worry about the Pitmans. It's the war, it puts people on edge.'

'Makes them paranoid, you mean,' said Hana, not attempting to hide the irritation in her voice.

'Somewhat. Anyway, enough of that. Back to business,' said Hopkins. 'For security, a lot of your father's work was written in his own code. We need that deciphered and you're best placed to do that.'

'But he never spoke to me about it,' replied Hana.

'No. But you are familiar with your father's coding style and with the Japanese language,' said Hopkins. 'We don't know how long your father is going to be in hospital for and, if I may say, we don't know if he will be able to return to work. We've come too far to call a halt to it now or wait for someone to work out your father's coding. As I said, we want you to pick up where he left off.'

Hana opened her mouth to speak but then closed it again. She was flattered that they thought so highly of her ability, but she was also apprehensive. She knew only a fraction of what her father knew. 'I . . . I don't know if I can,' she said honestly. 'I can't pretend to be anywhere near my father's standard of the language. It's complex and multi-layered. It's hard to directly translate it because a lot of it is nuanced and embedded in their culture.' She stopped talking, realising neither man was quite understanding what she was saying.

'You won't know until you try,' said Hopkins.

That was true. 'I suppose so,' said Hana. She mulled the idea over in her head for a few seconds, acknowledging the small ball of excitement in her stomach. She, of course, wished it was under different circumstances, but to be asked to fill in for her father . . . well, that was a huge compliment. She squared her shoulders and looked at Hopkins. 'When do you want me to start? And where?'

'Tomorrow,' said Hopkins. 'Arrive here in the morning at eight-thirty. Report to the hut to the left of the mansion house. You'll see it on your way out.'

'But I have work tomorrow,' said Hana, thinking how she couldn't possibly let the school and children down at such short notice. She thought she'd at least have to work a week's notice.

'Don't worry about that. We'll sort it all out,' said Hopkins.

'All right,' she replied, already feeling guilty for leaving without being able to say goodbye to the children. On the other hand, Mrs Pitman would be happy. No doubt, she'd think Hana had been sacked. Still, that was the least of Hana's worries. She would, of course, have to explain what she was doing to Gregory. 'What will I say to my husband? Am I allowed to tell him what I'm doing?'

'Only the bare necessities. That you've been seconded to cover your father's position, but he's to know no more than that,' said Hopkins. 'Now, the end of the day is around four p.m., but you may find yourself working late or through the night. All part of the job, I'm afraid.'

'Right, I see.' She wondered how Gregory would react to her being out all night.

'Of course, you can say no if it's going to cause a problem,' said Hopkins, as if reading her mind. 'But remember, this isn't about you and how it might upset your domestic life, it's far bigger than that. It's for peace in Europe. I really can't stress the importance of the work your father was doing.'

His statement was a contradiction. She couldn't say no, could she? Besides the fact, she didn't want to. 'I'm not allowed to tell a soul about what I'm really doing. Not even my husband?'

Hopkins eyed her. 'Not even your husband.'

'He's an officer in the RAF,' said Hana, not that she thought it would make any difference, but it was worth a try.

'You can tell him you're working here, but not what you're doing. It's the same rule for everyone who works at Bletchley Park.' Hopkins gave a sympathetic smile. 'If it helps, I can have a word with your husband, but it will probably be better coming from you.'

'I'll speak to him.' She was a little affronted that Hopkins thought a man-to-man chat about the little wife was necessary. She refused to be patronised in such a way.

'I'm sure he will understand,' said Hopkins.

Hana wasn't quite so sure Gregory would actually understand, but although Hopkins said she could decline, she didn't want to. Blow Gregory, she was honoured to have been asked to carry on her father's work. Her heart both swelled with pride and contracted with worry at this thought. Her father would be so proud of her; to know she was carrying on his work. Gosh, his were big boots to fill. She wasn't sure she was up to the job, but she'd give it a damn good try, with or without Gregory's blessing. She took a deep breath and addressed Hopkins. 'I'll be here at eight-thirty in the morning.'

'Good,' said Hopkins. 'Now, one last thing before you leave.' He nodded to his colleague who rose from his seat at the desk and produced a sheet of paper which he handed to Hopkins. 'I need you to sign this. It's the Official Secrets Act.'

'Oh, right.' Hana took the pen and paper. She had imagined signing the Official Secrets Act would be rather more ceremonial, but here she was, in an office tucked away in a seconded mansion house, being presented with the document. She skimmed across the wording and then added her signature to the bottom of the paper, before handing it and the pen back to Hopkins.

'Thank you,' he said, taking them and passing the paper straight to his colleague for safekeeping. 'I'll see you tomorrow, Mrs Phillips. Don't be late. We are depending on you.'

*

A car and driver had been made available to take Hana home. Once indoors, she telephoned Pamela.

'Is everything all right?' asked Pamela.

'Everything is fine,' replied Hana. 'I'm going to be covering for Dad. At his work.' She hated lying to her mother, but she had no choice.

'At the printers? Really? What about the school?' Pamela didn't sound convinced.

'It's all to do with the war effort, Mum. I don't really have a lot of choice.'

There was a small silence before Pamela spoke again. 'Well, I'm sure your father will be pleased to know you're standing in for him. Doing whatever it is you might be doing.'

There was a tone to her voice that Hana couldn't quite decipher. She wanted to describe it as understanding, and wondered just how much Pamela knew about Alfred's work. Although, she couldn't imagine her dad would have broken the Official Secrets Act. Her mother was an intelligent woman, and maybe she, like Hana, suspected there was more to the work at the printers than they were told about.

After Hana had finished her call to Pamela, Gregory telephoned to say he'd be home at six o'clock for tea and offered to call the hospital to see how her father was that evening. Hana appreciated the gesture. She didn't mention the conversation with Hopkins. She'd wait until Gregory was home and tell him face-to-face. She wasn't looking forward to breaking the news. She was already anticipating his disapproval.

Finally, at seven o'clock, she heard Gregory's key in the front door. Hana took the dinner out of the oven, where she'd been keeping it warm for the past forty-five minutes, and tried not to be cross that it was dried up. It happened often and she really shouldn't be annoyed by it.

'Hello,' said Gregory, coming to stand in the doorway of the dining room where Hana was setting his plate down on the table. 'I spoke to the hospital. They said your father is comfortable. How is your mother?'

'Upset, of course, but you know what she's like. Puts on a brave face.'

'And I assume you're doing the same.'

Hana looked up at him. There was a softness in his voice that had been absent in recent times. She was surprised at how moved she was by it. 'I'm no help to anyone sitting around crying,' she said, wiping her hands needlessly down her apron. She thought for a moment Gregory was going to approach her and offer some sort of comfort, but he paused halfway across the room and then moved to the table.

'Sorry I couldn't get back sooner,' he said, sitting down and flicking his napkin over his lap.

Hana sat down adjacent to him. 'It's all right. It doesn't matter now.'

There was a small silence while they began their meal. Hana went to speak at the same time as Gregory did. 'You go first,' she said.

'What were you going to say?' asked Gregory.

Hana popped the last carrot slice into her mouth, buying a few seconds while she swallowed it. 'I've been asked to cover Dad at work,' she said, attempting to sound nonchalant. Rather like Gregory had when he'd informed her about their house guest. 'Someone from his work came to the hospital and asked me to stand in for him.'

Gregory nearly spat his food across the table as he spluttered at her comment. 'Say that again.'

Hana tried not to bristle and reminded herself this was as out of the blue for Gregory as it was for her. 'Apparently, Dad was working on something important, and they want me to take over. I'm going to be standing in for him while he's recovering,' she said, meeting her husband's gaze. Gregory's once bright summer-blue eyes were more of a grey colour these days, like an overcast January afternoon. His whole demeanour screamed of a cold, harsh winter. She missed the man she had married, who was spring and summer all at once, bright, warm and fun. She was sure the Gregory of old, would have been enthusiastic for her, encouraged her. He would have been proud she'd been asked to stand in for her father, even if he didn't know what it was really all about.

'It's a ridiculous idea,' he scoffed, putting his cutlery together on the now empty plate. 'They should have asked someone else. What about your job at the school? I thought you liked working there.'

'I do like it at the school,' said Hana, getting to her feet and beginning to clear the dinner plates away. 'But I've been specifically asked because I understand Dad's system and so on.' She turned away, hoping Gregory wouldn't see the guilt in her eyes. It was kind of true what she was saying, but she was very aware she was intentionally misleading her husband.

'Exactly what do they need you for? What project are they talking about?'

'I don't know. I'll find out when I get there.'

'Speak to them again and tell them you've reconsidered and won't be able to take up the position.'

Hana took a sharp intake of breath as she dumped the plates into the washing-up bowl and then gripped the edge of the sink. 'No,' she said.

The silence between them filled the space. Hana could feel the sharp gaze of her husband's eyes boring into her back through the kitchen doorway.

'Ring them up and decline the offer,' Gregory persisted; his voice ice-cold.

'I can't,' she said, still not turning around. 'I've already accepted. I have to be there first thing in the morning—'

She flinched at the sound of Gregory slamming his hand down on the table. 'This is not open for discussion,' he said. 'I will not allow this.'

Hana spun around, unable to keep her anger at bay. 'I don't need your permission to do this,' she retorted.

'I'm your husband—' he began.

'Yes, and I'm your wife,' cut in Hana, striding across the kitchen to the open doorway of the dining room. 'But I have the right to make my own decisions.'

Gregory's hand was still stretched across the table where he'd slammed it down. His forefinger tapped furiously against the wood – the only telltale sign of how agitated he was. His finger stopped drumming. The ticking of the clock on the mantlepiece was the only sound in the room. It was Gregory who broke the silence. 'What happened to love, honour and obey?' he asked quietly, emphasising the last word.

Hana's heart jolted at his words. 'I think the question is, what happened to love and honour?' she replied, unable to hide the sadness in her voice.

She watched as Gregory got up from the chair and, using his walking stick to support and steady himself, limped around the table, pausing in front of her. He kept his face turned away from her, hiding the scars he hated so much, which fanned his neck above his shirt collar.

He was so close, she only had to move her head a fraction and she'd be kissing him. There was a time when that would have been such a natural thing for them to do, but since the accident there had been minimal physical contact. When Gregory had first come home from hospital, Hana had moved into the spare room, so she didn't knock his leg in the night or catch his tender and raw skin. That had been nearly two years ago, and neither of them had ever suggested she should move back into the marital bed. How tragic it was that Gregory should survive the accident, only for their marriage to be torn apart.

'Do what you want, Hana,' he said. 'You always have. Why would you listen to half a man, such as me? Why would you want to take someone like me into consideration?' He limped out of the room, across the hallway and into his study.

Chapter 5

Hana didn't see Gregory for the rest of the evening. She'd sat alone in the living room, her gaze flicking towards the doorway every so often, when she found herself wishing he'd appear from his study. She wanted him to come and sit beside her, to tell her that of course she should step in for her father. He'd take her hand and tell her he was sorry. He'd hold her, and she'd feel the gentle pressure of his hand around her shoulders, hear the beat of his heart as she leaned into him, feel the warmth of his body against her and his breath on her skin. But those were fanciful ideas fuelled only by distant memories.

Unsurprisingly, when Hana finally went to bed, she found it hard to sleep. She was worried about her father, filled with trepidation about her new job and upset about her argument with Gregory. She really wanted to clear the air before she left for work.

She got up earlier than usual on Wednesday morning and made some fresh coffee. When she heard Gregory moving about upstairs, she boiled the eggs her mother had given her the day before. Normally, Hana would call into see her parents and Gwen before going into work but today would be different. If only she could find out how her father was, that would be one less worry.

Gregory came downstairs a short time later and seated himself at the dining table. 'Good morning,' he said as Hana came into the room with the teapot.

'Morning,' she said, placing it down on the table. At the start of every day, Hana had to gauge what sort of mood her husband was in. More often than not, it was one of disinterest, but after their argument last night, things felt different today.

As she turned to go back out to the kitchen for the toast and eggs, Gregory cleared his throat. 'Hana,' he began. 'I'm sorry I was so cross yesterday.'

She nodded and let out a small sigh. 'I'm sorry, too.'

'Let's blame it on a difficult day,' he said.

'Yes. Let's,' she agreed, as attempting to talk about it in any detail would be met by a wall of silence. Since the accident, silence was the way Gregory dealt with problems. Internally, by himself. They no longer had long, heartfelt, emotional discussions. It saddened Hana immensely, but this morning wasn't the right time to get into any kind of debate.

Gregory smiled up at her and she returned the smile. She went to reach for his hand, but he swiftly picked up his knife and turned his attention to buttering his toast.

'You can still say no to the job,' he said, nonchalantly.

Hana steeled herself, closing her eyes for a brief moment as she composed a cordial reply. 'I know,' she said.

'But you're not going to, are you?' asked Gregory.

She shook her head. 'No. I'm not.'

*

Half an hour later, after tidying away the breakfast dishes and making sure she was ready for her new job, Hana called out a goodbye to Gregory. She didn't get an answer. It was disappointing, if not unsurprising. She went out to the garden shed and retrieved her bicycle. She estimated it was about a fifteen-minute cycle ride to Bletchley from home.

She was just about to wheel her bike down the driveway, when Gregory appeared. He looked at the bike. 'Why don't I give you a lift today?'

Hana was taken aback. What was she supposed to say to that? 'Erm . . . It's all right. I can cycle.' How on earth was she going to keep this deception up? Gregory thought she was going to work at a printers near the train station.

Gregory gave a sigh. 'Look, Hana. I know you're heading for Bletchley Park.'

'What?' She looked up at her husband in surprise.

'Don't worry. It's perfectly fine for me to know.'

'How do you know? Who told you?' She certainly hadn't breathed a word to anyone about the location.

'It doesn't matter. I'll drive you. Put the bike away for today.' With that, he unlocked the car and got behind the wheel, placing his stick on the back seat.

Hana was still rooted to the spot, still wondering how on earth he knew she was going there. He looked at her through the windscreen and beckoned for her to hurry up.

Hana wheeled the bike back into the garage and then got into the passenger seat. She still wasn't sure she should actually say outright that he was correct. If she didn't say anything, then technically she wasn't breaking the Official Secrets Act.

'So, your new job,' began Gregory as they drove out of the village. 'It happens to be my place of work, too.'

'What on earth do you mean?' asked Hana. 'You work at RAF Halton. Dad didn't work there.' This was all so confusing, she couldn't make any sense of what Gregory was saying.

Gregory glanced over and raised his eyebrows. 'I work at Halton in the same way your father worked at the printers, and in the same way you are going to be standing in for him there.'

Hana took a moment to let it sink in. 'You mean . . .'

'Yes.'

'Wait. You mean you work at Bletchley Park?'

'Yes.'

'And you know my father worked there?'

'Yes.'

'And you never said?'

'No. How could I? Official Secrets Act,' replied Gregory. 'And that's all we can say. We can't discuss it any further.'

Hana studied her husband for a long moment. Who was this man she was married to? Was this why he was so withdrawn and secretive? Was it his work that had made him even more detached? 'I had no idea,' she said eventually finding her voice.

'That's the whole point of Bletchley,' said Gregory, changing gear and accelerating. 'No one is supposed to have any idea.'

'Did they tell you I was going to be taking over Dad's role?'

'Last night. I had a brief telephone conversation with the people that be,' said Gregory.

'Is that why you were sorry this morning?' asked Hana. 'Because your bosses have pacified you?' It also irked her that someone, no doubt Hopkins, had taken it upon themselves to smooth the way with Gregory. She should be grateful, but it irritated her. She was perfectly capable of standing up for herself.

Gregory looked at her. 'In part, yes. Why? Does that bother you? It shouldn't. You've got what you wanted, a job at Bletchley. Why should it matter what I think about it?'

'It's not that, it would be nice to know these things,' she countered. 'Who phoned you?' Gregory remained silent, looking ahead through the windscreen. 'You're only agreeing to this because your bosses have ordered you to. That's right, isn't it?'

Gregory steadfastly refused to look at her or answer her. Honestly, he was so frustrating when he closed up like this. It made Hana want to scream and shake a response out of him. She never did, though. It would be pointless trying to get any more information out of Gregory.

They travelled the rest of the journey in silence. Hana didn't know what to say. Of course, her father and her husband wouldn't have been able to tell her where they were working, just as she hadn't been able to tell Gregory, and yet here she and he were, on their way to work, with neither being able to discuss what they were doing. No wonder their conversations were limited these days. And they looked to be even more limited now.

After having their papers checked on the gate, Gregory drove up the driveway of Bletchley Park, coming to a stop at the front of the old mansion house. It looked no more sophisticated than it had done the day before, and it was hard to believe so many secrets were behind the front doors.

'I'll take you to reception,' said Gregory.

'Will I see you at all today?' Hana asked. 'Maybe we could have lunch.'

There was that smile again. The pitying one. 'I don't usually take lunch. I'll see you this evening at home.'

'I assume we won't necessarily be travelling home at the same time.'

'Probably not. You know I often work late,' replied Gregory. 'And you might find you are, too.'

He accompanied Hana to the hut at the side of the property where Hopkins had told her to report. 'I'll speak to you later.'

They stood there, looking at each other. For a moment, she thought Gregory was going to give her a peck on the cheek goodbye, but he simply gave a small nod of his head. 'Have a good day.'

And then he was gone, leaving Hana standing outside the hut, nursing a ball of disappointment in her throat. As he disappeared around the corner, she gave herself a mental shake. She had better go and report to the powers that be. She really didn't know what to expect at this point. Oh, how her life had changed in just twenty-four hours.

Inside the hut, two women in grey overcoats sat side by side at a desk. One of them looked up and smiled. 'Hello. I assume you're new here.'

'That's right,' replied Hana. It was then she noticed two other women sitting on chairs in what appeared to be the waiting area. They were both in civilian clothing, each with a suitcase at their feet. One of them looked quite young, twenty years old at the most, and the other woman looked to be in her early thirties. The older one smiled and Hana gave a nod of acknowledgement. She handed over the papers Hopkins had given her.

The woman on reception inspected them briefly. 'Jolly good. If you take a seat, someone will come for you shortly.'

Hana sat down in one of the chairs opposite the two women. They were sitting a seat apart so Hana assumed they didn't know each other. The younger one was now busy reading a book, although her upright posture and tight grip on the cover made Hana think she wasn't as relaxed as she wanted to appear. The older woman's nerves were a little more apparent.

She looked over at Hana. 'Hello. Are you new here, too?'

'Yes. First day.'

'Do you know anyone who works here already, or are you in the dark like me?'

Hana didn't want to say her husband was here. Gregory hadn't even told her what he was doing, so she shouldn't really share that information, either. Fortunately, one of the women from the desk saved her having to answer.

'Ladies.' She looked up over the rim of her spectacles. 'It's best not to discuss any details. Even when you're working here, you mustn't just share information.'

'Sorry,' said the other woman, then grimaced at Hana.

They sat in silence for several more minutes before someone came in and instructed the older woman to follow them.

'Good luck,' said Hana.

It was another twenty minutes before Hana was collected. The other young woman had been whisked off a few minutes after the first.

Hana was taken over to the main house and led through the oak panelled hallway to a room which was being used as an office. The fireplace with its decorative plaster was still intact and looked out of place with the desks, typewriters, telephones and filing cabinets.

Hana was introduced to the Commander of Bletchley Park.

'Good morning, Mrs Phillips,' he said. 'Please sit down.'

Hana took the chair on one side of the desk. 'Good morning.'

'Now, I understand that you're Captain Phillips's wife and daughter of Alfred Castle one of our esteemed Japanese translators?'

'Yes, that's right.' Hana couldn't help feeling rather proud of both men being acknowledged by the Park's commander.

'I gather from your father's superiors that he spoke about you often. He was very proud of the fact that you could speak the language, and loved to tell his colleagues about how you competed against each other to complete the crossword.'

Hana couldn't help smiling. Bless her dad. He was such a sweetheart. 'I had the best teacher in my father.'

The commander smiled. 'I have no doubt.' He glanced down at the paper on his desk. 'And you were, up until yesterday, teaching at a village school.'

'That's right,' said Hana. 'Newton Longville, it's just a few miles down the road. I must admit, I wasn't expecting to leave there quite so suddenly.'

'No. I don't suppose you were but your knowledge and expertise in the language is invaluable, so I'm told by Hopkins. And if he says you're vital, then I won't be arguing with him.' The commander sat back in his chair. 'Your route to being recruited here at the Park, is a little different to most. A little "unorthodox", shall we say.'

'I didn't know anything about it until yesterday, when my father was involved in an accident.'

'Yes. I was sorry to hear about that. Try not to worry, he's in the best place and we've made sure he's getting the best care.'

'Thank you,' replied Hana. She was beginning to appreciate just how important her father was to the work being done here. She wasn't sure everyone would have the same level of care from their employer.

'All the work done here is of the utmost importance and highly confidential,' continued the commander. 'I cannot stress that enough. You've already signed the Official Secrets Act, and you know that any breach of that will be seen as treason.'

'Yes, sir,' said Hana, feeling it was the correct way to address the commander.

'And you understand the penalty of treason? Imprisonment at best, death by hanging at worst. And don't think it can't or won't happen just because you're a woman. I can assure you, it certainly can. Am I making myself clear?'

Hana swallowed. 'Yes. Crystal clear.' She'd rather the images of being taken to the gallows and hung weren't quite so clear. She gave an involuntary shiver at the thought.

'Normally, at this point you would be sent on a seven-week training course, but things are hotting up in the Pacific and we need you to continue your father's work as quickly as possible.'

Hana nodded trying to remain composed. Inside, her stomach was somersaulting. The weight of expectation being placed on her was palpable.

'You will be fast-tracked through training and simultaneously work in your father's department, so you will be learning on the job, too.' He gave her a long look. 'You're a very intelligent young woman. Gaining a first-class honours degree in languages at Cambridge is not to be sniffed at.'

'Thank you,' said Hana.

The commander cleared his throat. 'Just remember how capable you are. No getting all flaky on us now. If you don't think you can do it, or you're not committed, then tell me now and you can go home and forget you ever came here.'

If he was goading her, then it wasn't working. Hana never shied away from a challenge, and she wasn't about to now. She sat up a little straighter in her chair and looked the commander in the eye when she replied. 'Not at all. I'm quite prepared to put the extra effort in and carry on with the work my father was doing.'

A satisfied glint flickered in the older man's eyes. 'Good.' He picked up the telephone on his desk and informed his secretary the meeting was over.

As Hana was leaving, he called to her. 'Mrs Phillips . . . your father will be very proud when he hears what you're doing. Don't let him down.' He gave a nod and turned his attention to some paperwork on his desk.

'His bark is worse than his bite,' said the secretary quietly as she led Hana back through the hallways of the mansion house.

Hana followed the secretary out of the main building and across the grounds to where a group of huts were situated, coming to a stop outside one of them. 'This is Hut Seven. Naval Section,' the secretary informed Hana, as she opened the door and went inside. A corridor ran down the centre of the hut with doors opening onto rooms on either side. The secretary popped her head around the door of the first room.

'New recruit for you,' she said. 'This is Hana Phillips. Translator. Alfred's daughter.' She beckoned for Hana to follow her into the room. 'And this is Graham Chatfield,' she told her. 'He's the supervisor of Hut Seven. I will leave you in his capable hands.'

The gentleman sitting behind the desk rose to his feet and held out a hand to Hana. 'Pleased to meet you.' He smiled broadly and shook Hana's hand robustly. He was probably around the same age as her father, with white, thinning hair and round glasses. His shirt sleeves were rolled up and his tie loosened from around the unbuttoned collar. There were grey-and-white flecks of stubble across his chin and jaw. Hana got the feeling he had been working all night. He certainly didn't look like he'd just got up, anyway. 'I'm sorry to hear about Alfred,' he said, this time looking rather more serious. 'I do hope he makes a speedy recovery.'

'Thank you,' said Hana.

'I was at Cambridge at the same time as Alfred,' continued Chatfield. 'Jolly good chap. He was one of the best Japanese speakers I knew. I hear you've inherited the skill from him.'

'I can't claim to be as good as my father,' said Hana, another swell of pride rising inside her chest.

'Pretty damn good, from what I hear. He was always singing your praises,' replied Chatfield. 'Right, I'd better introduce you to the rest of the team. This way.'

They went back out in the hallway and bypassed several rooms, before entering one at the end. This room was much larger than the office where Chatfield had first greeted her. There were three rows of tables, almost like workbenches in a science lab, one behind each other, down the centre of the room, with four individual desks running down one side under the windows. A bank of filing cabinets sat against the opposite wall, and at the far end of the room was a blackboard.

There were several people scattered around the room at different desks, all working intently amongst stacks of papers, which were in various different trays lined up along the workbenches.

'Can I just have everyone's attention for a moment?' said Chatfield. He paused, while the team stopped working and looked up. 'This is Hana Phillips. She's going to be working with us while Alfred is recovering. Hana is actually Alfred's daughter and, like her father, has rather a knack for languages, especially Japanese. So, she's going to be taking over his role.' He smiled at Hana. 'Let me introduce you to everyone.' He indicated a man, probably in his mid-forties, on the other side of the room. 'Derek Smythe.'

Derek gave a smile and a nod. 'Welcome aboard,' he said. 'Yes, sorry to hear about your father.'

'And this is Jenny Denton,' carried on Chatfield. 'She's from Cambridge, too. Languages also her speciality. She is your father's assistant so she will now be assisting you.'

'Hello. I've heard a lot about you,' said Jenny.

Hana was flattered that her father had spoken about her to his colleagues. 'Well, unfortunately, I can't say the same,' she said, pitching for humour but the look on Jenny's face told her she had missed it. Hana tried to recover the situation. 'I mean, I wouldn't have heard about you because Dad – Alfred – never spoke about his work here. In fact, the first I knew about it was yesterday.' She stopped talking at the deadpan expression on Jenny's face.

Derek gave a polite chuckle, but Hana still wished she hadn't said anything.

'This here is Audrey Brookes. We've pinched her from the Wrens.'

'Hello,' said Audrey, her smile rather warmer than Jenny's greeting. 'Good to have you here. Sorry to hear about Alfred.'

'Thank you,' said Hana.

Chatfield continued. 'We also have Lottie Rawlins working in this room. She's our filing clerk. We'd be lost without her. You'll get to meet her later.' Chatfield indicated the desk in front of Jenny's. 'That's your father's seat, there,' he said. 'For now it will be yours. As I said, Jenny is your assistant, but we'll have a team meeting now to go through everything and bring you up to speed with what we are doing. Jenny, why don't you make Hana a cup of tea?'

Hana didn't need to look at Jenny to know her colleague would not be happy about being instructed to make the new girl a cup of tea. 'It's fine. I can make it,' said Hana quickly. She dumped her handbag on the desk. 'New-girl initiation test: see if I can make a decent cuppa.'

'Challenge accepted,' said Jenny, dryly.

Hana wasn't quite sure why the younger woman was so hostile towards her, but for now she'd ignore that and go on a charm offensive. If she was going to have to work with Jenny, they needed to get on.

Chapter 6

In the end, Hana offered to make tea for everyone in the hut and sat down at what was her father's desk while Chatfield headed up the group meeting.

'So, basically, what we're doing here is translating and filling in the missing words. We receive decrypted messages which are often incomplete.'

'Usually, incomplete,' said Jenny.

Chatfield nodded. 'Yes, as Jenny said, usually incomplete and sometimes—'

'No one can make head nor tail of them,' interjected Jenny a second time, which earned her a reproachful raise of his eyebrows from Chatfield. She gave a shrug. 'Just saying.'

Chatfield turned his attention back to Hana. 'The messages are often in foreign languages. Now, there's enough German speakers to fill in the gaps on those ones, but here in the naval section, we're working closely with the Americans at listening to what's going on in the Pacific. Little do the Japanese know, we've cracked JN-25 – their naval code. Now we can monitor their communications, troop movements, supply lines etc. It all helps to predict what they're going to do next.'

'Ah, now I see,' said Hana, as it began to fall into place.

Chatfield took out a pipe from the pocket of his cardigan and chewed on the mouthpiece without lighting it. 'Now, the Japanese diplomats are very chatty and tend to send lengthy messages, which usefully outline the full strategies of the Axis powers. Breaking those codes has been far easier than the higher command messages. The information contained in those messages are our utmost priority.'

'How successful have you been so far in cracking those codes?' asked Hana.

'Running at about fifty per cent,' said Chatfield. 'Needs to be higher. We're missing out on crucial information.'

'How many translators have we got in the hut?' she asked.

'This hut? There are over twenty. This room, it's just us five, although I've been promised an extra pair of hands.' Chatfield paced back and forth in front of the blackboard, sucking on the unlit pipe, before speaking again. 'Whilst a lot of the linguists here are learning Japanese, you, like your father, are ahead of the game since you already have a substantial command of the language. The encryptions change on a daily basis and radio messages are being intercepted around the clock. That's why we need to fill in the gaps as soon as possible. We could break a message which has a huge impact on what our troops are doing in Europe and beyond. I can't stress enough, how urgent it is for us to crack the messages in their entirety.'

There was a small silence as Chatfield let his words sink in. Hana looked around at her colleagues who were all studying her. 'Right. Where do I start?' she asked.

'That's the spirit,' said Chatfield. 'Jenny will go through some of the messages with you, show you what we're up against.' He looked over at Jenny. 'Show Hana the record cards and translations Alfred was working on. Those are the higher command codes.'

Hana took the seat next to her father's assistant.

'So, you're a Japanese speaker like Alfred?' said Jenny.

'That's right, although I'm not at his level. But I did spend a lot of time in the country when I was younger,' replied Hana.

Jenny slid a ledger book towards Hana. 'This is the codebook Alfred was working on and one we use if we're stuck. We are looking at words to represent some of the key military terms here, as well as identifying new ones.' She flicked through the pages. 'I don't know how up-to-date your language skills are or how much you've learned from training, but you might want to familiarise yourself with these first before you jump in at any actual translation.'

'My father, I mean, Alfred, and I practised Japanese every day,' said Hana. 'Though obviously in a different context. So, yes, I'd like some time to look through the book.'

'You would have been given some key military words when you were training,' said Jenny. 'I expect you'll recognise some of them.'

Hana bit her lip. She didn't want to pretend she'd completed training, but it was also awkward that she was being fast-tracked. 'I'm learning as I go.'

Jenny paused and eyed her. 'You have completed your training, haven't you?'

'Not exactly. Well, no. Not at all. I'm doing both.'

Derek gave a low whistle. 'Fast-tracked. Impressive.'

Jenny's huff was less complimentary. 'That's highly irregular.'

'But necessary,' cut in Chatfield, before anyone could say anything. 'Hana can cope with the challenge.'

'Let's hope so,' said Jenny under her breath.

'Right, everyone get back to work,' instructed Chatfield, signifying that was the end of the conversation.

Hana felt decidedly uncomfortable at the obvious special treatment, or rather, dispensation, she'd been given.

Getting off on the wrong foot with her colleagues was the last thing she wanted.

*

Hana was pleased when lunchtime came, and Graham told her to take a break for an hour. 'We stagger our breaks so there's always someone in the hut carrying on the work,' he explained. 'Be back in an hour, yes? The canteen is just out of the main gates in Wiltern Avenue, where the hostel is. But I assume you're not staying in the hostel as you live locally.'

'That's right. I live in Newton Longville.'

Chatfield nodded. 'Well, you should head over to the canteen at lunchtime. Just around the corner from there on Church Green Road is where you'll be doing your training. It's all nice and close.'

Hana went into the canteen and grabbed some food, which she ate at one of the long tables in the dining hall. She watched others coming and going. They were a mix of people. Some were clearly civilians, like herself, in their everyday clothes. Others were military personnel from all branches. She was still in shock that Gregory was working here and she'd had no idea. Her father working here in secret she could understand, but her husband? Surely, she should have known somehow or at least suspected. It made her wonder what other secrets Gregory was keeping from her. And yet, she had no right to ask him to betray his country. Like her, he had signed the Official Secrets Act, and the restriction to sharing classified information extended to spouses. There were no exceptions. Still, it hurt her somewhat.

As if by thinking of Gregory, she conjured him up. He slid into the seat opposite her.

'Hello, Hana,' he said. 'Thought I'd take lunch today to see if I could find you. How is it going?'

He sounded chirpier than he usually did, which took Hana a little by surprise but also warmed her heart. It was a small glimpse of the buoyant and charming man she had fallen in love with and married.

She offered a warm smile in return. 'It's going all right, I think,' she said. 'There's a lot to take in. New people to meet.'

'It's bound to feel strange at first.' Gregory's face grew serious. 'You don't have to do this if you don't want to.'

Hana withheld the frustrated sigh that threatened to escape. 'I want to,' she said finally.

'Let me rephrase that.' Gregory pushed the mashed potato around on his plate with his fork, before looking up at her. 'You don't have to do this if it's not for you. You may want to, but it may not be quite what's right for you.'

This time Hana didn't withhold her exasperation. 'For a moment there, I thought you'd come to offer me words of encouragement, not discouragement.'

Gregory placed his fork on the edge of his plate. 'I'm offering you a way out. You're very stubborn and bloody-minded at times, Hana. I was simply giving you a chance not to lose face.'

She eyed her husband across the table. 'I'm perfectly capable of doing the job I've been asked to do,' she said, wishing she could say more. 'I have highly desirable skills and knowledge. The work I'm doing is crucial.'

'That's all well and good, but don't underestimate how difficult it might be.'

'Anyone would think you found me being here a threat.'

Gregory's eyes narrowed a fraction, and he leaned across the table towards her, his voice low. 'I do not find you a threat. I'm just trying to stop you making a fool of yourself by trying to live up to your father's reputation. You don't have the same expertise and knowledge as him. They are expecting a lot from you, and I don't want you to be embarrassed because I care about you, believe it or not.' With that he got to his feet, leaving his tray on the table and grabbing his stick he left the canteen.

Hana glanced around her, hoping their marital altercation had gone unnoticed. Two young Wrens in their uniform to her right hurriedly averted their gaze. So much for no one seeing them argue. Hana pushed her plate away, feeling guilty for leaving the food but knowing she wouldn't be able to stomach it. Not after the low blow Gregory had just delivered. He didn't think she was good enough. That was the bottom line. And as for embarrassing herself, he was clearly more worried about her embarrassing him. For a moment there, she had been reeled in; she thought his happy demeanour was genuine. She really didn't know her husband anymore.

'Hey, don't look so glum,' came a woman's voice, breaking Hana's thoughts. 'You don't mind if I sit here, do you?'

Hana looked up as Audrey sat down in the seat recently vacated by Gregory. 'Not at all,' she replied.

'So, who was that handsome looking RAF chap you were just talking to?' Audrey spooned sugar into her tea before stirring it around, her spoon clinking against the cup, before taking a large gulp from the cup.

'Oh, him. Erm, that's . . . that's my husband, actually.'

Audrey nearly spat her tea across the table. She swallowed hard. 'Your husband?'

'Very ladylike,' came another voice. It was Jenny. She took the seat next to Audrey. 'What's going on?'

'Well,' began Audrey. 'See that rather handsome RAF officer who's just disappearing out of the door.'

Jenny looked over. 'With the stick?'

'Yep. Well, he is Hana's husband.' Audrey looked pleased with herself.

Jenny's head snapped back around to Hana. 'Your husband? My, you really are connected. We'd better watch ourselves around you. Pillow talk and all that.'

Hana tried not to look as affronted as she felt. 'Don't worry. There won't be any of that. I didn't even know he was working here until this morning.'

Jenny gave a look that said she found it hard to believe.

'You are a dark horse,' said Audrey, who clearly was teasing.

'Look, if you don't mind, can you just keep that to yourselves?' asked Hana. 'It's awkward otherwise and people jump to conclusions. I'm here on my own merits.'

'Yes, of course you are,' said Jenny. 'Just like us.'

Again, Hana couldn't quite tell if Jenny was being sincere or not. She chose to ignore any spite that had been laced within the comment.

Audrey tapped her nose and winked. 'Your secret is safe with us, after all, keeping secrets at this place is what we do best.'

Hana couldn't help warming to Audrey. She hoped Jenny's frostiness would thaw. The idea of having friends at work appealed to Hana. Apart from her mother and Gwen, she didn't have many friends in the village. Her job as a schoolteacher meant most of the parents thought of her in a professional way rather than a personal way. It didn't trouble Hana greatly, but as the war had gone on and her relationship with Gregory diminished, she missed the light-heartedness of female friendship.

The conversation turned to other things. Audrey explained that she had lived in London before working at the Park and was now billeted in the village with a darling landlady, Mrs Kidson, who had a young baby, who was a darling, too, except when he cried in the middle of the night.

'You could ask to be moved,' said Jenny.

'I know but despite what I say about the baby, I do like living with June. That's Mrs Kidson. We get on well and it keeps her company. Her husband was home on leave, and it was soon after he'd gone back she had found out she was pregnant. He hasn't seen the little fella yet.'

'All these children growing up without their fathers around,' said Hana. 'It's horrible. My brother is a POW. His little boy is growing up so fast, and he's missing it all.'

'He won't be the only one,' said Jenny needlessly.

Hana again ignored any kind of dig Jenny was making. 'Do you live in the village too, Jenny?' she asked.

'Yes. Thankfully, there are no babies in the house, and even though there are two other girls billeted there, I have a room to myself.'

'She's showing off now,' said Audrey, with a wink. 'Anyway, where are you living?'

'Oh, I'm local, actually. Just down the road at Newton Longville,' replied Hana. 'So, I'll just be commuting in.'

'Not on the dreaded Bletchley buses,' said Audrey.

'I'm not sure yet. I got a lift in today.'

'Of course you did,' said Jenny. 'Can't have an officer's wife, bussing it in.'

'You know there are a selection of free bicycles to use if you ever get stuck,' said Audrey. 'In the bike shed near Hut Six.'

'That's handy to know,' said Hana. She checked her watch. 'Right, I suppose we'd better head back.'

They got up and stacked their trays and plates on the collection station. Just as they were about to leave the dining room, the door swung open and in strode a man in civilian clothing. He stopped dead in his tracks and then smiled. Hana realised Audrey was grinning back at the man, although neither had acknowledged each other it was clear this was not their first meeting.

'Ladies,' said the man, who looked to be in his early thirties. He held the door wide open with an exaggerated bow and a wave of his hand. 'Please, allow me.'

'Why thank you, kind sir,' said Audrey as she took her time to walk past him.

'My pleasure,' he replied with a wink, to which Audrey giggled.

Hana followed Jenny and Audrey through the door and out onto Wiltern Avenue.

'Well, it seems you aren't the only one with romantic connections here, Hana,' said Jenny. 'I've seen him about the Park. Come on, Audrey, spill the beans.'

'Fair's fair,' said Hana, enjoying the banter between them. She slipped her arm through Audrey's and Jenny did the same on the other side.

Audrey gave another laugh. 'That was Bill Crosslands,' she said, unable to control the grin spreading across her face. 'He's in Hut Three. Don't ask me what they do in there. I have no idea.'

'I don't suppose you do,' said Jenny. 'You two obviously know each other.'

'He's very good-looking,' said Hana.

'He is, isn't he?' replied Audrey enthusiastically. 'We've had a drink a couple of times at the pub in the village, The Eight Bells. Nothing serious, not yet anyway.'

'I don't think it will be long, judging by the way he smiled at you,' said Jenny.'

They reached the gates to the Park and showed their passes to the guard, who nodded and waved them through.

'Heads up,' said Audrey under her breath. 'Here comes the spook.'

'What?' Hana looked up to see Hopkins coming out of one of the buildings.

'MI5,' supplied Jenny.

'Ah, just the person,' said Hopkins as he approached them. 'Mrs Phillips, may I have a word, please?'

'I don't think that's a question,' muttered Audrey.

'New girl in trouble already,' said Jenny.

'We'll see you back at the hut,' said Audrey. 'Hopefully, anyway. Don't want them whisking you away.'

'Don't look so worried.' Hopkins offered up a smile. 'I just wanted a word in private. Shall we walk around the lake?'

It seemed a strange choice for a chat with MI5, but Hana was beginning to realise that here at the Park, nothing was strange.

'I'm supposed to be back at the hut,' said Hana.

'Don't worry about that,' assured Hopkins. 'Your friends will vouch for you.' He took out a pack of Player's cigarettes and offered one to Hana.

'No, thank you. I don't smoke.'

'Ah, yes. I remember. Good for you. Terrible habit.' Hopkins proceeded to light his cigarette and take a long draw, before slowly exhaling the smoke. He slipped the packet back into his pocket. 'I'll get straight to the point,' he began. 'Your reason for being here is twofold. One of those reasons being to carry on your father's work. The other is even more sensitive. What I'm about to tell you is highly confidential. You cannot talk about it to anyone, only me.'

'All right,' said Hana, feeling Hopkins wouldn't proceed without her acknowledgement. 'When you say "only you", does that exclude Chatfield and the commander?'

'Absolutely no one else other than me.' Hopkins stopped walking and looked at her. 'Only me means just that. *Only me*. Do you understand?'

Hana nodded. 'Yes. Very much so.'

'Good.' He reassumed his walking and Hana fell into step with him. 'There's a spy in the hut,' said Hopkins quietly. 'A mole.'

Hana gave a sharp intake of breath. She had not been expecting that. 'A spy? Are you certain?'

'Of course I'm certain. I don't make a habit of throwing such serious allegations around without certainty.'

'Yes. Sorry. Do you know who?'

'No. That's the problem.' Hopkins took a final draw on his cigarette before dropping it to the ground and grinding it out with the toe of his highly polished, black leather shoe. 'We approached your father a couple of weeks ago. We had, and still have, reason to believe information was being leaked. Information that could only have come from his room. We asked him to find out who the mole was.'

'Right,' said Hana, taking it all in. 'Can I ask why you approached my father? Why not Chatfield or one of the others?'

'Good question. Chatfield is not close enough to the action. We needed someone working in that room where the higher-command Japanese communications were being decrypted. Chatfield would have to start paying particular attention to the room and it would arouse suspicions.'

'So why my father?' Hana pushed again for a more definitive answer.

'He's the most trustworthy. He has proved that several times when dealing with highly sensitive translations. He'd also been to us earlier about protecting such information and we consulted him in putting in further precautions. He has been instrumental in shoring up security in the room and in the hut overall.'

'My father is quite a particular person,' said Hana. 'He likes things done in certain ways.' It was no surprise to Hana that Alfred had assessed the security and suggested improvements. 'Did he ever say who he suspected?'

'No. But he left a message for me the night before last – the night before his accident. I didn't speak to him personally as I was in a meeting, but the message he left was a pre-agreed coded message, saying that he had information on the mole. I phoned him back first thing yesterday morning and we arranged a meeting. We didn't discuss names over the telephone. Security reasons.'

'Hold on, you telephoned yesterday morning?'

'Yes, that's right. He was at home.'

'I know,' said Hana. 'I was there when he took the call.'

'Interesting. I assume he didn't say anything about it.'

'No. Just that he had to go into work early,' said Hana, thinking back to the previous morning. Was it really only then? Things had moved so fast.

'And nothing else?'

Hana shook her head. Then the realisation dawned on her. She looked up at Hopkins. 'Do you think the accident . . .' It was difficult to even voice her thoughts. She steeled herself. 'Do you think the accident wasn't an accident? Do you think . . . he was targeted because of what he was about to tell you?'

'We believe so,' said Hopkins. He fixed Hana with a look, as if weighing up her reaction.

Hana took several deep, steadying breaths. 'Were they trying to kill him? To stop him for exposing the spy?'

'Again, that is what we believe.'

She felt her heart thump harder. The fact that someone had intentionally set out to murder her father made her shiver. 'Poor Dad,' she said, to herself more than to Hopkins.

'Are you all right?' he asked.

'Yes. I'm fine.' She paused while a couple of Wrens passed by, chatting away about a night out. Once they were out of earshot she spoke again. 'Why are you telling me all this?'

'In a nutshell, we need you to find the information your father had gathered. We need to know who the spy is and whatever else he had found out. It was much more than just a name. Alfred had compiled a file – names, times, locations, et cetera. Everything we need to close the spy ring down. I cannot stress how important it is that we, at MI5, get this information as quickly as possible.'

'Can't you just go and look for it?' asked Hana.

'If only it were that simple.' Hopkins lit another cigarette. 'If we go charging in there, searching through all the papers, we're going to arouse suspicion and alert the spy we're onto them. They will run. Or even find the evidence and destroy it. That's the worst-case scenario to be honest. They could carry on with what they're doing for longer. We need to find out who is involved before we show our hand.'

'What exactly am I looking for?' asked Hana.

'That's just it. We're not sure how Alfred collected the information. I believe he would have written it in code, so that if it was found no one would think anything of it, or if they did, they wouldn't be able to read it. That's where you come in. You are the perfect solution.'

'I am?'

'For a start, bringing you into the hut, under the guise of replacing your father is totally reasonable. After all, you have extensive knowledge of Japanese. You're Cambridge-educated. You have first-hand experience of living in Japan, so you have a deeper understanding of the culture.'

Hopkins paused to take a long draw on his cigarette, before slowly releasing the smoke from his lungs. 'And, probably most importantly, you more than anyone else will understand your father's coding. We know from his lectures at Cambridge that he often spoke about how you and he made up your own coding, your own ciphers. You, more than anyone else understand his logic, his way of thinking. There couldn't be anyone better than you to find the information your father had gathered. We're relying on you, Hana. And who knows, you might crack a couple of Japanese messages along the way.'

Chapter 7

The rest of the afternoon Hana spent working alongside Jenny, who showed her the ropes, explaining to her how her father was working out the code and what progress they had made so far.

'These are messages from the Japanese diplomats to one another,' Jenny explained. 'They are very long-winded. They do like to chat. It can be quite laborious decoding everything, only to find they're talking about things that have already happened or that we know about.'

'That must be frustrating,' said Hana, picking up one of the messages that was waiting to be decoded.

'You could do some of those,' said Jenny. 'They're easy ones, and not so vital.'

'Erm, is that what Alfred was doing?' The idea of trawling through diplomats' chit-chat was not appealing, and if it wasn't what her father was doing, then what was the point of her being there?

'Well . . . no. He was decoding the higher-command messages.'

'Then that's what I should be doing,' said Hana, purposefully, returning the diplomat's message to the tray. 'I'm here to do Alfred's work. It's not a great use of resources if I'm doing less important messages.'

Jenny raised her eyebrows. 'My, we don't lack confidence, do we?'

'It's not that—' Hana was ready to defend her corner, but before she could go on, Derek Smythe spoke.

'It makes sense what Hana is saying. We need her expertise with the more complicated codes.'

'But she hasn't completed the training,' protested Jenny.

'There isn't time to wait for me to do all the training first,' said Hana, silently thanking Derek for sticking up for her. 'I'm doing it simultaneously.' She looked around the desk. 'Where are the higher-command messages?'

Jenny didn't reply as they entered into something of a stand-off. Hana wasn't about to be bossed around, especially now Hopkins had given her the extra and somewhat more urgent task of finding her father's notes so they could find out who the spy was. She eyed Alfred's assistant and wondered whether Jenny was being obstructive on purpose, or whether it was simply because her nose was a little out of joint at Hana's arrival.

Jenny let out a huff and broke the deadlock. 'Over there in the red basket.'

'Thank you,' said Hana and reached across the desk, plucking a piece of paper from the basket. 'Right, can you tell me where to start?'

It wasn't without reticence that Jenny moved her chair next to Hana's to look at the code.

'First thing we do is look at the letter-frequency charts from the previous fifty Japanese naval-transmissions,' she said, going over to the wooden filing drawers which lined the back wall. She took out an index card. 'This is our records system. We keep things like common Japanese phrases, crib sheets and frequency tables.' She came back over to Hana and slid the index card along the desk towards her, before taking a file from another filing cabinet on the back wall. 'This is where we keep a tally of letter occurrences.' She dumped the file down on the desk next to Hana, before reaching for another file. 'And these are our worksheets where we record our progress with cracking codes. We also have to complete daily logs to record which messages have been broken and anything of note that will help with breaking future codes.'

'It's a lot to take in all at once,' said Audrey, giving Hana a sympathetic smile.

Hana appreciated the gesture. She had a feeling Jenny was making a point of how much there was to learn. It was most definitely going to be a steep learning curve for Hana.

'Here's a book with the common Japanese naval terms,' Jenny was saying, dumping another book in front of Hana. 'With the messages, we're looking for repeat patterns across the transmission. Particularly vowels. Locating them within the messages makes it a lot easier to take educated guesses at the rest of it. We often get half-decoded messages here, and because we are the experts, we get the task of cracking the rest of the code.'

'You'll soon get the hang of it all,' said Audrey. 'Unless they change the codes before we break them.'

'What happens then?' asked Hana, looking through the pages of the codebook and the ledger in front of her and secretly feeling a little daunted by the prospect. The enormity of the task was beginning to sink in.

'We start again from scratch,' said Audrey.

'So, the ability to work quickly and accurately under pressure is paramount,' concluded Jenny. 'Not as easy as you thought?' Jenny looked pleased with her observation.

'I didn't expect it to be easy at all,' said Hana. 'On the contrary, I'm looking forward to the challenge.'

'We can start off by me showing you some of the codes we've cracked and how,' said Jenny. 'After that, you can have a try at the higher-command ones. But, and I don't mean to be rude, I think you'll find you're in over your head to start with.'

Hana bristled at the comment. Rather than dent her confidence, as she was sure it was designed to, Jenny's scepticism actually made her even more determined. She wasn't going to let Jenny have the satisfaction of gloating over her lack of experience. She thought of Alfred lying in the hospital bed. She owed it to him and herself to be able to do this. She also thought of Hopkins and her secret mission. She wasn't prepared to let anyone down.

So Hana chose to rise above Jenny's sniping and listened attentively as the assistant explained how they had cracked some of the codes.

'So, there you are,' said Jenny, when she'd finished. 'I need to get on with some work now. Shout if you need any help.'

'Thanks,' said Hana. She really hoped she wouldn't have to ask Jenny for help, that would mean swallowing an awful lot of pride.

Hana spent the next thirty minutes or so getting to grips with the filing system, seeing how their work and findings were recorded. There was an awful lot of paperwork, and this was just the information they had within their room of the hut. It was hard to imagine how much information was held across the whole of the Park.

She flicked through the index cards, marvelling at what had been learned so far.

'Oh, admiring my filing system, are you?' came a woman's voice from behind Hana.

She spun around to see a young woman in civilian clothes, smiling at her. 'Your filing system?' asked Hana.

The young woman had white-blonde hair, styled perfectly into curls and pinned back behind her ears. She held out her hand to Hana. 'Lottie Rawlins,' she said. 'I'm your walking, talking filing system.'

Hana shook hands. 'Hana Phillips. I'm here to stand in for Alfred.'

'Oh, my word. I heard what happened to him,' said Lottie. 'Does anyone know how he is?' She looked around the room.

'You're talking to the right person,' said Derek. 'Hana is his daughter.'

'What?' Lottie's expression was one of surprise. 'Really?'

'Yes, that's right,' replied Hana.

'Wow. This is a surprise.' And then more seriously, 'I am sorry to hear about your father. How is he doing?'

Lottie was open and warm. Hana liked her instantly. 'I'm going to see him after work today,' she said. 'If there's time, that is. I don't really know much yet.'

Lottie gave a sympathetic smile. 'If anyone can come back from something like that, then it's Alfred. He's a very quietly determined man.'

'Thank you,' said Hana. 'I really appreciate that.'

'Now, to work, I'm afraid,' said Lottie, patting the back of her blonde hair which must have taken ages to arrange into the perfect curls. She looked like she should be on the cover of a fashion magazine. Far too glamorous to be a filing clerk, Hana couldn't help thinking.

As Hana worked her way through the afternoon, her conversation with Hopkins was ever present in her mind. She couldn't help taking the odd glance around the room, her gaze travelling over her colleagues. Which one of them was the mole? Which one of them was the reason her father was lying seriously injured in a hospital bed right now? Who had betrayed Alfred?

She could feel the anger rising from the pit of her stomach. She gripped the pencil she was holding, pushing down hard on the paper. There was a crack as the lead broke.

'Pencil sharpener's over there,' said Jenny, not looking up from the code she was working on.

Hana was glad of the excuse to get up from her desk. She took several deep breaths as she went over to the end of the workbench where the sharpener was clamped. She shoved the pencil in and wound the handle of the sharpener around and around, faster and faster.

She looked up and realised Jenny was staring at her. Hana stopped turning the handle and withdrew the pencil, which had been sharpened to within an inch of its life. Jenny eyed the pencil before returning to her work.

Hana forced herself to take yet another deep breath. She had to keep calm. She couldn't let her personal feelings get in the way of doing her work. If she stayed calm, she had a better chance of not only cracking any codes but, more importantly, finding out who had betrayed their country and was responsible for trying to silence her father.

Hana sat back down at her desk, forcing herself to think about where Alfred might have recorded or hidden the information about the spy. Hopkins seemed sure it had been recorded in code, and knowing her father, Hana was inclined to agree. Highly confidential and sensitive information like that needed to be protected. There was no point writing it in Japanese as everyone in the room would be able to read it.

Would he have kept it here at the Park though? Was this the safest place to keep that sort of information, coded or otherwise?

She glanced up and everyone seemed to be busy, not paying her any attention. Trying to act casual, Hana opened the drawer to her father's desk. It was very neat and tidy, which didn't surprise her in the least. Alfred was an organised man. A place for everything and everything in its place, he would often say. Indeed, his desk showed exactly that and was a replica of the one in his study at home, in terms of where things were kept. Pens and pencils all neatly set out in trays, paper for notes stacked precisely in another drawer. In the second drawer were several books. She lifted them out. They were Japanese to English dictionaries. Other than that, there wasn't anything that looked remotely like what Hopkins was after.

She had to think like her father. If she had secret information, where would she hide it? Not at work, she decided. Home was the obvious place that sprang to mind. She'd have to look in her father's study at home as soon as she got the chance.

By the time four o'clock came around, Hana was exhausted. There had been so much information to take in, which, whilst challenging, wasn't beyond her capabilities but tiring.

'No luck cracking the code, then?' said Jenny, looking at the paper in front of Hana.

'Not yet,' said Hana. 'Early days.'

'Better luck tomorrow,' said Jenny, shrugging on her coat. She called out goodnight to everyone and headed out of the hut.

'Don't worry about it,' said Audrey. 'It can take days or even weeks to decipher some of these messages. Go home. Get some sleep and tomorrow we start all over again.'

'Thanks,' said Hana. She said goodbye to everyone and headed out of the hut. As she needed to make her own way home, she opted to take one of the bicycles Audrey had mentioned. However, as she rounded the corner, she was pleased to see her husband waiting for her.

'I was just thinking about you,' said Hana. 'I didn't know if I'd have to take one of those to get home.' She nodded to the assortment of second-hand bikes under the corrugated roof.

'Not today, at least,' said Gregory. 'How was your day?'

'It was interesting to say the least,' she replied. She had to stop herself mentioning Hopkins. 'What about yours?'

'The usual.'

Hana realised that this would be the extent of their conversation about their working days. There wasn't much else they could really talk about. Besides, Gregory looked deep in thought. She couldn't help wondering what he was working on and whether this was also having an effect on his mood. Maybe he couldn't stop thinking about his work because it was highly important. But of course she couldn't quiz him about it.

'Have you heard any more news about Dad?' she asked as they walked to the car.

Gregory shook his head. 'No, sorry. Not had time to call today,' he said. 'But we have time to take a detour to the hospital if you want to see your father.'

'Oh, yes, please,' said Hana, falling into step on Gregory's right-hand side, something he was pedantic about her doing. He said it was so she didn't bump against his walking stick, but Hana had long suspected it was so she couldn't see the scars on his hand and neck. His 'disfigurements', as he called them.

Gregory took the car keys from his pocket and tossed them about in his palm. He walked around and got into the driver's seat, and soon they were zipping out of the grounds of the Park and heading over to the hospital.

They travelled in silence and Hana's thoughts again turned to her father. She felt a little guilty she had been somewhat preoccupied by her new job that she hadn't had time to think about him too much, but now with Bletchley Park behind her, the seriousness of her father's condition filled her mind.

*

'You've only got ten minutes before visiting hours are over,' said the nurse as they reached the nurses' desk.

'How has he been?' asked Gregory.

'He's been drifting in and out of consciousness, but he's not really spoken,' she said, adopting a more sympathetic response.

'Has he said anything?' Gregory pressed.

The nurse glanced at Hana and then addressed Gregory. 'The doctor will be able to answer your questions more fully once he's done his rounds in the morning. At the moment, Mr Castle hasn't said anything particularly coherent.'

Hana's breath hitched in her throat as the nurse responded to Gregory's questions. The thought of her father finding it difficult or even impossible to communicate was awful. He would be devastated. As a linguist, speech and communication were everything to him. She realised she was inadvertently gripping Gregory's arm and he looked down at her hand. She thought for a moment he was going to shirk away from the contact, but instead, he braced his arm to offer both physical and mental support, before they walked down the corridor to Alfred's private room.

Gregory opened the door and stepped back, allowing Hana to enter first.

The curtains were drawn, and a small, bedside lamp cast a soft orange glow across the room. Alfred's eyes were closed, but at the sound of the door swishing across the lino floor, his eyes fluttered and opened and his gaze found Hana. She broke from Gregory's hand and rushed to his bedside, a ball of emotion tumbling in her stomach. She blinked back the tears.

'Hello, Dad,' she said, leaning down and kissing his cheek. She studied his face for any sign of recognition or acknowledgement, but Alfred's face remained expressionless as he held her gaze.

'Hello, Alfred,' said Gregory coming around to the other side of the bed. He rested his hand on his father-in-law's shoulder. Alfred's gaze moved across to Gregory, before looking back at his daughter.

'We've been so worried about you,' said Hana, sliding her hand over her father's.

Alfred opened his mouth as if he was going to speak, but only a gruff rasping sound emitted. 'Don't try to talk,' said Gregory. 'It may be a few days before you're up to speaking.'

Hana wanted to burst into tears. Her beautiful, strong father looked so vulnerable and sad lying there. She dipped her head momentarily to gulp back the lump in her throat, before looking back at him and forcing a smile. Positivity. That's what Alfred needed right now. 'It's all right, Dad. Everything is going to be all right. Mum is fine. Worried about you, of course. She was here earlier. I don't know if you were awake.' Hana was gabbling, she knew, but the silence was heavy and she didn't want her dad to get upset if he couldn't speak. She had no idea how much he knew, or indeed, how much he understood. The need to try to communicate with him was strong. Even if her father couldn't talk, surely the sound of someone speaking to him would be a comfort.

'Why don't you let your father rest?' suggested Gregory.

Hana shook her head. She checked it was just the three of them in the room, before she leaned in closer to Alfred. 'You'll never guess what, Dad,' she said quietly. 'I've been asked to work at Bletchley Park.'

Alfred's hand twitched, almost as if in response.

'Hana, I really don't think this is a good idea,' said Gregory.

'It's fine,' replied Hana, not breaking her gaze with her father. He had heard her, she was sure. He understood what she had said. The helplessness she had felt on first seeing him was replaced by hope. 'It's all right for him to know. Isn't it, Dad?'

Alfred's hand twitched again and he opened his mouth, but still no words came. Hana pushed on.

'They've asked me to carry on with the work you were doing. To stand in for you.' She smiled broadly at her father. 'Gregory knows and I now know he works there, too, but of course, we can't talk about it to each other.'

'You really need to stop,' said Gregory.

'I really don't,' snapped back Hana. She looked back at Alfred, smiling broadly at him at first, but he began moving his head from side to side on the pillow. His hand was jerking more violently now and some sort of muffled grunt came from his throat.

Gregory put his hand on Alfred's shoulder. 'It's all right, Alfred. Don't get worked up now.' He threw Hana a look somewhere between concern and annoyance.

'Dad, come on, now. It's all right. Calm down,' coaxed Hana, the few seconds of joy that he had heard her, now completely extinguished. 'Everything is all right.'

Alfred continued to thrash for a few more seconds, before his eyes rolled back in his head. He gasped, and then his whole body slumped.

'Dad!' cried Hana, leaping to her feet.

Gregory leaned over, putting his ear close to Alfred's mouth and nose, and placed his hand on the older man's chest. Hana was frozen to the spot. Gregory stood up and looked over at her. 'He's breathing.'

'Oh, thank God for that,' cried Hana, before a sob escaped. She held her face in her hands. For an awful moment, she'd thought her father had died. She dropped her hands. 'That was my fault. I shouldn't have told him about Bletchley,' she said quietly.

Gregory came around to her side of the bed, cupping her elbow in his hand. 'We should let your father rest now. Come on, let's get you home.'

As they left the room, Hana thought her heart was going to break. They reached the car park, and she burst into tears. Gregory put an arm around her and comforting as it was, it was no balm to the heartache she was experiencing.

*

As soon as they arrived home, Hana rustled up some supper for them both, although she had very little appetite. It was only the fact that she knew it was terrible to waste food when rationing was in full swing that made her eat it.

After she had cleared the dishes and washed up, Hana telephoned her mother. She didn't mention about Alfred getting upset. She felt too ashamed.

Besides, she had to assume Pamela knew nothing about what Alfred was really doing for work, so trying to explain about Bletchley without compromising herself and the Official Secrets Act she had signed would be impossible. So she opted to say nothing.

Hana sat down in the living room. Gregory had already disappeared into his study. Of all the opportunities for him to spend just a few minutes with her, she thought it would have been today. Her heart, heavy already, somehow sank a bit lower. She tried listening to the radio then attempted to read a book, she even picked up some knitting that had been stuffed in her sewing bag for weeks, but none of these activities distracted her from thinking about her father. She felt so helpless. Surely there was something she could do.

It was said that even when people are unconscious, they can sometimes hear what's going on around them. Maybe she could take a newspaper with her next time and read some of the stories. He always liked to keep up to date with what was going on in the world. She could maybe even do the crossword, read out the clues and share the answers with him. Yes, that's what she'd do, she decided.

Hana dumped the knitting back in the bag and closed her eyes, resting her head against the back of the sofa. She'd make sure she grabbed a copy of tomorrow's newspaper and take it into the hospital so she could read to him about all the latest goings on.

The telephone rang out, making Hana startle. She jumped to her feet and rushed out to the hallway to answer it in case it was the hospital or her mother.

She was just about to lift the receiver, when it stopped ringing. Gregory must have taken it in the study. She could hear his voice coming from behind the closed door. It was low and muffled so she couldn't make out what he was saying, but it sounded urgent. Her stomach somersaulted at the idea it might be bad news about her father. Hana stepped quietly towards the door of the study and strained to hear what was being said. She wasn't one to eavesdrop on her husband's conversations, and she'd certainly never felt the urge to before, but something made her do it today. Maybe it was all the worry about her father that made her do it. She didn't know, but she was right outside the study door now and could just about make out what her husband was saying.

'You're not to call my home again . . . My wife is here . . . Yes. I'll come now but this can't happen again . . . I . . .' The rest of his words were lost as he lowered his voice even further.

Instinct made Hana step away from the door and hurry back to the living room. She heard the ding of the telephone as the handset extension in the study was replaced in its cradle. She grabbed her book and pretended to be reading it as the study door opened and she heard Gregory step into the hall. She turned to look over her shoulder.

'Everything all right?' she asked, trying to sound casual. 'Would you like a cup of tea?'

Gregory paused, frowned and looked up at her. 'No. I've got to go out.' He moved out of her eyesight towards the front door.

Hana hopped up and went out to the hall. 'What, you're going out now? It's late. Where are you going?'

Gregory didn't meet her gaze as he took his hat from the hall stand and shrugged on his coat. 'It's work,' he said, placing his hat on his head. 'I won't be long.'

She was about to protest, then remembered that the nature of their work often meant long and odd hours. Still, it seemed strange.

Gregory had his back to her now, his hand on the lock. She saw his shoulders rise as he took in a deep breath, releasing it slowly before speaking. 'Sorry, darling. I can't talk about it,' he said, turning and offering her something akin to a smile.

'Right.' She nodded.

Her husband opened the front door and stepped out onto the path, pulling the door closed behind him.

Hana stared at the closed door. She hadn't known Gregory to have to go out in the evenings before. It all seemed so out of the blue. She walked back into the living room and looked out of the bay window, watching as the car pulled away and out of the drive.

Hana thought back to the conversation she'd overheard. Gregory had sounded rather brusque and impatient. As if he was annoyed to have been called. That wasn't the reaction of someone who was meeting a lover. She gave herself a mental shake at the ridiculous idea that he was having an affair. No, it definitely sounded more like a work call. She'd just have to trust him, which she did, but she couldn't help being intrigued now by what he was doing.

Hana let out a sigh. All this suspicion and guesswork was tiring, to say the least. She wandered over to the sideboard where several family photographs were on display in various different frames. She picked up the silver-framed one of her and her father. She was about ten years old and they hadn't long been in Japan. It was their second visit. She was holding her father's hand, her mother on his other side and next to her was Amaya, one of the Japanese women who had welcomed them into her home and introduced them to the wider community. Hana smiled fondly at the memory. She replaced the photograph on the sideboard. Amaya had passed away in 1930, just before Hana and her family had returned to England. She had taught Hana many Japanese words in the time the Castle family were out there.

Thinking about it, with his in-depth knowledge of Japanese, it was no wonder Alfred had been asked to work at Bletchley. She couldn't help wondering why she hadn't been approached by them before. They obviously knew she could speak the language, otherwise they wouldn't have approached her now. Unless it was something to do with a father and daughter working together having the potential for compromise or conflict of interest. She had no idea.

Whatever the reason, it didn't really matter now. She was at the Park and she had been asked by Hopkins to find the information Alfred had uncovered about the spy.

She let out a sigh. After going to see her father and all the upset, she had completely forgotten she'd meant to look in his study for the information.

Hana looked at the clock on the mantelpiece. She decided to ignore the time of night and going out to the hallway, phoned her mother at home.

'Hello, Mum. Me again. Look, erm, I need to pop over this evening . . . Yes. Now . . . I know it's late but I need to look for something in Dad's study . . . to do with work. I won't be long. See you soon.'

Pamela had sounded tired and Hana felt guilty for bothering her, but she knew she wouldn't be able to settle without checking the study. It would be a feather in her cap if she could turn up tomorrow with the information Hopkins required. That would prove her worth, and hopefully they would think about keeping her on at the Park.

Hana dragged her bicycle out from the depths of the garage and cycled to her parents' home. It was dark and more difficult to navigate the roads with no streetlamps or bicycle lights which had all been banned due to the bombing raids.

It wasn't long before she was at Bramble House. It was Gwen who let her in, but her mother met her in the hall, looking tired and less than enthusiastic at Hana's late visit to Alfred's study.

'Is it absolutely necessary tonight?' Pamela asked her. 'I can't think what the printers need so urgently. Couldn't it have waited until the morning?'

'Sorry, Mum,' said Hana, giving her mother a quick kiss on the cheek. 'I won't be long.'

Pamela sighed, suggesting she still wasn't happy about it, but wasn't going to labour the point. 'All right, then. I'll put the kettle on for a quick cuppa,' she said, turning and heading down the hallway to the kitchen.

'I'll help you,' said Gwen, throwing Hana a brief smile.

Hana stepped into her father's study. It was only yesterday she'd been in here looking for the telephone number for Alfred's work. Since then, her world had been dislodged from its familiar and secure foothold. Methodically, she began to search through her father's papers. She started with the desk drawers. The top drawer had several pens and pencils lined up neatly in a row, and two notebooks. The second drawer contained Alfred's diary, along with an address book. The third drawer contained several manila files, all labelled with their contents. No surprises. Everything was as she'd expected – highly organised, in Alfred's usual fastidious manner.

A quick rummage through all four drawers of the filing cabinet yielded no results, either, though she smiled as she opened the bottom drawer of the cabinet where Alfred kept every single copy of *The Daily Telegraph* he'd read in the last twelve months. When a new one was placed in the filing cabinet, he would remove the oldest copy. Hana was aware of Alfred's little idiosyncrasies and his need for order, and though she didn't know why he kept the newspapers for twelve months, it was what he always did, so she'd never really questioned it. In the same way, she had never questioned his need to line his pens and pencils up in a particular order on his desk before he started work.

Hana quickly flicked through the newspapers and checked underneath the pile, in case he'd hidden a book of some description there but found nothing. She made sure the newspapers were left as neat as she'd found them and closed the drawer.

The last place she could think to look was the bookcase on the back wall. She opened the glass doors and, tilting her head to one side, carefully scanned each of the spines. Seeing nothing, she looked again, but the result was the same. Gosh, it would really help if she knew where he'd written down the vital information she needed. Hana closed the doors of the cabinet with a frustrated sigh.

There was a tap at the door and Gwen poked her head into the room. 'Sorry, but your mum's made the tea. I can't distract her any longer.'

'It's all right. I've finished in here now,' said Hana, taking one last look around the study in case she'd missed it somehow.

'Anything I can help with?' asked Gwen.

'No. Just looking for a file for Dad's work,' replied Hana. 'Not to worry. Right, let's have that cup of tea.'

*

When Hana returned home an hour later, there was still no sign of Gregory. She waited up for as long as possible for his return, but when the hands of the clock crawled their way to midnight, she gave up. Part of her was worried about where he was, but another part of her, a much larger part was resigned to the fact that he was probably caught up with work. Now she actually knew what he did, that it could run into the small hours, or even all night, was a distinct possibility. She took herself to bed and was just drifting off to sleep when she heard the sound of a car approaching and wheels crunching on the gravel drive. A few moments later, the sound of the key in the front door, reassured her it was Gregory.

Despite his ascent of the stairs being somewhat cumbersome, Gregory made surprisingly little noise as he made his way to the first floor. Hana hopped out of bed and opened her bedroom door as he appeared on the landing. In the soft pale light of the moon seeping through the doorway and onto the landing, she noted the frown on her husband's face. An expression she saw far more these days than she liked. It made her sad. Not just for her, but for him, too. He always looked like he was lugging the worries of the world behind him.

'Is everything all right?' she asked, opening the door wider.

Gregory came to a halt. 'Sorry. I didn't mean to disturb you,' he said, his eyes taking in Hana in her short satin nightdress.

She realised she hadn't put on her dressing gown when she'd jumped out of bed and now felt strangely self-conscious. It had been a long time since they had seen each other anything less than fully clothed. 'I wasn't really asleep.' Hana folded her arms across her body and then, feeling ridiculous at suddenly being modest in front of her husband, she dropped her arms to her side. She met Gregory's gaze. She had an unexpected desire to reach out to him.

A look of indecision dashed across Gregory's face, quickly replaced by his all too familiar frown. He gave a nod. 'Goodnight, Hana.' Then he limped across the hallway to what was now his bedroom, closing the door behind him.

Hana let her gaze rest on the bedroom door. She couldn't deny that for a moment she had wanted to be back in their bedroom, in their marital bed, but the rejection burned deep. He hadn't needed to outrightly say no to her, the look on his face said it all. Louder than any words he could have spoken.

Chapter 8

Hana was pleased with the distraction of work the following morning. She and Gregory had shared breakfast in virtual silence, apart from her asking if he would change his mind about coming to Freddie's birthday party.

'I'm surprised you're still having the party, considering your father's in hospital,' said Gregory.

'Well, it's for Freddie more than anything,' replied Hana, niggled at the inference. 'And Dad would still want us to celebrate.'

'I can't change my plans, though,' he said. 'We've got the American coming today.'

'I haven't had time to prepare the guest room,' said Hana, feeling irritated all over again that they would be accommodating a guest and she had been given little to no warning about it, let alone even be consulted. But what with everything that had happened in the past few days, she'd forgotten about it, until Gregory had reminded her this morning.

'Is there anywhere else he could stay?' she asked. 'Just while Dad is in hospital and I'm working. I'm not really in the right frame of mind for a house guest.'

'You'll barely notice he's here,' said Gregory, without looking up from the newspaper he was reading.

Hana rather doubted that, but she didn't want to start the day off with an argument. She got up from the table and quickly cleared away the breakfast plates. 'I need to go in early today,' she said. 'So I thought I'd cycle.'

'It's cold out there.'

'I don't mind.'

'Why don't you wait, I'll drive us in?'

Hana had been hoping to get in early, before Jenny or Audrey, and have a more thorough poke around of her father's desk and the ledgers, including Alfred's personal ledger book. She had come to the conclusion the information must, after all, be at the Park and that he must have written it in code, as Hopkins had suggested. That meant, it might be hidden in plain sight and be right under her nose.

'Got a lot of work to get through,' she said, teasing her hair in the mirror to avoid looking at her husband. 'Trying to make a good impression and get myself up to speed with everything. I start training this afternoon, as well, so I have even less time in the hut.'

'Like I said. I can drive us in.' He got up. 'I'll just fetch my coat, and we can go.'

*

Derek was already in Hut 7 when Hana arrived. 'Didn't you go home last night?' she asked, hanging her jacket up on the coat stand in the corner of the room.

Derek rubbed his eyes and yawned. 'Now that you come to mention it . . .'

Hana stopped mid-stride and turned to look at her colleague, taking in his ruffled hair and stubble around his chin. 'Oh, gosh,' she said. 'You really have been here all night.'

'Got caught up in something and didn't want to break off.' Derek stretched his arms above his head. 'Must admit, it's catching up with me now.'

'Here, let me make you a coffee,' said Hana, going over to the kitchenette at the back of the room. 'Strong black coffee is what you need. You must be starving, as well.' A few minutes later, she brought the hot drink over to Derek and next to it placed a couple of biscuits. 'To keep you going,' she said.

'Ooh, biscuits. There's a luxury.'

'Don't tell my husband,' said Hana with a wink. 'They're from his stash at home. Anyway, what were you working on that was so important?'

Derek pushed his notebook over to her, along with the partially decrypted message. 'I've been looking at these three last intercepted messages,' said Derek. 'The first group of letters – SFPR – appear in exactly the same position in all three messages. And that's the same for the third group – POBN. They all appear in the third set.'

'Right,' said Hana, studying the codes.

SFPR AYDT POBN RZXY
SFPR WMG POBN VAQQ
SFPR LVXC POBN JHKC

'So, I'm guessing the first and third blocks all mean the same thing,' she said. 'Some sort of standard phrase, instruction or grouping.'

Derek smiled. 'Exactly that.' He rested his elbows on the desk. 'So, what do you think I did next?'

Hana gave a laugh. 'I'm not sure I know.'

'Yes, you do. Just think about it for a moment.'

Hana pursed her lips as she considered the options, which to be honest were quite limited, she wasn't sure what the protocol was. 'Well, without knowing how things work here,' she said after a while, 'I'd check these against some codes and words that we know don't change. I don't know, like a port or a place? Or try to identify vowel placement.'

'Good. And we can also identify the radio operator by the codename they use,' said Derek. 'This is their codename, here.' He pointed at a letter grouping above the main body of the message. 'We take this code and check it against our list of operators. Of course, we don't know their name. We label them for our own records – and in this book here, we've got a list of codenames. The radio operator, in this case from Penang, we refer to as Operator Seven.'

'How does that help?' asked Hana.

'We look at our records for Operator Seven, Penang station and see what habits we've noticed, what patterns. Quite often the operators develop habits or are a bit lazy and use the same technique. It's like having their own style of handwriting.'

'And Operator Seven?' asked Hana. She was fascinated by this. She loved patterns and analysing. It was one of the reasons why she found languages so engaging and the study of syntax and language coding so addictive.

'Operator Seven keeps vowels in predictable positions. It's a common operator error.'

'And from this what did you do next?'

'Cross-referenced against our database of known Japanese naval terminology. If we assume the fixed position of the vowels is correct, then we can start matching potential words against our frequency tables.'

Hana looked over at Derek's desk and the numerous sheets of paper strewn across it. 'I know you're making it sound very easy, but I'm guessing by the number of scribblings and notes you've made, plus the fact you've been up all night at it, the decoding took a long time.'

Derek rubbed his eyes. 'You can say that again.'

'And have you discovered anything important?' she asked.

'Not on its own,' admitted Derek. 'It's still not complete and not everything makes sense. I need to double-check it, but at the moment, from what I can work out, it's advising of the movement of a submarine.'

'What do we do with it now?'

'I can work on it some more and in the meantime, Chatfield will send a copy through to someone higher up who will analyse what we've decoded and decide whether it's important or not.'

'Do you ever get any feedback?'

'Nope. If you think someone's going to come along and pat you on the back, then you're mistaken.' Derek gave a big yawn. 'I need another coffee. Do you want one?'

'No. I'm fine, thank you,' said Hana. She was conscious that time was pushing on and Jenny would be here before she'd had time to study Alfred's codebook. 'Thank you for showing me all this, though. I really appreciate it.' She began gathering up the pieces of paper.

'Any time,' replied Derek, taking the papers from her. 'Just need to pop this down to Chatfield's office.' He waved a summary update sheet in his hand.

As soon as he was out of the room, Hana took the chance to have more thorough look through the desk drawers. Maybe she'd missed a specific book Alfred had been using, other than his codebook.

She had visions of it stuffed at the back or even stuck somehow to the underside of the drawer. If it wasn't in his study at home, then it had to be here. But her search resulted in nothing.

Hana picked up Alfred's codebook and carefully began looking through the pages. In Alfred's usual style, everything was set out neatly. Pages titled and numbered with an index in the back of the book. Hana ran her finger down the index, looking for something that might be a clue as to where he'd written down the information about the spy, but there was nothing apparent.

She paused, reminding herself to think like her father. If it was such sensitive information, it wouldn't be obvious. There were several pages written solely in Japanese. Hana began reading but it seemed like random words. She couldn't see any sort of pattern in the lettering to indicate it might be written in a code.

She could hear voices coming from the hallway of the hut – it was Jenny and Audrey.

She quickly closed the notebook and grabbed the nearest file, opening it in front of her just as Audrey and Jenny walked into the room, followed by Derek.

Jenny and Audrey greeted Hana and settled down in their seats.

'Everything all right?' asked Jenny. 'You look worried.'

'Me? No. I'm fine,' replied Hana. 'I was just thinking about the codes. Derek just showed me what he'd been doing.'

'I see,' said Jenny. 'Well, that saves me the trouble.' She took a message out of the wire basket and passed it over to Hana. 'There you go. See what you make of this.'

Hana took the piece of paper. Challenge accepted. If Jenny thought she was going to catch Hana out, then she was sorely mistaken. She was her father's daughter and with that came a tenacity. She'd crack this code, if it was the last thing she did, and without the help of Jenny.

The morning passed quickly and although progress was slow, Hana did feel she was making headway with the code. Derek had come over at one point to see how she was doing and made a couple of suggestions, without making her feel incompetent. She had forgone her tea break to carry on working on the message, knowing that after lunch she was expected to go over to the hall at Church Green Road for her training session. She wanted to have something tangible to show for her morning's work.

All the time, though, she was keeping an eye on what was going on in the room by covertly watching her colleagues – Derek, Jenny, Audrey, Lottie and even Chatfield – mentally noting how often they might leave the room or talk to one another, or maybe she'd catch a secretive communication between two people. She wasn't sure what she was looking for specifically, but just as with the codebreaking, Hana was looking for patterns and irregularities of patterns. Someone in the room was a spy, and should she not find where Alfred had logged that information, she was determined to do her best to find out who it was herself. She owed it to Alfred, if nothing else.

Chapter 9

It was the end of the week, and in the few days she had been working at the Park, Hana's days already had a routine. Mornings were spent codebreaking, and her training was in the afternoons. In the evenings, she was exhausted, making supper for her and Gregory and then falling into bed.

Conversation with Gregory was limited. She didn't even have the school to talk about now. She missed the children especially. Even though the world looked bleak, they'd never failed to bring a smile to her face with their ability to stay positive. There was nothing she enjoyed listening to more than the sounds of their laughter, shouts and squeals in the playground.

It was another reason to spur her on to finding out who the spy at the Park was, and to try to decode the transcripts. It may only be a small part in the war effort, but all the smaller parts put together had potential to make a much bigger impact. She could only hope that impact would bring an end to the war sooner rather than later.

On the Thursday evening, Hana had gone home expecting to meet the American serviceman, only to be told he had been delayed by a couple of days. She was relieved. It gave her a bit more time to prepare for his arrival and wrap some presents for Freddie's party the next day, though to her disappointment she would have to miss it, too. She didn't have to ask Hopkins to know he wouldn't take kindly to her leaving the Park at three p.m. for a tea party.

*

Saturday arrived – Hana's last working day of the week before she had the next day off. The hours at the Park were typically spread over three shifts of eight in the morning to four in the afternoon, then four to midnight and finally midnight to eight, with one day off a week. Although, in reality, as Derek had demonstrated, the need to work beyond the end of a shift was not unusual. From her own experience, Hana knew having to break off in the middle of something when your thoughts were in full flow made it difficult to pick things up again the next day.

Today was a prime example. She was working on a code she'd been given earlier in the week, and she was very nearly there with it. Admittedly, it was taking her longer than both she and Jenny had liked, and she'd had to leave it on Friday afternoon to go to her training session. When she'd come back to it this morning, it had taken her ages to pick up where she'd left off.

Finally, though, she had decoded it and with a deep sense of satisfaction handed it over to Jenny, who had insisted on checking it. The message had then been put into a tray where it would be taken somewhere else, somewhere Hana didn't know, where it would be deemed important or not. And that was that. Gone. Just like that.

Now she had been given another intercept to decode. It was Derek's day off, so it was just herself, Jenny and Audrey.

It was mid-morning when Chatfield appeared from the hallway.

'If I could have your attention, please?' commanded the former Cambridge don. 'We have a—'

'Sorry, excuse me,' came Audrey's voice as she squeezed through the doorway and into the room, having just returned from her tea break. 'Sorry.' She gave a grimace towards Hana, before sliding into her seat.

'Right, I'll start again,' said Chatfield. He moved further into the room, followed by another man in American military uniform. Hana noted the officer rank on the sleeve of the drab, olive coloured jacket. He was striking, with dark hair and a honey-toned, olive complexion, which set off his deep brown eyes.

Audrey nudged Hana's arm with her elbow. 'Well, hello,' she whispered so only Hana could hear.

The two men stood in front of the blackboard. 'This is Captain Robert Becker of the US Army,' informed Chatfield. 'He's on secondment to help with our translation work. He's had experience in the East and his knowledge will be invaluable.'

'Good morning,' said Robert with a nod to the rest of the room.

Chatfield continued, 'Captain Becker is familiar with the Japanese language. It's probably best if I let him tell you a bit more about himself.' He turned to Becker. 'Over to you.'

'Thank you, Graham,' said Robert. He looked at the team. 'So, here goes . . . I actually joined the army as a medic but my knowledge of Japanese through my father and grandfather, has meant my medical skills have taken a back seat. Whenever I mention my heritage, I often get grilled on the details, so I thought it best to save anyone the trouble of asking and me having to explain several times.' He gave a confident but warm smile before continuing. 'My grandfather was Japanese, so obviously fluent in the language, which he passed down to my father, who in turn passed down to me. The bloodline has reached me, but not in full as my grandfather married an American woman and moved to New York. My father was born in New York – Brooklyn, to be specific – as was my mother, and then me. So, in a nutshell, I'm a regular American with Japanese heritage.'

Jenny put her hand up and the captain paused.

'Please, go ahead . . . uh . . .?'

'Jenny,' she said. 'Jenny Denton. I'm a translator here.' She flashed a smile at the officer. 'You say the knowledge of the Japanese language has been passed down to you, just how fluent does that make you if you've learned it second-hand, as it were?'

'Good question,' he replied. 'And, please, call me Robert. We're all equal here. No need for military rank when it's just us in the hut.' Another charming smile to the team followed before he replied to the question. 'I may not be fluent as a native speaker, but I'm pretty good.'

'Captain Becker . . . Robert . . . is being very modest here,' put in Chatfield. 'In linguistic circles, he'd be classed as fluent. He certainly has an advanced knowledge of the language which is exactly why he's here to help us. And this will prove very timely, in light of Alfred currently being out of action.'

'Yes. I was sorry to hear about Alfred,' said Robert. 'I had the pleasure of hearing him talk a few years ago when he was in America discussing the research work he was doing in some of the more remote parts of Japan.'

'Oh, then you might remember his daughter,' said Chatfield. 'She's here with us now. Hana Phillips.'

Hana smiled at the officer. 'I would have been a teenager, and probably hanging around behind the scenes or in a hotel room with my mother, so I'm sure you have no recollection of me whatsoever,' she said, remembering when the family had accompanied Alfred to the USA six months after they'd returned from Japan. Hana was seventeen at the time.

'It's an honour to meet you today,' said Robert. 'And your name, Hana, is Japanese for flower; it's a metaphor for beauty.'

Hana liked that he pronounced her name as it was said in Japanese, like a shortened version of the name Hannah, which most people defaulted to. She didn't mind especially. Her brother was known as Tom, even though his actual name was Tomoki. She felt herself blush a little and wanted to kick herself for doing so. Robert was definitely a charmer. Very American.

Chatfield cleared his throat. 'You'll actually be working closely with Hana,' he said to Robert. 'She and Jenny have been carrying on Alfred's work from where he left off, so that's where you come in.'

'I shall look forward to it,' said Robert.

'Right, well, in at the deep end,' replied Chatfield. 'I'll leave you in the hands of Hana.'

'Perfect.' Robert smiled again.

The rest of the morning passed quickly as Jenny brought Robert up to speed with their decrypting and the methods they were using. Hana noticed her dad's assistant was far more forthcoming with the information than she had been with Hana. Though Jenny hadn't held anything back from Hana, her approach to sharing and informing had been with a certain amount of reluctance, whereas with Robert, she was very enthusiastic in her approach. Several times, Robert addressed a question in Hana's direction, only for Jenny to jump in with the answer before Hana could even speak. Hana let it slide. She wasn't about to get into some kind of competition with her colleague.

Lunchtime came around and under Chatfield's instruction, Robert took his lunch the same time as Hana, who'd been asked to show Robert the delights of the canteen.

'Don't get your hopes up too high,' she warned as they made their way out to the canteen just outside the gates on Wiltern Avenue. 'Not sure what you're used to, but it's pretty basic. You won't go hungry, though.'

'Oh, I'm easy,' replied Robert. 'Besides, the diet doesn't seem to have done you any harm.'

Hana shot him a sideways look, uncertain as to what he meant. 'They do their best,' she said, not knowing what to say. She could see the look of mischief in the American's eyes, accompanied by a cheeky wink. She averted her gaze, making sure she looked straight ahead as they made their way to the canteen. Was he flirting with her? She didn't much care for it if he was. She'd heard plenty of stories about the American GIs being over in England and how they were sweeping young women off their feet with their charm, chocolate and apparently never-ending supply of nylon stockings.

As they neared the canteen building, Hana caught the familiar sight of Gregory as he made his way along the path. 'Gregory!' she called out and waved as he looked over. He actually looked quite pleased to see her. Or so Hana thought. Then she realised Gregory was smiling broadly at Robert.

'Hello, there,' greeted Gregory. 'I see you've met my wife.'

'Your wife?' repeated Robert. 'Oh, I'm sorry. I had no idea.'

'You know each other?' Hana was confused.

'Yes,' said Gregory. 'Captain Becker here is going to be our house guest.' Hana was aware her mouth had dropped open as she processed the news. Gregory gave a chuckle. 'Come along, Hana, it's not like you to be lost for words.'

'Sorry. It's just taken me by surprise, that's all,' said Hana. So this was the house guest. Why hadn't it occurred to her sooner?

'Right, I take it you're on your way for some lunch,' said Gregory. 'Come on, before all the good stuff goes.'

Hana followed Gregory and Robert out through the gates and into the canteen. It gave her a couple of minutes to adjust to what she'd just learned. Robert seemed a nice chap, though, and despite him being a little flirty, he also seemed dedicated and good at his job.

'So, what's it like, being husband and wife and working at the same place?' asked Robert, dubiously poking at the mashed potato on his plate with his fork. 'Does that make things difficult?'

'Actually, it wasn't until this week that we knew we'd both be working here,' said Hana. 'I've only been asked to stand in while my father is unwell.'

'Oh, of course,' said Robert. 'How is Alfred?'

'Hard to say,' said Hana, thinking back to how grey her father had looked the previous day. 'He's got some broken bones, which will heal, but he took a nasty blow to his head. It's something of a waiting game.'

'The mind and body are amazing things,' said Robert. 'Try to stay as positive as you can.'

Hana was touched by his words. 'Thank you.' She took a deep breath. 'And back to your original question about Gregory and I working at the same place. It really doesn't make any difference as we still can't talk about our work.'

'Yeah. Of course. I didn't think about that. So, no pillow-talk for you two,' said Robert.

Hana wanted to laugh, despite it not being the first time someone had mentioned pillow-talk, but seeing Gregory's poker face, she restrained herself. The rest of the lunch conversation stayed on safer ground: how they thought the war was going and the impact on the country generally. Hana was interested to hear an American perspective on the war, but each time she spoke, Gregory veered the conversation in another direction. In the end, she gave up and only listened politely.

She was glad when lunch was over and she was back in Hut 7.

'Sorry, if I embarrassed you back there about pillow talk,' said Robert, once both Jenny and Audrey had gone for their lunch.

'Oh, it's all right,' said Hana. 'No harm done.' At least that's what she hoped anyway. She was aware of Robert looking at her, but she avoided making eye contact. Instead, she picked up a dictionary from Jenny's desk and took it over to her own desk. 'Right, we'd better get on,' she said, looking at the paperwork in front of her. 'I've got an hour and then I have to head over to Church Green Road for training.'

'Training?'

'To bring me up to speed with some of the technical terms. I'm being fast-tracked because of my knowledge of Japanese.'

Robert raised his eyebrows. 'Fast-tracked, eh? They must think highly of you.'

'Oh don't,' she said with a grimace. 'I'm not sure everyone is pleased that I'm here getting some sort of special treatment.'

'I can always help you with any revision,' said Robert.

'Thank you. I'm sure I'll be fine, though.' Hana wasn't sure if revision sessions with Robert were a good idea, it might create some tension within her new colleagues if they thought she was getting even more special treatment.

Chapter 10

Hana found concentrating during the training session particularly hard that afternoon. When the fifteen-minute break came, she was more than glad for some fresh air. Even though it was chilly outside, she chose to take a walk around the churchyard opposite the training centre.

It wasn't just the pressure of training and work that was exhausting, but the pressure and expectation to find the information Alfred had collated was unrelenting. With her father being seriously ill in hospital, Robert's arrival and Gregory's distanced behaviour, it was a lot to deal with. Hana knew she needed to make a concerted effort to cope with whatever was in front of her at the time. Whatever situation presented itself, she'd deal with it then and try not to look at everything as a whole. It was difficult, but necessary.

Apart from Alfred's recovery, the most pressing thing was finding his notebook, or whatever it was she was supposed to be finding and give that to Hopkins. That, at least, would be one less thing for her to contend with.

The doctors kept saying Alfred needed to rest and sleep was the best thing for him. It was hard not to let her mind wander to all the dark places of what this could ultimately mean for her father's recovery, but equally Hana didn't want to dwell on such negative thoughts.

The fresh air, together with the space to mentally unload her worries, helped Hana get through the afternoon. She was glad when the day came to an end and even more appreciative when Gregory came to find her to give her a lift home, though she realised the gesture was also because he was bringing Robert back, along with a rather large-looking kitbag that took up one half of the back seat.

Hana offered to sit in the back along with the kitbag, but Robert wouldn't hear of it. 'I'm just grateful for the ride,' he said, climbing into the back of the car.

'I'd like to go to see Dad this evening,' Hana told Gregory as they drove home. 'Would I be able to take the car?'

'Ah, I'm sorry but I need it tonight,' said Gregory as he navigated the vehicle along the lanes. 'I've got to go out.'

'Again?'

'Yes. Again,' replied Gregory tersely.

Hana sank back into the red leather of the seat, feeling embarrassed at the way he had replied to her in front of Robert. Still, she wasn't about to make matters worse and pick him up on it. 'Don't worry. I'll see if I can go with Mum,' she said. 'Or take Mum's car, at least.'

Gregory gave a grunt of acknowledgement.

Hana was glad when they pulled up onto the driveway and she could busy herself with showing Robert to his room. She opened the double doors and stepped out onto the veranda which swept around the first floor of the house.

'Nice view,' said Robert joining her. 'It's beautiful.'

'Thank you,' she replied. 'I can't take credit for the garden, though. It was all here before. Tall Trees is Gregory's family home. He grew up here and the house has been in his family for quite some time. I believe his mother did most of the gardening.'

Robert let out a low whistle. 'He's not like a lord or something, is he? Do I have to start bowing and all that business?'

'No. Don't worry, no bowing needed.' She couldn't help laughing at Robert's mock shock. 'His family are quite normal.'

'Just wealthy. Sorry, I didn't mean to offend you,' said Robert rapidly. 'Money is a vulgar topic for you Brits. Or so I've heard.'

Hana gave a shrug. 'Whilst it might be pleasant to be rich in money, my father always said it's far better to be rich in heart.'

'Your father is a very wise man.'

Again, there was that intense look from Robert that made Hana avert her gaze. She looked down at her shoes and then out at the Douglas fir ahead of her, which dominated the lawn. She heard Robert give a small chuckle, but she ignored it.

'Ah, that's where the house gets its name from,' he said, following her gaze. 'Tall Trees.'

'Yes, I suppose it is,' said Hana, glad of the change in direction of the conversation.

'I guess when they named it, the tree wasn't that tall, but they obviously had high hopes – no pun intended.'

Hana smiled. She liked Robert's humour. 'I've never really thought about it,' she replied. 'But yes, I suppose you're right there, too.'

They stood in silence for a moment, both looking out at the tree.

Robert spoke first. 'I guess, though, technically, there should be more than one tall tree.'

Hana smiled. 'Actually, there were two but a storm some years ago put paid to that. The house was already named by then, so they just stuck with it.'

'Makes sense.'

A comfortable silence lapsed between them again, as they looked out across the mature grounds of Tall Trees.

It was a companionable moment and reminded Hana of when she and Gregory were first married. She missed those days of easy company, shared jokes, wishes and dreams. She let out a sigh and forced melancholy thoughts away. 'I'd better get supper ready,' she said.

*

Gregory may have been putting on a bit of a show for Robert during their meal, being more jovial and chatty, but Hana wasn't fooled. There was an underlying, subtle tension that was not so subtle that she didn't notice. She could only assume it was to do with work and whatever Gregory had to do this evening.

'So, do you have any family other than your parents?' Robert's voice broke through her thoughts.

'Oh, sorry. Yes. A brother. Tom. He's a POW.' She felt the words catch in her throat.

'I'm sorry,' said Robert. 'Do you know where he's being held?'

'*Stalag Luft* Three, Poland.'

'*Stalag Luft* Three? That's run by the Luftwaffe,' he said. 'If it's any comfort, the conditions in the Luftwaffe-run camps are much better than the regular German-army-run ones.'

'Really?' The tiny nugget of information filled Hana with some hope.

'That's what we've heard anyway,' said Robert, obviously erring on the side of caution.

'I do hope it's true,' said Hana. 'We've written to him via the Red Cross, but I don't know if he's received our letters. We've not heard anything from him.'

'Don't give up hope,' said Robert. 'Things like that can take months and months.'

'Thank you.' Hana put her cutlery together. 'Do you have any family, back home in America?'

'My folks. Three brothers and one sister.'

'Three brothers. And where are you in the pecking order?' Hana took a sip of her water.

'Right in the middle. Two older brothers and a younger brother and sister.'

'Where are they? Are they all in the military?' asked Gregory.

'Yes. Well, my brothers are. Two in the Navy and two of us in the army. And, thank God, we are all so far safe and well.'

'Lucky you and your brothers,' said Gregory.

Hana inwardly winced at Gregory's comment.

Robert gave a shrug. 'I'm not sure I believe in luck, but it certainly doesn't do any harm.' He looked towards Gregory's hand. 'What happened to you, if you don't mind me asking?'

The unapologetic directness of the question made Hana wince even more than before.

Gregory ran his finger around the collar of his shirt. 'Emergency landing. Got caught in the flames.'

'You couldn't bail out?' asked Robert.

Gregory fixed Robert with a stony look. 'Obviously not.'

'But you made it out alive. That's the important thing,' said Robert, seemingly unperturbed by Gregory's starchy response. 'Better that than not, I guess.'

'I guess so,' replied Gregory.

Hana couldn't bear sitting there any longer. She got up from the table. 'I really should get moving. I don't want to be too late getting to the hospital.' She started clearing the table, but Robert got to his feet.

'Allow me. I can do this for you.'

'No. You don't have to,' said Hana but he was already taking the plates from her.

'I insist,' he said. 'You've been good enough to host me. It's the least I can do. Besides, I have to do it when I'm home. My mother would have something to say about it if I sat back and didn't help.'

Hana glanced at Gregory but the expression on his face was indecipherable. She turned to Robert. 'I don't want to get you in trouble with your mother.' She released her hold on the crockery. 'Thank you. That's very kind.'

Twenty minutes later, she was cycling over to her mother's house. As she pedalled down the darkened lane, she couldn't help wondering if Gregory would complain about her letting Robert do the dishes, especially as it was his first night with them. But in all honesty, she didn't care. Hana had never been brought up to believe a woman's role was purely in the home, and she liked that Robert had offered. Alfred had always advocated for equality for both his children, hence why Hana had gone to study at Cambridge.

As she reached her mother's house and propped her bicycle up against the garage, Pamela was already at the door. She looked ashen and shaky.

Hana's heart lurched. Her mother wasn't one for histrionics, but Hana could tell she was deeply worried. 'What is it, Mum?' Though it could really only be one thing.

'I've just had a call from the hospital to say your father's taken a turn for the worse,' her mother told her. 'I was hanging on for you. Get in the car quickly.'

Gwen came out of the house. 'Be careful,' she said, giving Pamela a quick hug and squeezing Hana's hand in a gesture of support.

Hana gave a small smile. 'I'll drive,' she said, taking the keys from her mother. The fact that Pamela didn't argue, only served to convince Hana that she was extremely concerned about Alfred.

Hana drove as fast as she dared in the diminishing light and ignored her mother's small intakes of breath as they sped their way to the hospital. There weren't many other cars on the road, which made driving fast a lot easier. With fuel being rationed, a car was something of a luxury, which, so far, her parents had managed to maintain.

As they hurried into the hospital, Hana could see the nurse's shoulders sag somewhat at their arrival.

'We know it's late,' said Hana, 'but my mother had a call to say my father had taken a turn.'

'Yes. Of course,' replied the nurse. 'Come this way. Matron will speak to you.'

They entered Alfred's room. The curtains were drawn and a small sidelight had been left on, casting a shadow across Alfred's face. Matron was in the room with another nurse who was smoothing out the bedsheets. The latter nodded at Hana and Pamela before leaving the room.

'How is he?' asked Pamela, going straight over to Alfred and studying him. She lightly brushed her hand across his forehead, smoothing his hair down.

'He's resting,' said Matron. 'He's in a stable condition now, but his blood pressure dropped significantly earlier and his breathing was very weak.'

Hana gripped the end of the bed for support. This did not sound good. 'Have things improved now?' she asked.

'Yes. As I said, his condition is stable. We're sorry to have worried you. My Ward Sister was a little previous calling you.'

'No. It's fine,' said Pamela. 'We're glad she did.'

'You can stay a little while, if you want,' said Matron.

'Thank you.' Pamela sat down in the chair beside Alfred's bed, taking his hand in hers. 'Now, Alfred, none of this worrying the staff anymore. We were all in a flap for a minute there.'

The matron left the room and Hana sat down in the chair on the other side of the bed. 'Hello, Dad,' she said. 'Now that we're here, we might as well stay for a bit. I forgot to bring the newspaper with me. I was going to see if we could do the crossword.'

Alfred's eyes flickered but didn't open.

'Oh, yes. We must remember it tomorrow,' said Pamela, injecting a lightness to her voice as if they were having a normal conversation.

'I've been at work all week,' said Hana. 'At the printers, doing your job.' She wished she could speak openly about what she was really doing, but that would mean telling her mother. Although, Pamela was an intelligent woman and Hana was certain she had her suspicions about it all, anyway. 'It's been very busy. I'm working alongside Jenny, Audrey, Derek, Chatfield and Lottie.' Hana hoped that mentioning these names wasn't breaching any official secret.

Just as before, when she'd mentioned continuing his work, Alfred reacted strongly. He took a sudden and sharp intake of breath and his eyes pinged open and his whole body convulsed.

'Alfred,' said Pamela, getting to her feet. 'Alfred. Breathe. Take a breath.'

'Dad, come on, Dad.' Hana stood up. Alfred still hadn't taken a breath. 'Mum, get the nurse,' she urged.

Pamela hurried out of the room and Hana stood over her father. 'Dad! Breathe!' She was tapping his cheek with her face, trying to get him to look at her but it wasn't working. She grabbed his shoulders and shook him firmly and then harder again. 'Dad!' Panic was coursing through her. 'Please, Dad. Breathe.' She shook him again.

Then, as suddenly as he had gasped, Alfred let out a deep breath. His eyes closed but his body was still tense. He was fighting for breath now and his arms and legs were thrashing around wildly.

Hana had never been so relieved to see two nurses rush into the room, followed by Pamela.

'Please wait outside,' one of them instructed.

No sooner had they stepped out into the corridor when a doctor came hurrying through and into the room. Hana gripped Pamela's hand. They could hear the doctor issuing instructions in a calm and collected manner, the nurses responding in kind to the backdrop of the sound of a struggle as Alfred was restrained. And then, it all went quiet. It was as if the room itself had sucked in a deep breath, only letting it out when the doors finally opened and the nurse appeared in front of them with a reassuring smile.

The doctor followed her out. 'Mrs Castle?' he said, addressing Pamela, who nodded. 'We've administered a sedative to your husband. We will review the situation again in the morning, but it's likely we will keep him sedated. His brain needs to rest to heal and to allow the swelling to go down. I don't know what caused him to become so distressed, but to avoid it happening again, we are likely to keep him sedated.'

'Is he going to be all right?' asked Hana.

'I don't want to make false promises,' said the doctor. 'But at this given time, he's comfortable and that is the best we can do at the moment.'

'Thank you, Doctor,' said Pamela. 'Can we say goodnight to him?'

The doctor looked undecided for a moment before relenting. 'Very quickly and quietly.'

*

The drive home was subdued and taken at a much lesser speed than their outward-bound journey. 'I'm sorry,' said Hana as they pulled up outside Bramble House.

'Sorry? What are you sorry for?' asked Pamela as they got out of the car.

'It was my fault Dad got upset,' explained Hana, locking the car door. 'It kind of happened a bit last time I went to see him. I mentioned I was standing in for him and he got a little agitated.'

'Nonsense,' said Pamela, standing in front of Hana. 'It's just a coincidence. Don't be blaming yourself now.'

'But he was fine until I mentioned what I was doing,' said Hana.

Pamela held her at arm's length and studied her face. 'I don't know what it was your father was doing at work,' she emphasised the last word, 'but I'm not stupid and I'm sure it was more than printing leaflets.'

Hana looked at her. 'He . . . erm . . . I . . .' What could she say? She didn't want to lie but she couldn't tell the truth either.

Pamela held up a finger. 'Don't say anything. There's no need. I have no doubt your father was doing something very important. Important enough that they now need you to cover for him. Since you have no experience whatsoever with printing, I have my own ideas about the kind of work you're doing, but I'm not about to share them.' She smiled gently. 'Whatever it is, I know you can do it and your father will be very proud of you.'

'But the way he reacted,' began Hana.

'He's suffered a serious brain injury,' said Pamela. 'Things might not be working quite as they should. It stands to reason that his reactions might not be as we expect.' She patted Hana's arm. 'So, no more feeling guilty, all right?'

'I'll try not to.'

'Do you want to come in for a cup of tea?'

'I'd better get back,' replied Hana. 'We've got a house guest, and both Gregory and I have abandoned him on his first night.' Hana gave her mother a kiss on the cheek and hopped on her bicycle, waving as she cycled down the drive and out onto the lane. It made sense what Pamela had said, but even so, Hana still couldn't help feeling partly to blame. Mentioning work would have to be strictly off the agenda now.

The wind had picked up during the course of the evening, making the cycle home rather more arduous as she battled against the headwind. Hana was glad when she finally made it home.

'Hello!' she called out as she slipped off her coat and hung it on the hall stand. She went down to the kitchen and put the kettle on.

'Evening,' came a voice behind her.

Hana startled at the sound of Robert's voice. 'Oh, I didn't realise you were there,' she said. 'I thought you might have gone to bed.'

'Sorry, I didn't mean to make you jump.'

'Tea? Or would you prefer coffee?' She held the tea canister in one hand and the coffee tin in the other.

'Coffee. Thank you.'

'Oh, don't thank me too soon. You haven't tried it yet.' Hana spooned some of the ground beans into a cup. 'This is the emergency blend of coffee.' She pushed the lid back on and handed it to Robert to inspect.

'Some ingredients are not available at the moment,' he read on the label. 'Sounds ominous. Although, it can't be any worse than the ration pack we get from the military.'

Hana made their drinks – coffee for him and tea for her – and sat down at the table, watching his face as he brought the cup to his mouth and took a sip. She couldn't help laughing at his expression as the liquid assaulted his taste buds. 'I did warn you,' she said.

Robert took another sip. 'It's gonna be an acquired taste, for sure.'

'Sorry. Maybe you should convert to tea.'

'It's not that bad.' He laughed and his eyes crinkled in the corners. After another sip, which Hana was convinced was out of politeness rather than desire, he put the cup on the table. 'How is your father?'

Hana looked down at her hands wrapped around her cup. 'He's been sedated,' she said. 'I know it's for the best but . . .' She looked up at the ceiling and blinked several times, taking a deep breath. 'It's just . . . there's swelling on his brain, and they aren't making reassuring enough noises. I feel like they aren't telling us everything . . . I'm so worried about him.' She pulled a handkerchief from her pocket and dabbed at her nose and eyes. 'Sorry. It's been a long day.' She got up and tipped the remains of her tea down the sink, leaving the cup in the washing up bowl. Goodness, she felt all at once physically and emotionally exhausted. She rested her hands on the edge of the Belfast sink, taking a moment to compose herself. What would Robert think if she broke down in tears on his first night?

'Hey, I'm sorry,' said Robert. The legs of his chair scraped on the red quarry tiles. Hana was aware he had come to stand next to her. 'It's OK to cry,' he said.

Even though it was the last thing she wanted to do, her tears had other ideas and sprung from her eyes. Hana struggled to stop herself from collapsing in a bawling mess. She was going to need another handkerchief at this rate – man-sized. It was only the touch of Robert's hand on her back that jolted her to an abrupt stop.

'I'm so sorry,' she mumbled into her handkerchief.

'Don't be. It's only natural.' He rubbed his hand up and down her back a couple of times. 'Would you like me to make you a fresh cup of tea?'

Hana blew out a breath. 'Sod the tea,' she said, standing more upright. 'I'm going to have something stronger. Come on.'

Without hesitation, she strode down the hall, glancing briefly at the study door, which was firmly shut, before she went into the sitting room, Robert following her. 'Push the door,' she said, going over to the drinks cabinet. 'Port or whisky?'

'Is this like the tea and coffee option?'

She couldn't help smiling. 'No. Both options are equally good. No emergency stuff here.'

'Whisky it is.'

Hana poured the drinks and handed Robert his as he stood in front of the fireplace. 'Cheers,' she said, holding her glass up.

'Cheers.'

They both slugged their drinks back at the same time. 'Same again?' Hana was already taking his glass.

'I should say no.'

'Should is an auxiliary verb, used to express necessity or possibility. It's not a definitive response.'

Robert chuckled. 'OK. Then my definitive response is yes.'

'Excellent.' Hana poured them both another drink, but this time took herself to the sofa and sipped it in a rather more refined manner. 'Again. Sorry about that just now.'

Robert sat down next to her. 'Like I said, you don't have to be sorry.'

She smiled, appreciating his sincerity. They sat in a comfortable silence while they finished their drinks. 'I should go to bed, really,' said Hana.

'Should? What was it you said? Something about it being an auxiliary verb?' There was a twinkle of amusement in Robert's eyes.

Hana got to her feet. 'Correction. I am going to bed.'

Robert stood. 'Hope you get a good night's sleep.'

Hana reached out and lightly touched his arm. 'Thank you, Robert. Goodnight.'

He placed his hand over hers. 'Try not to worry.'

It was amazing how the small act of listening and saying a few reassuring words, could make a person feel comforted. Maybe it wouldn't be so bad having Robert as a house guest after all.

Chapter 11

Over the next few weeks, Robert proved himself the perfect house guest and Hana liked having him around. He'd brought a different sort of energy to the place with his friendly easy-going, kind nature, and often offered to help out around the house, particularly clearing up the kitchen after their evening meal.

Spending time with Robert had become a welcome distraction from the reality of what was going on around her, and Hana found herself looking forward to the sound of Gregory closing his study door behind him after supper. It was an hour or two when the company was easy, when she felt lighter in her heart than she had for a long time. It was a reminder of who she was before the war, and she no longer felt lonely in the evenings now that she had someone to chat to about things other than the war.

She and Robert had a lot in common. They shared a love for Big Band music, which she had to play quietly after Gregory had come out the first time she'd put the radiogram on and snapped at her to turn the 'ruddy music down'. It had been embarrassing, to say the least, but Hana refused to turn it off completely. The war brought small pleasures, and she was determined to find them where she could.

One evening a few days after he'd arrived, Hana had put a record on and been surprised when Robert asked her if she wanted to dance.

'Only if you want to,' he'd said, softly, glancing towards the closed door of the sitting room. 'I know I shouldn't really ask, but it's been a long time since I've been to any kind of dance.'

Hana had followed his gaze to the door. She couldn't remember the last time she and Gregory had danced. He had refused to since his accident, and she did understand that, even though it made her sad. But she loved dancing, and she missed it.

She looked back at Robert and got to her feet, taking his outstretched hand. 'Thank you. I'd love to.'

As she rested her hand on his shoulder and he slid his hand around her waist, a wave of butterflies flitted through her stomach. She wasn't sure if this was the excitement of dancing or who she was dancing with.

It felt a little awkward at first, but as the music filled the room, Hana felt herself relax. She closed her eyes and imagined herself at a dance, in a ballroom filled with people, where there was no war, bunting was strung across the ceiling and the sound of laughter and chatting filtered through the music of the band.

She opened her eyes, and Robert was smiling down at her. She smiled back and allowed him to draw her a little closer to his body.

Hana could have stayed there in his arms all night, but as the record came to an end, she looked at the clock. 'Gosh. I didn't realise it was so late,' she said, reluctantly pulling away. 'Thank you, though. I've missed this so much.'

'Any time you wanna dance, just say the word,' Robert replied softly.

*

Hana and Robert had danced each night since then, and now, as she sat at Alfred's bedside, she found herself reliving the previous evening's dance. Instead of the upbeat, Big Band music, it had been a softer slower song and Robert had held her closer than before, his jaw resting just above her ear. She had closed her eyes and found herself leaning into him as his hand spread wide across her back and his thumb had softly stroked her spine.

It had felt intimate and yet so natural. Reliving that moment in the quiet of the hospital room brought a smile to her face.

'You look like the cat who got the cream.' Her mother's voice crashed through her thoughts.

'What? Oh. No. Sorry.' Hana wasn't even sure what she was saying. 'I mean. I was miles away.'

'I could see that.' Pamela eyed her daughter, but Hana wasn't about to confess anything to her mother. She made a conscious effort not to think about Robert for the rest of their visit.

Soon enough, it was time to leave and after driving back to Bramble House with her mother, Hana cycled back to Tall Trees.

It was only now that she allowed herself to think of Robert again. The prospect of a late-night dance spurred her on down the darkened lane.

She heard a car coming up from behind her. She could hear the fluctuating sound as gears were changed and revs dropped, then increased. The vehicle didn't sound to be in a particular hurry, though, and Hana moved closer to the side of the road. She glanced back over her shoulder. The dark shadowy shape of the car loomed up behind her. It slowed and then began to accelerate.

It was heading straight for her.

The headlights flicked on and Hana was blinded by the dazzling light. She wobbled, came to a halt and hopped off her bike.

The driver must be able to see her.

The car continued to accelerate.

Hana squinted against the glare of the headlights. She waved her hand furiously to get the driver's attention.

'Hey!' she yelled. 'Hey! Look out!'

The car was bearing down on her. It wasn't going to stop.

Hana's bike was between her and the grass verge. She threw the bicycle down and hurled herself towards the opposite side of the road, hitting the gritty surface, stones biting into the palms of her hands and knees.

Seconds later, there was a horrific sound of crunching metal as the car ran straight over her bicycle and she felt the wheel brush her foot.

Hana lay there for a moment, certain the car was going to stop.

It did. A few metres down the road.

She rolled herself over so that she was in a sitting position, expecting the door to open and the occupant to climb out.

But to her horror, the car began to reverse. At speed.

Hana scrambled to her feet and somehow managed to reach a gap in the hedge. She charged through it, ignoring the brambles scratching at her legs and snagging at the heavy fabric of her coat.

She heard the car screech to a stop once again. And then, with a rev of its engine, it sped off into the night.

Hana rushed out into the road. Anger coursing through her. She shouted at the car's disappearing taillights as she chased it down the road.

As it vanished out of sight, Hana ground to a halt, bending over double and panting hard to catch her breath.

Then the tears came. Tears of anger and of relief.

*

'Jeez, what happened to you?' asked Robert as Hana hobbled through the door sometime later.

'I fell off my bike,' she muttered, shrugging off her coat and hanging it on the hall's coat stand. She held onto the coat hook for a moment, closing her eyes. She was not going to cry again in front of their guest. 'I need to get cleaned up.' She headed for the stairs, but her knee was throbbing, and she could barely bend it. She sucked in air between her teeth, not wanting to make a fuss. She grabbed hold of the newel post to steady herself and then winced as the cuts on her hand reopened.

'Let me help you,' said Robert, hurrying over to her. 'Please.'

Hana relented. She was tired, and in too much pain and discomfort to argue. 'Thank you.' They made their way down the hall and into the kitchen. 'I need to boil some water.'

'No. What you need to do is sit down here and let me do that,' said Robert. 'Remember I'm actually a trained doctor. It's what I did before I joined up. I was originally with the medical corps. So, just to reassure you, I do know what I'm doing.'

'Oh yes, I forgot.'

He gave a quick grin. 'Now, be a good patient and sit down.'

She did as she was told while Robert boiled the kettle and, under direction from Hana, gathered up the TCP, a clean flannel and some plasters.

'This is going to sting a bit,' he said, kneeling in front of her. 'Sorry, can you . . .' He gestured to her skirt.

'Oh. Yes.' Hana pulled up her skirt and then remembered she was wearing stockings. The nylon was shredded around both knees. 'Oh.'

'Er . . . I'll . . .' Robert turned so that he had his back to her.

Well, this was rather awkward but necessary. Hana kicked off both shoes and deftly unclipped her stockings and slipped them down. It was rather painful as some of the blood had dried into the nylon. She bundled them up into a ball and shoved them onto the seat of one of the chairs, throwing a tea towel over them. 'You can turn around now,' she said.

Robert set about cleaning her knees. 'How did you manage to fall off your bike?'

Hana shrugged. She hadn't planned to say anything until she'd told Gregory about the incident first, but her resolve to remain stoic had reached its limit. A tear forced its way from her eye and trickled down her cheek. She swiped it away and swallowed hard trying to keep her composure. 'Sorry,' she said, when she realised Robert had stopped what he was doing to look up at her.

'Don't apologise,' he said. 'You've taken a nasty fall. It's dark out in those lanes. You shouldn't really be out there riding your bike.'

'It's not that,' said Hana cutting him off. 'I didn't exactly fall off my bike. I jumped off.'

Robert looked confused. 'Why did you jump off a perfectly good bicycle?'

She gave a small laugh despite herself. 'A car was coming at me. It was my only option.'

'Damn. The driver didn't see you at all?'

Hana took a deep breath. 'Oh, they saw me. They ran straight over my bike. Fortunately, for me, I had already dived out of the way, but then they reversed up. I'm sure they were trying to run me over.' As she said the words, she shook, and another tear leaked its way from her eye. Again, she wiped it away. 'Gosh, what am I like? I'm not usually a wreck like this.'

'Please, don't apologise,' said Robert gently. 'Are you quite sure they deliberately tried to run you over?'

She nodded. 'Whoever it was aimed straight for me. Sped up, in actual fact, as they got nearer.'

'Why the hell would someone do that?'

'I've no idea. And I know how ridiculous it sounds,' said Hana, looking up at the ceiling for a moment and then back down at Robert. 'But it's true.'

Robert shook his head slowly and dabbed at her knee again. Hana winced. 'Sorry,' he said. 'There's a bit of grit in here. Put your foot up on my thigh.' He gently cupped the back of her calf with one hand to steady her leg and then wiped at the cut on her knee. When she flinched, he held a little tighter. 'Sorry,' he said again.

After he had put a plaster on one of her knees, he tended to her hands. 'Look at the state of me,' said Hana, inspecting her grazed and torn palms.

Robert got some clean water and then very attentively began to bathe her wounds.

Hana was very aware of his hand holding hers. She looked at him and he looked up, meeting her gaze. 'Thank you,' she said, her voice almost a whisper. To have someone care for her, to show her even a small amount of compassion, to feel the comforting touch of another human. It almost brought her to tears again.

'It's the least I could do,' said Robert, his voice matching hers in volume. His eyes searched her face as if trying to decipher what she was thinking.

The sound of the door opening and closing, snapped the tension in the kitchen.

'Gregory,' said Hana, needlessly. She looked down the hall at the figure of her husband, illuminated by the hall light.

Gregory got to the doorway and frowned. 'What's happened here?'

Robert got to his feet, dropping the flannel into the bowl, before drying his hands on the towel.

'I came off my bike,' said Hana. 'Robert was just patching me up.' She held up the palms of her hands to reveal her wounds and then nodded at her knees. 'The road is pretty unforgiving it seems.'

'How on earth did you manage that?' asked Gregory, coming over and stepping between Robert and Hana.

'It wasn't an accident,' said Robert.

Gregory didn't look at Robert. 'Thank you for helping my wife. I'm sure she can explain,' he said, his tone cold.

Hana wanted to die at Gregory's rudeness. How embarrassing. She went to say something, but Robert beat her to it.

'It's all right,' he said. 'I have a few things to attend to.'

'Thank you, Robert,' said Hana. She nudged Gregory's arm.

'Yes. Thank you.' Gregory was terse, which made Hana cringe even more.

She looked up at Robert, hoping to convey her apologies without having to say anything. He gave her a subtle wink and left the room.

'Well. You didn't have to be quite so rude,' she hissed at Gregory. 'He was just helping me.'

'I could see that,' snapped back Gregory. He pulled out the chair where one of her stockings was hanging over the edge, before hooking it up with the end of his walking stick. 'Really, Hana.' He spoke like a disappointed parent.

'My knees were bleeding. The stockings are shredded,' said Hana, feeling the burn of embarrassment, not to mention a certain outrage at what her husband was suggesting. She snatched up the stockings and, opening the Aga, threw them inside. They shrivelled to nothing in seconds.

'And you let him . . .' Gregory gestured with his stick again towards her knees.

'Touch me,' hissed Hana. 'Yes. I did, as a matter of fact. I was upset. I still am. He cleaned and dressed my wounds. What's so wrong with that? He's a medic for goodness' sake.'

'You could have done it yourself is all I'm saying.'

'I appreciated someone doing it for me.' They stared at each other for a moment. Hana spoke again. 'And just in case you were wondering, I didn't just fall off my bike. Someone tried to run me over.'

'What on earth are you talking about?'

'Exactly what I said, but let's not worry about that tonight. Of course, if you hadn't had to go out in the car, I could have taken it and none of this would have happened.' She felt churlish for saying it, but her anger, frustration and the sheer emotional exhaustion of the past couple of weeks was taking over. 'Tomorrow, if it's not too much trouble, we can go and retrieve the mangled wreck of a bike that is currently on the side of the road where I had my accident.' Hana brushed passed her husband and marched, as best as she could, out of the kitchen. Despite the pain in her knee, she got herself upstairs and into her bedroom, relieved she didn't bump into Robert on the way. That would only add to her humiliation. She flung herself down on the bed, trying to control the anger and embarrassment that were vying for pole position.

A few minutes later, she heard Gregory's laboured ascent of the stairs and let out a sigh. Here she was, frustrated that she couldn't get up the stairs quick enough because her knee was hurting her, but at least her injury would heal. Gregory, on the other hand, would never have that privilege. He would have to live with his pain and inconvenience for the rest of his life.

She got up from the bed and went over to the door, hesitating for a moment. She wanted to say goodnight to him. To clear the air but it was so awkward, especially with someone else in the house. And what must Robert think of them? She didn't even want to consider that too deeply. But with the sound of Gregory's bedroom door opening and then closing, she'd missed her chance.

As she undressed for bed, she could hear Robert moving around in his room. Then the door opening and his footsteps going down the stairs. His tread was soft, as if trying not to disturb anyone. Maybe he was going to get a glass of water. She felt very rude not saying goodnight to him, but she was in her nightdress and had no intention of facing him now.

She brushed her teeth at the bedroom sink, and as she dried her face, she heard the creak of the back door being opened and closed. Hana crossed the room to the window, peeking out to look down at the garden. She could see Robert standing on the edge of the lawn, smoking a cigarette.

He must have sensed her gaze, as he turned and looked up at her. Hana darted away from the window but then felt foolish. Of course he would have seen her. She moved to the window again and tentatively peered out.

Robert was still looking up. He smiled and mouthed, 'You OK?'

Hana found herself smiling back at him, touched by his concern. She nodded and then raised her hand a fraction to give a small wave.

Robert tipped his forehead in a lazy salute.

Chapter 12

Hana awoke the next morning to the smell of cooking. She was confused. Cooking? That wasn't something Gregory did. She drew back the bedcovers and moved her legs to get out of bed, then winced as the pain brought back last night's near-miss.

Hana carefully straightened her knee, relieved to see that the dressing was still in place, and although she could see a little blood had seeped through, it didn't look fresh.

She shivered at the chilly autumn morning and, limping a little, went to open her curtains. She rubbed at the condensation on the inside of the windowpane and saw a silvery frost across the lawn.

Hana washed and dressed, choosing a woollen dress to keep her warm while she was at work. The huts were made of wood and apart from a small heater in the corner, they didn't provide much comfort against the cold mornings and evenings.

As she crossed the landing, she could hear Gregory moving about in his room. That answered her question as to who was cooking. She continued on downstairs and into the kitchen.

'You're up bright and early,' she said looking at Robert standing at the Aga with a frying pan in one hand and an egg in the other.

He looked around at her and smiled. 'Good morning. How are you feeling today?'

'A little stiff. But also surprised. No, make that curious.' She nodded towards the frying pan.

'I figured you might need to take it easy this morning. Let me fix breakfast.' He placed the pan on the hot plate and went to crack the egg, then paused. 'That's if you don't mind? I don't wanna overstep the mark here.'

Hana smiled, going over and taking the egg from him. 'I don't mind at all, but you might want to cook the bacon first. It takes longer.' She put the egg to one side and took the last of the bacon ration from the pantry, inwardly sighing that it would be another week before they could get any more bacon – the meat was such a luxury these days. 'Anyone would think you hadn't cooked breakfast for yourself before.' She raised an eyebrow.

'Ah. Busted.' Robert dragged his hand down his face. 'No, I can cook a few things, and I think I could have managed bacon and eggs, even if the eggs would have been a little overdone.'

She took the bowl of lard and with a spoon, dug into the set fat. She scrunched her face up in discomfort as the knife handle pressed against her sore palm.

'Here, let me,' said Robert. He reached over and covered her hand with his. 'I'll bet you're a little sore this morning?'

Hana let go of the spoon as he turned her hand over. 'Yes,' she admitted. 'But only if I press on my hand too hard.'

He frowned. 'You should report what happened to the police.'

'Do you think so?'

'Yes. I do.' He inspected her palm. 'The wound looks clean. It should heal fine.'

'Good. It's a bloody nuisance, I know that.' She avoided looking at him – very much aware of his closeness, his touch. 'The other one's not so bad.'

'And your knees?' He was still holding her hand.

Hana wasn't about to lift the hem of her dress to show him, although just his gaze was making her feel exposed. She heard Gregory on the stairs and quickly pulled her hand away, snatching up the spoon with the lard and sliding it into the frying pan. 'They're not too bad. Like my hand, a little sore.'

Robert looked right back at her for several seconds, both aware of Gregory's footsteps nearing the bottom of the stairs.

Robert moved to the table and sat down just as Gregory entered the kitchen. 'Morning,' Robert greeted him, taking a sip of his coffee.

'Morning,' echoed Hana, feeling guilty and yet also feeling cross for being so. She hadn't done anything wrong.

'Good morning. I see I'm the last one up today,' said Gregory, taking his usual seat at the end of the table. 'Did you sleep well?' He directed his question towards Robert.

'Very well,' replied their guest. 'I was just saying to Hana that she should report what happened last night to the police, or at least to somebody at the Park.'

Hana tensed. She placed the bacon rashers into the frying pan.

'I don't think there's any need for that,' said Gregory, picking up his newspaper.

'But she was pretty much deliberately knocked off her bike,' said Robert. 'The intention was there, anyway.'

Gregory opened the broadsheet. Sighed. And then closed it, folding it carefully before returning it to the table. He looked up at Hana. 'And what do you think?'

Hana's shoulders tensed some more. 'I'm not sure.'

'Do you agree with me, or do you want to take Robert's side?'

'It's not a case of sides,' she said.

'I was only offering advice,' said Robert.

'Well, thanks for that,' said Gregory. 'Things work a little differently here in England. We're not in the United States of America now where we call the "cops" for the slightest thing. There's currently a war on, and I'm sure the police have better things to do. Besides, what can they do? Unless Hana got the registration plate. Did you, dear?'

Hana felt mortified. Why was Gregory still being so hostile towards Robert? She looked at the two men, eye-balling each other. 'Er. No. I didn't. I'm not even sure what car it was.' She knew damn well it was an Austin Ten, it was the same car they had. But right now, she needed to defuse the tension that was building between her husband and their guest. 'Thinking about it, I might have made a mistake. It was all a bit of a blur, and I did catch my head on the road. We should just forget about it,' she said. Privately, though, she was going to mention it to Hopkins. It had to be more than a coincidence – first her father, then her. Both targeted by a black Austin Ten.

Gregory smiled. 'I agree with you.' He gave what was clearly a faux smile at Robert. 'Thanks for your concern, though. Now, is that coffee I can smell?'

Robert shot Hana a glance before turning back to Gregory. 'It sure is. I'm not so keen on your British coffee so I managed to get this from a friend of mine. He brought it over with him, right from the United States of America.'

Hana inwardly groaned at the jibe. They were as bad as each other.

'Right, who would like eggs? Did I tell you Mum said one of her chickens has stopped laying. We might not be getting fresh eggs for breakfast much longer.' She rambled on about the chickens for a few minutes, ensuring the conversation about her accident wasn't brought up again.

Once breakfast was over, Robert left for Bletchley, explaining he had to be in early and a car was waiting outside to take him. 'Got a briefing before we start today,' he said.

And then he was gone. Hana braced herself. She knew Gregory had been quietly seething for the past thirty minutes.

He barely waited for the door to close before speaking. 'I'd appreciate it if, in future, you didn't consult with an American who's only been here five minutes about whether or not you should go to the police,' he said, putting his coffee cup down on the table.

'I didn't ask him, it was just conversation,' said Hana and then hated herself for sounding so pathetic.

'It's a ridiculous idea. You should realise that.'

'Explain why it is ridiculous?' Hana could feel her own temper rising now. She was cross with Gregory, as well as herself.

'Because of where you work,' said Gregory as if explaining to a child. 'The bosses at the Park won't thank you for bringing the local bobbies poking around asking questions, like "Is there anyone who would wish to cause you harm? Why were you cycling around at night-time? Why don't you visit your father during the day? Oh, because you work. Where do you work? Blah. Blah. Blah.'

She hadn't actually thought that far ahead, but she prickled at his tone. 'You don't have to speak like that.'

Gregory sighed. 'I apologise but it's frustrating that I need to spell everything out. If you're going to tell anyone, it's Chatfield, not the police. I wish you'd come to me first.'

'I was going to but, like I said, you weren't here,' replied Hana. 'Besides all that, you were actually quite rude to Robert. It was embarrassing.'

'Oh, I'm embarrassing you now. You've finally plucked up the courage to say it to my face – I'm an embarrassment.'

Indignation swirled inside her. She knew exactly what Gregory was implying. She hated the way he was twisting her words. She had never been embarrassed about Gregory and the way he looked or that he had to walk with a stick. 'That was uncalled for,' she said. 'You're being petulant.' He didn't reply and she knew he knew it, too. 'We all are going to have to live together under one roof, please don't make it any more difficult than it has to be.' She got to her feet and marched out of the kitchen. Stuff the washing-up. She was going to work. Alone. Not with Gregory.

It wasn't until several minutes later when she had slammed the door behind her and was standing on the gravel driveway that she remembered she didn't have her bike. She wasn't about to go back indoors and ask for a lift from Gregory. Her pride wouldn't let her. She'd just have to catch the bus and walk at the other end. Then she realised she'd left her purse indoors. Walk it was.

Hana wasn't one for being a hothead but Gregory had really got under her skin. By the time she was out of the village and walking along the road though, her temper had subsided, her knee was making its displeasure known. She really shouldn't have stormed off so petulantly.

The sound of a car engine approaching from further down the lane startled her. A surge of panic rose up through her chest. What if they, whoever that might be, were coming back again to do the job properly?

She looked over her shoulder as the car rounded the bend. She gave a sharp intake of breath. It was an Austin

Ten. She looked around for somewhere to jump out of the way, but the engine slowed and as it neared, she recognised the driver. It was Gregory.

Hana stood to the edge of the road waiting for him to reach her. For a moment, she didn't think he was going to stop, but the car drew to a halt. Gregory climbed out and walked around to the other side of the car, where he opened the passenger door. He raised his eyebrows questioningly at her.

She sighed as she walked over to the car. 'Thank you,' she said, accepting his hand to guide her in.

'I'm sorry for biting your head off,' said Gregory as he settled himself back behind the wheel.

'I'm sorry, too,' replied Hana. She looked at him, hoping he would turn to her, maybe even smile in that way they used to when they knew they'd both overreacted about something. The way couples who loved each other did, who, once their tempers had died down, felt rueful about any outbursts. Maybe he would lean over and kiss her and tell her it was a silly argument. But none of those scenarios played out anywhere other than in her imagination these days. Gregory put the car into gear and pulled away.

Hana looked out of the window at the passing hedgerows, all but bare of their foliage, exposed now to the oncoming winter. She wanted to pass it off as a minor disagreement, but she knew it went deeper than that. It wasn't about whether she should or shouldn't report the incident, it was about how Gregory saw himself next to Robert's easy yet caring manner, his confidence, his stride . . . his unmarked skin. Gregory was comparing himself to the American and was convinced he fell short of the mark. It was as if his scars burned fresh all over again, marking him as something less. Hana had tried so many times since the accident to persuade him that his scars were proof of survival, not failure but her words were rebuffed. She couldn't break through the wall he'd built around himself. And now, as she watched the skeletal branches blur past the window, she felt the fight leaching from her bones. She didn't have the energy anymore. The constant rejection had worn her down.

'I'll tell Chatfield about last night and see what he thinks,' she said as they reached Bletchley Park.

'Thank you,' said Gregory, seemingly accepting the olive branch that represented. He drove through the gates and parked the car. 'Look, I didn't get a chance to tell you earlier, but I'm going to be in London for the next few days.'

'Over the best part of the weekend and my day off,' protested Hana.

'I know that, but the war doesn't stop at weekends, my dear.' He got out of the car.

Hana was already gingerly climbing out, too, not waiting for him to open the door for her. 'Why? Why have you got to go to London?'

He gave her a look as if to say did he really have to spell it out. 'Work,' he said simply. He came around to her. 'I'm heading off there shortly, in fact.' He took his wallet from his pocket and took out a pound note which he gave to Hana. 'Bus fare and whatever else you need.'

'Right.' She took the money and slipped it into her handbag.

'I'll be back Tuesday evening.' He hesitated, and for a moment, Hana thought he was going to kiss her goodbye, but he didn't move towards her. 'Have a good weekend.'

Hana watched him head over towards the mansion. He didn't turn to look at her once. She pressed her lips together as a sadness engulfed her. What had become of their marriage? It was held together by a tatty old thread, and she didn't know how to fix it.

*

'You look like you've lost a pound and found a shilling,' said Audrey as Hana entered their room in the hut.

'What? Oh, sorry,' said Hana. She smiled at her colleague as she walked around to her desk. She hated to admit it to herself but there was a certain amount of relief at Gregory's departure. Sometimes she felt quite exhausted from his sour manner. It would be nice not to have to worry about it for a few days. Of course, this immediately made her feel guilty, but she pushed that emotion away.

'My goodness, what on earth happened to you?' It was Jenny's voice breaking Hana from her thoughts. Jenny was peering at Hana's knees, which had peeped out from the hem of her skirt as she sat down.

'Fell off my bike,' said Hana. She hesitated for a split second as she contemplated how much to share with her colleagues. Nothing, at this stage, she decided. 'I was cycling home after visiting Alfred in hospital. It was dark. I must have hit something in the road.'

'Why were you on your bike?' asked Audrey, peering over the desk to inspect Hana's knees.

'No car available,' said Hana. She held up her hands to show the palms. 'Managed to do this, too.'

Derek and Chatfield came into the room, and they, too, fussed over Hana's injuries. 'Are you sure you're all right?' asked Chatfield.

'I'm perfectly fine,' she replied. 'Now, can we all stop worrying and get on with what we're here for?'

'I second that,' said Robert, coming into the room.

'Ah, Becker,' said Chatfield. 'Have you seen what Hana's done to herself?'

'Erm, yes, I have actually,' replied Robert. 'Nothing too serious, though.'

'There, you've heard it from the medic yourself,' said Hana. 'I'm fine.'

'Hmm.' Chatfield didn't look convinced. 'Is that your medical opinion, Becker, or one that Hana insists you have?' He looked speculatively over the top of his glasses at her.

'Yes,' confirmed Robert. 'It's mine.'

'Right, well, as long as you think you can continue to work.'

'I've a few scrapes and grazes, that's all,' said Hana, peeved that everyone was making such a fuss about it. She returned to her work. She had a new message to decipher and was keen to break this one quicker than her previous ones.

Jenny shuffled up next to her. 'You and Robert seem to have hit it off,' she said quietly.

Hana gave a shrug as if to say it was no big deal.

Jenny obviously didn't speak quietly enough, as the next thing Hana knew, Audrey was sprawling across the desk to join the huddle. 'He is rather handsome, isn't he?'

'Well, you two are welcome to fight over him,' said Hana. 'Just in case you've forgotten, I am actually married.'

'It's a two-horse race, then,' said Audrey, with a wink.

'Who are you calling a horse?' whispered Jenny with mock indignation. 'You speak for yourself. I like to think of myself as a beautiful young filly.'

The three of them laughed at the comment, which earned a reproachful look from Chatfield as he left the room.

'You'll get us shot,' whispered Hana.

As they returned to their work, Hana couldn't help thinking how nice it was to hear Jenny making a joke. Maybe things would be better from now on. It would be much nicer working with her if they got on well. In fact, the whole atmosphere in the room that day was the best it had been since Hana had started. Maybe they were all getting used to each other and beginning to relax as they worked in a team. Hana had to take what joy she could and where she could get it, especially as home life was so difficult at the moment.

However, she soon reminded herself that whilst it was nice to make friends, ultimately, she had to be conscious that any one of them could be the spy. She mustn't let herself be distracted. Any self-respecting spy would make sure they ingratiated themselves with their colleagues to avoid suspicion and keep abreast of any rumours.

Hana was pleased when it was time for a quick tea break. Her head was still hurting from her fall and a headache was threatening. 'I'm just going to nip out for some fresh air,' she said to Jenny.

'Right-o. See you in a bit,' said Jenny, not looking up from her work.

Hana slipped out of the room and along the corridor. As she stepped outside, she breathed in deeply. The air was a little damp, and the earthy autumnal smell filled her nostrils. The leaves were already falling from the trees, and it wouldn't be long before she'd need to dig out her winter coat, hat and gloves. She walked around the side of the hut, which backed onto the wooded gardens of Bletchley Park, and leaned against the trunk of an impressive oak tree, closing her eyes for a moment. She suddenly felt fatigued, and if there had been a bench to sit down upon, she was certain she would fall asleep.

As Hana stood there peacefully, the sound of voices drifted her way. At first, she didn't think anything of it but inadvertently tuned into the conversation when she realised they were coming closer to her. She opened her eyes and strained to hear more. The voices were low, almost secretive and one was definitely male. She couldn't be certain of the second person, who didn't seem to be doing so much talking.

Hana stood stock still. Some primal instinct told her to stay hidden as the voices got nearer and louder. She could hear what they were saying now.

'We need to be careful. It can't be obvious. Wait a few more days and try again,' came one of the voices. 'Phillips will be back by then. He's gone off to London today. And before you say anything, yes, we can trust him.'

Hana had to stop herself from gasping out loud. There was no doubt they were referring to Gregory. What did he have to do with anything? Whatever was going on, it didn't sound to be above board.

There was the scrunch of leaves underfoot as the pair got even closer to Hana. She was certain they must only be a few feet away from her on the other side to the oak tree. Seeing her breath puff into the cool air, she buried her mouth in the collar of her jacket.

'I need to get back before anyone misses me,' said the man again. 'We should go.'

And then they were walking off, away from Hana, who stayed exactly where she was for several more minutes, not daring to move nor make a sound. She wasn't quite sure what to make of what she'd just heard.

Then, with much reluctance, Hana made her way back to the hut. Just before she got there, she heard a familiar voice.

'Hey!' Robert called out, jogging across the grass to catch her up. He stopped in front of her. 'You look tired.'

'You know how to make a girl feel good about herself,' said Hana with a laugh.

Robert smiled and cocked his head to one side. 'Who said a woman can't look tired and beautiful at the same time?'

Hana felt herself blush at the compliment. 'Thank you,' she said, awkwardly and pulled open the hut door. 'Better get back to it.' She managed a smile and then headed inside, already scolding herself for her reaction. At the same time, her stomach was doing a silly little jumpy thing.

*

Hana concentrated again on the message she'd been given to decrypt. She had tried several methods of decoding it, but none of them were working.

She leaned back in her chair, stretching out the cramps that were threatening in her fingers. She'd been staring at the same blasted Japanese intercept for three hours now and was making no headway whatsoever. She rolled her head around in small circles and rubbed the back of her neck, before returning her attention back to the code.

NKRA JNLP EKYX WRKY GRTN
HYLC KYFD JIWP BAWR KRPO

It was a Japanese fleet intercept, sent at 0300 hours. Something was off about it, but she couldn't quite place it. She had been spending the past weeks at the Park, tracking routine submarine movements and their supply orders from Germany, which ranged from things like, extra diesel, medical supplies, radio equipment which matched German frequencies, to name but a few. It was tedious work and on its own almost felt insignificant, but it was supply routes like this that helped feed into the bigger picture of how Japan was fairing in the war overall. A lot of it was nuanced, and guesswork, but it was all important. Not that Hana saw the direct result of all the decrypts, that was above her paygrade and anyone else's in the hut, to be honest, but she was the supplier of information and, as always, it was on a need-to-know basis.

The sound of rain pattered on the roof of the hut and tapped against the windowpanes. Glad she wasn't cycling home tonight. She looked back at the intercept. Not that whoever sent it had to worry about her cycling home in the rain.

She took another look at what she had decoded so far. It wasn't making sense, and that in itself put her on high alert. She double-checked what she had done so far.

'Everything all right?' asked Jenny.

'I don't know,' replied Hana. She didn't really want to share information with anyone in the hut, seeing as they were all under suspicion of being a spy, but at the same time, she couldn't withhold crucial information. She glanced around the room where everyone else was heads-down busy. There had been a rapid increase in decrypts in the last week or so, which again was sounding alarm bells to the room. Everyone was working longer hours to try to work out what was going on. 'Look at this,' she said eventually.

Jenny moved her chair closer to Hana and took the intercept and Hana's notes. She spent several minutes checking and rechecking what Hana had done. 'It all looks good to me,' she said at last. 'I'm guessing this part about "snow falling" is what's bothering you.'

'Exactly. I've checked the weather in Japan at this time of year and it's similar to our autumn. Not a snowflake in sight.'

'Make a note of it. Check previous similar intercepts and see if that's been mentioned before,' said Jenny. 'Sometimes we get an anomaly we can't apply. When Lottie comes back, ask her if she's remembered seeing this at all. It's most likely a codeword, but for what, who knows.'

Jenny returned to her work, Hana to hers but although she appeared to be looking at the code, in reality her mind had shifted to who the spy was. Hopkins was growing impatient, and she couldn't blame him. She might be having some success at cracking the codes but finding the crucial information they needed about the spy, or indeed working out who the spy was, that particular gift was eluding her.

She sat back in her chair, feeling deflated. Maybe she wasn't as astute as she thought she was. Just because her father was an absolute ace at words and codes, it didn't mean she had inherited those skills to an equal extent. It made her feel guilty. She didn't want to let him down. How embarrassing for her and disappointing for him if the daughter he had boasted about to everyone turned out to be a flop.

She pressed her lips together as a wave of sadness washed over her. She wished there was something tangible she could do to help her dad. He would be mortified if he could see himself now. The man lying sedated in the hospital bed was not the man who had loved, nurtured and educated her all her life.

The need to see her father engulfed her and she glanced up at the clock. There were another ten minutes until the end of her shift. Instead of going home, she'd get the bus over to the hospital. She knew Alfred wouldn't be able to communicate with her, but just being in his presence, holding his hand, hearing him breathe, was all she could think about.

Chapter 13

At the stroke of four, Hana was tidying up her desk and filing away her daily logs. Bidding a hurried goodbye to everyone, she rushed out of the hut. She was sure there was a bus in ten minutes from Bletchley and she had no intention of missing it.

The past few weeks had been exhausting both mentally and emotionally. Work at the Park had been intense and she'd put in some longer shifts as the messages from the Japanese continued to be intercepted and partially decoded. The Japanese officials sure liked to talk. Their messages between one another could hardly be described as brief, but scanning the conversations and picking out the vital nuggets of information was proving invaluable to the Pacific operations. She just wished she could crack the current intercept she was working on which had come from somewhere higher up the command chain and, therefore, was likely to contain much more sensitive information

She had just reached the end of Wiltern Avenue when a car pulled up alongside her. It was Robert.

'Do you want a ride?' he asked, leaning across the front seat to call out of the passenger window.

'Since when did you have a car?' asked Hana.

'Since about four hours ago,' said Robert. 'Been issued with it.'

'Impressive.'

'I like to think so.' He gave a grin. 'You wanna get in?'

'Thank you but I'm not going home right away,' said Hana. 'Look, I must dash. I'll miss my bus. I'll see you later.' She began walking again, her heels clipping swiftly on the pavement.

Robert drew up alongside her again. 'You don't need to get the bus. I'll take you wherever it is you're going.'

She didn't stop walking. 'I'm going to the hospital. It's about half an hour away. Thank you again.'

This time Robert drove off, but only as far as the end of the road. He jumped out of the car, went around to the passenger side and held the door open. Hana drew to a halt as she reached him.

'Please, Hana, allow me the pleasure of driving you to see your father,' he said. 'Also, please don't say no otherwise I'll have to throw you over my shoulder and forcibly put you in the car.'

'That sounds a lot like kidnap to me,' said Hana.

'If you just accept the lift then it's not kidnap.'

Hana found herself laughing. 'Far be it from me to cause an international incident,' she said. 'Thank you.'

With some navigation from Hana, Robert drove them swiftly through the Buckinghamshire countryside, pulling up outside the hospital some thirty minutes later. Apart from giving Robert directions, they hadn't spoken in the car. It was if Robert understood that she needed time to be alone with her thoughts. She appreciated his understanding and lack of offence.

'Thank you, Robert,' Hana said. 'I won't be long.'

The nurse reported that Alfred was comfortable and still sedated, but that Hana wasn't to worry. 'He just needs time,' she explained. 'And head injuries are best healed by rest.'

Hana slipped into her father's room. 'Hello, Dad,' she said quietly as she reached his bedside. She leaned over and kissed his cheek. 'Just wanted to come and see you.' She sat next to the bed and held his hand in hers. 'I've been at the Park today. I didn't get a chance to tell you before, but I've been approached by MI5.' She paused, waiting for any kind of acknowledgement that he had heard her. She looked down at his limp hand in her palm, willing him to respond with a squeeze or a tap of his finger, but his hand remained still. 'They want to know where the information that you've been gathering is.' She looked over her shoulder to make sure no one had slipped into the room without her noticing. 'The information about the spy . . . Dad, they want me to find it and give it to them. A chap named Hopkins told me it was top secret.' She paused again, but again there was no indication that Alfred was even aware of her presence. 'I don't know where to look. Who to ask. Who to trust.'

Hana sat back in her seat. She hadn't really expected Alfred to suddenly regain consciousness and tell her everything she needed to know, but speaking to his serene form brought a familiar comfort she couldn't quite identify. The sound of his steady breathing marked time as she recalled all the times he had been there for her, anchoring her through choppy waters. When she'd first learned of Gregory's injuries, when she had struggled to know how to help her husband. She thought of the way her father's eyes crinkled at the corners when he smiled, the way he could distil her worries and fears with a few words that gave her comfort and strength. Now, in the small hospital room, she craved his wisdom more than ever. Would she ever see that gentle reassuring smile again, the one he proffered just before he delivered his profound advice?

She sat quietly for several more minutes, soaking up the strange sense of peace that seemed to come from just being in his presence. He may not be able to offer words of wisdom, or even a hug, but being here with him made Hana feel safe. Over the last few weeks, her little cocoon of safety had been ripped open at the seams, and she didn't know how to patch it up. She didn't even have Gregory to turn to. He was still battling his own demons and continuing to shut Hana out. It was sad to realise that one could be with someone one loved, a husband, and yet feel alone.

There was a tap at the door and the nurse poked her head into the room. 'Can I get you a cup of tea?'

Hana smiled. 'No. I'm fine, thank you. I only called in quickly.' She got to her feet and, giving Alfred a kiss goodbye, she left the room and headed out the car park.

'How is your father?' asked Robert as she got back into the car.

'No change,' said Hana. 'He's still sedated. I just wanted to see him, to let him know I was there.'

'Look, it may not feel like you're doing any good, but I have no doubt that somewhere in his subconscious he knew you were there at his side.'

Hana didn't know if that was scientifically true, but she liked the thought and took comfort from it.

When they got back home, Hana excused herself and went upstairs just to have a few minutes to herself before she had to go back downstairs and play hostess. Her mind was whirring with everything that had gone on and she really did feel quite tired. She lay down on the bed and closed her eyes for a moment, searching for some kind of escape from all her thoughts. She must have nodded off because when she awoke, it was dark outside. As she came around, she was aware of the smell of cooking wafting up the stairs. She sat up. It smelled like chicken and potatoes, the kind of supper her mother would make. Her stomach rumbled in appreciation and anticipation.

Hana ventured downstairs expecting to see Pamela in the kitchen and was wholly surprised to see Robert straining potatoes over the sink.

'Ah, there you are,' he said, looking back at her over his shoulder. 'I was going to come and wake you in a minute. I hope you don't mind, but I thought I'd cook dinner.'

Hana raised her eyebrows. 'So, you can cook after all?'

'As I said, my skills are limited and yeah, the bacon and eggs went off-plan, but I can cook a stew. I have my mom to thank for that. She said it wasn't right that we should expect a woman to always be there to cook for us. By us, I mean my three brothers and myself.'

'I like the sound of your mother,' said Hana. 'And in her honour, I won't offer to help.'

Robert smiled. 'Good, because I would politely decline any help.' He nodded towards the table. 'Are you any good at opening wine?'

Hana noticed the green wine bottle on the table for the first time. 'Wine? Wow. That is a luxury.' She went over to the kitchen drawer and rummaged around for the corkscrew. 'Where did that come from?'

'A friend of mine.' Robert gave a wink and moved closer to her. 'I can't disclose my source,' he said in a low whisper, 'but I have contacts.'

Hana was very aware of his shoulder brushing against her own. 'Contacts?'

'Yep. And don't try to torture me into revealing who they are.'

'I can't imagine you'd give in to my interrogation.'

'Depends what methods you used.'

There was a beat of silence and Hana wasn't sure she was even breathing at that point.

Then Robert stepped to one side, putting space back between them, humming a tune Hana didn't recognise. She managed to uncork the wine and stood it on the table, then busied herself with setting the table and putting the plates into the bottom shelf of the Aga to warm. Gradually, the fizzle of energy that was zapping between her and Robert died down.

Soon they were sitting opposite each other at the table, enjoying the meal and especially enjoying the wine.

Maybe a little too much.

Hana was aware it was going to her head rather rapidly, but it was such a luxury these days that she didn't want to put a stop to it.

'That was the most delicious meal I've had in a long time.' Hana gave a sigh of satisfaction as she put her cutlery together on the plate and leaned back in her chair, taking another sip of wine. 'It's always so much nicer when someone else cooks.'

'Good to see you relaxing,' said Robert.

'Not for much longer. It's your turn to relax now.' Hana got to her feet to begin clearing the dishes.

As she stood at Robert's side, reaching to take his plate, he put his hand out and caught her wrist. 'Let me,' he said, getting to his feet and taking her plate from her. 'You need a proper night off.' He picked up the other plate. 'And no arguing.'

Hana thought about standing her ground, but only for a second. She wasn't sure she had the energy and, to be honest, it was nice being looked after for a change. 'All right,' she said. 'Thank you.'

'You're welcome.' He put the plates on the worktop and went back to the table, where he topped up her wine and passed the glass to her.

'Anyone would think you were trying to get me drunk,' said Hana, eyeing the full glass he held between them.

'Is that a bad thing?'

'Some might say you could take advantage of me.' She looked up at him.

'I would never do that,' he replied softly.

Hana took another deep breath and stepped away, reminding herself that whatever the state of her marriage, she should not be flirting with another man, even if he was desperately attractive and attentive.

When she went into the living room, Hana purposely sat in the armchair by the fireside that Gregory usually occupied. She really needed to put some physical distance between her and Robert.

'All done,' he said, coming into the living room. 'I hope the dishes are done to your satisfaction.'

He had an easy smile, one that was hard to ignore. Hana found herself smiling at him. 'I'm sure you've done them perfectly well. I can't imagine your mother would have let you get away with dirty dishes.'

'She most certainly did not,' said Robert. He held up the wine bottle towards her. 'Top up?'

Hana covered the glass with her hand. 'No. Thank you. I shall have an awful headache in the morning if I drink any more.'

Robert sat down on the sofa. 'Where did Gregory say he was going?' His tone was casual as he refilled his own glass.

'Just to London,' Hana said. 'No more detail than that.' She turned on the radio, twiddling the dial until the voice of Fred Astaire singing 'Cheek to Cheek' played softly in the background.

'Aren't you curious?' asked Robert. 'Or even worried?'

Hana looked at the American. 'Curious, yes. Worried, no.' She took a sip of her drink to hide her face. Her statement wasn't strictly true, but she wasn't worried for the reasons Robert might think she was.

'He doesn't tell you much, does he?'

Hana shrugged. 'A lot of what he does is secret. He can't tell me. The same way I can't tell him what we're doing at the Park. I know you said it before, but I can assure you there's no pillow talk.'

Robert rested his elbows on his knees. 'I don't think there's any pillow talk going on at all.'

She shot him a look. 'We take our jobs very seriously.'

'Plus, you don't share a room.'

'That's really none of your business.' She was more than niggled now. That was downright impertinent of him. 'But, no, we don't as it happens.' She finished her drink and rose. 'I think I'll go to bed now.'

Robert jumped to his feet. 'I'm sorry, Hana,' he said, standing in front of her. 'I didn't mean to offend you.'

'As I said, it's none of your business.' Unexpected tears came to her eyes, and she cast her gaze down, dipping her head. She really shouldn't have had that last glass of wine; it was making her very emotional.

Robert rested his hands on her arms. 'I don't mean to upset you.'

She went to reply but her words stuck in her throat. A tear fell down her cheek. Then another. And another. Where on earth had this outpouring of emotion come from? She couldn't stop herself as sobs racked up in her chest. 'I'm sorry,' she managed to croak out before another sob engulfed her.

Then Robert was tipping her head up, dabbing her tears with his clean white handkerchief. 'Hey, don't be sorry.' He put his arms around her and pulled her in close to him.

Hana felt herself sink into his chest. She could hear the beat of his heart. The warmth of his embrace just made her cry even more. She couldn't remember the last time Gregory had held her like this. Had made her feel cared for. She was so used to being stoic and strong, she'd forgotten what it was like to *feel*. And now she was feeling that raw emotion of relief that someone was caring for her. It wasn't her husband, but she didn't care.

Robert kissed the top of her head and murmured comforting words that a parent might say to a child. Words that brought reassurance and comfort. Words that made her feel she wasn't alone.

Eventually, the tears subsided, and Robert wiped her damp face again. 'It's OK. Everything is gonna be OK. Trust me.'

'I'm so sorry,' said Hana, finally finding her own hanky in her pocket.

'You don't have to apologise,' said Robert, in that soft reassuring voice.

For a moment, Hana couldn't tear her eyes away from his. The urge to reach for him was strong and it felt as if, as he gazed down at her, that at any second he was going to kiss her. If he did, she didn't think she'd be able to stop herself from kissing him back. His mouth was moving closer to hers; there was just a hair's breadth between their lips.

But then Robert let out a sigh, lifting his chin and kissing her on top of her head.

'You've had a tough few days,' he said. 'You should get some sleep.' He took a step back from her. 'I'm going outside for a smoke. I'll lock up. Goodnight, Hana.'

Chapter 14

Hana had lain awake in bed for a long time, thinking about that moment with Robert, when he had comforted her, she was certain he was about to kiss her, but something had stopped him. Part of her was relieved, but another part of her was disappointed. She was surprised by this feeling. She felt guilty for wanting him to kiss her, but she also acknowledged the feeling of happiness and excitement the thought had brought her. His embrace had given her comfort. She missed that sensation and wished it could have been Gregory making her feel like that.

She had finally drifted off to sleep, and when she awoke in the morning she was still confused over her feelings. She tiptoed downstairs and set about making breakfast as she usually would. There was no point trying to avoid Robert, she'd have to face him sooner or later and better here at home than at work.

'Morning.' Robert's voice broke through her thoughts.

She spun around to see him leaning against the doorframe. 'Good morning. Coffee?' she asked trying not to appear flustered. Just him standing there was enough to send her pulse racing.

'Thank you.'

Hana was very aware Robert was tracking her movements even though she had her back to him. She could feel his gaze on her. Unnerved, she fumbled the cup and just managed to catch it before it fell onto the quarry tiles.

'Gosh. I'm all fingers and thumbs,' she said trying to laugh, but failing.

He came over, took the cup and turned her around to look at him. 'Hana,' he began.

Hana looked down. 'We should forget about last night,' she said. It would be easier for both of them if she took the lead and let him know that what happened last night between them was nothing either of them should be concerned about. She could at least save some dignity this way.

'We should, I guess,' replied Robert. 'But what was it you said about should? That it's a possibility. Well, I'm not sure forgetting about last night is possible. To be honest, it's not something I ever want to forget.'

Heat raced up Hana's neck and her cheeks burned. 'Nothing happened. It was nothing.'

'You and I both know it was close enough to be something.'

'We can't . . . I mean . . . I'm married.' She looked down as shame consumed her.

Robert put the cup on the side and took her hands in his. 'We don't have to get into all this right now. One of us might say something we regret.' He brought up her hands and gently kissed each palm.

'Did you learn that at medical school?' asked Hana, trying for humour to defuse the tension between them.

'It's my secret remedy.' Robert was still holding her hands.

'It must have been charm school in that case,' said Hana.

The kettle's shrill whistle cut through the air. 'I guess you'd better get that off the stove,' said Robert.

'I suppose I should.' Hana sidestepped away from him. She heard him sigh and then heard the scrape of the kitchen chair as he sat down.

'Are you at the Park today?' he asked once she'd made the coffee and placed the cup on the table in front of him.

Hana took a seat. 'Yes. I work six days on and one day off, which is tomorrow.'

'Shame. I was going to propose a picnic today.'

'In this weather?' Hana glanced out of the window at the grey and drizzly morning. 'Have you seen it outside?'

'I could have improvised on the picnic,' said Robert. He took the plate she handed him. 'I'll drive you to work and pick you up when you're done. You'll get soaked otherwise.'

'You don't have to do that,' said Hana, even though the thought of a lift over taking the bus was appealing.

'I know I don't have to,' he replied, 'but I want to.'

'Thank you.' It was easier not to argue.

'Once you're done with breakfast, I'd like to take a look at your knee,' said Robert. 'I couldn't help noticing some blood has seeped through the dressing.'

Again, Hana didn't argue.

At least this time she hadn't yet put on her stockings, so once breakfast was over, Hana remained in her seat while Robert pulled a chair up in front of her. Hana was very much aware of his touch as he lifted her leg to rest her ankle over his knee, so he could remove the old dressing, clean the wound and redress it. His touch was both tender and electrifying. Hana fought to control her breathing. He was just dressing the wound, that was all.

Robert applied the plaster and smoothed the edges either side with his thumbs in a slow and deliberate motion. He paused. 'How does that feel?'

Honestly, how was she supposed to answer that question? Hana nodded. 'Good. I mean, fine. Thank you.'

There was a small twitch to the corners of his mouth, before Robert ran his hands down to her calf and lowered her foot to the floor. He really didn't need to linger, but Hana was very aware that he did. She didn't move away. Robert gave her leg a small squeeze, before sitting back in his chair. 'You probably won't need the dressing on tomorrow.'

'That's good,' said Hana, although part of her was genuinely disappointed. It was nice being cared for and looked after for a change. Who was she kidding? It was nice, more than nice, to feel seen for who she was – a woman. Not a wife, or a glorified companion but a woman who was capable, intelligent and, dare she say it, desirable? She hadn't experienced the latter, at least, for a long time.

'Look, I don't want to come between a man and his wife and go against Gregory's opinion,' Robert said. 'But have you thought any more about reporting almost getting knocked off your bike to the police? Or at least to someone at the Park?'

'I'm going to mention it,' said Hana. Although she had told Gregory she would tell Chatfield the truth, she had held off doing so. He was the wrong person to tell, she had decided in the end. If anyone, it was Hopkins who needed to know. She looked at Robert. 'Can you answer me something honestly?'

'Sure.'

'Do you think me being almost run over was deliberate or just a coincidence, bearing in mind my father was knocked down by a car just a few days ago?'

Robert looked thoughtful for a moment. 'I'm not sure I believe in coincidences like that,' he said eventually. 'I mean, you were brought into the Park to pick up where your father left off, with the decoding and so on. In my mind that's more than a coincidence.'

'That's what I've been thinking.' Hana couldn't deny the small rush of relief that Robert thought the same as she did.

'Can you think of a reason why you and your father are being targeted?' asked Robert.

'Gosh. Put like that, it all sounds rather more serious than even I was thinking,' said Hana. 'I've never considered myself as a target.'

'Everyone and anyone can be targeted all the time we're at war. Especially so with what your father, and now you, are doing.'

Hana had to fight the desire to confide in Robert about the spy at the Park, but she knew she couldn't. 'I suppose, being at Bletchley, it feels quite removed from what's going on in Europe and beyond.'

'It's all very closely related,' said Robert. He shifted position on the chair, leaning into Hana some more. 'I'm going to hazard a guess that your father was involved in something that no one else in the hut knew about. And as you've now taken on his role, by default, that means you have taken over this secret assignment of his.'

Hana avoided eye contact with Robert. 'We're not supposed to talk about things like this,' she said.

'I know. I'm not asking you to breach the Official Secrets Act or anything like that,' replied Robert. He rested his forearms on his knees. 'I'm worried about your safety. If it was just decrypting the Japanese messages, then why isn't anyone else in the room, or the hut, being targeted? It appears to be something specific to you. And I don't wanna see you hurt.'

Hana was sure her heart skipped a beat at that moment. Robert's reaction to this was so very different to Gregory's. Robert actually cared about her. Not just about the war.

'I wish I could tell you more,' said Hana, genuinely regretting not being able to share the details of her assignment.

'I wish you could, too,' said Robert. 'Then I'd be able to help you.' He lifted his hand and brushed her cheek with his knuckles. 'Promise me, if it all gets too much, whatever it is you're doing, then you'll get help?'

He looked so sincere and so full of concern. She reached for his hand, entwining her fingers with his. 'I promise.'

Robert nodded. 'Thank you.' He got to his feet. 'I guess we'd better head over to the Park.'

The five-minute car journey to Bletchley Park was over far too quickly for Hana's liking. When Robert wasn't changing gear or having to use both hands to turn the wheel, he was holding Hana's hand. She wasn't entirely sure what was happening between them, but she relished the comfort it provided. In fact, it wasn't just comfort Robert was giving her, he was giving her confidencc in herself as a woman. For the first time in a long time, she felt wanted.

'What are you going to do today with your day off?' she asked as Robert pulled up outside the main gates to the Park.

'I could mope around feeling lonely and sorry for myself,' said Robert, twisting in his seat towards her.

'That would be a waste, and I can't imagine you moping anywhere.'

'True. No. I'm going to head over to Bassingbourn,' said Robert, referring to an RAF base south of Cambridge. 'Going to catch up with an old buddy of mine who's stationed there. I'll pick you up on my way back through.'

'That sounds good,' said Hana. 'Have a good day.' She resisted the urge to kiss him goodbye. 'See you here at four.'

She hopped out of the car and with a light step, headed over to the hut.

'Morning,' she said, to Audrey and Lottie who were already there.

'You look very happy this morning,' said Lottie.

'That's because her husband is away and she's at home with the dishy Captain Becker,' said Audrey.

'Honestly, Audrey, I do wonder what goes through your mind at times,' scolded Hana good-naturedly, though internally scolding herself for giving too much away from just her expression. 'Anyway, you're the one who's love's young dream.' She hoped to deflect the attention away from herself. 'How is . . . what's his name, with the little taches and blond hair?'

'Oh, yes, that's Bill Crosslands,' said Lottie. 'Hut Three, I do believe.'

'Bravo,' said Audrey, giving a small round of applause to her colleague. 'I'm impressed you remembered.'

Lottie winked at Hana. 'It's my job to remember things like that. There's a reason why I'm a much sought records clerk.'

'And modest with it,' piped up Derek who had just entered the room. 'So, who are we talking about?'

'Never you mind,' said Audrey. 'That's for me to know and you to find out.'

Hana laughed at the easy banter between her colleagues. Her mood dipped, though, when she remembered the task Hopkins had set her, work that if successful would mean exposing one them as a spy who'd been leaking secrets to the enemy. For a moment, she had forgotten what she was supposed to be doing, and the reality was a sobering thought.

This was reinforced later on that morning when she stepped outside on her break and, instead of heading to the tearoom, she took a stroll around the lake. She needed to stretch her legs after being sat at the desk for the past few hours. However, her moment of peace was soon disturbed when, seemingly out of nowhere, Hopkins appeared at her side.

'Hana, how are you getting on?' he asked, adding starkly, 'With your assignment.'

'No luck so far,' said Hana. 'I've checked all the places I can think of for a notebook. I'm beginning to wonder if I should be looking for something else. Something smaller.'

'Such as?'

I'm not really sure,' confessed Hana. 'Maybe my father photographed his notes and then destroyed them.'

'That's a possibility,' said Hopkins. 'Where have you looked?'

'In the room in Hut Seven, and in Dad's study at home.'

'Well, look again. For something other than a notebook,' instructed Hopkins. 'And get on with it. Every day that passes is another day the mole is leaking secrets. They need to be found. I cannot stress the importance of this enough.'

'Yes. Of course.'

'I need this information, Hana. Your ability to find it and decode it is vital. Am I making myself clear?'

'Yes.' Hana balked slightly at his authority, then said, 'There was something else.'

Hopkins turned to look at her. 'Spit it out.'

'Does anyone else, other than you, know I'm trying to find this information?'

'No. Why do you ask that?'

'You said my father was run down on purpose,' she said. 'Well, I nearly suffered the same fate when I was cycling home the other night. It seems quite a coincidence.'

Hopkins pursed his lips. 'You mean, someone wanted to silence your father and now they want to stop you finding his secrets, too?'

'Something like that,' said Hana.

Hopkins nodded gravely. 'I'm afraid this backs up further the importance of what your father had discovered, and how vital it is that the information he has is found, as soon as possible. Not just for the war effort but for your own personal safety, too.'

'Who is the spy spying for?' asked Hana.

'It could be a number of people, including other departments but considering we're codebreaking Japanese messages, it's likely to be for Japan. They will want to know what we know. Now, I really must get on.'

'There is one more thing,' said Hana. 'It's been bothering me. The timing of my father's accident. He took a phone call from you and then as he left the house he was run down. You didn't know until the night before that he had information. Whoever did that must have known he was about to hand that info over.'

Hopkins nodded his head. 'What's your question?'

'How?' Hana shrugged. 'How did they know that he was about to pass on the intelligence?'

'Your father suspected he had been compromised. That's why we were meeting. I can only assume whoever it was realised he was about to disclose their name. They needed to act fast and running him down by car was crude but effective.'

Hana winced at the terminology. 'If only he had been able to tell you the night before.'

'You can't think like that,' said Hopkins. 'We have to deal with what's happened, not what might have happened. We can't change anything.'

Hana nodded. The stark reality that she was a target rattled in her chest. She blew out a steadying breath. 'Why haven't they come after me again?'

'To be frank, they may be planning their next move. Or perhaps, for some reason they think they are safe,' said Hopkins.

'Or maybe they've now got the evidence my father had and I'm no longer a threat.'

Hopkins appeared to consider this suggestion as if it was the first time he'd thought about it. 'That's very true,' he said. 'In which case, if you can't find your father's evidence, then you need to find the spy yourself.'

'I'll do my best,' said Hana, not relishing the thought.

'Make sure you do,' said Hopkins. 'For all our sakes.' He gave her a pointed look before turning and walking off in the opposite direction.

Hopkins seemed more agitated than before. She needed to up her game. There must be something she was missing. Something obvious. Something hidden in plain sight. That's what her father always said about secrets and codes: once you saw whatever it was, it was so obvious you couldn't believe you hadn't spotted it sooner.

Even though it was a Saturday, weekends meant nothing at Bletchley Park, which included Hana's afternoon training sessions at the red-brick building opposite St Mary's Church. They were concentrating mostly on call signs, and so far, Hana had found learning what was essentially a new language in naval terms relatively easy to absorb. She was aware it would get more complicated as the weeks passed, especially as she was having to play catch-up from missing the morning sessions. Working in the hut was helping, though.

Initially, Hana's absence from the morning sessions had raised some discreet and not-so discreet questions from the other women on the course, but once the instructor had reminded them about the Official Secrets Act they had all signed, the questions had stopped.

After the afternoon's training, Hana had an hour to kill before Robert was picking her up, so she headed over to

The Eight Bells pub, where some of the others were going for a drink after their shift.

The pub wasn't too busy, and Hana found a seat near the window. It wasn't long before Audrey and Jenny turned up.

'Hana, you're here! Fabulous,' said Audrey, sitting down at the table and opening her bag. She pulled out a small bottle of fragrance and dabbed it to her wrists. 'Want a splash?' she asked holding the bottle out to Hana and Jenny.

'Why not?' said Hana with a smile, while Jenny answered with an eye roll. Hana put a drop behind each ear. 'Oh, that's nice. Lemony.'

'It's my favourite,' said Audrey, taking the bottle back as she finished applying a fresh layer of lipstick.

'Oh, look out,' said Hana as she caught sight of Bill Crosslands striding towards the pub. The others followed her gaze.

'So that's the reason for the perfume and lipstick,' said Jenny, smirking at Audrey.

Bill entered the pub and made a big show of insisting on buying the three of them a drink. He pulled up a chair, which he squashed between Audrey and Jenny.

'A thorn between two roses,' he said, lifting his pint glass in something of a toast.

'You can say that again,' muttered Jenny. Then, with an unnaturally wide smile and barely veiled intolerance, she picked up her drink to join in the toast.

As Hana took a sip of her orange juice, Jenny caught her gaze and rolled her eyes. Hana managed to downplay her grin. It was strange, that small interaction with Jenny felt like a massive victory, or at least some sort of win. Jenny was hard to get to know, and didn't tolerate anyone, let alone fools, gladly. But Hana felt like she'd just made a small breakthrough.

'Oh, here's Lottie,' said Audrey, waving the younger woman over. They all shuffled around so Lottie could squeeze in, too.

'So, do all you lovely ladies work together?' asked Bill.

'Yes, but Hana here is mornings only.'

'Really?' said Bill, eyeing Hana over the top of his glass. 'How come?'

'Special privileges,' said Audrey. 'She's something of a genius, is our Hana. Her father is Alfred Castle, you know the one who had the accident—'

'Audrey,' butted in Jenny. 'Probably not the best place to discuss these things.'

'Probably best not to discuss it at all,' corrected Hana.

Audrey laughed. 'Oh, come on, you two. It's not exactly classified information, and it's only Bill.'

'It's all right,' said Bill. 'This bloody war makes everyone nervous.'

'I'll be so glad when it's over,' said Audrey. 'Life can go back to normal then and no one has to sneak around.'

'Hear, hear,' said Jenny.

'Don't anyone hold their breath,' said Lottie. 'Honestly, this war is far from over. It's not just Europe, is it? Look what's happening in the Soviet Union with the Germans trying to take Stalingrad.'

'The Russians won't stand for that,' said Bill. 'They'll hit back any time now, you mark my words.'

'The Russians are our best defence against fascism,' continued Lottie.

'That's enough,' said Jenny, looking around the pub. 'Keep your voices down.'

Lottie looked around at the sparsely populated bar. 'Not exactly Leicester Square on a Saturday night, is it?'

'No, but Jenny's right,' said Bill. He leaned forward towards Hana with a mischievous grin. 'I can interrogate you another time about what you're doing here.'

'I don't think anyone will be interrogating Mrs Phillips any time soon?' came a voice from behind Bill.

Everyone looked around. Hana was surprised to see Robert standing there. She wasn't quite sure how she felt about his intervention. She was supposed to be keeping her head down and not drawing any attention to herself.

Audrey let out a laugh. 'Bill was only teasing,' she said. 'It's called the British sense of humour.'

Bill put up a hand in acknowledgement to the American. 'Yes, old chap, just teasing.' He got to his feet. 'Anyway, I need to head off now. Enjoy the rest of the evening.' He turned to Audrey and rested his hand on her shoulder. 'See you tomorrow.'

Hana was relieved that Bill had left, but now she had Robert to contend with. She really didn't want him to join them. Audrey would have a field day questioning him.

Robert clearly had the same idea as Hana. 'Would you like that lift home now?' he asked.

'Yes, please.'

Hana said her goodbyes and followed Robert out to his car. 'Your timing couldn't have been better. Although I'm impressed you knew where to find me.'

'I was early so thought I'd kill a bit of time at the pub,' replied Robert, starting the engine. 'Who was the guy there with you?'

His voice sounded rather too casual, and Hana couldn't help throwing a sideways look at him. 'He wasn't with me. He was with Audrey.'

Robert made some sort of grunt, as if he was reluctantly accepting her explanation. 'I don't like him much,' he said.

'Neither do I.'

Ten minutes later they were pulling into the driveway of Tall Trees.

'What the hell?' said Robert.

Hana, who had been fishing in her handbag for her front door key, looked up and gave a small gasp.

A policeman was standing outside the property and judging by his stance with his feet apart and his hands behind his back, he had been standing there for some time.

'Mr and Mrs Phillips? he asked as Hana stepped out of the car.

'I'm Mrs Phillips,' she said.

Hana's heart began to race as a thread of panic began to wind itself around her stomach. She felt Robert's hand on her elbow and was grateful for his support, both literally and figuratively. A stampede of thoughts assaulted her. Why was there a policeman there? Was she in trouble for talking about work at the pub? Was there news on Tom? Why wasn't her mother here? She looked at Robert and then at the policeman, as the worst-case scenario dominated her thoughts.

'Has something happened to my father?'

Chapter 15

'What's happening?' asked Robert.

'I'm afraid there's been a break-in at the property,' replied the policeman. 'We were alerted by a neighbour who saw the front door had been left open. When they came over, they called out to you, obviously got no answer and then came in. That's when they saw the house had been burgled.'

Hana let out a gasp. 'Burgled. Oh, no. Who was the neighbour?'

'Mrs Marsden across the road. My sergeant asked me to stay here until you came back.'

'Is there . . . much damage?' Hana looked at the house, angry that someone would do something like that.

'Broken pane of glass in the back door,' said the policeman. 'That's how they got in. The house has been checked and there's no one in there.'

Hana hated the thought of someone being in her house, rummaging through her belongings. And then she thought of Gregory's study. 'I need to go inside.'

'If you can make a note of anything that's missing and let us know,' said the policeman.

'Yes, of course,' replied Hana. 'You don't need to stay. I'll call by the station tomorrow.'

'Right-o. If you're sure you don't need me.'

'Positive. Thank you.' Hana watched the policeman climb on his bicycle and head off. She took a deep breath before crossing the threshold. It was strange how the house now felt different, knowing someone unwelcome had been inside.

She pushed open the door to Gregory's study. The room was a complete mess, drawers pulled open, the contents scattered across the floor, books pulled out of the bookshelves, papers littering the parquet flooring. Nothing had been left untouched.

The sitting room had received much the same treatment. Cushions were upturned, the side table tipped over, drawers pulled open, and books tossed to the floor. Hana stooped to pick up a broken photograph frame. It was a picture of her and Gregory on their wedding day. The glass was shattered. Hana felt tears rush to her eyes. She blinked hard. She did not want to cry. She didn't want whoever had been here to have that effect on her. She was angry. She needed to hold onto that anger so she wouldn't break down.

'Hey.' It was Robert. His hand rested on her shoulder, before turning her around to face him. 'Mind you don't cut yourself.' He took the frame from her and placed it on the sideboard.

'This is just awful,' said Hana, resting her head momentarily against Robert's chest. Something on the floor caught her eye. It was the newspaper her father had given her the morning of his accident. She bent down and picked it up, remembering how he'd told her to finish it. She placed it on the sideboard, making a mental note to take it with her next time she went to see him.

'I had a look at the back door,' said Robert. 'It's just a small pane of glass. I'll see if there's something in the shed to board it up with until someone can fix it.'

She nodded, giving herself a moment to regain her composure. 'Thank you. There's probably a hammer and nails in there somewhere, too. I need to check the rest of the house to see if anything has been taken.'

The dining room wasn't quite as bad as the living room. The sideboard in there had been rifled through, as had the cupboards. Upstairs, the bedrooms had not been spared either. Gregory's bedroom door had been left open, and Hana could see his bedding thrown on the floor. She stepped inside.

She picked up the sheets and blankets and remade his bed, before folding the clothes that were hanging out of the drawers and putting everything back in its place. She had no idea if anything was missing.

After Gregory's room, she turned her attention to her own. Unsurprisingly, pillows were strewn across the carpet, the bedside drawers rummaged through and worst of all, her underwear drawer had been yanked open and rifled through. She pushed it closed, wondering how many of her clothing-ration coupons she would need to replace the underwear. Just the thought of someone touching it made her skin crawl. She paused at the window, which overlooked the rear garden, and could see Robert coming out of the shed, carrying a piece of hardboard and a hammer. As she began to tidy up her things, she could hear the gentle banging as Robert made the repair to the door.

Hana briefly considered letting Gregory know what had happened but reminded herself that she didn't actually know how to get hold of him directly. It all had to go through his work, which she now knew to be at the Park. Anyway, there wasn't anything he could do from wherever he was in London. At least, that's where he'd told her he was going.

She checked her dressing table and jewellery box and was relieved nothing appeared to be missing.

The box room needed minimal tidying. There wasn't much in the room for the intruder to look through. She picked up the teddy bear from the floor and placed it back on the wicker chair in the corner. It had belonged to Gregory as a child and his mother had insisted they keep it for the yet to be born, or even conceived, Phillips baby.

When they were first married and had moved into Tall Trees, Hana had imagined this room as a nursery. She'd pictured herself sitting in the wicker chair, nursing her child. In her mind it was a little boy, and he had a crown of blond hair just like Gregory's. Tonight was probably one of the first times she was glad the room wasn't a nursery, although the thought that someone had been in here still left a sour taste in her mouth.

She pulled the door closed behind her. Robert would need to check his own room.

Hana made her way downstairs where he was just finishing repairing the door.

'That should be all right for the night,' he said. 'Or until Monday when someone can come out to fix it. How's it looking upstairs?'

'Much the same as it does down here. I didn't go into your room, though.'

'I wouldn't have minded if you had.'

'It's strange,' said Hana, sitting down on the kitchen chair. 'I can't see a single thing missing. Not even my jewellery. Every piece is still there.'

'Doesn't sound like a regular break-in.'

'That's what's bothering me,' replied Hana.

The telephone ringing cut through their conversation and Hana got up to answer it.

'Hana. It's me, Gwen.'

'Oh, Gwen, You heard?'

'Yes. When Pamela and I came back from shopping earlier.'

'How did you find out?'

'The police were here. Your mum is so upset. I've not seen her like that before.'

'Oh, poor Mum. Tell her not to worry. Everything's fine. Nothing is missing and I've tidied up now.'

'What do you mean, you've tidied up?'

'The house. I've tidied the rooms up,' said Hana. 'I've just got Gregory's study to do. He'll be furious to think someone has been through all his belongings.'

There was a silence down the line. Gwen eventually spoke. 'His belongings?' she said. 'I wasn't talking about your house.'

'What? I'm confused.' Hana shook her head. 'Then, why did you ring me?'

'Because there's been a break-in, here, at your parents' house,' said Gwen, speaking slowly, as if Hana was a child.

'You've had a break-in, too?' Hana closed her eyes.

'Oh, my goodness,' said Gwen. 'You mean—'

'We've both had break-ins.' Hana gripped the receiver tighter. One was suspicious enough, given her circumstances, but two breaks-ins . . . that was no coincidence at all. 'I'll be right over.' She put the phone back in its cradle.

Robert was standing in the doorway. 'What's going on?'

'I'll tell you in the car,' she said, and at Robert's arched eyebrow, added, 'I need you to drive me to my parents' house, please. Straightaway.'

He fished in his pocket for his car key. 'Let's go, then,' he said.

After making sure the house was secure, they were speeding out of the drive and over to Bramble House. Grateful that Robert did not fire questions at her, Hana nonetheless filled him in, repeating her telephone conversation with Gwen.

'Now you tell me that's not a coincidence,' she said.

'You're right, sweetheart. No coincidence.' Robert slowed down and pulled the car over to the side of the road.

'What are you doing?' asked Hana. 'Is there something wrong with the car?'

Robert turned in his seat to face her. 'I need to say something before we get to your parents' house,' he began. 'I'll get straight to the point. I'm worried for your safety. First of all, your father gets run over, then you nearly get knocked off your bike, there's a break-in at your house and your parents' house. All this at the same time you take over your father's work at the Park. Something is going on.'

Hana blew out a breath. 'I know.'

'What do you mean, you know?'

'I know something is going on.'

There was a pause. 'And is that all you're gonna say?'

Hana looked up at Robert. His dark brown eyes were full of concern, and a frown was creasing his brow. 'I can't say anything else.'

Robert's gaze searched her own, as if trying to read what was going on in her mind. 'I'll say it again, I'm worried about you.' He reached over and took her hand, bringing it to his lips.

There was so much he wasn't verbalising. Maybe he was like her and didn't know where to start. How even to describe this connection between them. He lowered her hand, and Hana gave a gentle squeeze. 'Thank you,' she said softly. 'But I need to get to my mum's.'

He continued to study her for another moment before nodding. 'Sure. But we need to talk at some point.'

'I know.'

A few minutes later they arrived at her parents' home and Hana was upset to see the house had received the same treatment as her own, with particular disarray in her father's study.

'Dad would hate to see it like this,' she said, standing in the room looking at all the papers, books, pens and personal items callously discarded everywhere. Somehow this was even worse than walking into the mess at her own home.

'They certainly did a job here,' commented Robert. When they'd arrived, he at first loitered outside, saying he didn't want to intrude, but Hana insisted he came in. Somehow just his presence near her was comforting.

'The police said we can tidy up now,' said Gwen coming into the room. 'They're still talking to Pamela.'

Hana had already spoken to them; in fact to the same sergeant who had been out to Tall Trees.

'He thinks what happened here and at yours is connected,' continued Gwen. 'Especially as no one else in the village has been targeted.'

There was that expression again, targeted. First, her father, then her, then their homes. The anger and indignation bubbled away inside Hana as she began picking up some of the papers and books. Whoever it was had been through the filing cabinet and thrown a few files onto the floor, but for the most part everything in the cabinet was still there. The newspapers in the bottom drawer had been disturbed, but that was all. It was a small comfort. Hana knew it was strange to feel emotionally attached to a stack of newspapers but completing the crossword each day with her father had been something that had reinforced their bond. She shuffled them back into a neat stack and closed the drawer.

Hana spent the next half an hour or so tidying her father's study. It made her feel better, and in a strange way, closer to Alfred. She might not be able to communicate with him at the moment, but sitting in his chair, touching his pens and pencils and putting them in the order he liked – restoring order to the disorder – gave her a deep sense of connection, as if just by holding the pen, she was holding her father's hand.

When she'd finished, she went to find her mum who was in the kitchen with Robert and Gwen.

'Just in time for a cup of tea,' said Gwen.

'Ana! Ana!' It was little Freddie greeting her. He hadn't yet mastered the art of saying the first letter of her name. Hana swooped him up for a cuddle. 'Well, hello, young man,' she said, kissing his cheek before turning to her sister-in-law. 'At least no one was here when all this happened. I take it Freddie was with you.'

Gwen nodded. 'Thank goodness. I nearly asked Mrs Harris to come and sit with him. Glad I didn't now.'

'Yes, we have to be thankful for small mercies,' said Pamela. She put her cup down. 'While I was tidying up, I kept thinking who would do this. I don't believe for one minute it was a break-in.' She looked directly at Hana. 'As you know, I'm not daft enough to think your father's talents were being used at a printing company. And by default, that means the work you're doing, Hana, isn't just at the printers.'

'You never said anything to me,' said Gwen.

'Some things you can't talk about,' said Pamela. 'But given the circumstances of what's happened today, I need to say something.'

'Mum—' began Hana.

'Don't worry, I'm not going to put you in a difficult position. As I said, I'm not daft.'

'No one is implying you are,' said Hana.

'Hana, please. Let me speak.' Pamela paused to ensure she had Hana's full attention. 'I have no idea what your father was doing, and he never breathed a word. I've never asked him. And I won't ever ask you. All I will say is, you need to raise this at . . . the printers . . . and you need to be careful. We don't know who did this, or what they were looking for, or if they found it. They might come back.' She paused again. 'Now, seeing as none of us are going anywhere in a hurry, we all need to be extra vigilant. Although I'm grateful that Captain Becker is here while Gregory is away, I think you should stay here with us.'

Hana exchanged a glance with Robert, before replying. 'I'd sooner stay at home. Gregory will be back in a couple of days and, as you say, Robert will be at Tall Trees with me. But I will contact work and let them know what's happened.'

This seemed to pacify Pamela, and although Hana could tell Gwen was concerned, her sister-in-law stated she wasn't going anywhere, either. 'I could only go to my mum's,' she said. 'But she's in London and that's not safe either, albeit for different reasons. Besides, I'm not leaving you on your own.' She patted Pamela's arm.

Reluctantly, Pamela agreed that they should carry on as usual. 'I suppose that's the best thing to do,' she sighed.

After staying to help Pamela and Gwen put the rest of the house back together, Robert finally drove back to Tall Trees with Hana.

'Thank you for everything you've done today,' said Hana as they hung their coats up in the hallway.

'I'm not sure I've done too much,' replied Robert.

'Just being here has been nice,' replied Hana.

'Nice? Is that all?' There was a playfulness to his voice.

Hana looked up at him. 'More than nice.'

Robert exhaled slowly. 'Much as I want to show you just how nice I can be, we do need to talk about what's happened today.'

Hana wasn't sure if she felt relieved or disappointed at the need to talk. 'No time like the present,' she said with false cheer.

They sat in the sitting room and Robert poured Hana a sherry. 'You probably need this. You look exhausted.'

'Thank you. Now that I've sat down, I must admit, exhausted is exactly how I'm feeling.'

'That's the adrenaline subsiding.' Robert took the seat next to her on the sofa, sitting at an angle so he was half facing her. He stretched his arm out along the back of the furniture and his fingers brushed Hana's shoulder.

She leaned her head back and closed her eyes, allowing Robert to gently pull her towards him so that her head was resting on his shoulder. He kissed the top of her head. 'If only life were this simple,' she said, more to herself than to Robert, before sitting up. 'Right, let's get this over with. What did you want to talk about?'

He gave a soft smile. 'I'm not about to interrogate you.'

'Shame.' She laughed and then adopted a more serious expression.

Robert placed his glass on the coffee table. 'I'm going to level with you about why I'm here at the Park. And what I'm about to tell you is highly confidential. You can't let on to anyone that you know. No one.'

'All right,' said Hana, an uneasy feeling pitching in her stomach. 'Does this break the Official Secrets Act?'

'Let's not go there. Right now, your safety is my priority.'

'That's very noble of you,' replied Hana.

'Noble sucks sometimes,' said Robert. 'I'm not just here on a sharing knowledge exercise about what's going down in the Pacific. I'm part of the OSS – Office of Strategic Services. You've heard of them, right?'

Hana gave a slow nod as she took in this information and translated its meaning. 'You're a spy.' She realised she had subconsciously edged a little away from Robert.

'Not exactly. Not in the way you're thinking.'

'In what way, then?'

Robert hesitated a moment before he answered. 'I think you and I are at Bletchley for the same reason.'

Chapter 16

'What do you mean?' asked Hana, her heart thumping.

'We, by whom I mean the United States, have had our suspicions for a long time that there's a mole at the Park – in the NSJI section in particular. Someone is passing on information to the Russians. Passing on naval intelligence.'

Hana frowned. 'All right. But why did they have to send you over. I mean if, hypothetically, what you suspect is true, why aren't you liaising with British intelligence and letting them find the mole?'

'Because the mole is not working alone. It goes further than the hut.' Robert fixed her with a look. 'Do you understand what I mean?'

'I think so,' said Hana, keeping her voice emotionless. If what Robert was saying was true, where did Hopkins and MI5 come into all this? 'Does British intelligence know why you're here?'

Robert paused. 'Probably best if you don't ask me that.'

'So why are you telling me all this?'

'Because I want to keep you safe. I want to be your back-up. We could work together on this.'

'I don't know how,' said Hana. 'I'm just standing in for my father.'

'You can trust me,' said Robert. 'I wouldn't do anything to hurt you. I just want to keep you safe. I'm risking everything by even talking to you. All you need to do, is go to Chatfield and that's game over for me.'

'We shouldn't be having this conversation.'

'But we are.' Robert rubbed his face with his hand. 'Look, Hana,' he said. 'If you're trying to find out who the mole is then two heads are better than one. We can work together and when we find out, we can pass the information on to whoever it is that needs it.'

'What makes you think I know anything about this?'

'You're not denying it, so I'm gonna assume everything I've said is true.'

'How do you know the mole's not me?'

Robert gave a small smile. 'This all started before you even arrived at the Park. You're not the mole, sweetheart. I know that for a fact.' He moved around to face her again. 'I repeat, I need to know you're safe. Once this mole is found, you will be. We just need to find the information your father had.'

She shifted uncomfortably. 'What makes you think he had any information?'

'He must have done, otherwise why did they try to kill him?'

It was a good point, but Hana still couldn't bring herself to say anything. She thought of Alfred and how he had remained silent, never uttering a word to any of them about what he was doing. That, together with the Park commander's stark warning about what happened to those who broke the Official Secrets Act, was enough to stop Hana from saying anything, even to Robert. 'As I said, we shouldn't be having this conversation.'

Robert let out a frustrated sigh. 'I get it,' he said eventually. 'I get why you don't want to talk about it. And I can't force you.' Another sigh. 'I'm only telling you all this because I care. We may have only known each other a short time but, my God, Hana, I wish it could be in different circumstances.'

Before she could reply, Robert was pressing a kiss to her mouth. A strong, passionate and deep kiss. She wanted to resist, to push him away. She should, but she knew she couldn't as she relaxed and wrapped her arms around his neck. He somehow made her feel safe and yet alive at the same time. Robert made her feel like someone. Someone special.

After a few minutes, Robert gently pulled away. 'Come on,' he said, getting to his feet. He pulled her up with one hand and led her out to the hall and up the stairs.

With an enormous effort, Hana let her moral compass take over. As they stopped outside his door, she drew her hand from his. He gave her a questioning look. Hana looked down and then back up at him. 'I can't,' she said. 'I'm sorry. Really, I am.'

It was one thing having a passionate kiss with him on the sofa and being lost in the moment, but it was quite another to move from the sofa to Robert's bedroom.

How could she sleep with another man in the house she shared with her husband? Her marriage might be in tatters, but what an insult to Gregory that she should commit adultery in their marital home. She just couldn't bring herself to do that, whether Gregory ever found out or not was neither here nor there. She also had her own pride and dignity. Much as the idea of sex with Robert was more than appealing, if she did sleep with him, she didn't want it to be some sordid little affair. She deserved better than that. They all did.

'What's wrong?' Robert's gentle voice broke through her thoughts.

'I can't do this,' she repeated.

He lifted her chin with his finger. 'Sometimes, Hana, you have to think of yourself. You have to give yourself permission to find your own happiness.'

'I'm scared,' she admitted in almost a whisper. 'I feel overwhelmed by my own emotions, which I can tell you now are definitely at war with each other.'

'Don't be scared, sweetheart. Trust yourself. Trust your heart. Trust me with your heart.'

Trust. There was that word again. A word Robert put so much meaning on. Hana had trusted Gregory with her heart and look how that had ended. He had dragged her into his self-fulfilling prophecy of misery. She had gone willingly, like a good wife should, not realising she would lose herself. That she would be part of the problem for Gregory. She would be just as much a burden to him as his injured leg and scarred skin. She wasn't sure when she had stopped becoming Hana Phillips and just become Gregory's wife. She missed herself. And now here she was, about to turn down a man who could give her all those things she craved, who would let her be her whole self again. But she couldn't go through with it, and she wasn't quite sure why.

'I see you, Hana,' Robert said softly. He pulled her close, holding her to him in those warm, safe arms of his. He kissed her head. 'I see a woman who deserves to be whole again but also a woman who isn't quite ready to be seen.'

His words nearly broke her. It was as if he really could see right into her very soul. He understood her. 'Robert . . .' she began, lifting her head to look at him.

He dipped his head, his mouth finding hers and kissed her again – tenderly as if she was the most fragile thing in the world. Then he pulled back. His hand cupped her face, and he ran his thumb across her bottom lip. 'Sometimes the hardest truths to face are the lies we tell ourselves about who we need to be for others.' He dropped a butterfly touch of a kiss on her forehead, before moving away. 'Goodnight, Hana.'

*

Hana must have been even more tired than she thought. As soon as she got into bed, she fell straight to sleep. She woke in the morning, realising that for the first time in a long time, she had slept the night through.

Her next thought was of what happened the previous night. Did she have any regrets turning Robert down? Yes, she did in one respect. She was deeply attracted to him. He was kind, thoughtful, caring and generous. All the same things that had attracted her to Gregory when they had first started seeing each other. But it was Gregory she was married to, so on the other hand, she didn't regret saying no to Robert. The problem was, she didn't know how long she could keep saying no.

Her next thought was of the break-ins at Tall Trees and Bramble House the day before. She would have quite happily stayed in bed for longer, but she wanted to finish cleaning the house before she did anything else. The need to scrub the house clean of the intrusion was too strong to ignore. If it were at all practical or affordable, she would have replaced everything possible in her home. As it was, she had to make do with cleaning everything and she was grateful to Robert for rolling up his sleeves and helping her with the task.

Nearly two hours later, Robert convinced Hana she'd done enough. She was too tired to put up a fight.

'Thank you,' she said to Robert when they finally sat down with toast and honey. 'I do appreciate your help.'

'It's the least I could do. I hate to see you distressed by it all.'

'Not sure how Gregory will take the news.'

'I want to say, it might make him think twice about leaving you for days on end,' said Robert. 'But, for purely selfish reasons, I don't want that.'

'Me neither,' replied Hana. She ignored the prickle of guilt in her heart.

'So, how about we go for a walk today?' suggested Robert. 'It would be nice to spend some time together away from the house or work.'

Hana looked out of the kitchen window where they were now having breakfast. 'It's a bit chilly out there,' she said. 'It's nearly November.'

'I thought you Brits would be used to your weather by now,' he said. 'And the Fall is beautiful here.'

Hana smiled at the Americanism. 'It is rather tempting.' She put down her cup. 'But I did say to Mum that we would call in today. Perhaps we could pop over to see her first.'

'I don't want to upset your mother by just turning up,' said Robert.

'It will only be for a quick cup of tea and then we'll have the rest of the day to ourselves.' It felt exciting and not without a hint of danger, spending the day with Robert, but Hana was aware that the bubble would burst when Gregory returned home. She didn't want to think about that, it would mar the day if she dwelled on the inevitable. She should just enjoy the moment and relish in the little fantasy she was having where Robert was concerned.

*

Her mother was pleased to see them, and Hana was relieved to find Pamela back in her usual, positive and capable mood after the break-in.

'Gwen and I have been through the whole house from top to bottom,' her mother said. 'We've given it all an impromptu autumn-clean.' She sat down in the living room. 'What about you?'

Hana took the chair next to the fireplace. Not only because it was the chair her father usually sat in and it made her feel close to him, but it also meant she didn't end up sitting next to Robert on the sofa. She didn't want to give her mother or Gwen any reason to suspect something was happening between her and the American.

Freddie had positioned himself next to Robert with a book.

'You want me to read you a story, huh?' said Robert, picking up the two-year-old and sitting him on his knee. He opened the cardboard picture book. 'Right, what do we have here?'

Gwen came in with the tea, placing the tray on the coffee table. 'He will have you reading to him all day long if you're not careful,' she said, setting out the cups and pouring the tea into each one.

'I don't mind. I have five nephews and one niece,' said Robert. 'I'm used to it.'

Hana smiled as Robert turned the pages, pointing out the animals and making the appropriate noises. She looked across at Gwen who was studying her. Gwen raised her eyebrows. Hana couldn't quite decipher the meaning, but she was too enchanted with Robert's interaction with Freddie to give it another thought.

As was becoming Pamela's new routine for the past few weeks, she said she was driving over to the hospital to see Alfred, whose condition remained serious but stable.

'Would you like me to come with you?' asked Hana. 'I haven't seen Dad for a couple of days.'

'That would be lovely, but Mrs Harris from across the road wants to come and you know the hospital are strict about their rule of only two visitors at a time,' replied Pamela. 'I can tell Mrs Harris not to come, though, if you really want to.'

'No, don't do that. I'll go after my shift tomorrow,' said Hana. 'I'm on eight to four this week.'

'When's Gregory due home?' asked Gwen.

'Tuesday. At least that's what he said. You know it can change at the drop of a hat,' replied Hana.

'That will be nice to have him home,' continued Gwen.

Hana stole a glance at her sister-in-law, who returned her look with an innocent smile. She wasn't quite sure why Gwen would say something like that. She knew the state of her marriage, or what was left of it. It was a marriage purely in name and had been for some time.

Gwen got to her feet and began collecting the teacups. 'Would you mind giving me a hand?' she said to Hana.

'Of course.' Hana got up and took the tray Gwen held out, before carrying it out to the kitchen. Gwen followed her with the teapot and sugar bowl, which Hana reasoned could easily have gone on the tray. She put it down on the worktop and turned to face Gwen, who had closed the kitchen door behind her. Hana put her hands on her hips. 'Right, do you want to tell me what this is all about?'

Gwen placed the teapot and sugar bowl down next to the tray. 'Maybe I should be asking you that?'

'What does that mean?'

'You and Mr America out there,' said Gwen, darting her index finger between the direction of the living room and Hana. 'And don't look like you have no idea what I mean. I saw the way you looked at him. Not to mention the couple of glances that he threw your way and you could bet, if I noticed, so did your mother.'

Hana was momentarily stunned by Gwen's all too accurate observation and took a moment to compose her answer. 'It's really no one's business,' she said simply.

'So, you're not denying it.'

'I'm not saying anything. I don't even know why you're concerned.'

'Because I don't want to see you make a fool of yourself,' replied Gwen, this time with rather more compassion in her voice. She stepped closer to Hana. 'I know Gregory is being an absolute pig at the moment.'

Hana gave a snort. 'At the moment? That moment has been going on for two years.'

'Even so,' carried on Gwen, 'he is still your husband. And Robert, he's only temporary. He's not here long-term. I just don't want to see you get hurt. That's all.'

'You don't have to worry. I'm not about to do anything stupid.' Hana wasn't sure if that was strictly true, but it was what Gwen wanted to hear. 'I'm just enjoying Robert's company. We work together. We're living under the same roof. We're bound to spend time together. And after yesterday, to be honest, Gwen, I could do with some enjoyment on my day off.' She stepped forward and gave the other woman a hug. 'Don't worry. Everything will be all right.'

Hana wasn't sure if Gwen was pacified or not, though she didn't pursue the matter any further. Still, Hana was relieved when, a short time later, she was sitting next to Robert in his car as they drove away from Bramble House.

'All OK?' asked Robert.

'It is now,' said Hana with a sigh. She looked across at Robert. 'Gwen was warning me about the dangers of getting involved with you.'

'Ah. I guessed as much. Your mother was of the same opinion.'

'My mother?' Hana groaned. 'What did she say?'

'Just that you had been through a lot the last few years, and whilst it was nice to see you happy for a change, it wouldn't be nice for anyone to take advantage of you. She used the word "vulnerable".'

'She said that?'

'Your mother fires from the hip,' said Robert. 'A very formidable woman.'

Hana felt an unexpected pang of emotion hit her chest. 'You know, Mum would never say that to me. She's very much of the stiff-upper-lip brigade. Don't complain sort of thing. Roll up your sleeves and get on with the dishes.'

'What?' Robert gave a laugh.

'Oh, it's something she says. Means, stop making a fuss, life is hard work.'

'That is so British.'

'So, for her to say something like that to you is a novelty. The same with Gwen. I'm usually the one comforting her about my brother being held as a prisoner of war. For Gwen to show concern towards me, it's not something I'm used to.'

'What about your father?'

'He loves me. I know that. Same way I know Mum and Gwen do,' said Hana. 'But Dad, he has his funny ways. He's a very gentle man and a gentleman, but sometimes, it's like he's half in this world, and half in another – one filled with dusty pages of a dictionary, words, elegant phrases and cryptic clues. He's never been one for grand gestures, but whenever I need advice, I can feel the love in his carefully chosen words, delivered with such care. On a day-to-day basis, we bond over crosswords, puzzles and languages.'

'Just not the language of love.'

Hana thought for a moment. 'That language is not simply words, though, it's more about emotions.'

'Emotions that you don't talk about.'

'I'm not sure we know how to do that,' she said.

Robert let out a sigh. 'I think that might just be the saddest thing I've ever heard.'

Chapter 17

After leaving her mother's house, Hana and Robert detoured away from Newton Longville and went for a walk along the river in a nearby village. Hana had linked her arm through Robert's as if it was the most natural thing in the world. Then he had put his arm around her shoulder, holding her close to his side as they continued their walk. It was damp and a little cold in the autumn air, but Hana didn't mind, in fact, she barely noticed it.

Afterwards they had stopped off at a pub for a drink, and for a few hours Hana let herself believe in the fantasy she was living, that she and Robert were a couple and madly in love. That this could become her normal life. One where her love was welcomed and where she felt loved in return.

*

'I've had a lovely day,' said Hana as they arrived back at Tall Trees. 'It's been so nice to do something, well, normal for a change.' She hung her coat up and turned to go down the hall to the kitchen, but Robert was in her way.

He casually tossed his coat on the seat of the hallstand, before placing his hands on her upper arms. 'I've had one of the best days in a long time,' he said softly. Then he leaned his head down and kissed her. A small, tender kiss on her mouth, only pulling back a fraction.

Hana's heart thumped in her chest. She couldn't deny the fizzle of excitement that coursed through her as her breathing quickened. Before she had time to consider her actions any further, he was kissing her again. This time she responded, her hands reaching up to wrap around his neck while his arms encircled her waist, pulling her against him. She could feel his body against her and crikey, it felt good.

Their kiss became deeper and more passionate and for a moment she was lost to everything around her, every thought in her mind, every word whispering a warning. All she could think about was the sensation of being cherished and being wanted.

Hana didn't know how, but all of a sudden, she came to her senses. She pulled back from kissing Robert, pushing her hands against his chest.

She felt an awful tease and Robert would have every right to be frustrated with her, but in that moment of desire, when she thought she was lost to everything around her, from nowhere, all she could think about was Gregory.

'I'm sorry,' she muttered, feeling embarrassed – not at her desire but at her unwillingness to fully surrender to her emotions. The weight of her betrayal of Gregory was heavy.

'We can just go at your pace,' Robert said. 'I understand and it doesn't make me think any less of you. In fact, it makes me respect you even more.'

'Thank you.' Hana wasn't sure she deserved anyone's respect.

'I'm a patient man,' said Robert. He leaned down and kissed her briefly on the mouth.

*

Monday passed quickly. Hana had risen early and left for work without seeing Robert, and she'd worked late. When she'd arrived home at about eight, she'd had some bread and margarine and gone to bed early, claiming a busy day. She certainly wasn't stand-offish with Robert, and he seemed to understand that she needed some time for herself.

Reality was far too near for Hana to ignore it. Twice now she had stood at the precipice with Robert, and twice she had pulled back from the edge. Why? What was stopping her? It certainly wasn't anything lacking in him. He was charming, attentive, kind, considerate and extremely attractive. He was all of those things and more. But, and this was the bit she couldn't quite understand, he wasn't Gregory.

Why did that matter so much to her? She had considered her marriage more or less over a long time ago. But was it? For so long she had simply cohabited with Gregory. They shared space but never touched; breathed the same air but didn't speak the same language. The last time her husband had spontaneously been physical with her was to offer his arm in support when she was at the hospital. It made her sad while simultaneously offering a sliver of hope that maybe there still might be a chance for them.

Hana wanted to believe that was true, but was it really just wishful thinking? She knew she shouldn't feel guilty for wanting to be loved and wanting to love. Both these things she felt denied in her marriage. But something was still stopping her, and she wasn't convinced it was anything to do with her marriage vows or the shame of adultery. It felt more than that. There was guilt which didn't align itself with being unfaithful. It was knowing it would shatter Gregory's already fragile sense of self-worth and how it would confirm all the dark thoughts he ever had about himself since the accident.

In Robert she was finding the warmth and human kindness she craved for, but it wasn't love.

Did she still love Gregory? She didn't think she did. But what if she was wrong? The question was like looking at a half-completed crossword, where some clues had been answered, others crossed out and amended, and she couldn't solve the one vital clue which would open up the answers to all the intersecting questions.

*

On Tuesday morning, Hana washed and dressed before going downstairs where Robert was already sitting in the kitchen.

'Hey,' he said softly.

'Morning.'

He reached over and held her hand. 'Don't try to analyse everything,' he said. 'We're human. We're not a puzzle that has some sort of code to be deciphered. There is no formula where people's feelings are concerned. Don't try to break the code.'

She couldn't help smiling as his analogy was not dissimilar to her own, but she grew serious again. 'I need to say something.'

'OK.'

'I like you, like you a lot. You make me happy. You make me feel like there's something good to look forward to.'

'I'm glad, although I can feel a "but" coming on.'

Hana nodded. 'But I'm not ready to take things any further. I need to slow things down,' she said. 'We've only known each other a short time and you've come into my life when my marriage is at a low point. What's going on between us now can't be a measure for the future.'

Robert frowned. 'If you want to call a halt to this, I understand. I can't pretend that's what I want.' He blew out a breath. 'I think we have a future, but I'm prepared to wait until you're ready.'

'I don't know if I'll ever be ready.'

'I think right now, you're scared to take that step.' He held up his hand at Hana's protest. 'You have a lot to think about. And you've got a lot going on right now. I'm not putting any pressure on you, and I don't think you should put it on yourself, either. We need to walk our way through all this, not run.'

'Thank you,' she said.

Robert gave a smile. 'Let's just not panic or make any hasty decisions,' he said. 'All I'll say is that you deserve better than what Gregory has been giving you. Don't forget that. You deserve better.'

Hana knew he was right. She did deserve better but so did Gregory. 'I should get ready for work,' she said after a moment. 'I've got to call in at the police station on my way home to let them know nothing is missing from either here or Mum's house after the break-ins.'

'You'll be all right doing that on your own?'

Hana appreciated the concern. 'I'll be fine. Won't take a minute.'

'OK. I'd better head off,' said Robert. He had a meeting over at RAF Halton that day. 'Gregory is back tonight, right?'

'Yes. I'm not sure what time.'

'It's gonna be hard being around you knowing I have to look on from afar.' He kissed her hand. 'I need to go.'

While Robert nipped upstairs to grab his case, Hana went into the living room to look for the book she was reading. She was taking the Bletchley bus that day, which, although convenient, did take a rather convoluted route as it stopped off in several of the surrounding villages to pick people up – mostly women – from the various hostels and digs they had been billeted to. Diving into a book was another form of escape for Hana.

She found her book on the sideboard, next to the broken photo frame of her and Gregory's wedding. She slipped the photograph and frame into the drawer of the sideboard. Like her marriage, the frame was beyond repair.

As she grabbed her book, she noticed the newspaper her father had given her the morning of the accident. She hadn't been able to bring herself to do any of the crosswords over the past few weeks, but today, for some reason, she felt compelled to take it with her. She'd just take the crossword page, though, so she didn't have to carry the bulky newspaper with her.

Hana spread the newspaper out on the sideboard and leafed through to the barely completed crossword. The words 'Sea Kale' and 'Taffy' printed out in her father's precise handwriting within the crossword grid. Then Hana saw one of the answers had been completed in Japanese. She frowned as she looked at the symbols. Why had he done that? And more to the point, when?

She cast her mind back to that morning and the order of events.

Collecting eggs with Freddie. Coming into the kitchen. Her dad starting the crossword. Mum dishing up breakfast. The phone call. Alfred leaving suddenly. Him handing her the newspaper. Then the accident.

She gave an involuntary shudder at that part. The image of Alfred being tossed in the air like a rag doll would haunt her forever.

She backtracked to the newspaper. He'd told her to finish it. Of course, she hadn't. She'd totally forgotten about it and even when she'd picked the newspaper up the other day, she hadn't thought anything of his instructions. They had just been a casual remark.

Today was different. Now that she'd seen he'd written in Japanese, she felt sure it was all intentional. Alfred had wanted her to see this.

'Hana, I'm off now!' It was Robert's voice coming from the hallway.

Hana quickly closed the newspaper. She didn't know why, but she wasn't ready to share this with Robert yet.

He appeared in the doorway. He stopped and looked at her.

Hana smiled, gave a laugh and rolled her eyes. 'I was just looking at the crossword and got all distracted with it.'

'Right.' He didn't sound convinced. 'I was just coming to say goodbye.' He walked over and kissed her.

Hana tried to relax but she was a bundle of nerves. 'Have a good day,' she said, realising they sounded like a married couple saying their goodbyes for the day, rather than the secret almost-lovers they were.

Hana watched Robert leave, before going back to the newspaper and taking out the page with the crossword. She folded the page in half and then half again, before slipping it into her bag.

Realising she was going to miss the bus, she hurriedly locked the front door and quickly made her way to the bus stop, arriving just as the bus pulled up. Bletchley Park employed so many people and yet no one spoke about it. There were even rumours locally that it was a lunatic asylum, such were the rather eccentric looking people coming and going all the time.

Once Hana was seated on the bus, she took out the crossword, and with a new sense of purpose, had another look at it. Her father had deliberately given her this crossword. Oh, why hadn't she thought of this sooner? She had been sitting on it for several weeks now. It might hold the key to what Hopkins was looking for. She needed to try to understand what her father was telling her before she did anything else.

She wasn't sure why she hadn't told Robert about the newspaper. It had been a knee-jerk reaction to keep it a secret. Not a lot got past him, though, and she was sure he was suspicious, even though he didn't say outright. She hated keeping things from him. It wasn't how she wanted their relationship to be. But at the same time, this was of national importance, and she certainly wasn't going to put herself in a position where she'd be arrested for breaking the Official Secrets Act. The commander had made the consequences of that perfectly clear to her.

Hana studied the Japanese symbols. She was definitely interpreting them correctly, of that she was sure, but what did they mean? That was the problem. She could easily translate the letters, but they didn't make sense. They didn't form a word. She had to assume that Alfred had used a code when he wrote down the symbols. But what code? Something that she would be able to work out but not so simple that anyone else would. She needed to approach this logically and the first thing would be to double-check she had translated the letters properly. She could use the dictionary at the hut, the one Alfred had been compiling.

'Oh, what you got there? Crossword?' It was the young woman sitting next to Hana. 'I'm good at those.'

'I haven't had chance to finish it yet,' said Hana, folding up the paper.

'Pass it here, I'll help you,' the woman continued.

Hana slipped it into her handbag. 'Thanks, but I like a challenge. I'll have another go at it during my tea break.'

'Suit yourself.' She turned away from Hana and resumed her conversation with a girl across the aisle. Hana would have to be careful when brandishing the crossword about at the Park. There were plenty of people who loved a puzzle, and she certainly didn't want anyone else offering to finish it for her. She would need to be very discreet when checking the Japanese against the dictionary Alfred had compiled.

As it happened, the room was very busy that morning. There was a lot of chatter over the airwaves from the Far East between the Japanese officials. It felt like something was brewing, it was just a case of finding out what.

Hana looked at the intercept she was working on, forcing herself to focus on that. She'd have to be very discreet about the crossword clue, so for now needed to carry on as normal, until she got a chance to look at Alfred's dictionary.

Hana looked over at Lottie who was busy collecting index cards and sorting them into order before putting them in the ever-increasing number of wooden filing boxes in the room.

'Wind. Heavy cloud. More wind. Wind again,' she was saying to herself as she sorted the cards. 'Oh, rain, this time. The whole world is obsessed with the weather.'

'Isn't that the truth,' said Jenny, not looking up from what she was doing. 'More rain forecast here today. Super.'

A thought suddenly struck Hana. She looked at the intercept. The one where it mentioned snow. 'Lottie?' she said, trying to keep the excitement from her voice. 'Are there any mentions of snow?'

'Snow?' Lottie frowned. 'There have been a few. Let me see. Hang on.' She began flicking through the cards.

While she did that, Hana began marking down the known patterns for when the Japanese sent their weather reports. They were usually sent between 0600 and 1800 hours, at dawn and dusk.

'Snow has been mentioned three times in the past five days,' said Lottie.

Hana realised that Audrey was looking over at her. 'You on to something?' the WREN asked.

'I'm not sure,' said Hana, wary about giving anything away at this point. She hated not trusting anyone in the hut, but if she broke this intercept and it was highly classified information, she couldn't risk letting on to whoever the spy was. In her early days of being in the hut, Hana had welcomed the support and guidance, but as she had become more confident, she was more reluctant to share her thoughts. She just didn't know who to trust.

'Can I help?' asked Audrey.

'Thanks, but it's fine,' said Hana, giving her a smile.

'Do you need to know anything else?' called over Lottie.

'No. Thank you.' Hana went back to the intercept. She had to force her hands to stop shaking. The intercept had been sent at 0300 hours. This was highly irregular. And it mentioned snow, again, something that was just not compatible with the weather in Japan at this time of year.

She spent the next few minutes looking through the weather log for the past five days for all stations in the Pacific sector. She wasn't quite sure what she was looking for but there had to be something unusual.

The weather reports all began with FATL, and they all appeared to be legitimate reports. However, there were some, like the one she had in her hand that began with FOTL. A slight but significant variation. These were not weather reports, she was sure. They were some sort of instruction. She checked through the ones beginning FOTL. Her eyes nearly bulged from her head as she looked again. Snow was mentioned. A delivery of snow? It couldn't be actual snow, so it must represent a thing or maybe even a person.

They were moving something unusual through their supply chains, masking it within the weather reports.

Hana sought out the logbook, which recorded all the standard, fleet deployment messages. What or who was being moved?

She thought back to the submarine supply orders that were being tracked. There had been some unusual requests, if she remembered rightly. They had been noted but not attributed anywhere. Often, they received scraps of information that on their own meant nothing, but when put together with other scraps began to reveal the picture.

Hana spent the next two hours, studying all the information she had in front of her. Something important was being moved, from Germany to Japan.

'Any luck?' asked Audrey.

Hana looked up from her paperwork. 'Not yet.'

'I'm going to lunch. You coming?' asked Audrey.

Hana wanted to say no, but thought it might arouse suspicions. 'All right. Give me a few minutes to put this lot away.'

Soon the two of them were sitting in the canteen on Wiltern Avenue. Fish was the order of the day and although a little dry, it was a welcome treat.

'So, are you going to tell me what you're working on?' asked Audrey.

'It's nothing, just the usual boring weather reports and tracking supply movements,' said Hana, trying to sound uninterested.

'Rubbish,' said Audrey. 'You're onto something, I can tell.'

Hana gave a small laugh. 'If I was onto something, as you put it, don't you think I'd be rather more excited?' She took a sip of her tea. Was Audrey onto her was a more pressing question? And why was Audrey concerned about what Hana was doing?

'You don't fool me,' said Audrey. 'But have it your way. Just let me know if you need any help.'

'Sure. Now, tell me all about you and Bill Crosslands,' Hana said, trying to move the subject onto something else. 'When are you next seeing him?'

It did the trick and Audrey chatted away for the rest of the lunchbreak about how they were going to the cinema at the weekend. Hana listened politely, but her mind wandered back to the intercept. She was itching to get back to it. She was also aware she still hadn't had time to check the crossword answer against Alfred's dictionary.

The chance to do so came almost as soon as she returned to the hut from lunch when Jenny nipped out to the toilets.

With no one sitting right next to her, Hana took her opportunity to flick through the dictionary Alfred had been putting together. She checked and double-checked the symbols against his definition. She should have trusted herself. She had translated it correctly earlier, but the letters and syllables still didn't make sense.

As Jenny came back into the room, Hana slipped the crossword into her pocket.

'Everything all right?' asked Jenny as she took her seat next to Hana.

'Yes. Fine.' Hana didn't make eye contact but carried on studying the latest partially decoded message in front of her. She was aware that Jenny was looking at her, but eventually she turned to her own work. Hana had to force herself to concentrate on the work to hand. She couldn't get distracted and make a mistake with the decoding of the Japanese messages. She looked over at Audrey who was head-down and busy with her work. They worked on in silence to the backdrop of noises from the machines in the other rooms of the hut as they printed out the radio messages.

'I'm going for a break,' Jenny announced later that afternoon. 'What are you doing, Hana?'

Hana checked the clock on the wall. 'I'll come as well. I could do with some fresh air. Audrey? What about you?'

'I just want to finish this. You two go ahead. I'll catch you up.'

Hana followed Jenny out of the room and down the corridor of the hut, stepping out in the fresh autumnal air. Hana shivered. 'I'm going to grab my cardigan. Won't be a minute.'

She hurried back into the room just as Audrey, who was standing at her desk, shoved a piece of paper into her pocket. She looked up at Hana and for a split second there was a look of guilt on her face which she quickly managed to mask with a smile. 'Back so soon,' said Audrey, pushing in her chair and slipping on her jacket.

'I forgot my cardigan,' said Hana. 'You joining us?' She hadn't imagined it, had she? Audrey had definitely put a piece of paper into her pocket.

'Actually, I'm going to nip over to the main house. I need to put in a request for a new uniform blouse. I managed to burn mine with my landlady's iron. Horrible old thing it is. I scorched one of my own blouses as well. Terribly annoying, it was my favourite, and I was hoping to wear it when Bill takes me to the cinema.'

'Oh yes, your date with Bill.' She smiled at her friend as they made their way out of the hut.

'What?' asked Audrey.

'Nothing. Nothing bad anyway,' said Hana. 'It's just heartwarming to know that despite the war, people are still falling in love.'

'Falling in love? I'm not sure I'm doing that,' said Audrey.

'But you're keen on him?'

'I am,' Audrey replied. 'Probably no different to you and a certain American who happens to be lodging with you.'

Hana felt herself blush, wishing she'd never said anything in the first place about Crosslands. 'You're forgetting that I'm a married woman,' she said.

Audrey stopped and gave Hana a look. 'Just be careful,' she said. 'I wouldn't want you to make a fool of yourself.'

'What's that supposed to mean?'

'I don't trust him, that's all,' said Audrey. She looked down at the ground before returning her gaze to Hana. 'Look, Hana, I like you a lot and I would hate to see you get hurt or for your husband to get wind of something.'

'Get wind of what exactly?' Hana could feel panic and anger rising up in her chest. How on earth did Audrey know, or even suspect, something was going on between her and Robert?

'I don't want to upset you,' said Audrey, 'but as your friend, I think there's something you should know about Captain Becker.'

'I'm all ears.' Hana wanted to shake the words from Audrey but at the same time, dreaded what her colleague was about to say.

Audrey, linked arms with her again, drawing Hana towards the lake where Jenny was waiting for them. 'I saw him with Jenny in the village early this morning.'

Hana frowned. 'This morning? That can't be right. He was—' She stopped. She didn't actually know where he'd gone after he'd left her Tall Trees that morning. Not categorically.

'It's not the first time I've seen them together.'

Hana's first thought was how ludicrous it was that Audrey was even taking the trouble to tell her this. She gave a laugh. 'What are you doing, going around spying on everyone?' Then realising what she said, she checked herself. 'I didn't mean spying like that . . .' Hana stopped talking. Audrey's expression was deadpan. An unease spread across Hana's skin causing her arms to prickle.

'I can't say anything,' said Audrey, her tone serious. 'Use your imagination, though. Why do you think I'm so concerned about you and him?'

Hana felt her heart lurch as realisation dawned on her. Audrey was spying, or at least she certainly wasn't denying it. But was she the spy Hana was looking for? 'You've been asked to keep tabs on Robert?'

'Like I said, I can't say anything. But if that *was* the case, there'd be a reason why I might have been asked to do that.'

Hana looked out at the grey water of the lake and the mansion house beyond. The whole place held so many secrets, despite the amount of people who worked here every day. No one really knew what someone else was doing, saying or thinking.

Had Audrey been asked to spy on the team as well as Hana? Were they on the same side or opposing sides? She couldn't ask without showing her hand. And what of Robert? It seemed Audrey was warning her about him, but was it about her personal relationship or her professional relationship? He was constantly telling Hana to trust him. Did he mean that or was he just trying to gain her confidence? After all, Robert had said quite openly to her what his real role at the Park was.

All these mixed messages. How on earth was she supposed to work out who to believe and trust?

She stopped walking and turned to Audrey. 'When I came back into the hut just now, you put a piece of paper in your pocket.'

Audrey eyes widened a fraction. 'Is that what you think you saw?'

'I know it was,' replied Hana. 'What was it?'

'It's actually none of your business.'

Hana looked down at Audrey's pocket. 'Show me,' she said.

'Hey! You two!' Jenny was calling to them. She was a little further around the lake than they were and began to make her way back to them.

'Show me what's in your pocket,' said Hana more forcefully. When Audrey didn't move, she made a grab for her pocket, stuffing her hand inside.

'Get off,' cried Audrey. 'What on earth are you doing?'

'Just show me what's in your pocket,' demanded Hana. She could feel the paper between her fingers, but Audrey had a tight hold on Hana's wrist.

Out of nowhere, a pair of hands gripped Hana's shoulders from behind and yanked her away from Audrey, pushing her to one side. Hana stumbled but regained her balance. She spun around to see Bill Crosslands standing there.

He stepped in front of Audrey, in an act of protection and folded his arms across his chest. 'What the hell do you think you're doing?'

At that point, Jenny had reached them. 'Someone care to let me know what's going on?'

'You may well ask,' said Bill.

Hana glared at Audrey, who returned the look, but said nothing.

'Hana?' prompted Jenny.

'Show me what's in your pocket.' Hana didn't take her gaze away from Audrey.

Audrey looked uncertain. 'Hana, please . . .' she began.

'Just show me that piece of paper. You're hiding something and I want to know what it is.' Hana fought to keep her voice under control.

'Very well,' said Audrey. She dipped her hand into her pocket and withdrew the piece of paper, before holding it out to Hana.

Hana snatched it from her and unfolded it. She read the words in Audrey's handwriting.

Darling Bill

So you may wonder why I'm writing to you when I could be speaking to you in person. But being someone who loves words, it felt it far more fitting that I should write my thoughts down. Except, it's not just thoughts. It's my feelings, too. I have grown very fond of you over the past few weeks, I think it might even be something more. Something called love. I'm falling in love with you, Bill and I rather think, you feel the same about me.

Audrey

Hana read the letter again. She was mortified. What a fool she had made of herself.

'Happy now?' asked Audrey stepping forwards and snatching the letter back from her. She held it up for Jenny to see. 'It's a love letter. To Bill.'

'I'm sorry,' said Hana. 'Really, I am.'

'Come on, darling,' said Bill, putting his arm around Audrey. He led her away, glancing back over his shoulder to scowl at Hana.

Jenny shepherded Hana back towards the huts. 'What was that all about?'

Hana kept walking, looking straight ahead. 'We argued over men, would you believe?'

Jenny sighed. 'Men. They cause far too many problems. I can't say I'm a big fan of Crosslands. I think he's stringing Audrey along. I saw him at the Shoulder of Mutton the other night, he was sitting next to a WREN, looking very smug with himself.'

Hana did look at Jenny then. 'Did you tell Audrey?'

'Haven't had a chance. What do you think about him?'

'I don't know. There's something about him I don't trust.'

'Your father didn't like him.'

Before Hana had a chance to ask Jenny to elaborate, they were back in the hut.

'Why didn't my father like him?' whispered Hana.

If Jenny heard the question, she chose to ignore it.

Chapter 18

The events of the day plagued Hana and she found it hard to concentrate on her work. She was aware, she was being slower than usual with completing the codes, but she couldn't help it. There was something about what had happened earlier that just wasn't sitting right, but she couldn't put her finger on it.

Was it possible Audrey was the spy, and she had suggested Robert was up to something just to deflect Hana's attention away? Did Audrey know Hana had been placed in the hut to flush out the spy? Or was she genuine in her concern about Robert and Jenny?

And what of Jenny? She was hard to work out. At times she seemed almost hostile to Hana, and at other times friendly. Jenny had been the closest person to Alfred, working side by side with him every day. If anyone knew what he'd been doing or thinking, then it would be her. Hana considered trying to test the waters a bit with her, to work out if Jenny was friend or foe. Just how she was going to do that, without giving her own agenda away, she didn't know. She needed to give it some thought.

And then, of course, there was Derek. Hana found it hard to imagine him as anything other than genuine. She had no hard facts to go on, other than the way he had helped her with the intercept when they had stayed late. He had been keen to crack some of the coding. But wouldn't that be the perfect bluff for a spy? Appear helpful, but only to win the trust of others and ultimately betray them without being suspected.

She couldn't rule out Lottie either who had access to all the indexing and therefore, access to all the intelligence the hut was gathering. It wouldn't be difficult for Lottie to pass on information and even hide, or accidentally wrongly file something so that it couldn't be found easily.

There was, of course, Chatfield, but again, Hana's instincts were telling her he wasn't the mole. And Robert obviously wasn't as he had only arrived a few weeks ago. Although, he was spying on the hut for different reasons, which made Hana uneasy. Her colleagues were oblivious to his real motive for being there and she was now party to that deceit.

What Hana needed was some solid evidence one way or the other about all of them. She had some serious thinking to do about how she was going to achieve this. A process of elimination seemed the best way.

It wasn't until they were leaving that Hana had a chance to speak to Audrey. She caught up with her as they left.

'I'm so sorry about earlier,' she said. 'I got carried away and I feel awful about it.'

Audrey stopped walking and turned to face Hana. 'Apology accepted – given the circumstances.'

'Thank you.'

Audrey resumed walking. 'What I said earlier, about Robert, it was just to warn you,' she said in a low voice. 'I like you a lot, Hana. And I'm just looking out for you as my friend.'

Hana nodded. 'I realise. Sorry. I've had time to think about it. I shouldn't have reacted like that.'

Audrey slipped her arm through Hana's. 'It's this place,' she said. 'It's starting to make us all paranoid.'

'I think you're right,' said Hana.

They parted company at the front of the house, Audrey was heading back to her digs and Hana was waiting for the bus. Her nerves were kicking in at the thought of Gregory coming home that night. It had been a long time since she had missed him while he was away and an even longer time that she had looked forward to being in his company. Now, with the added complication of what was happening between her and Robert, she was practically dreading seeing him.

'Ah, there you are,' came a voice. Hana looked around to see Robert at her side. He smiled broadly at her. 'I was hoping to catch you. Come on, I've got the car.'

Soon, she was sitting in the passenger seat as Robert whisked them out through the back gates of the Park.

'Hey, why don't we stop at a pub on the way home?' said Robert. 'I admit, I'm being very selfish because when we get back to the house, I know you go back to being Mrs Gregory Phillips and I go back to being the American house guest.'

'I'm all for delaying the inevitable,' she said, trying to push away the guilt that had pitched up recently and taken root. She should really put a stop to this fling she was having with Robert, it wasn't right to deceive Gregory. But at the same time, Hana didn't want to deny herself the happiness Robert was bringing to her life.

They stopped at the next village to Bletchley and found a seat in the corner, tucked away from prying eyes.

While Robert ordered their drinks at the bar, Hana rummaged in her handbag looking for her compact mirror. She took out the folded crossword page of the newspaper and placed it on the seat beside her while she delved into the depths of her bag. Finding her lipstick, she reapplied it and was just putting everything back in her bag when Robert slipped into the bench seat of the booth next to her.

'Gin and tonic for the lady.' He slid the glass in front of her. 'So, did you finish the crossword?'

'I've not had a chance yet,' replied Hana, trying to appear casual as she picked up the newspaper. Somehow it slipped from her fingers and onto the floor.

Before she could reach for it, Robert was already stretching his arm down to pick it up. 'I'm good at crosswords. Why don't you let me take a look?'

Hana's heart picked up its pace as she gave a laugh and went to take the newspaper from him. 'If I get stuck, I'll be sure to ask for your help.' For a moment she didn't think Robert was going to let go as each of them held tightly to their corner of the paper.

'Sure,' said Robert, releasing his hold.

Hana popped the crossword back into her bag and took a long sip of her drink. 'Can I ask you something?'

'Of course.'

'It's a bit awkward, but Audrey happened to mention she saw you in Bletchley village this morning, with Jenny.' She took another sip of her drink to hide her awkwardness at asking.

'Are you checking up on me?'

'No. I mean, not really . . . I just thought you were going . . .' She trailed off, feeling highly embarrassed.

To her surprise Robert gave a chuckle. He leaned in towards her. 'You're not jealous by any chance, are you?'

'No!' She paused, realising he was teasing her. 'Maybe a little.'

Robert slipped his arm around her shoulder and kissed her, rather longer than necessary. Hana wriggled away, feeling embarrassed for a different reason now. Robert grinned at her. 'I remembered I had to drop something off at the Park, and on my way out I stopped at the shop for cigarettes. Jenny was just coming out of the shop as I was going in. We chatted, that was all.'

'I'm sorry. I didn't mean to sound prickly.'

'You don't have to apologise. I quite like the fact it caused a reaction.'

'You do?'

'Sure. It tells me you care.' He dipped his head to look at her. 'And it makes me worry just a little less about Gregory being home.'

'Talking of which, we should probably head home now,' Hana said reluctantly. 'It's been a much-welcome hour of escapism, but I do need to go home.'

'What time is he due back?' asked Robert, as they got to their feet.

'Around nine, I think he said.'

'At least we get to have dinner together on our own, then.'

As they walked out of the pub, Robert took her hand. 'I meant what I said about trusting me. With everything. Not just at the Park, but at home, with your heart. I am sincere, Hana. I promise.'

They arrived back at the house a short time later, but it wasn't until Hana had opened the door and stepped inside, laughing at a joke Robert had made about a bombastic colonel he'd had to deal with that day, that she saw the light on in Gregory's study.

Her breath caught in her throat at the prospect of another intruder. Instinctively, she grabbed Robert's arm.

'Stay there,' whispered Robert, stepping in front of her. He picked up an umbrella from the hall stand and holding it like a baseball bat ready to strike an incoming ball, he pushed the study door open with his foot. Then stepped into the room.

Hana watched as he lowered the umbrella and then she heard the familiar voice of Gregory.

'Bang. You're dead.'

'Gregory!' Hana rushed into the study. Gregory was sitting at his desk with his service revolver in his hand, pointed at Robert. 'Put that down,' she said. 'What on earth are you doing?'

'Defending myself against an intruder. Armed with . . .' he looked at Robert, 'an umbrella. Not a fair fight, I must admit.' He got to his feet and slipped the gun into the top drawer of the desk, before using his stick for support walked around to Hana. 'Hello, darling.' He kissed her on the mouth, holding her to him for a few more seconds than Hana was comfortable with. It was unlike Gregory to show affection like that.

She went to pull away, but Gregory kept his arm around her waist. 'I wasn't expecting you back this early,' she said.

'Thought I'd surprise you,' replied Gregory. 'And judging by the reception, I succeeded.' He looked over at Robert. 'Sorry, have I ruined any plans?'

Robert shook his head. 'No. Not at all.'

'I heard about the break-in,' said Gregory. 'Your mother telephoned me. She was a bit upset but she seems all right now. She brought me up to date on your father.'

'I've no idea what they were looking for, I—' Hana began, then stopped herself saying anything more. She'd had time to think about the break-in and what Robert had said. She was sure it was linked to her father knowing who the spy was and wanting to get their hands on the information before she did.

There was a long silence as Gregory looked at her as if he was deciding to say something. He looked over at Robert. 'Care for a drink?' He gestured with his head towards the decanter on the side.

'Not for me, thank you,' replied Robert. 'I need to sort a few things out. I won't intrude.'

'Don't let us distract you,' said Gregory.

'Dinner will be in hour,' said Hana, wanting to free herself from Gregory's hold, but not wanting to make a fuss, either.

'See you, then,' said Robert.

'Yes. I'll look forward to it,' said Gregory.

Robert nodded at Gregory and then with a fleeting glance in Hana's direction, left the room. She hadn't missed the dark look in Robert's eyes.

'So, darling,' said Gregory once they were alone. 'What have you been up to this weekend?' He let go of her and went to sit down at his desk again.

'Nothing. I was working Saturday. And then I had all this burglary to deal with. Poor Mum was quite shaken.'

Gregory eyed her from his chair. 'She seemed to think it was to do with the work your father was doing. Does she know he was working at the Park?'

'Not from me, but I think she's more or less worked it out for herself.'

'And she knows you're doing your father's work, which would explain why she said she was worried about you.'

'I haven't said anything to her, but you know Mum, she's not stupid.'

'No. Woe betide anyone to underestimate her,' said Gregory. 'That's always a fatal flaw in any kind of relationship.'

He picked up his pen, his attention now on the work in front of him. He paused. 'Oh, thank you for tidying up the study. I appreciate that.'

'You're welcome,' said Hana as the feeling of awkwardness between them prevailed. 'I really need to make the dinner.' She was out of the door before he could say another word.

*

Dinner turned out to be a rather strained affair. Gregory appeared intent on asking awkward questions and giving hostile answers.

'Hana, you never did tell me what you did on your day off, yesterday,' he asked as they were nearing the end of their meal.

He may be smiling at her, but Hana could tell from the tone of his voice that he had another agenda. 'We called in to see Mum,' she replied.

'Nice, was it?' Gregory gave a tight smile.

'Yes. I think she was glad to see me after the break-in.'

'I expect she was,' Gregory replied, putting his cutlery together as he finished his last mouthful of food. 'Then what did you do?'

'Why all the questions?' asked Hana. She really didn't want to confess that her and Robert had gone for a walk and had a drink in a pub. She knew Gregory wouldn't like it.

'Where did you go after you left your mother's?' Gregory's voice was firmer and any pretence that this was a pleasant conversation was over.

Before Hana could answer, Robert spoke up. 'I asked Hana to show me around some of the countryside. I thought it might take her mind off what had happened.'

'I was asking my wife.' Gregory ground each word out, his eyes never leaving Hana's.

'We had a drive out,' said Hana, trying to stop her voice from wobbling. 'And we went for a walk along the river.'

'And after that?'

'Look, I'm sorry if I've caused any problems,' said Robert. 'I was rather insistent when I asked Hana to take me sight-seeing.'

'Again, I'm asking my wife,' said Gregory.

'We stopped at a pub for a drink and then came home,' said Hana.

'At last, the truth! There that wasn't so difficult, was it?' said Gregory. 'Maybe next time, choose a pub where no one will recognise you and feel they have to report back to me. And then I won't have to pretend I know all about it.'

With that Gregory got to his feet, knocking the chair backwards as he did so, before exiting the dining room.

Hana closed her eyes as shame and embarrassment clawed at every inch of her skin. She could feel the tears gathering in her eyes.

'I'm so sorry,' said Robert quietly. 'Sorry that I've caused you problems, that is, not that we went out together.' He got up and came around to her, but Hana shied away from his touch.

She shook her head. 'Don't. Please.' If he showed her any sort of compassion or sympathy, she knew she was going to crumble in a heap.

She could sense Robert tensing at her words as a strained silence filled the room.

'OK, sweetheart,' he said, touching her shoulder briefly. 'I wish I could take you away from all this.'

Hana reached up and brushed his hand with her fingertips. She couldn't bring herself to speak.

After Robert had left, she remained sitting there for a long time, listening to him go out to the back garden for a smoke, before coming back in. He had paused at the doorway to the dining room, but hadn't come in, before retiring up to bed.

Only then did Hana get up and clear the table. It took her another half an hour or so to wash up and put the crockery away. The light was still on in the study, but she didn't want to disturb Gregory. She wasn't even sure what she would say to him anyway.

Hana took herself upstairs to bed. It had been a long day. So much had happened, it was hard to process it all. Once she was washed and in her nightdress, she sat in bed with her book hoping to distract herself, but she couldn't concentrate. Her mind was jumping from one thing to another. Tender moments with Robert, strained moments with Gregory, her altercation with Audrey and her suspicions of everyone in Hut 7. Not to mention Alfred's condition, which remained stable, neither deteriorating nor improving. How complicated her life had become.

She switched off the light and closed her eyes, trying to let her thoughts float freely around in her mind rather than pin down any particular thought and analyse it too closely. She longed talk to her dad. He had been her constant in life. The person she could relate to the most, the person she could confide in and the person who was unwavering in his support and love for her.

Her mind drifted back to happier times when she was a child, when they were living in Japan. She smiled when memories of Amaya found their way to the fore of her mind. Sitting there being taught how to use chopsticks and how to cook some of the most amazing food and playing with Amaya's grandchildren. It was so sad to know the two countries Hana felt she belonged to were now at war with each other.

Still, the memories were comforting, and she could feel her body finally begin to relax. Another memory, slightly hazier this time, came to her. She was sitting in the garden one day on a picnic blanket, surrounded by books and a Japanese dictionary. Alfred was next to her, and they were taking it in turns writing Japanese words in a notebook before passing it back to the other one to translate.

Hana sat bolt upright in bed as the memory suddenly became crystal clear. She was wide awake now, no longer in that half waking, half dreaming, state of mind.

She and Alfred hadn't been simply practising their language skills. She remembered now, they had been creating their own secret code. They had been writing messages to each other using the Japanese symbols. They had created a cipher all of their own.

'Oh, my God,' said Hana out loud. She threw back the bedclothes and jumped to her feet, scrambling to find her dressing gown. 'Oh, my God. Dad, you are a genius, and I am such an idiot.'

Chapter 19

Hana shrugged on her dressing gown and eased the bedroom door open. She could see a light coming from underneath Robert's door, but she had no idea if Gregory had made it to bed yet.

As she reached the bottom of the stairs, Gregory's study door was ajar, which was unusual, and it was all in darkness. She poked her head into the room, half expecting to see Gregory sitting there in the shadows, but the room was empty. She gently closed the door behind her and headed down the hallway. Through the glass of the door, she could just see the silhouette of someone moving around in the kitchen.

The doorknob was always a little sticky, hence why they never made a habit of closing the kitchen door. The trick was to turn it, wiggle it and turn it again, before nudging it with your foot. The door finally released on the second nudge and sprang open.

'That blasted door,' sighed Hana. Then stopped. Robert was standing at the kitchen table, with his cigarettes in his hand. He smiled but there was a slight awkwardness about him.

'Hey,' he said softly. 'I've just been out for a smoke.'

Hana nodded. Of course that's what he was doing. 'I'm sorry about Gregory earlier,' she said, pushing the door behind her, but not closing it fully. She wanted to go to him, to have him hold her, but there was a strange tension in the room. Maybe Robert was having second thoughts about her. She wouldn't blame him if he did. Hana didn't exactly see herself as a prize catch for anyone. Not least because she was a married woman.

Robert gave a shrug. 'He has every right to be angry with me. I just don't want him taking it out on you.'

'I'm fine.'

'Are you? Is that why you're up in the middle of the night?'

'I left my bag down here,' said Hana, picking it up from the table.

Robert looked like he didn't quite believe her. 'You need to get some rest,' he said, walking around the table and coming to stand in front of her. He cupped her face in his palm and ran his thumb across her cheek, before leaning his forehead against hers. 'I'll miss you tonight.'

Hana breathed deeply, wanting to soak up as much of Robert as she could, even if tonight it meant only his scent and touch. 'Me too,' she whispered. They stayed liked that for a moment before Hana pulled away. 'I really should go to bed. I'll be no use to anyone tomorrow otherwise.'

'Yeah. I should as well. Night, sweetheart.'

Hana listened to Robert's footsteps climb the stairs and go into his room, closing the door softly as he went. How on earth was she going to carry on living under the same roof as both Gregory and Robert? Maybe she should go and stay with her mother for a few days. Everything was so intense at the moment. Every aspect of her life was squeezing her and she was running out of energy and breath for it all.

Then, the little buzz of excitement that had caused her to come down to the kitchen in the middle of the night, reignited. Opening her bag, Hana took out the newspaper page and unfolded it, taking a moment to rein in her excitement. She needed to look at this calmly and analytically.

It had been a long time since she'd used the childhood code she and Alfred had devised. She smiled as she remembered Alfred saying that technically it wasn't a code but a cipher. The former, simply put, changed the meaning of a message by changing the meaning of individual words, whereas the latter, converted the message by a rule known only to the sender and recipient. Hana just had to remember that rule now.

Using her notebook, Hana wrote down the Japanese alphabet using the hiragana language. It was the first Japanese style of language she had learned and the one she and Alfred had used to create their cipher. She could see at a glance that Alfred had used hiragana when he'd completed the crossword as it was softer in style, the symbols more fluid, whereas katakana was more angular and was used for words that weren't in the Japanese language but had been borrowed from other countries. Her work at Bletchley incorporated both these styles.

Starting with the first letter or sound, Hana marked the number one next to it and carried on through all forty-six symbols of the Japanese hiragana alphabet. That was the easy part. The more difficult part was knowing the algorithm Alfred had employed. When they had created their own cipher, they had used the date as the deciding factor. Whatever the date was the day the cipher was created would be where the first letter/symbol began.

It took her a moment to work it out. It would be the date of the newspaper. There wasn't any other factor that could be used. The newspaper was dated October 6th, 1942. Hana wrote the date out in digits – 10, 6, 1, 9, 4, 2 – and added them up coming to the answer of thirty-two. If the sum total was in excess of forty-six, then the rule was to half the number until it came to forty-six or lower. However, that wasn't necessary today. Hana quickly worked out that for this message, the first letter of the alphabet started at the thirty-fourth letter/syllable of the hiragana alphabet. Once she had a starting point, cracking the cipher was easy

Within a couple of minutes, the meaning of the message was all too clear.

RAT. NAME. REPEAT.

Anyone else might have been amazed that Alfred had been able to implement the cipher so quickly, but his ability for words and numbers was unlike anything Hana had ever seen before or since.

She looked at the words. She had half expected them to spell out a name, the name of the spy but when she thought about it, that would be too easy. From what Hopkins had said, there was information against this person. It would be too much to put into a crossword clue hastily completed. No, Alfred was leaving a trail for her so she could find all the information. A name on its own meant nothing, and if someone else cracked this code, then the person named might be tipped off or even put in more danger. If they were killed because of their knowledge, then British intelligence wouldn't be able to interrogate them.

Hana rattled the end of the pencil between her teeth as she contemplated the cryptic clue.

Was her father asking her to repeat the name of the rat to Hopkins? If so, where was she supposed to find this name?

She tried to put herself in her father's position. He was trying to tell her something or give her an instruction but what that was, she had no idea. It was extremely frustrating.

*

Hana was awake bright and early on Wednesday morning. Excitement and anticipation being her alarm clock for the day.

Despite being earlier than usual, by the time she got downstairs, Robert was sitting at the table with a freshly made pot of tea and some toast.

'I heard you moving around, so figured I'd make you breakfast today.' He got to his feet and went to greet Hana, who stiffened at his touch. The last thing she wanted was to be caught in a clinch by her husband. Robert didn't seem bothered. He put his arms around her. 'Don't worry. He's already gone.'

'Oh, right. That was early,' said Hana, relaxing a fraction. She smiled up at Robert and relished the morning kiss he gave her, but also aware there was a sliver of guilt that Gregory had felt hounded out of his own home at the crack of dawn. He obviously didn't want to see either her or Robert, and to be honest, she couldn't blame him.

'Hey, don't look so sad,' said Robert.

She plastered on a smile. 'I'm fine. Right, cup of tea.'

After breakfast, Robert insisted on driving Hana to the Park. 'It makes sense. Why take the bus when I have a car and I'm going there anyway?'

Hana relented.

'Look, I'll get the bus home this afternoon. I'm going to call over to Mum's and then we're going to see Dad at the hospital,' she said, as Robert brought the car to a halt at the Park.

Robert didn't quite manage to hide his disappointment. 'Sure. I'll probably eat here. I don't think Gregory will relish the thought of dining with me tonight. And I don't want to sit through another meal with him being so uptight.'

'Gosh, this is awful,' said Hana. It truly was. Worse than she imagined. She had such conflicting emotions about it all.

'Hey, sweetheart,' said Robert, catching her hand as she went to exit the car. 'Don't panic. You can do this. We'll be all right. I'll make sure of it.'

'I'm fine. Honest.' That was a lie, if ever she'd told one.

'Don't go getting flaky on me now,' said Robert.

Hana hopped out of the car. Something about what Robert had just said grated on her nerves.

She saw Audrey walking across the grounds from the other side of the lake. Audrey looked up and waved, then waited for Hana to reach her.

'Morning. How are you?' asked Audrey.

'Oh, you know. Tired.' Hana was relieved everything seemed all right with Audrey now. 'Again, I am sorry about yesterday.'

'It's fine, really. I was upset at the time, but I'm all right now.' Audrey slipped her arm through Hana's and they moved to one side as a car came through the gates. 'Oh, look there's Robert over there,' said Audrey. Not that Hana needed telling but she looked over, nevertheless. Audrey continued. 'Did you ask him about Jenny?'

'He said he had bumped into her when he stopped at the shop.'

'That's his version of events, I suppose.' Audrey gave a shrug. 'But who am I to comment?'

Hana slowed her pace. 'Is there something I need to know?'

'Look, all I was saying yesterday, and I stand by that today, is just to be careful who you trust around here.'

'That's just it. Who does anyone trust? I mean, we've all signed the Official Secrets Act, so none of us should even be having any kind of discussion that will put us in danger of breaking it.'

'That doesn't mean to say it doesn't happen.' Audrey paused before continuing. 'I need to ask you something,' she said, and there was a hesitancy in her voice.

'All right, but I can't promise I'll be able to answer it,' said Hana.

'Was you asked to do more than just cover Alfred's work?'

'Why are you asking that?'

Audrey looked around furtively. 'Something is going on in the hut, in our room. I think someone is sharing information, and not to the right people.'

Hana's eyes widened at the candid confession. She wasn't sure how to respond to that. Was Audrey being truthful or was she double-bluffing to try to get information from Hana? 'What makes you think that?' she finally replied.

There were nearing the hut now. 'I can't say here,' whispered Audrey. 'Meet me this evening by the pavilion, around the back of the Methodist Church.'

'I can't. I'm going to see my father tonight.'

'On your way back. Seven o'clock. Make sure you come alone. Yes?'

'Yes. All right. But can't you tell me now?'

'No. Not here. It's not safe,' whispered Audrey. They were at the hut now. 'I've got something to show you.'

'Can't you quickly show me now?'

'Like I said, it's not safe here. Besides, I haven't got it with me for that exact reason. Now, not another word.'

Then they were entering the hut, and the conversation was over.

The building was a hive of activity as usual. The Soviet Union was in the middle of a heavily fought battle with the Germans over Stalingrad. From the monitoring of Japanese radio communications, it was obvious the Japanese rumour mill and gossip between officials were running high, and the outcome of the battle would have huge implications on how Japan moved forward. Of course, everyone in the hut was picking up bits of information from the messages they were deciphering, but even amongst themselves, they weren't supposed to talk about it. Hana could only guess from the messages she had seen herself. She really hoped this war would be over soon. She was exhausted from it. The whole country was.

Derek looked over at her. 'Are you all right? You look shattered.'

'Thanks. Just what a girl needs to hear,' said Hana with a wry smile. She hooked her bag on the coat rack along with her jacket. 'I didn't sleep very well.'

'Why's that?' asked Jenny.

'A lot on my mind. Training. You know, worrying about Alfred. I'm going to see him tonight.' Hana took her seat at her desk and looked at the stack of messages that needed her attention. She was also still bothered about Audrey's account of seeing Jenny and Robert together. He had dismissed it as an innocent encounter, and as much as Hana wanted to believe him, it niggled at the back of her mind. But she didn't know how to broach the subject again without sounding like she was jealous. Something he had teased her about. Was she jealous? She wasn't sure if that was the emotion she was experiencing or just one of general distrust. Audrey was right. The Park made everyone paranoid in the end.

'Good morning, ladies, and Derek,' came Lottie's singsong voice as she entered the room. 'How are we all today?' She looked around. 'Oh, such glum faces. Are you always like this in the mornings or is it just because I'm working full-time now?' She put her hands on her hips. 'Dear, oh dear. Shall I make us all a cup of tea?'

It wasn't so much a question as a statement and while Hana and the others got down to some work, Lottie went over to the tea urn and made drinks for everyone. She handed them out and was just passing Hana her cup, when she stumbled, spilling the tea down Hana's dress.

'Agh!' Hana leaped up from her chair, dumping the message she was working on onto the table. She looked down at the skirt of her dress. It was soaked.

'Oh, my goodness, I'm so sorry!' cried Lottie. 'Hana. Please, I'm sorry.' She grabbed a handkerchief from her pocket and started mopping up the tea which had splashed across the desk. 'I'm so clumsy.'

'It's all right,' said Hana. She looked down at her soaking wet skirt.

'Go and sponge it out,' said Audrey. 'And use the paper towels to dry it. Honestly, Lottie, what a mess you've made.'

'I'm sorry,' said Lottie, looking down and sniffling as she wiped her eyes with her fingertips.

'Oh, don't cry,' said Hana, feeling sorry for the young girl. 'It's only a drop of tea. It will wash out.' She put her arm around the younger woman and hugged her. 'Please, Lottie. It really doesn't matter.'

'Lottie, why don't you go and have a cup of tea yourself?' said Jenny. 'Hana, get yourself cleaned up. Audrey and I will sort this out.'

Hana managed to sponge most of it from her dress. Fortunately, she was wearing a dark-coloured wool dress, and the tea was disguised somewhat.

When she returned to her desk, all evidence of the little mishap was gone. Robert had appeared in the hut and he gave Hana a sympathetic smile, obviously having already been briefed on the mini disaster.

'I'm really sorry, Hana.' Lottie apologised again.

'Honestly, don't worry about it anymore,' reassured Hana, giving her another hug.

'Can we all get back to work now the drama is over?' It was Chatfield who spoke. 'Lottie, haven't you got some index cards to file?'

'Yes. Of course.' Lottie gave Hana another apologetic look, before heading over to the filing cabinets.

A silence fell over the room as everyone returned to their work. Hana looked around for the message she had just been working on. That was odd. It was nowhere to be seen. She looked in her tray, just in case it had been placed in there by mistake. Still no luck.

'Sorry but did anyone pick up the message I was working on?' she asked. 'I was just about to pass it over when the tea ended up in my lap.'

'Did it get wet?' asked Jenny.

'Nope.'

'I expect it was put in the basket,' said Audrey. 'It's probably gone off by now.'

Hana looked at the empty basket, the contents of which were now in another room being sorted into unimportant, important and urgent piles. 'I expect it will come back if anyone has a query on it.'

'Yes. Don't worry now. It's not like we haven't got any others to get on with.' Audrey rolled her eyes as she indicated towards the rapidly growing pile of messages waiting to be fully translated.

Hana sighed and picked out the message on the top of the pile. It was going to be a long day.

And she wasn't wrong. The afternoon training session seemed to drag on forever. She was so pleased when four o'clock finally came around.

She had opted to take the bus direct to the hospital to see Alfred. The Bletchley buses went in all directions ferrying their workers to and from the park, and it saved Hana having to wait around for public transport.

The four-thirty bus was packed, but Hana managed to grab a seat before it was standing room only. Squashed up against the window, she tracked the raindrops as they wove their way down the pane of glass. The only joy of the day, and that was stretching it somewhat, was the thought of seeing her father that evening. It was, of course, bittersweet. She hoped, like she did every day, that today would bring some better news of his condition.

The hospital visit didn't bring the happy news she was hoping. Alfred was still in a stable condition and still under sedation, but there was a suggestion that they might start to reduce the amount of sedative they were giving him, so he could gradually be brought out of the coma. Whether his brain was able to deal with that and had recovered enough to do so, they wouldn't know until they tried.

Hana had never felt so helpless. She'd give anything to have her father well again. In that moment, she didn't even care about the bloody coded message she'd discovered or finding the spy in the hut. None of it mattered, she just wanted her dad back. She rested her head on his hand she was holding and allowed herself the indulgence of a few tears.

All too soon it was time to leave. There was no Bletchley bus to take her back to the village this time, so public transport it was.

Just as she got off the bus, the rain that had been threatening all day finally put in an appearance. Hana opened her umbrella and hurried across the street to the pavilion, pausing as she reached the edge of the cricket field where the pavilion was situated. She looked around to see if she could spot Audrey anywhere, but it was far too dark to see clearly, and the rain didn't help matters either.

Hana made her way around to the pavilion. The wooden building was in darkness, but Hana tried the door anyway, in case Audrey was waiting inside. Unsurprisingly, it was locked. Hana checked her watch. It was exactly seven o'clock.

The minutes ticked by and still no sign of Audrey. Hana had completed two laps around the building, just in case Audrey was waiting on the other side, but no luck. It was now seven-fifteen. Hana's fingers drummed on the handle of her umbrella as she debated how long she should wait.

A sound of rustling from around the side of the pavilion, made Hana startle. She listened, expecting to see Audrey appear. The rustling came again. And then from around the corner appeared at cat.

'Oh, for goodness' sake,' sighed Hana in relief. 'Hello, kitty.'

The cat eyed Hana for a moment before darting back off into the bushes.

Hana checked her watch. Another ten minutes had passed. She'd give it until seven-thirty and then go. She couldn't stand around in the dark, cold and rain all night. The moon broke free from the heavy rain clouds, casting a soft white glow across the field.

As Hana looked over towards the entrance to the cricket field, she saw a figure hurrying through the gates. It was a woman, and although Hana couldn't see clearly in the darkness, as the figure neared, she was certain it was Audrey.

Hana was just about to step out of the shadows of the pavilion veranda and call out a greeting, when Audrey stopped in her tracks. Instinctively, Hana moved back closer to the building. Something had spooked Audrey. Hana scanned the cricket pitch and had she not been looking for whatever or whoever Audrey had spotted, she might have missed them. Someone was standing on the far side of the field, under the canopy of a large oak tree. It was the silhouette of a man, in a long overcoat and wearing a trilby hat. He was too far away for Hana to make out anything else.

Hana flicked her gaze back Audrey, who started to back away, retracing a couple of steps, before turning and running along the path and out of the gates. The man had moved out from the cover of the oak tree and was striding across the grass. Hana's heart thumped hard in her chest. She daren't move in case she caught his attention. She wasn't sure if he'd seen her or not. How long had he been there? Or had he followed Audrey and darted around to the other side of the field?

The man slowed his pace and came to a halt.

Hana held her breath. She desperately wanted to fold down her umbrella, but she daren't move. She watched as the man turned to look towards the pavilion. The moon had clouded over again, and she couldn't see his face at all, but it felt like he was looking straight at her.

For several, agonisingly long seconds, the man continued to look towards the pavilion, before finally turning away and striding out of the gates.

Chapter 20

Back at Tall Trees, Hana sat on the edge of her bed, giving herself a moment to try to make sense of what had happened earlier that evening.

After the man had left the cricket field, she had fled in the other direction, exiting through the west gate and running all the way back to Bletchley. A rather surprised guard had greeted her at the gates, and Hana had made up an excuse about missing the bus and needing to borrow one of the bicycles.

'Make sure the lights work,' said the guard.

That had been the least of her worries. Hana's only goal was to get back home as quickly as possible. Which she had managed. She had been pleased to come home to an empty house. She had no idea where either Gregory or Robert were, but she didn't care. She was just grateful to be home and safe.

She had gone to bed and remembered hearing Gregory come home. He had paused outside her bedroom door, before gently knocking and then opening it. Hana had pretended to be asleep.

'Goodnight, Hana,' he'd whispered, so quietly that Hana almost missed it, and her heart had performed some strange contraction.

Despite being tired, Hana was finding it increasingly hard to sleep at night. It was becoming more and more difficult to switch off when she left the Park. Some nights she felt exhausted and was certain she'd sleep all night, but, more often than not, she was awake again after just a few hours' sleep.

Tonight was no different. Here she was, wide awake. And although the blackout blinds made it impossible to tell what time of night or day it was, she was certain from the stillness of the house, that it was not time to get up.

She rolled over and groped for the bedside light. It took a couple of seconds for her eyes to adjust to the brightness before she was able to make out the time on her watch. It was nearly three in the morning. She gave a sigh as she remembered the night before. She had gone to bed with no clearer idea of who had spooked Audrey. At least she'd be able to find out when she saw her at work later.

Her thoughts turned to the work she was doing, and that intercept she had been trying to crack, not to mention the strange message Alfred had written in the newspaper. She had no time whatsoever to even attempt to work out what he meant.

There was no way she'd be able to get back to sleep now and resigned herself to getting up. She pulled on her dressing gown and tiptoed downstairs to the kitchen, where she made herself a cup of tea and sat down at the table.

The previous day, she'd copied the code she'd been trying to crack into her notebook. It was strictly forbidden to take any kind of paperwork out of the Park, and although copying the code down would probably be frowned upon, Hana was prepared to take the risk. If she broke the encryption, it would be worth it.

She looked at the groups of letters, and cross checked them with some of the naval terms she had already worked out. This was going to be a long and laborious process without access to all the codebooks and crib sheets held at the hut, but at least it kept her mind busy. She wouldn't be able to concentrate on anything else. This blasted intercept was consuming her every waking moment currently, even coming before trying to work out Alfred's message.

Minutes ticked by, then hours. She was so focused on what she was doing, that she barely registered the sound of the kitchen door opening and someone entering.

It was only when a hand reached over to cover her own, she looked up from what she was doing and was startled to see Gregory. She looked back down as he moved her hand away from the cup of tea. She realised she had been stirring her tea with her pencil.

She let out a sigh.

Gregory looked amused, there was even a small smile playing at the corners of his mouth. 'I haven't seen you do that for a long time,' he said, nodding at the pencil. It was something she'd done in the past – a little habit she often found herself doing when deep in thought. She remembered preparing for her interview with the school, when she had done the exact same thing, and Gregory had rescued the pencil from the tea that evening too.

'I was so distracted,' said Hana, shaking her head at herself as tea dripped from the end of the pencil.

Gregory let go of her hand and took the pencil from her. 'I'll make you a fresh cup.'

She met his gaze, resisting the urge to jump up and declare she'd do it herself. It was nice that he was offering. It was a long time since he'd done that. 'Thank you,' she said.

A minute or so later, Gregory set a fresh cup of tea down in front of her. He nodded at her notebook. 'Bringing work home?'

'Oh!' Hana turned the paper over. 'You're not meant to see that.' He gave her a curious look. 'I mean, I'm not meant to be doing this at home. Chatfield would have a fit if he knew.'

Again, Gregory gave a small smile of amusement. 'Don't worry, your secret is safe with me.'

Hana's heart gave a heavier thud. Secrets. She hated them. There were so many all around her. And with the secrets came lies and then the hurt that followed.

'Hana,' began Gregory. 'About the other day at dinner. When I was . . . well . . . quite frankly, rude. I'm sorry.'

Hana stilled. There was a softness in Gregory's demeanour that had been missing for so long that she was taken aback. She cupped her hands around the hot drink. 'I'm sorry, too,' she said. Sorrier than she could begin to explain. Sorry in ways that stretched far beyond the dinner table argument. Sorry for the distance that had spread like frost across a wintery grass and sorry that she had sought the warmth from someone else to counter it.

Gregory fixed her with a gaze, as if he knew the apology from both of them went far deeper. Hana wanted him to say he was jealous, that he still cared about her. She wanted him to throw their marriage a lifeline, but he said nothing.

The awkwardness between them which had become synonymous with their marriage had disappeared momentarily, but it was back in no time.

Hana pushed her chair back and got to her feet, her untouched tea still on the table. 'I should get ready for work.'

After washing and putting on fresh clothes, she came back downstairs to find that Gregory must have already left for work and she was now alone in the house.

After having a slice of toast, Hana prepared to leave for work. She'd have to cycle in on the bike she'd borrowed the night before. Not ideal. It was drizzling outside, and she didn't want to get wet, but she didn't have a lot of choice. She picked up her bag and opened it to look for her lipstick. Her hand paused mid-dip. Something was missing.

She let out a gasp. Where was the crossword? Hana leafed through the contents and checked the inside pocket. Then tipped the whole bag upside-down, the contents spewing out across the table. The crossword was missing. She whirled around the kitchen, in case she'd taken it out and left it on the table or worktop but she knew she hadn't done that. Another check of the bag proved fruitless.

Hana thought back to when she'd last looked at the crossword. It had been the previous morning. She hadn't had a chance to look at it since then. What with everything that had happened last night, it had been the last thing on her mind.

She sat down heavily on the kitchen chair. She'd either lost it, or someone had taken it.

Hana considered the consequences of both scenarios. If she'd lost it, the chances were that if someone found it, they would just throw it away. If, on the other hand, someone had taken it, then that meant whoever it was knew it held value. But it would still be meaningless because without knowing the deciding factor from which to base the code, they wouldn't be able to crack it. Well, not immediately anyway. She had no doubt someone at the Park wouldn't take too long to work it out, but on its own the crossword was useless. The translated words meant nothing.

Thankfully the rain had stopped by the time she left for work, and she arrived at the Park nice and dry. She popped the bicycle into the cycle rack along with an assortment of other bikes the Park had acquired.

There was another ten minutes before she was due to start work and Hana took the opportunity to wait over by the lake. She was hoping she'd catch Audrey on her way in so that she could ask her about the man last night and try to arrange another time to talk to her. Hana was going to suggest she went home with Audrey after work, and they could talk confidentially in the safety of Audrey's room.

It was a couple of minutes to eight o'clock and no sign of Audrey. Hana wondered if her friend had arrived at work earlier and was already in the hut. As she walked over to Hut 7, she saw Robert. Her heart gave a little flutter of excitement, but then immediately her stomach countered it with a roll of guilt.

'God, I wish I could wrap you in my arms and kiss the life out of you,' muttered Robert.

A few days ago she might have been thrilled at the suggestion, but today Hana's mind shied away from the idea. 'You didn't come back to the house last night.'

'I got a room above The Eight Bells. I thought I should give you and Gregory some breathing space,' replied Robert. 'I got the feeling he wasn't too happy to see me when he got back from London.'

'It's not you, honestly,' said Hana. 'It's me he's annoyed with. Will you come tonight?'

'I'll come over, but I'm not sure if I'll stay.' He opened the door to the hut, letting her walk ahead of him so the night-shift workers could pass in the narrow corridor, as they left to get some well-deserved sleep.

Hana looked around the room as she went inside, expecting to see Audrey already at her desk, but there was an empty place. 'Morning,' she said, slipping her bag from her shoulder and unbuttoning her coat. 'Anyone seen Audrey?'

Derek spun around in his chair, taking in the room. 'She should be here soon.'

'She's not in yet,' said Jenny. She looked over at the roster. 'It's not her day off, is it?'

'Not as far as I know,' said Chatfield. He flicked through the messages on his desk. 'No one has advised me she's not well, so I assume she hasn't phoned in ill.'

The door burst open, and in rushed Lottie. 'Sorry I'm late,' she said. 'Blasted alarm clock didn't go off.'

Chatfield looked over his glasses at her. 'Make sure you get a new one so this doesn't happen again. There is a bloody war on, in case no one's noticed.'

'Miserable bugger,' whispered Lottie as she hung up her coat.

Hana gave a theatrical eye roll as she slipped off her own coat and hung it on the peg next to Lottie's. Her hand brushed against the thick wool fabric which was peppered with tiny droplets of rain.

'Chop, chop,' came Chatfield's voice and Hana hurried over to her desk.

The supervisor seemed in a particular tetchy mood that morning and the mood in the room was sombre as Hana began her decoding. She glanced up at Robert who was sitting opposite her, and he sent a wink her way. Hana looked down. She didn't want to encourage him. She was aware she was taking a step back. As tempting as it was to rush headlong into a full-blown affair with him, it really wasn't something that sat comfortably with her. She was having a hard-enough time dealing with how she felt after just kissing him. Whichever way she tried to look at it, she had been disloyal to Gregory.

When it came to ten o'clock and tea-break time, Hana was relieved, but just as she was about to leave the room,

Chatfield called her back. 'I need you to do something for me,' he said as Hana stood at the side of his desk. He picked up a piece of paper with an address scribbled on it. 'Go and see if Audrey is all right. That's her address there. It's only five minutes around the corner.'

'All right. I'll go now,' replied Hana. It was an unusual request, but then nothing about the Park conformed to normal life.

'Maybe I should go with Hana?' said Robert.

Chatfield pursed his lips. 'Good idea. Although, I'm sure it's nothing to worry about.'

'Looks like it's about to rain again,' said Robert as they headed out of the hut. 'We'll take the car.'

Less than five minutes later, they were pulling up outside a modest looking semi-detached property. The rain had carried out its threat now and Hana wished she'd brought her umbrella. They huddled under the porch after knocking on the door.

A young woman, who looked to be in her early thirties, opened the door. She was wearing an apron and holding a baby on her hip. This was the six-month-old who kept Audrey awake at nights.

'Good morning. Mrs Kidson, is it?' asked Hana.

'Yes, that's me.'

'Sorry to bother you. I'm Hana Philips and this is Captain Becker. We work with Audrey Brookes. We just wondered if she was home. She didn't turn up for work today, so we've popped by to see if she is all right.'

Mrs Kidson took a moment to look Hana and Robert up and down as she shifted the baby to her other hip. Hana knew without looking at Robert that he would be flashing the landlady his most disarming smile. It clearly worked. Mrs Kidson smiled back and almost looked a little shy. 'I haven't seen her this morning. I don't usually as I have an early-morning cleaning job. I drop Kenneth off with my mum. I don't get back until nine-thirty.'

Hana smiled at the little boy before replying to Mrs Kidson. 'Would you mind if I just nipped up to her room to check if she's all right?'

Mrs Kidson hesitated, but then stepped to one side, opening the door wider. 'Top of the stairs. It's the room directly in front of you.' She looked at Robert. 'Come in, but wait down here.'

'Of course, ma'am. Thank you,' said Robert, taking off his cap and stepping into the hallway.

Hana smiled to herself on hearing Robert turning on his all-American charm.

She reached Audrey's room and gently tapped on the door. 'Audrey? Are you there? It's me, Hana.' She waited a few seconds, before tapping again. There was silence. She glanced back down the stairs to where Robert and Mrs Kidson were both standing.

'Go in,' said Mrs Kidson. The baby wriggled in her arms. 'I'll be in the kitchen. Shout if you need me.'

Hana turned the doorknob and stepped into the bedroom.

It was a small, single room, with a window overlooking the back of the property. The curtains were drawn but Hana could make out Audrey asleep in bed.

'Audrey,' she said softly, and then again a bit louder. She went over to the bed and switched on the bedside lamp.

Hana stared at the pale, translucent complexion of her friend; she was paler than she'd ever seen. Poor Audrey must be unwell.

'Hey, Audrey. Are you all right?' Hana reached out and touched Audrey's bare shoulder to give her a gentle shake.

But touching her, she gasped and jumped back. Audrey's skin was stone cold. Hana swallowed hard, her eyes darted to the bedside table and the empty glass of water alongside an empty bottle of pills.

'Oh, my God, Audrey. No!' Hana grabbed Audrey's limp hand, rapidly patting it. 'Robert!' she cried out, as she grasped Audrey's shoulders and began shaking her violently. 'Audrey. Audrey. Wake up.'

Then Robert was gently pulling her away from the bed and stepping in front of her. Hana watched in silence as he quickly examined Audrey, feeling for a pulse at her neck and then bending over to listen for her breathing. When he stopped, but didn't turn around immediately, Hana knew it was too late. Audrey was dead.

'I'm so sorry,' said Robert, facing her now. He went to put his arms around her, but Hana stepped back.

'I'm all right,' she said. 'It's . . . it's just a shock.'

'Looks like she took some pills,' said Robert. He went back over to the bed and respectfully lifted the sheet to cover Audrey's face.

'We should call the police,' said Hana, feeling like she wasn't really there, that it wasn't really happening. She worried her wedding ring around her finger. Her mouth was dry and she had a nauseating sensation in her stomach.

'Not just yet. We need to let Chatfield know first. They might not want the local police poking around too much.'

Hana was a little surprised, but Robert did have a point. It was then that she noticed a folded piece of paper propped up on the chest of drawers. Hana unfolded the note which simply read – *I'm sorry but it had to be this way. Audrey*

'What on earth does she mean by that?' asked Hana.

'It's no good trying to work out the thoughts of someone who takes their own life,' replied Robert. 'They don't think rationally.'

'We need to let Chatfield know.' Hana needed to be doing something. She avoided looking over towards the bed in case she lost her composure. She was only just keeping herself together.

They went downstairs, and on discovering that Mrs Kidson didn't have a telephone, Hana sent Robert off to the telephone box at the end of the road, while she comforted the landlady who was naturally shocked and upset at the news.

'I feel awful,' she was saying, whilst nursing a mug of hot tea in her hands. Her little boy was napping in his pram outside the back door, snuggled up in several layers of blankets. 'Audrey laying up there . . . you know . . . dead. And I didn't know a thing about it. I should have checked.'

'You weren't to know,' said Hana. She hesitated before adding, 'I'm sure the police will ask you some questions about Audrey, but can I ask, when you last saw her?'

Mrs Kidson wiped her nose and gave a little sniff. 'Well, it must have been yesterday at teatime. I cooked us a meal, like I always do and then she went up to her room.'

'What time was that?'

'Six o'clock. That's when I always do tea.'

'And you didn't see her after that?'

'Not saw her, no. I heard her go out at about a quarter to seven, but she was back by half past. I heard the door go and I called out to her. I said, "Is that you, Audrey?" She said, "Yes. Only me." In that cheerful way she does, and then she went up to her room. I didn't see or hear another peep out of her.'

'Nothing at all?'

Mrs Kidson thought for a moment. 'Actually, that's not true. I was in bed and heard the bottom stair creak and then the kitchen door open and close.'

'Was that Audrey?'

'Yes. It wasn't anyone else. I heard the tap run, so I assumed she was getting a glass of water . . .' Her voice trailed off for a moment. 'Oh, the water, oh do you think that's when she took those pills?' Mrs Kidson wiped her eyes. 'I wish I'd known. This is awful.'

Hana patted the other woman's arm, trying to reassure her it wasn't her fault. She was glad when Robert reappeared. He had Chatfield with him and two military policemen, as well as another man.

Chatfield introduced himself to Mrs Kidson, while the other men went upstairs. Hana wanted to go with them. She hated the thought of Audrey being surrounded by strangers, but Chatfield motioned for her to stay seated. 'The doctor is here to formally pronounce death,' he was explaining. 'And the military police are here to oversee everything is done correctly. There's a private ambulance out the front, and we'll discreetly remove the body from here to the mortuary. We'll deal with all the formalities from here on in.' He looked at Hana. 'Would you mind collecting all of Audrey's possessions, including clothes and bring them back to the Park? Meet me over at the mansion house. Captain Becker will wait with you to drive you back.'

It all seemed so clinical with no room for sentimentality. Hana supposed that's what war did to people. It desensitised them.

All too soon, Audrey's body was removed and taken away by the police to the hospital, where, according to Chatfield, there would be a postmortem to establish the cause of death, even though it did appear obvious. Chatfield left strict instructions that no one was to discuss what had happened today with anyone else. Hana was to return to work tomorrow and carry out her tasks as normal.

Clearing Audrey's belongings didn't take long. Like a lot of the women billeted, she had brought minimal possessions with her. It was only as Hana folded Audrey's clothes into her suitcase, that she allowed herself to cry. The next person to open this case would be Audrey's family. It was a heartbreaking thought. It made thoughts of her own brother, Tom, and where he was more painful. She hoped that her family would never be sent home a box of belongings for him.

Hana looked around at Audrey's room and the sum total of her possessions packed neatly into a cardboard box Mrs Kidson had found in her under-stairs cupboard. Hana let out a sigh. Now she'd never know what it was Audrey had wanted to tell her. Why she'd want to take her own life, Hana didn't understand. It just didn't make sense. She sat down on the bed, which she had already stripped so that Mrs Kidson could wash the sheets.

From Mrs Kidson's account of the night before, it was safe to assume that after Audrey had been spooked at the cricket field, she had come straight back to her lodgings. Had the person she'd seen followed her back here? Mrs Kidson said she hadn't seen Audrey, just heard her. Was it possible someone had followed Audrey into the house? No. That seemed unlikely, on reflection. Audrey wouldn't have willingly let someone in who she was running away from, and if the man had forced his way in, then it was highly unlikely to have happened in silence. Mrs Kidson would have heard a scuffle or arguing.

So, was it just the sight of the man that made Audrey take such drastic action? Hana wished she had followed Audrey home and somehow got to talk to her.

She bit her lip at the other possible scenario.

The man had somehow managed to gain access to the house and had forced Audrey to take those tablets, which Hana assumed were sleeping pills. But again, Mrs Kidson didn't mention hearing any disturbance. How could Audrey have been force-fed an overdose? Hana held her head in her hands, frustrated at not being able to come up with a plausible scenario.

And the more she thought about it, the more she was convinced Audrey had been murdered.

Chapter 21

Robert drove back to the Park and carried Audrey's belongings into the mansion house, with Hana following. They were directed by the commander's secretary to take the belongings through to one of the rooms at the back of the house. There, two military policemen were waiting for them, and both Hana and Robert had to give a written statement of finding Audrey. They were then told to wait for the commander for a debrief.

'Now, I don't want this getting out,' said the commander a short time later when they were called into his office. 'It's not good for morale. Don't go gossiping about it to all and sundry. If anyone asks you directly, you can tell them you are not at liberty to discuss the matter and that it is being dealt with by the appropriate authorities. Which, I might add, it is.'

'Yes, sir,' replied Robert.

'Yes, Commander,' Hana said, ignoring the gossiping comment. She did not consider herself a gossip.

The commander continued. 'Off the record, it is of course a tragedy that a young woman would take her own life, and I shall be sending my personal, as well as official, condolences to her family.' He sat back in his chair with a sigh. 'If you think of anything you'd like to add to the statements, then come to me first.'

Hana was glad to be out of the commander's office. By the time all the formalities and debriefs were done, it was mid-afternoon. The commander had told Robert to take Hana home early that day.

As they exited the mansion house, they almost ran straight into Gregory.

'Hana,' he said, his gaze flicking to Robert and then back. 'I was just coming to find you. I heard what happened.'

'You did?'

'Yes. The commander thought I should know, seeing as I'm your husband.' He shot another look at Robert, before turning his attention back to Hana again. 'Are you all right?'

'I think so. It was a shock.'

'No doubt. What are you doing now?'

'I've been told to take the rest of the afternoon off.' She looked up at him. 'I'm not sure whether to be offended or appreciative. I don't want them to think I can't cope with everything.'

'Not at all,' said Gregory. 'Like, you say, it's a shock.' He hesitated before he spoke again. 'I could see if they'll let me take you home.'

'Oh, don't worry. I'll be fine,' said Hana.

'The commander has instructed me to drive Hana home,' said Robert.

'Hmm. Right.' Gregory visibly bristled at the news. 'Well, you'd better carry out your orders, then.' Gregory moved around them without another word and entered the mansion house.

Hana didn't know whether to run after him or not, but what was she going to say to him?

She felt Robert's hand on her elbow. 'Come on, sweetheart.'

As Robert steered the car away from the Park, Hana wound down the window and let the fresh air parry against her face.

'You feeling OK?' asked Robert.

'I just can't stop seeing Audrey there in her bed,' admitted Hana. 'I don't want to think of her like that. I want to remember her smiling and laughing. Full of life.' Her voice cracked and she closed her eyes to hold back the tears. She felt Robert's hand reach for hers and she held it tightly. 'Do you really think she took her own life?' Hana asked after a few minutes had passed.

'It all points to suicide,' said Robert. 'I know it's hard to think she'd do that, but sometimes we have to face the truth, no matter how painful.'

'You know, she wanted to meet me last night,' said Hana. She couldn't see the harm in telling Robert that now.

'For a drink?'

'No. She wanted to meet me in secret. She didn't want anyone to know.' Hana looked across at Robert. 'We arranged a time and place. I was there first. I saw her coming, but there was someone else there, hiding in the trees. When Audrey saw him, she turned and ran away.'

Robert's eyes widened. 'Did you recognise the man?'

'No. It was too dark, and he was too far away.'

'Did he see you?'

'No. At least I don't think so. I left through the other exit.'

'Jesus Christ, Hana. Why are you only telling me this now?' Robert sounded agitated.

'I don't know. I was scared. Audrey made me promise not to say anything.'

'Did you put that in your statement?'

'No.' Hana wasn't sure if that was the right thing to have done, but she wanted to tell Hopkins first. She wasn't sure what had made her tell Robert. Maybe because she didn't want to keep secrets anymore. Life was hard enough, and all the secrecy surrounding the Park didn't help. She felt weighed down by the pressure of it all. 'I'm sorry. I shouldn't have said anything.'

'Hey, don't be sorry.' Robert squeezed her hand. 'Let's take a detour. Shame the pubs aren't open right now. I think you could do with a stiff drink.'

'The thought is not unappealing,' said Hana. 'Where are we going?'

'That place you took me before. We can get a hot drink at the tearoom and take a walk by the river. It will help clear your mind.'

A pot of tea and a strong coffee later, Hana and Robert were walking along the riverbank towards the woods. Her thoughts still very much on Audrey and how in just a few hours, everything had changed, and Audrey wouldn't see another day. Her life was over. She'd never feel the chill of the autumn air or see the weak hazy rays of an October sun, or smell the damp leaves all shades of brown and gold that were mulching on the ground or feel the light drizzle dampen her hair and wet her face. Hana could picture Audrey's smiling and laughing face – she had loved life, which just made it all the more difficult to accept that Audrey had wanted to end it.

'I've been thinking,' said Robert. 'This man you saw at the cricket field and Audrey wanting to meet with you, I don't think you should tell anyone just yet. Give me a few days to make some enquiries.'

'Some enquiries?'

'Yeah. I have contacts higher up the command chain. I might be able to find out a bit more about Audrey's death and whether they think it was suicide or something more sinister. I wanna know for my own peace of mind in case it now puts you in a dangerous position.'

It wasn't a nice thought to think she was in danger, but at the same time, it was nice to feel someone was looking after her. 'Thank you,' she said.

They walked on for a few more minutes, but the evening was closing in and with much reluctance, they turned and headed back to the car. All too soon, they were pulling up outside Tall Trees. The blackout blinds were all up at the windows, so Hana assumed Gregory was now home.

'Are you staying tonight?' asked Hana.

'No. I've still got the room at the pub. Now, please be careful.'

'I'll be safe at home. Stop worrying.'

'Easier said than done,' Robert muttered as she got out of the car.

Inside, the living-room table lamp was on, but the room was empty, as was the study. Hana put the kettle onto boil, and when Gregory still didn't appear, she went upstairs to look for him.

His bedroom door was open, and it was dark inside. A little flutter of nerves rattled in her stomach. 'Gregory!' she called out. 'Are you up here?'

As she turned away from the bedroom, she noticed the door to the box room was also ajar.

Hana stepped into the darkened room. The only light was from the table lamp and there in the corner, sitting in the wicker chair was Gregory. His head was down and his forearms resting on his knees. In his hands was the teddy bear. At Gregory's feet was the broken photo frame and their wedding picture.

'Gregory,' she said softly. When he didn't respond, Hana knelt in front of him. 'Gregory?' she said again. This time he did look up. The shadow from the lamp partially obscured his face, but nevertheless, she could see the anguish in his eyes, but it was different from the vulnerability of earlier in the kitchen. It was deeper than before. Almost knowing. 'What's the matter?' she asked. She went to hold his hand but stopped. He hated her touching his damaged skin.

'How long?' asked Gregory, his voice barely more than a whisper. The softness of his earlier apology had hardened into something else – resignation possibly? Or recognition?

'What do you mean?' She didn't know why she'd asked that. It was obvious what he meant.

'You and Robert. How long has it been going on?' He looked her directly in the eye.

It was only a matter of time before they got to this point. She couldn't insult his intelligence by denying it. Besides, that was the cowardly thing to do. She may not have had a full-blown affair with Robert, but she was certainly having an emotional affair with him. The difference was a mere technicality. 'Gregory . . .' she began but her voice trailed off, not knowing what to say.

'A chap I work with lost his wife yesterday,' he said, not waiting for her to continue. 'She was a nurse at a hotel on the south coast. It had been requisitioned by the RAF to use as a hospital. It took a direct hit. Killed nearly forty people.'

'That's terrible,' said Hana. The worst of the bombing might be over, but the Germans were still targeting the south of England.

Gregory got to his feet. 'The poor man is distraught. They had their future all mapped out.' He picked up his walking cane and looked down at the photograph on the floor. 'All their chances gone, in an instant.' Hana watched as her husband limped across the room, pausing in the doorway. 'Just like us, I suppose. I fear it's too late for us, too. I can't blame you, though. I mean, why would you want to stay with a cripple like me? A man with such a scarred body. A monster on the inside as well as the outside.'

'Gregory, don't.' She got to her feet, hating the fact that he thought of himself as a monster in any capacity.

He gave her a sad look, followed by a sigh. 'I've been many things in our marriage; more recently a fool, a selfish bastard and an absolute cuss to live with. But I've always loved you, Hana. Always.'

Hana opened her mouth to speak, but no words came out. Was it possible to love someone and not love them at the same time? Was loving someone and being in love two different things?

Gregory looked up at her. 'I love you, Hana, But I should have loved you more.' With that he left the room.

Hana stood in the middle of the room, clutching the teddy bear to her heart.

She heard his bedroom door open and then close and could only imagine what thoughts were going through his mind.

She went downstairs. Her appetite had disappeared, and she sagged down into the sofa in the living room. All she felt was a deep tiredness. She was tired of working at the Park, with all its secrets and distrust, the whispering in corridors and behind closed doors. She was not cut out to be a spy and she wanted out, but she was trapped.

Her mind went back to Audrey and what she had been going to tell her. There was something she'd wanted to show Hana. Something she couldn't bring to the Park. So whatever it was, Audrey must have kept in her room. Hana frowned as she thought back to Audrey's belongings. She had meticulously gone through everything as she had been instructed by Chatfield, and anything suspicious or sensitive was to be reported on a separate sheet. But Hana hadn't found a single thing that fitted that criteria. Damn, she must have missed something, and there was no way she could go through Audrey's things again, not now they were securely in the mansion.

Hana got to her feet. But what if it had been hidden in the room and she'd missed it? She needed to go through that room again, in case someone else found it, or whoever went through Audrey's belongings came to the same conclusion. Hana rushed out to the hall and grabbed her coat, pausing momentarily to look up the stairs and contemplate calling out to Gregory. She decided against it in case they got into an argument or discussion. There was no time for that right now.

The car keys were on the console table next to the telephone and without giving it another thought, she swiped them up. She hated driving in the dark without headlights, so her speed was minimal. Eventually, she pulled up outside Audrey's lodgings.

Mrs Kidson wasn't exactly pleased to see Hana that evening and made it clear that this was highly irregular.

'I'm so sorry,' said Hana. 'But I just wanted to check Audrey's room once more. I think I've forgotten something.'

Mrs Kidson's eyes narrowed. 'By rights, I'm supposed to get someone from Bletchley Park here if anyone turns up asking questions or wanting to go into Audrey's room – God rest her soul.'

'I know, but it's really important,' pleaded Hana. 'I hate asking, but please don't tell anyone. I'll get into awful trouble if they know I'm here. I was supposed to check and double-check, but I was rather upset earlier.' She put her hands together as if in prayer. 'Please, Mrs Kidson. Just this once.'

'Look, I really don't know what's going on,' said Mrs Kidson. 'But you seem a nice girl and I don't want to be the one to get you into trouble just because you forgot something.' She opened the door wide. 'Don't make a noise, though. I've only just got the baby to sleep.'

'Thank you, Mrs Kidson,' whispered Hana as she darted inside and up the stairs before the landlady had time to change her mind.

Hana shivered as she went into Audrey's room. It didn't feel any better being in here than it had earlier. The smell of TCP hung in the air and Hana assumed Mrs Kidson had already been up here, cleaning and wiping down the floor and surfaces. Poor woman had to carry on living in the same house where Audrey had died.

Hana flicked on the main light and cast her gaze around the room.

How sad for Audrey to end her life alone in a little room in a village far away from home. Hana slowly turned a full 360 degrees, her eyes examining the room in minute detail for something she might have missed.

For some reason, her gaze kept coming back to rest on the dressing table in front of the window. It had two drawers on either side, which she had emptied, but now she was looking at the furniture, she could see a gap between the pieces of wood which ran along the front.

Kneeling in front of the dressing table, Hana ran her fingers along the fake front, pushing it to try to release a hidden drawer. Then she slid her hand underneath, right to the back. She nearly missed what she was looking for, but her fingertips grazed a little metal cap. She pushed it back and the front drawer gently popped open.

The drawer was shallow and only about twenty inches deep, but inside was a little black notebook. Hana sat down on the floor and opened the book. She flicked through the pages. There were dates and times listed on each page, and underneath Audrey had written in Japanese. Hana smiled to herself. Audrey must have been jotting down things that only a few people would be able to translate. The information here wasn't just meant for anyone. Audrey had only intended certain people to be able to read this.

Hana felt a small sense of relief that finally she was getting somewhere. If she could translate this, she could take the information to Hopkins. She was sure Audrey knew who the spy was. As she leafed through to the back of the book, a photograph slipped out to the floor.

She picked it up and as she looked at the black-and-white image, she let out a gasp as her heart missed a beat and her stomach did some kind of somersault.

There was no mistaking the two people sitting in a cafe, apparently unaware their meeting was being photographed.

Hana dropped the photograph as if it was a hot potato. She looked down at the image staring back up at her, taking a moment to gather her thoughts.

'Find what you were looking for?' Mrs Kidson was standing in the doorway.

Hana jumped. She hadn't heard her come up. 'Yes, thanks. It was a photo album.' She popped the photograph and notebook into her bag. 'Right, I'd better get off. Thanks ever so much.'

With that she sailed past Mrs Kidson, down the stairs and out of the door, breathing a sigh of relief as she jumped into her car, before driving away. She had to stop when she got around the corner. Her hands were shaking so much from the adrenaline, she wouldn't be able to drive home at this rate.

She took out the notebook from her bag and flicked through the pages. Immediately, she could see some sort of pattern emerging. Each entry was dated and time-stamped in Audrey's neat and precise handwriting. There were names and locations, too. It looked like some sort of logbook.

As for the photograph. It must be important, or Audrey wouldn't have it and the possibilities crushed Hana's heart, even though she had no right to feel that way.

She drove home steadily and was relieved when she pulled up outside her house.

She was just fishing out her house keys, when suddenly she was aware of footsteps rushing towards her. Hana had barely turned when she was bundled to the ground in some sort of rugby tackle, her head making contact with the car as she went down. She let out a scream and then as her back thudded on the stony driveway, all the air was knocked from her lungs. She was aware of a dark figure grappling with her on the ground, jumping to their feet and trying to yank her bag from her hands.

Hana tried to hold onto the handle, but it was pulled free from her grasp before she had time to get a proper hold. The footsteps raced off down the driveway and out onto the street.

Hana gasped for breath as her lungs sucked in oxygen. She rolled over and managed to get to her hands and knees.

It was only then that she felt something wet on her eyebrow. She dabbed a finger to it. She was bleeding. She had a vague recollection of her head catching the wing mirror of the car as she was knocked to the ground.

'Hana!' The voice came from the end of the driveway.

She recognised it immediately. 'Robert.' She was so relieved to see him, she wanted to cry.

He reached her in seconds. 'What happened?' he asked, helping her to her feet. He held her at arm's length as he inspected her face. 'You're bleeding.'

'It's just a small cut, I think.' She felt her knees buckle. 'I'm so glad you're here. You're some sort of guardian angel,' she whispered as her body sagged.

Robert caught hold of her. 'You need to get inside.' He went to lift her up.

'No. I'm fine. I can walk,' she insisted. Besides she didn't want Gregory to be greeted with the sight of Robert carrying her across the threshold.

The door opened and Gregory appeared on the step, illuminated by the hall light behind him. 'What the hell's going on?' he demanded and then looked at Hana. 'Your head. It's bleeding.' He looked accusingly at Robert.

'Let's just get her inside,' said Robert. His words were calm and measured, as he guided Hana into the house.

'Someone care to explain what's going on?' Gregory was barely controlling his temper.

'I'd like to know that, too,' said Robert.

Hana watched the two men glare at each other. She sighed and rubbed her forefinger up the bridge of her nose to her forehead. She couldn't quite believe it had come to this.

It was Gregory who broke the stare first. 'I'll get you some warm water and a cloth. You need to clean that wound. I'll call thc doctor.'

'I don't need a doctor.'

'I'd sooner you were checked over,' insisted Gregory.

'I can do that,' said Robert. 'I am a medic.'

Gregory ignored him. 'Hana?'

'Can you just get the TCP from the cupboard and some water, please?'

Gregory went out of the room and Robert knelt down in front of her. 'You don't have to take orders from him anymore,' he whispered.

'I'm not taking orders,' replied Hana. 'From anyone.'

Gregory returned with the water and cloth. 'Do you want me to do that for you?'

Hana didn't need to look at Robert, to know he had bristled at the suggestion. She took the bowl and cloth. 'I'll do it myself.'

'So, what happened?' asked Gregory.

'I was just getting out of the car, when someone ran up to me from behind. Sent me flying and stole my handbag,' she said. 'I can barely believe it, really. Here in Newton Longville you don't expect that.'

'Did you get a look at them?' asked Gregory.

'No. It all happened so quickly. And it's dark out there. They ran off and were gone before I had even realised what had happened.'

'What was in your bag?' asked Robert.

'That's just it. Not much.' Hana winced as she dabbed some TCP onto her cut. 'My lipstick, compact mirror, a few bits and bobs and my purse with less than a pound in it.'

'Someone's going to be disappointed,' said Gregory. 'They must have just been walking by at the right moment and took the opportunity.' He paused. 'Where did you go?'

'I went back to Audrey's digs,' said Hana. 'I wanted to make sure I hadn't missed anything.'

'At this time of night? Why couldn't it wait until the morning?' Gregory asked.

'Because the landlady might have thrown anything out that I had missed.' She didn't meet Gregory's eyes. She was telling the truth, but not the whole truth.

'And did you find anything?' asked Robert.

'No. Nothing.'

'So, you didn't go there with her?' Gregory looked at Robert with narrowed eyes.

'No, I didn't.'

'What were you doing out here, then?' Gregory's hand gripped the cane a little tighter.

It was a good question. What was Robert doing there? Hana looked up at him waiting for an answer.

Robert shifted on his feet as he looked at Hana. 'I was in Bletchley village earlier. I saw you leaving Mrs Kidson's house.' He glanced uncomfortably at Gregory before looking back at Hana. 'I just wanted to make sure you got home safely.'

'You followed me?'

'Yeah. In my car. I parked across the road and got out for a smoke. That's when I heard you cry out.'

'You must have seen who attacked her,' said Gregory.

'They darted out of the driveway, just as I got there. I was more concerned about you, Hana.' He looked both apologetic and embarrassed at the same time. 'Sorry. Lousy timing. If I'd been a few seconds earlier . . .'

Gregory made a scoffing noise. 'Not such the great protector, after all.'

Robert took a deep breath. He looked down at Gregory's leg and then up to his face. 'That makes two of us.'

Hana inwardly winced at the barbed comment from Robert. That was pretty nasty. Despite what she thought about Gregory, he didn't deserve a low blow like that. 'It doesn't matter, anyway,' she said. 'No real harm done.'

'We should report it to the police,' said Gregory.

'We should let the Park know,' contradicted Robert.

'It's not really up to you,' snapped Gregory.

Hana got to her feet. She'd had enough of this sparring between the two men. 'It's up to me what I do, not either of you.' She looked from one of them to the other, her hands on her hips, waiting to make sure she had their full attention before continuing. 'I'll let the Park know tomorrow when I go into work and ask them what they think I should do. In the meantime, I don't want either of you two making any kind of decision on my behalf. I'm perfectly capable of thinking and deciding matters for myself.'

Robert's shoulders relaxed. 'Sure. No one is trying to tell you what to do. But yes, wait to see what they say at the Park.'

'Thank you. Now, it's late and I really need to go to bed.' She motioned with her head towards the door. For a moment she thought Robert wasn't going to leave, but if he had any crazy idea about staying, he soon rethought it.

'Right. I'll get off, then. Goodnight, Gregory.'

'Goodnight.' Gregory's reply was tight with not a single ounce of sincerity. Not that Hana could blame him.

She walked Robert to the door, still feeling upset at what he'd said. 'I'll see you tomorrow.'

Robert leaned down to kiss her, but Hana turned her head away. 'Not here.'

Robert straightened up. 'What's wrong?'

'You didn't need to say what you did to Gregory, about him not being able to protect me. I saw the way you looked at his leg.'

Robert looked surprised. 'He started it.'

Hana let out a huff. 'Now you sound like a child.'

He looked at her for a moment before taking her elbow and ushering her out onto the front doorstep. 'Come with me,' he said in a low voice.

Hana glanced back over her shoulder down the hallway, before pulling the door closed a little further. 'I can't,' she whispered back.

'You can. You just have to close that door properly and walk out to my car with me. It couldn't be easier.'

She shook her head. 'You need to go.'

Robert gave her a long look. 'We need to talk. I'll see you tomorrow.'

When she went back inside, Hana closed the door and locked it with a sense of relief.

Chapter 22

'Are you going to let me call the doctor?' asked Gregory as Hana came back into the living room. He was sitting in the chair next to the fire.

'I'd sooner you didn't,' replied Hana. 'There's something I need to ask you about.'

'That sounds serious.'

'It is.' She took the chair opposite him. 'When I went back to Audrey's room tonight, I found something. I think whoever stole my bag was trying to get what I had found.'

'And I don't suppose you're going to tell me what it is?'

'Actually, I am,' replied Hana. 'In fact, I'm going to show you. The thing is, what I found wasn't in my bag. I'd put it in my coat pocket.' She picked her coat up from the back of the chair and dived into the pocket. 'I found this notebook and photograph.' She flicked at the edges of the black and white image. 'It's a photograph of you and Lottie Rawlins. The filing clerk from Hut 7. My hut.' She passed the photograph to Gregory and watched him look at it, pursing his lips before letting out a long sigh. 'Looks like you both are having a cosy chat in a tearoom, somewhere,' she said.

'What do you want me to say?'

'Why were you meeting her?'

'If I was to say it was work related, work at the Park that I cannot discuss, would that satisfy you?' asked Gregory.

Hana shook her head. 'No. It wouldn't.'

'Didn't think so.' He tapped the arm of the chair with his fingertips, the burnt skin across the top of his hand tightening and relaxing as he did so. 'If you think—'

'You're having an affair?' Hana cut in. 'No, Gregory, I don't,' she said. Then softer. 'I know you better than that. Even now.'

He looked up at her and she saw a flash of pain in his eyes, before he masked it. 'Even now?' He looked right into her eyes. 'What does that mean?'

'Even now, despite everything, despite how we've . . .' she gestured between them, the gap representing the wasteland that had once been their marriage, 'I know you're the same man who still values loyalty and protection.'

Gregory ran his finger around his shirt collar, easing the fabric from his skin. He still insisted on his collars being starched, even though they irritated the scar tissue from time to time. 'We used to be better at this,' he said eventually. 'At . . . at being us.'

Hana nodded. 'I know.' She looked down, not wishing him to see the tears gathering in her eyes. He may be the one she could trust, and the reason why she was here talking to him about work, but it was only work allowing that togetherness. As a couple, that unity had disappeared and yet, here they were – trusting each other. How could they trust each other with matters of national security, but not matters of the heart? 'I miss you.' The words were out before she'd even given them thought. 'I mean – I miss being us. I miss being able to tell you everything that I'm thinking and feeling.' The admission surprised Hana as much as it appeared to surprise Gregory. She met his gaze, and she could see so much of her own sorrow reflecting at her.

Gregory looked away first, turning his gaze back to the photograph, his hand trembling. 'I'm not that person anymore, Hana. I lost all that in the accident.'

'I wish it was different,' she whispered. 'I'm sorry.'

'You're not to blame. And I don't want your pity.'

Hana wiped at the tears from her face. 'I've never pitied you. I was always your ally,' she said softly. 'All I wanted was for you to let me in so I could be there for you.'

It was a long moment before Gregory spoke. 'I know. I rather think I pitied myself.' He took a deep breath. 'I've only ever wanted what's best for you, and I'm not that.'

Hana didn't know what to say. Gregory had spent the past two years building barriers around himself, shutting her out and now, at the eleventh hour, he was letting her in. She had a tiny glimpse into what he was thinking. There had been a time when she knew without him saying anything and vice versa. It was so tragic the way they had lost each other and what they had.

Gregory cleared his throat. 'Hana, about what happened just now, out on the drive.'

'What?' She forced herself to concentrate on what he was saying, disappointed the small moment of what felt so intimate had gone.

'Don't you think it's a bit of a coincidence that Robert was there?'

Hana frowned, not liking what she was about to say but compelled to be honest. The irony of that notion wasn't lost on her, either. 'It did cross my mind,' she confessed. 'But he was watching out for me.'

'Watching out for you or watching you? They're not the same thing.'

Hana twiddled her wedding ring, not wanting to face up to the nagging thought in the back of her mind that had been there since it happened. 'I know what you're saying, but how would he have known that I had found something?'

'Lucky guess? Spoke to the landlady after you left? Did you come straight home?'

Slowly Hana shook her head. 'I pulled over a little way up the road. Just for a few minutes.' Had that been enough time for Robert to speak to Mrs Kidson? Oh, God, she hated the thought that Robert was involved in what had happened. It couldn't be true. He'd already told her he was at the Park to find out what was going on. Had he been using her? Winning her trust? Letting her find the answers and bringing them to him on a plate? Had she really been played so easily? The thought made her want to be sick. She should have seen this coming a mile off.

'What's in the book?' asked Gregory.

'I don't know yet. It's all in Japanese. I haven't had time to translate it.' Hana dabbed at her nose with her hanky. 'I shouldn't even be telling you all this.'

'Then why are you?'

Hana met his gaze. 'Apart from my dad, you're the only person I can trust.'

Gregory raised an eyebrow. 'Even though I can't explain the photograph?'

'I don't know what your role in all this is,' replied Hana. 'But of all the things I've doubted in recent weeks, your integrity has never been one of them. It was one of the first things about you I fell in love with when we first met. Your integrity, and also your loyalty.' She ran her fingertip around the edge of the notebook. 'Even when you came back, changed, and you shut me out, you did it because you thought it was the right thing to do. You pushed me away because you thought, still think, it's best for me. And despite all that, you never once lied to me. You did all this because you truly believed it was right.'

'Hana . . .' Gregory began softly.

'I've watched you drag yourself through so much pain, just to walk again, and even when that wasn't enough, you carried on forcing yourself to do more, so you could return to work and do your duty.' Hana gripped the book. 'You've stayed loyal to your job and your country, even when it cost you so much. And cost us so much, too.'

She saw him physically wince at the reference to his injuries, and even though she knew he didn't like it, she reached out and held his scarred hand. For once he didn't pull away. She carried on, her voice steady. She didn't know if she'd ever get this moment to talk to him like this again. 'Whatever has broken between us, I still trust you. I've always trusted you. You've never lied to me, even when the lies might have been kinder than the truth.'

'I'm not sure I deserve your loyalty,' said Gregory softly.

'And I'm not sure I deserve yours, either,' replied Hana.

They sat in a heavy silence that was almost unbearable. There wasn't even the usual ticking of the clock. Hana noticed the hands hadn't moved in all the time they had been here. Time had stood still. It somehow felt appropriate.

It was Gregory who broke the silence first. He moved his hand from Hana's. 'I'm glad we were able to speak. I just wish we'd done this sooner.'

'Me too.'

'Look, I don't mean to sound harsh or callous, but your safety is a priority. I wouldn't be able to live with myself if something happened to you. No matter what our relationship is. So, listen carefully, all right?'

Hana forced herself to keep up with the switch in direction and pace of the conversation. There certainly wasn't much time for sentimentality in this game. 'All right,' she agreed, sitting up straighter, giving Gregory her full attention.

'There are some people who desperately want to know certain intelligence your father had been gathering,' he began.

'You know?'

'Yes.'

'Since when?'

'From the outset. That's why I was against you working at the Park. I knew it would be dangerous.'

'But you weren't allowed to say anything?'

'Not outright.' Gregory ran his hand through his hair. 'I'm using my discretionary powers now. I could probably get in a lot of trouble.'

'How much trouble?'

'That doesn't matter. Listen, there are at least three people who want that information, each for their own purposes,' said Gregory. 'Do not trust anyone. And I mean anyone. You are key to discovering the information, and some people will want to know it, others will want it kept quiet. Some people don't even want to run the risk of the information being discovered. I'm going to take an educated guess that your father has written the information down in code. A cipher even. And you are the only person who would know how to break that cipher. Which is why I assume you were approached by the Park in the first place.'

'Do you know what the information is? You seem to know an awful lot,' she said.

Gregory hesitated for a second. 'Yes. I do. It's a name. And I suspect there's some information to back that up.'

Hana nodded. 'The day Dad was run down, we had been doing a crossword together. Just before he left the house, he gave me the paper and said I needed to finish it.'

'And did you?'

'No. With all that happened, I totally forgot about it,' said Hana. 'Until the other day. I happened to pick it up and look at the crossword. He'd left me a message in Japanese. A coded message.'

'Why am I not surprised your father would do that?' Gregory said with a smile. 'Have you deciphered the code?'

'Yes, but it doesn't make sense. It just says, RAT. NAME. REPEAT.'

Gregory frowned. 'Can I see it?'

'That's another thing. It's missing. I don't know if I've lost it or if it's been stolen. But I can't work out what he was trying to tell me. He must have only had seconds to leave that code for me. RAT, that must mean a spy, doesn't it?'

'Yes. That's my thinking,' agreed Gregory. 'NAME. Alfred wants you to find the name or give you the name.'

'Yes, but what does the REPEAT bit mean?'

'I'm not sure.' A look of concern crossed Gregory's face. 'You know there are people who don't want you to find it.'

'They've not done a very good job of stopping me yet.'

'The emphasis on the word "yet",' said Gregory. 'There are others who want the information and are letting you do all the legwork. After which—'

'After which I'll no longer be of any use to them,' cut in Hana, as the severity of her situation began to dawn on her. 'How do I know who to trust?'

'You don't. When you've worked it out, you need to tell me immediately and I'll go to the commander with it. After that, you go to MI5. Bypass whoever recruited you. Go straight to the top. Once the information has been shared, you won't be in so much danger.'

'I was rather hoping I wouldn't be in any danger,' replied Hana.

Gregory gave a small smile at her attempted humour. 'You'll be out of danger once the person has been identified and removed, together with their contacts.'

They sat in silence while Hana absorbed everything Gregory had said. 'Thank you,' she said finally.

'For what?'

'For trusting me and being the one I can trust.'

A sadness filled his eyes. 'It's how it was always supposed to be,' he said quietly. Then before Hana could say anything, he was on his feet. 'I'd say look at the time, but the blasted thing has stopped. I'll sort it out now before I go to bed.'

Hana looked on as Gregory lifted the Japanese mantle clock down from its position on the shelf above the Aga, placing it on the table. She loved that clock. Her parents had brought it back from Japan with them and gifted it to Hana when she moved into Tall Trees. The casing was brass and looked almost like a lantern with gold scrollwork decorating the top. There was an intricate blue and gold decorated plate that sat behind the mechanism. It was a beautiful piece of art in its own right.

She watched as Gregory inserted the key. He went to turn it, then stopped. 'Ah, nearly forgot,' he said. 'This winds anticlockwise.' He began to turn the key. 'I always thought it was because it was Japanese, but apparently not. The one in my office is anticlockwise, too.'

Hana had stopped listening. She grabbed Gregory's arm. 'Oh, my goodness. I'm such an idiot!' She jumped to her feet.

'What's the matter?' asked Gregory, stopping what he was doing.

'Backwards. The clock is wound backwards. It's a Japanese clock.'

'Sorry, I'm still not following you.'

'I need to go to the Park,' said Hana, already racing towards the door.

'Hana, what's going on?'

'I'm sorry, I've got to go.'

'Hana! Wait! I'll drive you.' Gregory hurried out of the room, his stick clicking on the floorboards.

Less than fifteen minutes later, Hana was bursting into the room in Hut 7, where Chatfield and Derek were still working.

Hana rushed over to her desk. 'The Japanese intercept I've been working on,' she said, as she grabbed the papers from the tray.

Chatfield didn't seem at all surprised by her presence and came over to the desk, as did Derek.

'What are we looking at?' asked Derek once Hana had organised the pieces of paper.

Her hands were shaking as she picked up the intercept. 'We've been reading it wrong. Or at least I have,' she said. 'I knew there was something strange about these intercepts that all begin with the same code, but I couldn't work out what.'

'Care to enlighten us?' said Chatfield.

'The codes need to be reversed.' Hana was now writing the coded groups of letters backwards.

Derek took the sheet from her. 'I'll read it out to you.' He began reading the codes out in reverse.

'Now, we need to start again,' said Hana. 'OPRK. Derek, check that against the log. I'll bet that's the date code.'

Derek grabbed the log. 'Yes. You're right. That's the date and time window.'

Hana could feel the excitement building inside her. What if they could crack this code tonight? 'Right. Next one. RWAB.'

Derek immediately began looking through the logbooks. Chatfield picked up the naval codebook. 'Here we go,' he said after a while. 'Deep-water rendezvous point.'

They spent the next two hours mapping out the codes and working backwards to decode them. With each part of the intercept they broke, the excitement and tension mounted. Every now and then Hana had to take a moment to calm herself. They couldn't afford to make any mistakes.

'Let's just take stock of what we've got,' said Chatfield. He rolled his shoulders as they laid out the index cards on which they had been writing the decoded message. 'Snow is falling on the silver eel,' he read.

'Silver eel has to be a submarine,' said Derek.

'Snow? Either of you know what that could be?' asked Chatfield.

'It's come up a few times recently, but we don't know what it means yet,' said Hana.

Chatfield read some more of the message. 'There's a deep-water rendezvous, and then this part says they are rising to the sun. It sounds to me like they're surfacing.'

'Meeting another sub or a boat when they surface?' suggested Derek.

'Oh, my God,' said Hana. Both Derek and Chatfield looked at her. 'I think I know what snow is.'

'Well, don't keep it to yourself, girl,' said Chatfield.

'Wait a minute.' She rushed over to the index cards, flicking through them at speed. 'Snow. This has come up several times. I asked Lottie about it, but she thought it was to do with the weather.' Hana pulled out an index card and held it triumphantly in the air. 'She must have missed this one.' She hurried back to her desk and put it down for Chatfield and Derek to read. 'Snow is the nickname of a German scientist.' She looked from one man to the other. 'They are not talking about transporting supplies between Germany and Japan. They're talking about transporting a person. *Senshi.* That means an expert or specialist. Senshi Gruber.'

'And what does Senshi Gruber specialise in?' asked Chatfield.

Hana gulped. 'His background is pharmaceuticals.' She looked at the faces of the two men.

'Who is he meeting in Japan?' asked Derek.

Hana went back to the intercept and cross-referenced against their notes. It took several minutes but she came up with a name. '*Chishiki*.'

'Means knowledge,' said Derek.

'It's a codename,' said Hana. 'Do we have anything on who this might be?'

'Does it really matter, though?' asked Derek. 'I don't think it takes a genius to work out what's going on here.'

'Chemical warfare,' whispered Hana as Derek uttered an expletive under his breath.

'We need to pass on this information immediately,' said Chatfield. 'We've got the date, time, rendezvous point and confirmation that an expert in pharmaceuticals is being sent to Japan.'

Chatfield strode over to his desk and snatched up the secure telephone. 'I need naval intelligence.' He spoke into the receiver with authority. 'Priority One. High-value personnel transfer. Code Red.'

While he waited to be put through, he turned to Hana. 'Well done, Hana.'

'Yes, well done, old girl,' said Derek. 'With any luck the sub will be intercepted before Gruber is anywhere near the rendezvous point.'

'I hope so,' said Hana glibly. Although it was something to be celebrated, she didn't feel like doing so. Her decrypting may well save hundreds or thousands of lives but ultimately it also meant lives would be lost when the threat was removed.

'Tea? Coffee? asked Derek. 'Hang on a bit longer and you can get breakfast in the canteen.'

Hana hadn't realised how long she had been at the Park that night. Hours. It was pitch-black outside. In all the excitement of cracking the code, she remembered Gregory had said he would wait for her. Surely, he would have given up by now and gone home.

Chatfield had said she could go home or bed down under her desk for what was left of the night.

'I'll just double-check Gregory went home,' she said. 'If by some miracle he's still here, I'll see you in the morning. If not, I'll be back in a minute.'

She wasn't sure why she was checking; she was certain Gregory would have left. She stepped out of the hut, the cold of the night momentarily taking the air from her lungs, and tugged her coat tighter around her as she headed over to the car park. To her surprise, the Austin Ten was parked exactly where it always was.

She rushed over to it. The windows were all steamed up on the inside, but she could see Gregory's head leaning against the glass of the driver's door. She tapped on the window, and he jerked awake immediately. Hana hurried around to the other side of the car and jumped into the passenger seat.

'Please don't tell me you've been sitting in the car all this time?' she said, genuinely concerned for him.

'Not quite,' he said. 'I managed to blag a cup of tea from inside the mansion house.'

'How long have you been out here for?'

Gregory checked his watch. 'Long enough.'

'You're not answering my question.'

'It doesn't matter.' He smiled. 'Have you done whatever it was you needed to do?'

Hana couldn't help the beam of pride spreading across her face. 'I couldn't possibly say.'

Gregory smiled wider. 'I take it you're all right to go home now?'

'Yes. Not that I'll get much sleep, but yes, home.'

Gregory started the engine and headed out of the Park. Hana could feel her eyes closing before they'd even reached the main road. She allowed herself to be pulled into a sleep where she heard Gregory whisper, 'Well done, darling.'

Chapter 23

The following morning when Hana awoke, for a moment she couldn't work out what the heavy feeling in her heart was. Then she remembered Audrey, and a wave of sadness flooded her.

She got up and was strangely disappointed to find that Gregory had already left the house. She and Gregory had settled on some kind of truce, almost as if they had a new understanding of each other. It was a feeling of relief, but also heartbreaking that it had all come too late.

Hana sat in the kitchen with a freshly made cup of tea. Being alone gave her the time and space she needed to think what she was going to do now.

She couldn't go to the commander yet. What was she going to tell him? It wasn't like she had discovered anything significant last night. What she needed to do was to work out what was written in Audrey's book and try to find the cipher messages her dad had undoubtedly left for her somewhere.

The telephone ringing cut through her thoughts. It was her mother.

'Hello, dear. Is everything all right? I haven't heard from you for a couple of days?'

'Sorry, Mum,' said Hana, feeling immediately guilty for neglecting her. 'It's been really busy at work. I was going to call by later to see if you were going to the hospital today. I'd like to see Dad.'

'That's good. The hospital said it may take a couple of days for the sedatives to leave his system, and then after that, well, it's up to Dad.'

There was the tiniest of fractures in Pamela's voice as she spoke.

'Dad will do everything he can to come back to us,' said Hana. 'He won't leave us without a fight.'

And it was true. Hana had every faith in her father. He loved his family without condition, and if sheer willpower was all that he had to recover from his head injury, then she knew he would do it.

She had no sooner finished the call with her mother and put the phone back in its cradle when there was a knock at the door.

Hana was surprised to see Robert standing there. He was looking especially handsome, in his uniform, hands in his pockets, the cowlick of dark hair smoothed back, his rich brown eyes and a small smile playing at the corners of his mouth. He had no right to look quite so handsome.

'Good morning, ma'am,' he said, giving her a casual salute.

Hana laughed. 'Please, ma'am is sweet, but it makes me feel like an old lady.'

'Is . . .?' He nodded towards the house, not needing to finish his question.

'No. Gregory's already left. Anyway, what are you doing here? I wasn't expecting to see you.'

Robert stepped forward, scooped his arm around Hana's waist and edged her back into the hallway, kicking the door closed behind him, before kissing her.

Hana felt her body involuntarily stiffen, and she cut short the kiss. 'Don't, you'll have the neighbours talking.'

'I just wanted to check you were OK after yesterday.'

'I'm OK. Every time I think of Audrey, I can barely believe what happened.'

'I know. It's heartbreaking,' agreed Robert. He took a closer look at Hana. 'How's your eye feeling?'

'Not too bad,' replied Hana. 'The bruising is starting to come out already.'

'If I ever get my hands on who did this to you, they'll be sorry.'

'Thank you for your chivalry,' said Hana, with a smile. 'Look, I really need to get to work.'

'Which is exactly why I'm here. I'll take you in the car.'

'That's great. Thank you. I've just got to get a different handbag after mine was stolen last night.'

'Well, you might not have to,' said Robert. It was only then Hana noticed that he had one hand behind his back. With the flourish of a magician, Robert held aloft Hana's bag.

'Oh, my goodness!' Hana couldn't believe it. She took the bag from Robert and inspected it, just to be certain it was hers. She looked inside, surprised to see her mirror, lipstick and purse were still there. The money had gone from the purse, but she didn't care about that. She was more pleased to have her bag back. It was one of her favourites. Gregory had bought it for her several years ago, before the war, when they had gone to London for the weekend to celebrate their wedding anniversary. 'Where did you find it?'

'A couple of streets down,' replied Robert. 'I had a scout around the area last night. I saw it there, dumped on the grass verge. I didn't wanna come back with it. I figured Gregory wouldn't be too pleased to see me.'

He wasn't wrong there, but Hana chose not to acknowledge the remark. In some sort of strange way, it felt a little disloyal to Gregory. 'Seeing as there's just the money missing, I think it's safe to assume that's what they were after.'

'Seems that way. You didn't have anything else in there?'

Hana gave a shrug. 'No. Nothing.' She took her coat from the peg.

'You didn't find anything at Audrey's place last night, then?' asked Robert, taking the coat and helping her on with it.

Hana hesitated momentarily. 'No. Nothing,' she repeated, glad she had her back to him. She felt his hands rest on her shoulders. Hana turned around and buttoned up her coat. 'We should get a move on.'

'Yeah. Sure. Come on.'

'I suppose someone should tell Bill Crosslands about Audrey,' said Hana, as Robert turned out of the drive and onto the road. 'It should come from me really, before he hears it on the grapevine.'

'Best let the military police deal with that,' said Robert. 'Were he and Audrey that close?'

'I think she was very fond of him,' said Hana. 'I'm not sure how he felt about Audrey. He's quite the show off really. He likes the women to fuss over him.'

'I gathered that, from that time I met him in the pub. I haven't got competition, have I?'

'Not where Crosslands is concerned,' replied Hana.

'But somewhere else?'

Hana threw Robert a sideways look. Was he jealous? It was flattering that someone should feel that way over her, but at the same time, she wasn't sure she liked the sense of ownership that came with it. She made a display of laughing and theatrically rolling her eyes. 'A girl has to keep a man on his toes.'

Robert reached across and took her hand, kissing her knuckles as he drove along. She was glad he didn't pursue the conversation further.

By the time they'd reached the Park and gone into the hut, news of Audrey's death had already been broken.

'Chatfield just told us about Audrey,' said Jenny, coming up to Hana and giving her a hug in an unusual display of affection. 'Are you all right? It must have been awful for you.'

'It was such a shock,' admitted Hana, the emotion of the previous day rising back up.

'Oh, Hana,' it was Lottie. 'I can't believe it about Audrey.' She dabbed her handkerchief to her eyes. 'And you found her. You poor thing.' She too gave Hana a hug. As she did so, memories of the previous day and evening resurfaced in sharp focus.

Lottie pulled back. 'Whatever happened to your eye?'

'I caught it on the door,' said Hana quickly, not wanting to get into the detail of the assault. Compared to what happened to Audrey, it felt insignificant.

Derek gave Hana a nod from across the room, then chatted with Robert for a few minutes, before Chatfield told them they needed to get back to work, despite the difficult news of the morning. A quiet, respectful hush fell across the room as they went about their duties.

It wasn't until their mid-morning break, they got to speak again. Hana and Jenny were on the same break and took a walk around the grounds of the Park.

'No one would tell us anything yesterday,' said Jenny. 'When you didn't come back, I knew something was amiss, but I never for one moment thought Audrey was dead. I can't believe she took her own life. Poor thing. I knew she was homesick, but not suicidal.'

'None of it makes sense,' said Hana, as they rounded the corner. She let out a small groan. 'Oh, God, there's Bill Crosslands.'

Bill was sitting on a bench, smoking a cigarette, his head bowed. He looked up as they approached and got to his feet.

'Bill . . .' began Jenny.

'It's all right. I heard,' he said. He looked at Hana. 'You found her. It's so bloody awful. I can't take it in.' He stretched his finger and thumb across his brow line.

Hana reached out and rubbed Bill's arm. She might not be his biggest fan, but she wasn't totally heartless. 'We're all finding it hard to take in,' she said.

'Did she ever say anything to you about the way she was feeling?' asked Jenny.

Hana appreciated Jenny's forthright nature at that moment.

Bill shook his head. 'No. That's just it. I thought she was happy. We had been out for a drink a couple of times, you know . . . I'm not saying it was anything official, but it felt like we were on the brink of something.'

It seemed an odd thing to say, given that Hana had seen the love letter Audrey had written to Bill, but she didn't want to bring that up now and risk him closing up. Instead, encouraged by his willingness to talk, Hana took the opportunity to question him. 'Did Audrey ever mention anyone following her? Or seeing someone she knew, but wasn't keen to speak to?'

Bill frowned and gave Hana a look, as if she had just asked a ridiculous question. 'Someone following her? No. Not at all. Why are you even asking that?' He stopped in mid-rise of the cigarette to his mouth. 'Wait a minute, do you think it was foul play?'

'No. Not at all,' said Hana. 'She just mentioned to me once that she'd seen someone hanging around the cricket field. I wondered if it was a one-off.'

'She never said anything to me,' replied Bill. He blew out a long breath and ground his cigarette into the grass with his shoe. 'I need to get back to work.'

After saying their goodbyes, Hana and Jenny made their way back to the hut. Only a few more hours and then Hana would be over at the training centre. Gosh, she felt shattered. The intensity of the work was bad enough, but coupled with her personal life, finding out who the spy was and Audrey's death, not to mention Alfred's accident, she wasn't sure she had any room for anything else, let alone training. The only thing to look forward to was seeing her dad that evening. She hoped she'd see some signs of improvement, now that they were slowly bringing him out of his induced coma.

Lunchtime couldn't come soon enough. At least she'd have an hour to relax a little. Hana went over to the canteen and sat down with her tray of food. It was sausages and boiled potatoes with onions and a drop of gravy. The food wasn't exactly great at the Park, but the kitchen staff did their best with what they had and normally Hana enjoyed her food. Today, however, her appetite had deserted her. She had no mind for it whatsoever, but it felt criminal to waste it when so many people were going without, so she forced herself to eat as much as she could.

She was glad Jenny was on a different lunchbreak today. Hana wasn't feeling the best company and had left the canteen earlier than needed. Since the recent rain they'd had wasn't expected today, she took the long way out of the Park, not rushing to reach the training centre in Church Green Road. Instead, she found herself wandering in the direction of the pavilion. The last place she'd seen Audrey alive.

The thought caused a little stab at her heart.

The cricket field was empty as Hana followed the path around towards the pavilion. She thought of the other night when she'd stood on the porch. She stopped for a moment. She had assumed she hadn't been seen. She looked across the field to the tree the man had been standing under. She decided to test her theory and changed direction, walking over to the oak tree.

From the tree, she had a clear view of the entrance that Audrey had come through. Hana walked around the tree, spotting the other entrance directly behind her.

Hana's theory had been that the man had entered the park from this entrance so he could track Audrey without being seen. She looked towards the pavilion. Another tree obscured her line of sight to the building, but if she moved to the right, she could see it. Hana tested each sight line a couple of times, adjusting her position each time. There was no way she could see both the entrance that Audrey had taken and the pavilion at the same time. She hoped that meant the man hadn't seen her.

Hana checked her watch; she should make her way around to the training centre now. She was just about to leave, when movement from the pavilion caught her eye. Instinctively, she pushed herself back against the tree.

Slowly, she moved a fraction to the right. With it now being daylight, she could clearly see two figures on the porch of the pavilion. A man and a woman. They had come out of the pavilion and were now pausing to talk to each other. Then the man leaned down and drew the woman into a kiss. And not the sort of kiss you gave a friend. It was a full-on, mouth-to-mouth kiss that lasted for several seconds.

Then they pulled apart and the woman pulled on a hat before they went off in opposite directions.

'Wow,' said Hana out loud. Neither Bill nor Lottie looked as distraught just then, as they had made out earlier.

Chapter 24

When Hana came out of the training centre that afternoon, she wasn't at all surprised to find Robert waiting for her, his car parked in the road outside.

'People are going to start talking,' she said as she got in the passenger seat.

'Let them. Maybe we should give them something to talk about,' said Robert, leaning over and kissing her.

Again, Hana pulled back, looking around and relieved to see the road was empty. 'Not here,' she said and then noticed the hurt look on Robert's face. 'Sorry. I just don't want to be the subject of gossip. It's been a long day, and I'm shattered. I'm going to see my dad tonight.'

'On your own?'

'No. With my mum.'

'You want me to drop you straight to your mum's house?' asked Robert, starting the engine.

'I'll go home first,' said Hana. 'I want to get out of these work clothes and freshen up and have something to eat.'

'Will he be there?'

Hana had noticed that more and more often Robert didn't refer to Gregory by name. 'Who? Gregory? I've no idea.' She had secretly hoped he would be. After seeing Lottie and Bill together that afternoon, she had initially been shocked, but as she'd thought about it, she'd also been relieved. She wasn't quite sure how it all fitted in, but she was certain that whatever had been going on with Lottie and Gregory in that photograph, they weren't involved romantically. The same couldn't be said for Bill and Lottie. In fact, Hana was a little outraged that Bill was pretending to be upset about Audrey when he was carrying on with someone else. And as for Lottie, there was something bothering Hana that she couldn't quite put her finger on. She wanted to talk through her half-formed ideas with Gregory.

She looked across at Robert, trying to force a smile but falling short.

'Hopefully, you won't have to put up with the situation for much longer,' he said, mistaking her expression to be because Gregory might be there, rather than not. 'I had some good news this afternoon.'

'Oh, what's that?'

'I've got somewhere to live. A place of my own.' He grinned at Hana now, looking very pleased with himself. 'I pulled a few strings, applied a bit of leverage, and found a house here in Bletchley. I get the keys in the morning.'

'That's good,' said Hana. 'Better than living above the pub.'

'You don't seem too happy. I thought you'd be pleased.' He ran the tip of his finger down her cheek. 'You know, you could always move in. Maybe not right away, but in time.'

Hana had to stifle a gasp. 'Move in?'

Robert looked genuinely hurt. 'I was kinda hoping for a more enthusiastic response.'

'I'm just a bit shocked,' said Hana. 'We've not talked about this before. It's a bit further down the line.'

'Looks like we're talking about it now.' He ran his hand across his chin. 'I thought you'd jump at the chance to leave Scrooge.'

'Don't call him that,' said Hana.

'What? Scrooge? But he is.'

'He's not. He's just—'

'Miserable and bitter because he's got a mangled leg.' Robert started the car.

Hana might have privately, readily agreed with this before, but somehow, hearing Robert say it out loud made it sound . . . distasteful. Mean, even. 'He's had a lot to deal with.'

'Look, I get it. This is happening fast, I know that,' said Robert. 'But I thought it's what you wanted. I thought you were done with your marriage. Have I got that wrong?'

'I need time. It's a big deal for me and I don't want to rush into anything or feel pressured into a decision.'

They finished the journey in silence. When Robert pulled up outside Hana's house he turned to face her. 'Hey, sweetheart,' he said gently, cupping her face in his hand. 'We could be good together. Don't let guilt ruin everything.'

'It's too soon for us to think about anything like moving in together,' said Hana. She took a deep breath, summoning up the courage to be totally honest. 'Whatever this thing is between us, it could very well fizzle out as swiftly as it came. Let's not get ahead of ourselves.'

Robert lifted her chin so she had to look at him. 'Life is fragile. This war has taught me that you gotta grab your happiness where and when you can. Don't put it off because you might not get a tomorrow.'

Hana gave a small smile before getting out of the car. He blew a kiss in her direction and then drove off. She watched the car pull out of the drive before letting herself into the house and closing the door behind her, she rested her head against the oak. She wanted everything to be all right, she really did. She just wasn't sure what all right was anymore.

A noise behind her, had her spinning around.

'Sorry, I didn't mean to startle you.' It was Gregory coming down the stairs. 'I heard the car pull up.'

What he didn't say was that he'd probably not only heard the car but witnessed Hana and Robert in the vehicle. She felt a flush of embarrassment swoosh up her neck. 'I didn't realise you were home,' she said.

'I've only been in ten minutes.'

'Actually, I'm glad you're here,' said Hana. 'There's something I want to talk to you about.'

'That sounds serious.'

'Let's go through to the kitchen. I'll make a cup of tea and tell you.' Hana moved around Gregory, and he followed her through the house. 'I went for a walk at lunchtime today,' she began as she filled the kettle and put in on the Aga to boil. 'I ended up at the cricket field at Bletchley.'

'Right,' said Gregory, taking two cups from the cupboard and putting them out on the counter.

'I saw Lottie Rawlins there. She was coming out of the pavilion with someone. A man.'

Gregory raised his eyebrows. 'I take it she didn't see you.'

'No. The man was Bill Crosslands.' Hana looked at Gregory to try to gauge his reaction, but his expression was neutral.

'Was that the same Bill Crosslands who Audrey was keen on?'

Hana shouldn't be surprised that Gregory knew all this. 'Yes. It's just that when they went to say goodbye to each other, they kissed. And not a fleeting, peck-on-the-cheek type of kiss either.'

Again, she looked for a reaction, but still Gregory remained unreadable. 'Maybe he wasn't so keen on Audrey after all.'

'That's not how either of them were behaving this morning,' said Hana. 'This morning, Bill was very upset. And Lottie was crying.'

There was a small silence before Gregory spoke. 'This morning was how he wanted you to see him. And Lottie, too, for that matter. This afternoon, not so much.'

'Exactly.' Hana waited hoping Gregory would say something else, but as the kettle began to whistle, he lifted it from the Aga, sloshed a drop around in the pot to warm it, before adding the loose tea from the caddy and then filling it up with the boiling water. Hana gave an exasperated sigh. 'I don't know what to make of it.'

'It would seem Crosslands is something of a player,' said Gregory eventually.

'It makes me want to punch him right on the nose,' said Hana.

Gregory burst out laughing. 'I don't think I've ever heard you say that.'

Hana laughed despite herself. 'It just makes me angry, that's all.'

The smile dropped from Gregory's face. 'Love brings out the best and the worst in people.'

Hana couldn't reply to that. The comment struck her right in the heart. Whether it was intentional or not didn't matter, the sentiment applied to her. 'I should go and get ready,' she said, not looking at Gregory. 'Mum's going to pick me up soon. We're going to see Dad.'

'Ah, yes. They're beginning to take him off the sedatives, I believe.'

Hana was surprised Gregory was aware of this. 'Yes. That's right.'

'I . . . er . . . I've been keeping in touch with the hospital,' said Gregory.

'Oh, right.' She had no idea Gregory had been in direct contact with the hospital. It was a nice thought. 'I need to get freshened up.' They moved awkwardly around each other. She hated that the atmosphere between them had changed so quickly again.

'I need to get on with some work,' said Gregory, heading out of the kitchen.

'Did you want to come tonight – to see Dad?' She wasn't quite sure why she'd asked him. It was impulsive but also felt like the right thing to do.

Gregory hesitated before answering. 'Maybe not tonight. I think they only allow two people at a time,' he replied. 'I don't want to hog anyone's visiting time. But I would like to see Alfred, maybe another night when no one else can make it.'

'That sounds like a good idea.'

'Thank you for asking, though.' Gregory carried on down the hall.

There was a sadness in his eyes when he'd looked up at her just now. And watching him walk down the hallway, he was carrying himself differently. Not so upright and stiff as he usually did. Instead, his head was dipped and there was a sag to his shoulders.

Hana went upstairs and washed before slipping into a clean dress and brushing her hair, still contemplating the change in Gregory. Her hand paused, mid-brush, and she lowered it slowly as understanding settled over her like the evening shadow. It made her want to cry. The anger had been replaced by acceptance. A sad acceptance laced with defeat. Not the peaceful kind, but the devastating sort that comes with knowing that love isn't enough.

*

Pamela and Hana sat either side of Alfred's bed, watching his deep and regular breathing. Hana wasn't sure what she had expected, but she had hoped there would be some sort of notable difference to her father, now that the amount of sedative had been reduced. She held his hand, as she always did when she visited.

'It's been really busy at the Park, Dad,' she said, remembering that the nurse had told them to speak to him, that their voices would filter through to his subconscious and help to pull him out of the deep sleep he was in. If nothing else, it would be a comfort to his mind. 'I was looking at the crossword you gave me just before your accident.' Hana paused, checking for any reaction to what was potentially a difficult subject. She glanced over at her mother, to ensure she didn't think it inappropriate to mention it, but Pamela gave her an encouraging smile, so Hana continued. 'I saw the last clue you had written, and I think I've worked out the next bit, well, partly anyway.'

As her father's breathing continued, Hana realised that there wasn't going to be some fanciful miracle that evening. Her father wasn't going to suddenly wake up at the sound of her voice and explain all about the crossword clue. It had been a ridiculously naive thought of hers.

'I've got today's paper,' said her mother, looking at Alfred. 'I'll read you some of the headlines.'

Hana sat back and listened to her mother. She sounded like one of the BBC broadcasters as she read the top stories of the day. It reminded Hana of when she was a child and Pamela used to read to her and Tom each night, and then Alfred would take over and read a short story in Japanese. It was such a nostalgic and comforting memory of when life was simple, just the four of them. The Great War was over and the next five years had been bliss. But now, here they were in the middle of a second world war, and as a direct result, Alfred was unconscious in a coma and she, of all people, had been sent in to flush out a spy. It was all so surreal, and yet so very real at the same time.

Hana and her mother stayed with Alfred for another hour, then it was time to leave.

'Shall I drop you home?' asked Pamela as they neared the village.

'Actually, can I come to yours? I'd like to catch up with Gwen.' Hana was conscious she hadn't spent much time with her sister-in-law lately.

'Gwen was asking after you this morning, actually. She bumped into Gregory the other day.'

'Oh, really? Where was that?' Gregory hadn't mentioned it, but then it wasn't like she and Gregory shared the small details in their life anymore.

'It was outside the doctors. Gwen had to take Freddie, he's had an awful cough. She wanted to get him seen to. He's fine, though, nothing to worry about.'

'That's good,' said Hana. 'Had Gregory been to see Doctor Peters?'

'I really don't know. It's not the sort thing you ask, is it?' said Pamela, as if Hana was a child who needed reminding of their manners.

Hana didn't pursue the conversation, but it bothered her that there might be something wrong with Gregory. She made a mental note to ask him tomorrow.

They arrived at Bramble House and Gwen pulled open the door, pleased to see Hana.

'Hello, stranger,' she said, giving Hana a quick hug. 'How's it all going at work?'

'Oh, you know. Same old, same old,' replied Hana. 'Far too boring to even think about, let alone talk about.'

Over a cup of tea, Hana, Gwen and Pamela chatted some more about Alfred and the progress they hoped would happen but countered with caution as they all knew he was far from out of the woods yet. Coming out of the sedation would not be without its own problems.

'We just have to remain positive,' said her mother, getting up from the table. 'Now, you two stay there and chat all you like, I'm off to bed.' She gave them both a peck on the cheek and took herself off upstairs.

'How's Mum holding up?' asked Hana.

'Exactly how you imagine she would,' replied Gwen. 'She is the epitome of remaining positive and not wallowing in self-pity.' She gave Hana a reassuring smile. 'She's fine. Don't worry.'

'I don't know how she does it,' said Hana.

Gwen put her cup down and took a deep breath. 'Hana,' she began.

Hana looked at her sister-in-law, sensing a difficult conversation was about to be had. 'Yes?'

'I saw Gregory yesterday, outside the doctors.'

'I know. Mum said. And I'm glad you mentioned, it saves me the embarrassment of having to ask,' said Hana. 'Is he all right?'

'It depends how you define all right,' said Gwen.

'Physically?'

'Look, I don't know what he was at the doctor's for, if that's what you want to know. He was just coming out. I didn't like to ask.'

'No. Of course not.'

'He seemed sad, is what I noticed. As if he was carrying the weight of the world on his shoulders. I know he can be prickly, but there was something different about him. I just wanted to let you know.' Gwen took a sip of her tea.

Hana had noticed this for herself, but it felt starker having someone else mention it.

'Thank you,' replied Hana. 'He hasn't talked to me about it, but I suppose he's not likely to.'

'You could try asking him, he is your husband. Or at least I think he still is?'

Hana's gaze snapped towards her sister-in-law's. 'What's that supposed to mean?'

Gwen shrugged, seemingly unfazed by the question and tone. 'Has anything else happened between you and Robert Becker?'

Hana hesitated. 'He gives me a lift to work sometimes.'

'Is that all?'

Hana looked down at her now empty cup, as if the answer to all her problems was in the tea leaves. 'I think my marriage might be over, Gwen,' she said quietly. 'I feel like we've reached some sort of understanding, Gregory and I, almost a truce, I suppose, but . . .'

'But, what?'

'But we can't ever go back. We've strayed too far from where we started.'

Gwen looked at her for a long moment. 'Is any of this to do with Robert?'

'Yes and no. I think he has just highlighted how bad things have become between me and Gregory.' Hana put her head in her hands for a moment as she gathered her thoughts. 'I want some happiness in life,' she said. 'I miss being happy.'

'And you really don't think things are going to get better between you and Gregory?' asked Gwen.

'I don't honestly know.' Hana gave a sigh. 'I'm tired, Gwen. I'm tired of trying and getting nothing in return. I'm tired of the atmosphere between us. I'm tired of being alone and I'm tired of being lonely. I want more out of life than to rattle around and simply cohabit with Gregory, as if we are lodgers in the same house. I want to look forward to going home at night, and feel happy to go to bed with someone who loves me, to wake up next to that person. I don't want to be alone anymore. You must understand that, surely?'

Gwen dipped her head. 'Of course I understand that. What do you think I do every day and night?'

'Oh, God. I'm sorry. I didn't mean to be so thoughtless.' Hana sprang to her feet and was at Gwen's side, pulling her in for a hug. How bloody selfish, she was. Hana shouldn't be spouting about being lonely when Gwen was in the exact same boat except it was worse. Gwen loved Tom, and she wanted him back. She had no control over her situation whereas Hana had every control. 'I'm sorry,' she repeated.

'It's all right. Don't give me too much sympathy,' said Gwen, sitting up as Hana let go of her. 'The only way I keep going is not to think about it. Sometimes, though . . . it's just too difficult.'

Hana went over to the dresser and opened the bottom door, hooking out a bottle of port. She poured two glasses and sat back down at the table, sliding a glass over to Gwen. 'I think we both need this tonight.'

Gwen sipped her drink gratefully. 'Do you think you can get everything you're looking for from Robert? Is he really the answer to your happiness?'

'I just feel alive again when I'm with him. Everything seems so much more bearable, nothing seems drab and grey.' But as Hana was saying it, a little voice in the back of her mind reminded her of her doubts. Life with Robert was fun, but was it real? Were his feelings real? She didn't really know him that well and a couple of times recently, she hadn't liked the way he'd behaved. The catty remark directed at Gregory about his leg still bothered her.

'Do you love him?'

Hana's heart threw in a beat before she answered. 'No. I love being with him, but I don't love him.'

'And you don't love Gregory anymore?'

'Loving Gregory is complex and difficult.'

'You didn't answer the question.'

Hana had purposefully tried to swerve Gwen's probing, but she obviously wasn't going to be let off the hook so easily. 'I have never stopped caring about him,' she said at last.

'You still haven't answered the question,' persisted Gwen.

'What's there to say?'

'Gregory still loves you,' said Gwen with an undeniable certainty.

Hana looked at her sister-in-law, whose face was full of concern. There was no judgement. Hana sighed. 'You don't think getting involved with Robert is a good idea, do you?'

'If I'm honest, no. But then I'm not the one in your shoes.' Gwen took another sip of the port. 'Is it really what you want? Long-term, I mean? Or is this just a moment of hedonism? A moment in time where you don't have to think of anyone other than yourself, where there are no consequences? A whirlwind romance where you haven't even touched the surface of real life? I mean, do you really know him?'

'I just want to enjoy life again,' Hana said quietly, looking down at the red liquid in her glass. 'I want to be happy.'

'I know. Don't we all? Just make sure your happiness isn't really here with Gregory. That it isn't just clouded by the small bit of glamour that's walked into your life now and could easily walk right out again.'

'I know all that,' said Hana. 'If I'm honest, I'm not sure Gregory would care if I did leave him.'

'I wouldn't bet on that,' said Gwen.

'It's so hard to think straight at the moment,' confessed Hana. 'I feel hemmed in from all directions. It's like I'm suffocating. I need air but can't find any.'

'Have you thought about having a few days to yourself? To think things through?'

'You mean a holiday?' It was an idea that had been floating around the periphery of Hana's thoughts for several days, but she had pushed it away for it seemed self-indulgent.

'Exactly that,' said Gwen.

'But where would I go?'

Gwen gave a laugh. 'You'd come here, of course. Back in your old room. Pamela would understand. In fact, she'd probably love having you about for a few days.'

Hana mulled Gwen's suggestion over some more. Maybe it wasn't such a bad idea?

She eyed her sister -in-law. 'What are you not telling me?'

Gwen paused. 'I shouldn't be saying anything.'

Hana made a scoffing noise. 'It's a bit late for that.'

Gwen was then silent for few minutes. She finished her drink and then topped up her glass, taking another long sip, before she finally spoke. 'I did not tell you this, all right?'

'All right,' said Hana.

Chapter 25

When Hana came to leave, it was pouring with rain, so her mother insisted on driving her home.

Gregory came out of his study to greet her. 'How is your father?'

'About the same, to be honest. Too early for anything significant to happen.'

She took Audrey's notebook from her bag. 'I was going to try to translate what's in here,' she said.

'Good idea.'

'Do you want to help?' She wasn't quite sure why she wanted Gregory to help her and judging by the flicker of surprise on his face, he wasn't either.

'Yes. Why not?' he replied after a moment's pause.

They went into the living room and Gregory sat down next to Hana on the sofa where she had the notebook open on her lap.

'It's written in Japanese.' Hana moved the book over so Gregory could see.

'Since I know not a word of the language, shall I make notes while you translate?' suggested Gregory.

By all rights, it should have felt awkward sitting there with her husband who she was planning on leaving, albeit for a few days at first, but somehow it didn't. She couldn't remember when they'd last sat this close to one another either. But here they were.

Once Gregory had a pen and piece of paper to hand, Hana began reading the notes in the book.

'These numbers look pretty obvious,' she said. 'Dates and times. Underneath, it says . . . Eagle . . . Sparrow . . . Bench . . . Lake.'

'Seems like Audrey was a birdwatcher,' said Gregory.

Hana was about to dispute this, when she saw a small smile play at the corners of his mouth. She moved on to the next entry, which was a day later and in the evening. 'Hawk . . . Eagle . . . Mutton . . . Sandwich.' The next translation made no more sense than the previous two. 'Sparrow . . . Six . . . Oak . . . Hole.' And so the entries continued with seemingly random words with no connection whatsoever. After they had gone through two pages, Hana slumped back in the sofa. She loved a puzzle, but puzzles needed a pattern – a formula – in order to solve them, and she didn't know where to start. 'I need the key,' she sighed. 'If only Dad was all right. I'm sure he'd work it out.'

'You're overthinking it,' said Gregory, studying the piece of paper he was holding. 'I don't think it's as difficult as you're making it.'

This had Hana sitting forwards again. 'Really? Do you know what it means?'

'Well, not exactly, but I think she's using codenames for people. She's observing them meeting up and possibly noting what they're doing.' He pointed at the first page with his pencil. 'Hawk, Eagle, Sparrow, Nightingale, they're codenames for people. When there's more than one, they're meeting up. When there's only one bird mentioned, they're on their own. The next part could be where she's seen them. On the bench at the lake, that's possibly at the Park. Bletchley, that is, not just a random park.'

'So, Audrey saw two people, Eagle and Sparrow, meet at the bench by the lake at Bletchley,' said Hana. 'And the next entry is Hawk meeting Eagle, and Mutton is where they met, or is Mutton another person?'

'Mutton doesn't fit the pattern of birds,' said Gregory.

'It's a place, then.' Hana gave a small laugh as she unravelled the code. 'Mutton. That's the Shoulder of Mutton pub in the village.'

'Of course,' said Gregory. 'Sandwich, though, I've no idea on that.'

'No. Nor me.'

'And all this is well and good, but without knowing who these people are, it's meaningless.'

'Wait, if Audrey was following people from the Park and she had a photograph of you and Lottie, maybe it was her who took it and it stands to reason that the meeting would surely be in her book.'

'Yes, I suppose so.'

'So, when did you meet Lottie? If we can find the date and time in this book, and Audrey recorded it, we might be able to work out if either of you are mentioned. It might help us somehow.'

Gregory got up and went across the hallway to his study to get his diary, which he then laid out on the coffee table. 'I've met Lottie several times,' he said.

Hana wasn't sure why this bothered her. She had no right to be jealous, and yet it was the exact emotion she was feeling. 'You can't tell me why you met her?'

'You have to trust me,' said Gregory.

Hana took a deep breath, pushing her own feelings to one side. She looked at the date in the diary. Gregory had written "2.15. Dentist". 'Dentist? Whose benefit was that for?' she asked.

'Anyone who looked in my diary,' said Gregory without missing a beat.

'Including me.'

'It's the way it had to be.'

She knew that, but it still hurt. She flicked through the pages of Audrey's notebook and found the date and time. 'Sparrow . . .' She hesitated as she translated the next word, not wanting to say it out loud.

'What does it say?' asked Gregory. He looked at Hana. 'Don't worry about hurting my feelings. What's she called me, Old Buzzard or something?'

'Flamingo,' said Hana hesitantly.

'I can see where she got that idea from,' said Gregory. 'Come on, Hana. It's funny really.'

'Sort of.' Hana didn't really find it funny at all.

'What else does it say?'

'Mutton . . . Jaw.' She looked up at Gregory. 'What does it mean?'

'I met Lottie at the pub. The Shoulder of Mutton and we just talked.'

'Mutton. That was mentioned earlier,' said Hana.

'It's mentioned a couple of times, actually.' Gregory scanned his handwriting. 'Here. Up here and on this one, too.'

'So, the third word is the meeting place,' said Hana. 'What about Jaw?'

'We just spoke. We didn't do anything or go anywhere. And as you can see by the time at the bottom. Where it says Flamingo with an arrow, that's the time I left. I was there ten minutes, that's all.'

'She was spying on people,' said Hana. 'We just don't know who for or why.'

'But it most probably cost Audrey her life.'

'I still can't believe she's really gone,' said Hana, sitting back and closing her eyes. 'It doesn't seem possible.'

'Another casualty of the war,' said Gregory.

'I just keep thinking of all her plans, all the chances she'll never get,' continued Hana. 'We're all just marking time. Believing things will get better or we have another day, tomorrow or the day after to fix things. But Audrey hasn't got any tomorrows. Out of this, it's made me realise that we shouldn't put things off.'

'I suppose we've both been marking time,' said Gregory, his voice gentle, almost contemplative. 'We've been waiting for things to get better, but all the time our tomorrows have slipped away, without us noticing. We let ours go quietly, one by one, or at least I did. I thought there would be another and then there wasn't.'

He hauled himself up, holding his cane for support, before limping out of the room and across the hall to his study. Closing the door behind him.

Hana sat rooted to the spot, unable to speak as the truth of his words pressed heavy against her heart.

*

'Are you feeling all right, Hana?' It was Jenny. They were in Hut 7 the following week, carrying out their usual decoding work which was rather more exciting now they were working on the intercepts coming in about the personnel transfer via a submarine.

'I'm fine,' she replied, giving Jenny a smile. 'Just a little tired, that's all.'

'No time to be tired. There's a war on, in case you had forgotten,' said Jenny, mimicking Chatfield, before returning to her work.

Hana couldn't help raising a smile. Jenny was so deadpan at times with a quick, dry sense of humour. If you weren't quick enough, you'd miss it.

It momentarily took her mind off what she planned to do that evening. Her conversation with Gregory a few nights earlier had reinforced for Hana Gwen's idea of going to stay at Bramble House for a few days. Hana needed some time away from Tall Trees. She needed clear space to think about what her future might look like. The answer seemed clearer each day – her marriage was over, and she and Gregory couldn't continue to live with each other. She just needed some time to be certain this was the right decision.

There was also Robert to think about. Things with the American officer had moved very quickly, and it worried her. She was aware that with such instability in the world, making decisions sooner than a person normally would wasn't that unusual. There were women getting married all the time after whirlwind romances with soldiers, airmen and sailors. It was as if everyone was aware that life was fragile and could be taken away at any time; that one couldn't sit back passively and wait for the war to be over. People wanted their happiness immediately, to make the most of it while they could.

Hana wanted to convince herself that she was doing just that, but part of her wasn't so easily persuaded. After seeing Gregory so despondent, she was surprised by her strength of compassion for him. She was ignoring her guilt, because that wasn't a true measure of her feelings. Her heart was her measure, and at the moment, it was all over the place.

By the time 4p.m. came around, Hana was glad she was done for the day. She was walking along Church Green Road, when she heard her name being called. Looking around, she saw Robert jogging to catch her up. Before he even reached her, she could see there was a concerned expression on his face.

'What's wrong?' she asked.

'Nothing. I just wanted to see you.'

'Well, here I am.' She gave him a smile, though she sensed Robert wanted to say something else. She didn't have to wait long.

'I was kinda hoping you'd changed your mind about staying at your mother's.'

She gave him another smile, this time an apologetic one. 'Sorry, but no, I haven't changed my mind.'

'Is it me?'

'No, it's not actually.' It prickled her that he thought he was the centre of the universe.

'What is it, then?'

'I told you before. I need time to think. I don't want to rush into any decision. The village will be a hotbed of gossip, and I don't want to embarrass Gregory, or myself.'

Robert gave a small shake of his head. 'I don't get it. Why the hell are you worried about him?'

'Because I care about him. And both of us will still have to live in this village – my parents will continue living here, too. It's not just about me. What I do will have a ripple effect, and I'd be selfish if I didn't consider everyone else. There's no rush, is there?'

Robert looked at her for a long moment before replying. 'I guess not.'

He sounded like a sulky child, but Hana dug deep for her empathy. 'I'm sorry, but there are things we should have discussed before today. Things we don't know about each other that are really important.'

'So, you're hedging your bets.'

'No. I'm not actually. I'm making sure I'm doing the right thing.'

'You know I'm the right thing,' said Robert, leaning closer to her. 'Don't be scared, sweetheart.'

'I'm trying not to be. I've just got a lot of things happening all at once.'

Robert pulled her in for a hug. 'I know you have. Sorry. I guess now you know I can be impatient, but I get it.' He kissed the top of her head. 'I'm here for you. Lean on me, if you need anything.' He kissed her again. 'Let's go get your things.'

The journey back to the house was tense. Apprehension was building in Hana by the minute. She was actually going through with this. She was leaving Gregory. Her heart was hammering faster and faster with every mile. When Robert pulled up in the driveway, she felt physically sick. Gregory's car was parked outside the garage. She was glad he was in, so she could speak to him face-to-face, but at the same time, she was dreading it. She sat in the passenger seat unable to move.

'Do you want me to go in with you?' asked Robert.

'No. I need to do this alone. I owe that much to Gregory.'

'I'm not sure you owe him anything.'

'I'm walking away from five years of marriage,' said Hana, her voice a little sharper than she intended. 'I absolutely do owe it to him.'

'But come on, Hana, your marriage has only been in name for the past, what . . . two years?'

'You're being pedantic.'

'I'm being honest.'

Hana got out of the car, her feet carrying her forward on autopilot. Her brain was barely keeping up with her. She pushed her key into the lock. Gwen's words of warning hurtled around in her head about it being a whirlwind romance, that she barely knew Robert, that they hadn't discussed the important issues, only danced around the edges in some sort of hedonistic falsehood. Was that really true? Hana could hardly think straight. Was she about to make a huge mistake? She glanced back at Robert in the car, he dipped his head to meet her gaze and gave an encouraging smile.

Hana pushed the door open and stepped into the house, wondering if this would be the last time she'd cross the threshold.

She tapped on the door of the study, expecting to find Gregory in there, but the room was empty. She went through the whole of the ground floor, but there was no sign of him. She paused at the foot of the stairs and strained to listen, but there was no noise. She had an uncomfortable feeling of déjà vu from when she had gone to Audrey's house, which sent a shiver through her as she went upstairs.

'Gregory? Are you here?'

His bedroom door was open, and Hana poked her head into the room to see that he was standing at the window overlooking the front of the house, his back to her.

'You don't have to say anything,' he said in a monotone voice, not turning to look at her. 'I'll save you the trouble.'

Hana went to speak, but her voice lodged in her throat. She took an audible breath, trying to control the emotion rolling around inside her, clawing at her heart and churning her stomach. 'I . . . I wanted to tell you myself,' she heard herself saying.

Gregory made an almost choking noise in his throat. He turned to face her. 'You don't have to.'

'I'm sorry, Gregory.'

He shook his head. 'Don't apologise.' He glanced back out of the window. 'You don't need to be sorry, Hana. It's an end I deserve.'

'I never wanted it to end this way,' she said. 'I didn't want it to end, but things got so bad. I am sorry, though, about . . . about Robert.'

'Not as sorry as I am.' He blew out a long breath. 'Do you love him? No. Don't answer that. I don't want to know. I assume you do. Or I assume you don't love me anymore and I can't blame you.' He took a few steps closer to her. 'I'm not about to get into a big argument. You've made up your mind. I know I've left this all too late, but there's something I wanted to tell you, just so you know.' He looked down at the ground, uncertainty crossing his face.

'What?' whispered Hana.

'I went to see Doctor Peters. About my accident. About how it's affected me. Affected us.'

'Oh.' Hana wasn't quite sure what to say or how she even felt about that. 'Has it helped?' she asked finally.

'There's no quick fix but I'm working on it.' Gregory rubbed his jaw. 'After what happened to the wife of that chap I know, the nurse who was killed in the bombing, it got me thinking. That things could be a lot worse for me. That I had fallen into a spiral of self-pity and loathing. That I didn't think I was good enough for you anymore.'

'That wasn't true,' whispered Hana.

'I was a coward, though. I wasn't brave enough to tell you to leave. I was rotten to live with. I pushed you away. There's no wonder you found comfort with another man. That was my fault. I thought it was what I wanted because well, I wasn't what you wanted or needed.'

'Why would you think that?'

'Because I wasn't the man you married. I thought I wasn't worthy of your devotion, and you were staying out of pity.'

'I told you before, I have never pitied you,' said Hana, finding strength in her voice again.

'As I said, I've left this all too late and I'm going to have to live with the consequences,' said Gregory. 'But I want to tell you something I should have told you a long time ago.' He paused, holding her gaze. 'You have been the love of my life. I don't know how I would have got through the last few years without you, even though I've been utterly beastly. I don't deserve your patience or your love. So, although I never wanted this to happen, I'm glad you'll be happy now.'

'Don't,' said Hana, tears swamping her eyes.

'I'm not trying to make you feel guilty or sorry for me,' said Gregory. 'I just wanted you to know that I understand why. You can go and live your life with a clear conscience. I just wish I'd understood sooner so that I might have been able to change the course we found ourselves on. But that is for me to regret, not you.'

'I'm so sorry,' said Hana, not even attempting to hide her tears now.

'You have nothing to be sorry for,' said Gregory. 'I, on the other hand . . .'

They stood in the room looking at each other for a moment. So many confusing and conflicting feelings rushed through Hana. She couldn't think clearly.

Gregory broke the silence first. 'Look, I'm going out now.'

'Don't go on my account,' said Hana. She didn't want to force him to leave his home. 'I won't take long.'

Gregory shook his head. 'I'd sooner not witness you leaving. Take your time getting your things together. I won't be back until much later.'

He walked between Hana and the bed, pausing as he reached her, his shoulder touching hers. 'You know where I am if you need me.'

Hana nodded, causing more tears to fall from her eyes. She reached up her hand, lightly touching Gregory's shoulder. 'Thank you.'

It was now Hana's turn to stand at the window and witness the scene below. A few minutes later, Gregory stepped out of the house. She watched him pause and look towards the car where Robert was sitting. She couldn't see Robert's face, but Gregory stood for several seconds, before putting on his hat and walking away down the drive, his cane crunching on the gravel in time with his uneven footsteps.

Hana had underestimated quite how emotional she'd feel as she packed some clothes into her suitcase, enough for the week.

When she'd finished, she took the case down to the hall and paused to look at the photograph of her parents hanging on the wall, taken some time in Japan. Goodness only knows what her father would think about her leaving Gregory. The two men had always had a fond and mutual respect for one another. Alfred had always enquired after Gregory, and they'd often spent time in each other's company discussing their shared love of aircraft. Another of her father's idiosyncrasies. He loved people and the spoken word, but he was also fascinated with technology, especially aircraft.

Hana thought of mother, too, who hadn't been particularly thrilled when she'd asked if she could move back home.

'You want to do what?' Pamela had stared at Hana from across the kitchen table.

She had every right to be flabbergasted, Hana couldn't criticise her for that.

'I need some time to myself. A break,' repeated Hana.

Pamela blinked several times and let out a big sigh. 'I thought that's what you said, but I was hoping I'd misheard.'

Freddie chose that moment to gate-crash their tête-à-tête, toddling at almost a run into the room. Hana had never been so grateful to see her nephew. 'Hello, my darling,' she'd said, picking up the boy and sitting him on her knee. 'You're looking very smart in your trousers. Who have you got here? Bunny?' She took Bunny and tickled Freddie's tummy with the soft toy.

'Sorry!' said Gwen dashing into the kitchen. 'He's too fast for me.'

'Don't be sorry,' Pamela had shaken her head. 'In fact, you should join us. Hana has some news.'

Hana exchanged a glance with her sister-in-law, who grimaced.

Pamela's head shot up as she looked between the two young women. 'You know already.' It was a statement that didn't warrant an answer. 'I seem to be the last to know. I take it you approve, then?'

'What?' Gwen looked shocked. 'No. I . . . I mean . . .'

'No, Gwen doesn't approve,' cut in Hana, saving Gwen the awkwardness. 'I spoke to her about it and she said I needed to make sure I was doing the right thing.'

'And are you?' asked Pamela, with little sympathy in her voice.

'There are things I need to think about and talk over with Robert.'

Pamela sat back in her chair, folding her arms across her chest. 'Bloody Americans.'

'It's not Robert's fault,' said Hana. 'You know things have been difficult between me and Gregory for some time.'

'Yes. I know that. I'm not blind,' said Pamela. 'But all marriages go through difficult times. Don't you think I haven't wanted to throttle your father on more than one occasion?'

'It's not a case of Gregory being annoying,' said Hana feeling defensive. She knew her mother would give her a hard time, but she still felt the need to defend her actions.

'I'm sure it's not,' said Pamela. 'When your father told me we were going to Japan, do you think I just said, "Oh, all right. Jolly good. Let's go?" No. I didn't. We argued. Many times.'

'But you worked it out and still went,' said Hana. 'Believe me, Gregory and I can't work things out. We've tried.'

'Yes. We worked things out. Your father promised me it wouldn't be forever. Although, I didn't think I'd be there five years. And there was a time when I told him if he wanted to go that much, then he'd have to go on his own. Effectively, our marriage would have been over. But we compromised. Marriage is a partnership not a dictatorship. And not something to give up on just because it's a bit tough.'

Hana looked down at her teacup. 'Mum, I'm tired of trying. I don't know if I have the energy. I'm sad. I don't want to be sad anymore. I want to be happy.'

'How has Gregory taken this news?' asked Pamela, her tone a little softer.

How ironic. Her mother had sympathy for Gregory but not for her daughter. Hana was beginning to feel like the big bad wolf. 'He said he wouldn't try to stop me.'

'Well, short of holding you hostage, I don't suppose he could,' said Pamela. 'What I meant was, is he upset?'

Hana hesitated, hating to have to confess. 'Yes. He is.'

'Do you not love him anymore?'

'It's not a case of loving him or not.'

'Is it you don't love your marriage? Your situation?' pressed Pamela. 'Because that's fine. That happens. Just don't confuse it with not loving the person.'

Hana couldn't answer. She looked at her mother. She'd never known that Pamela hadn't wanted to go to Japan, she had just assumed her parents were in tune with everything. They always appeared to be in harmony, she couldn't imagine them disagreeing over something like that. 'What was your compromise for Japan?' she asked.

'That we came back to England before you were eighteen,' said Pamela. 'Your father would have been happy to stay there, but he'd made a promise to me.'

That made sense. They'd returned to England when Hana was seventeen. In all the years they'd been home, Hana couldn't ever remember Alfred complaining about being in England. But could she equate that to her own marriage? She wasn't sure. Hers and Gregory's issues ran far deeper than living abroad. If only it were that simple to compromise.

Standing in the hallway of Tall Trees now, Hana gave a big sigh as she thought back to that conversation with her mum. It was her mess, and she would have to face the consequences, which included not everyone being happy about what she was doing. But this wasn't about pleasing other people, she'd been doing that for far too long. This was about putting her own needs first for a change.

Despite the pep talk to herself, it was with a heavy heart that Hana closed the front door behind her.

Robert got out of the car and took her case and bag from her.

'It's going to be all right,' he said reassuringly as they drove away from the house. 'Trust me.'

Why was everyone talking about trust, when what she was doing was all about mistrust, both in her personal life and work life? She sank further into the seat, forcing a smile in Robert's direction, but she was anything other than content.

Chapter 26

It was Wednesday, the day after Hana had moved out of Tall Trees, and it felt strange being back in her old room with the same pink candlewick bedspread she'd had for years. The same pink-velvet curtains still hung at the window and her treasured rag doll sat on the chest of drawers. It was a time capsule of her childhood. Despite the nostalgia, the room didn't bring any comfort, and Hana had had an unsettled night.

She was glad when this morning had finally come and with a day off from work, she and Pamela had driven over to the hospital in the hope of seeing some sort of improvement in Alfred's condition.

'We're not administering any sedative at all today,' the nurse explained as they arrived at the ward. 'We were hoping to see some signs of Alfred coming around on his own, but it's early days.'

Hana and Pamela took their usual seats each side of the bed, holding Alfred's hands. Pamela was telling him about one of the chickens that had stopped laying and how she had given some eggs to Mrs Harris across the road. And Hana smiled as Pamela recounted, with great enjoyment, a story about the grandson of another of her friends, Mrs Watson, who was learning how to ride a bicycle, but hadn't yet mastered the brakes, and half the street had been chasing him down the hill, calling out warning shouts to unsuspecting pedestrians. In the end, the postman had been the one to catch him.

It was the easy chatter Hana had listened to many a time between her parents, only of course this time her father wasn't able to respond. She loved the relationship her mum and dad had, it was one she had aspired to in her own marriage. When she and Gregory were dating and then first married, Hana had been confident in their love and friendship, and that they would easily echo her parents' relationship. Those early days had been full of such joy. Even cooking for Gregory had been something she was proud to do, a chore that was now just that: a chore. Dining together had become impossibly difficult.

Honestly, she had to stop thinking about Gregory all the time. She had made her choice. She was doing what she wanted for a change. She should be looking forward, not backward. The future was exciting and full of promise. Yes. That's what she needed to remember.

She realised Pamela had finished her retelling of the runaway grandson. 'Anyway, Alfred,' said Pamela, pulling her bag onto her lap. She brought out a newspaper.

Hana recognised it immediately as *The Daily Telegraph*. Pamela carried on chatting away. 'I've got one of your old newspapers here. I thought we could do the crossword together.'

Hana gave her a curious look. Her mum had never done the crossword. Always said she disliked the cryptic clues. Pamela looked over at her. 'It's an old paper. One from the filing cabinet. No point me trying to do one from scratch. This way I can read out the clues and the answers because he's already filled them in.'

'Makes sense,' said Hana, amused at the idea.

'Right, where's the crossword page? Ah, here we are.' Pamela settled in her seat. 'Right, here we go. One down.' She read the clue out and then ran her finger down to the square marked with the corresponding number. 'Albatross,' she said, and repeated this for the next clue. 'Brother.'

Hana looked at Alfred for any flicker of acknowledgement, but there was none.

'Keep going,' she encouraged Pamela.

Pamela looked back down at the newspaper. 'That's odd,' she said.

'What's that?'

'Your father has crossed out a word here and written something in Japanese.'

Hana sat up straight. 'Let me see,' she said holding out her hand.

Pamela passed the newspaper over. Hana studied the Japanese symbols for a moment and just as before, they made no sense. They didn't spell a word.

'I need a pen and paper,' she said, scrambling in her handbag. Using the same method as she had before, she used the date of the newspaper as her starting point.

'What's wrong?' asked Pamela.

'Nothing,' said Hana, distractedly. 'I'm just working out a clue.' A minute later and Hana had the word in front of her. Or rather a name. She jumped to her feet. 'Have you got any other newspapers with you?'

Pamela shook her head. 'No. I just brought the one.'

Hana was getting to her feet. I'm really sorry, Mum, but I need to go.'

'Go? Why? We've only been here a short while.'

'It's to do with work,' said Hana, shoving the newspaper into her bag. She was sure now that Alfred had left more names and information in the other newspapers. 'You don't have to come with me. I'll get the bus.'

Pamela got to her feet. 'No. I'll take you. Your dad would want me to.' She leaned over and kissed her husband on the cheek. 'Sorry, dear, got to dash off and take Hana home. Apparently, she's got something important to do.'

Hana also gave her dad a kiss goodbye. 'I've found the crossword clues,' she said. 'You're a genius, Dad. Love you.'

Pamela didn't ask any questions and again Hana wondered if her mother knew more than she ever let on about what was going on around her. Soon they were speeding towards Bletchley, faster than Hana had ever known her mother to drive. Pamela took the corner wide and at speed.

Hana let out a small cry of alarm as a delivery truck blasted its horn. Pamela swung the car to the left, somehow avoiding contact with the truck. She carried on totally unfazed. Hana was speechless as she looked across at her mother again, who seemed totally obliviously to their near miss. Honestly, if there was one thing she'd learned these the last few weeks, it was that nothing was at it seemed. Her father, a top military asset, decoding Japanese messages and flushing out spies – and her mother, practically a getaway driver!

It wasn't long before they were home. Hana barely waited for Pamela to switch off the engine before she was jumping out and running indoors, much to Gwen's surprise.

Pamela followed her in, telling Gwen not to be alarmed and they should put the kettle on. Hana glanced in the living room as she dashed by. She did a double-take and came to an abrupt halt, just as Gwen was calling out her name. Gregory was sitting on the sofa, a cup of tea on the table in front of him. 'Gregory! What are you doing here?' asked

Hana, aware of the little flutter of something she didn't have time to identify ripple through her chest.

The next moment Gwen charged into the room behind her, almost knocking her off her feet. 'Sorry,' she said to Hana. 'I invited Gregory in for a cup of tea.'

'You did?' Hana looked between her sister-in-law and husband in total confusion.

'We bumped into each other at the play park. I was there with Freddie,' explained Gwen. 'I didn't think it would be a problem . . . I . . . Gregory looked . . .' She stopped talking.

'What Gwen's trying to say is that she felt sorry for me,' said Gregory, getting to his feet. 'I fear I must have looked terribly downcast, and she took pity on me.' He gave a wry smile as Gwen began to protest. 'It's all right, Gwen.' He looked at Hana. 'I needed some fresh air. Part of my new routine. Fresh air. Exercise.' He looked almost apologetic, and Hana's heart had that funny sensation again, but she still didn't have time for self-examination.

There was an awkward silence, which Pamela broke as she came back in with a cup of tea for Hana. She looked around at the cohort in the living room. 'What's this, musical statues? Hana, isn't there something important you need to do?'

'Oh, yes. Yes, there is.' Hana retreated from the living room and crossed the hall to her father's study. In the bottom drawer of the filing cabinet, she took out half a dozen newspapers and spread them out in chronological order across the floor.

'You've worked it out, haven't you?'

Hana looked up to see Gregory standing in the doorway of the study, one hand holding his stick and the other in his pocket.

'I hope so. I mean, I think I'm about to,' said Hana, scrabbling in her handbag for a pen. 'The first code Dad left me. RAT meant the spy. NAME, that's obvious, as we said before. REPEAT. That means repeat what I have just done.'

'Looking in the newspaper for clues,' said Gregory.

'Exactly. Other newspapers. Like all these ones that Dad has kept. There are codes in here.' Her hand trembled as she began to jot down the translations.

Gregory came over and with a little effort, sat down on the floor next to her. He placed his hand on hers. 'Shall I do the writing?'

The feel of his hand on her skin sent yet another strange sensation through her. 'Yes, please.'

They spent the next few minutes, decoding the cipher messages, ending up with several sentences and what looked like random words.

'What have you got?' asked Hana as she translated the last word.

Gregory turned the piece of paper around for her to see. 'Does that remind you of anything?'

Hana read the words Gregory had written, before looking up at him. 'Audrey,' she said.

Gregory nodded. 'Eagle. Sparrow. Flamingo. They're all here and more. Cuckoo. Swan. Finch.'

'So, Dad and Audrey were using the same identifiers,' said Hana.

'Yes. And you know what that means, don't you?' said Gregory, still maintaining eye contact.

'They were working together.' Hana's hand automatically gripped Gregory's. 'Audrey and Dad were sharing information.'

'Your father wasn't a spy, so that means Audrey wasn't either, unless she was a double-agent, but that doesn't make sense if you think about it.'

'No. It doesn't,' said Hana as she hurriedly sifted through all the information in her mind, trying to line it up. 'They tried to kill Dad because he had found out who the spy was. He hadn't told anyone at this point. But Audrey either knew, too, or had information that was incriminating – or she knew Dad had worked it out. She must have been working for him, with him – that's why she died.'

'It makes sense,' said Gregory. 'Her death was made to look like suicide. One murder and one attempted murder wouldn't look good. Questions would be asked. But Audrey taking her own life fits better with the idea that she was the spy and about to be exposed. Someone is trying very hard to not let the name of the real spy be discovered. How did you work this out, anyway?'

'It was Mum, really. She brought an old newspaper in to read to Dad. She was reading the crossword clues and answers to him. I just happened to be there at the right time.'

Gregory studied the newspapers in front of him. 'We must be missing some,' he said. 'Are there any more?'

Hana got to her feet and went over to the filing cabinet. There were three more coded crosswords. It didn't take too long to break the codes.

'It still doesn't make sense,' she said. 'Who is the spy? Where's the evidence?'

A knock at the door interrupted them. It was Gwen. 'Sorry, but Hana, could I have a quick word? In private.'

'Of course.' Hana got to her feet and followed Gwen into the living room. 'What's wrong?'

'I didn't want to say in front of Gregory,' said Gwen. 'But earlier, when you were out and before Gregory was here, I had a visitor. It was Robert.'

'What?'

'I know. Very strange. Took me by surprise and I was in a rush.'

'What did he want?'

'Well, that's just it. He said he wanted to talk about you.' He insisted on coming in and I felt obliged to offer him tea.'

'What happened, Gwen?' Hana could tell her sister-in-law was building up to something.

'I went to make the tea and when I came back with it, he said he couldn't stop after all and up and left. It was all very odd.'

'How strange.'

'There's something else.'

Hana didn't like the look on Gwen's face. 'What?'

'After he had gone, I realised the study door was open and so was the bottom drawer of the filing cabinet.' Gwen looked ashen. 'I'm so sorry, Hana. I didn't really know what to make of it, but your mum's just told me about the newspapers.'

'It's not your fault, Gwen,' said Hana. After reassuring Gwen she wasn't to worry, Hana returned to the study where Gregory was working his way through the rest of the newspapers from the filing cabinet.

As she relayed the story to him, she didn't miss the flicker of pain that crossed his face at the mention of Robert.

Gregory frowned. 'You think Robert took the missing newspapers?'

'I think so,' said Hana, even though she hated admitting it. 'But how would he know about them? Had you told him?'

'I'm not sure but I remember one particular time, hiding it from him when he came into the room. Don't ask me why – I just did. He gave me an odd look but didn't say anything. I assumed he hadn't noticed. The original crossword that Dad gave me went missing. I thought I'd lost it but maybe Robert took it. Maybe I wasn't as clever as I thought I was.' Again, the admission was painful. She felt such a fool.

'We need to get them back. But let's see what we've got here first,' said Gregory. 'We might not need them.'

They worked their way through the stack of newspapers, but it was only the most recent ones in the last three months that had any messages written on them.

'Let's see what we've got now,' said Gregory consulting the piece of paper where he'd been writing the deciphered messages. It read like a telegram. With codenames, dates and times, the same way Audrey had made her notes, but here there was more information. 'Have you seen this line?' asked Gregory pointing to the paper. 'Left a dummy message. The next day the Cuckoo was singing. This must have been how they confirmed there was a spy in the room.'

'Sparrow must be the spy in the room,' said Hana. 'They've told someone else called Cuckoo, who must have taken it higher up the chain to Hawk.'

'The Hawk obviously has serious clout. It has to be MI5. Possibly Hopkins,' said Gregory.

Hana groaned. 'And he was the one who recruited me to find all Dad's information.'

'So, let's assume Hawk is Hopkins,' said Hana. 'We need to find out who the mole is. It's not Audrey. That leaves, Jenny, Lottie or Derek.'

'Don't forget Chatfield,' said Gregory. 'I know it's a stretch, but no one can be ruled out.'

'Do you think someone in the room realised what Audrey was doing and killed her?'

'It seems that way.'

Something that had been bothering Hana for a long time, something she hadn't been able to put her finger on, suddenly came back to her. 'Oh, my God,' she gasped, putting her hand to her mouth. 'I think I know who killed Audrey.'

Chapter 27

'You're going too fast,' said Gregory, holding his hand up to stop Hana in mid flow of her theory. 'Start again. Slower, this time.'

'All right. The morning I found Audrey, I had cycled to the Park,' said Hana. 'I remember being worried about getting caught in the rain. It had rained earlier that morning but by the time I set off, it had stopped.'

'Right.'

'Lottie was late that morning and she came bursting into the hut. Chatfield told her off. When she hung her coat up, I remember brushing up against it when I went to hang up mine. Hers was wet. Mine wasn't.' She looked at Gregory.

'So, she got caught in the rain.'

'Yes. But I didn't. It wasn't raining when I left for work. Lottie came in after me. Her coat was wet? Why was that?' Hana didn't wait for Gregory to catch up. 'Because she'd been caught in the rain earlier. She said she'd come straight from home. That her alarm clock wasn't working.'

She could see Gregory putting the information together. 'Lottie lied about the reason she was late,' he said. 'She was out earlier in the rain.'

'Yes. What if she was out in the rain because she had gone to Audrey's place that morning?' She shivered at the thought of what happened.

'Do you think Lottie is capable of doing that?' asked Gregory. 'It would take quite a lot of strength to overpower someone. I know Audrey is, was, petite, but even assuming Lottie did manage to get the better of her physically, how did she force the sleeping tablets down Audrey's throat?'

'Audrey told me she took sleeping tablets to help her sleep. Maybe Lottie somehow made her take more.'

Gregory sighed. 'I don't know, Hana. I'm with you up until that point. But let's progress this line of thought, as if that happened.'

'There's something else. I'm sure Lottie was there,' said Hana. 'Audrey wore this lemony smelling perfume. I smelt that on Lottie.'

Gregory shrugged. 'So, they wore the same perfume.'

'Or was Lottie wearing Audrey's? I don't remember smelling that on Lottie before then and when I thought about it, I didn't remember packing away a scent bottle when I had to gather all Audrey's things together. What if Lottie took it?'

'Again, possible.'

'And she wasn't as bothered about Audrey's death as I thought she would be. I saw her and Crosslands kissing, remember?'

'Ah, yes. At the cricket pavilion.'

Once again, a realisation dawned on Hana. 'The hat!'

Gregory gave her a guarded look. 'What hat?'

'That photograph of you and Lottie together, there was a hat on the table, just like the one she was wearing at the pavilion.'

'I don't especially remember, but I'll take your word for it.'

'There were two hats on the table. One was yours and one was hers.' Hana could feel the excitement building up inside her. 'I saw someone follow Audrey out of the cricket field the night before she died. I assumed it was a man.

They had on an overcoat and a hat. I don't think it was a man, at all.'

'It was Lottie?'

'Yes. It must have been. And there's more. Mrs Kidson thought she heard Audrey go downstairs early in the morning. She thought it was to get some water or use the toilet. What if she was letting Lottie in for some reason and Lottie killed her? It would have been raining and that was why her coat was wet.'

'We are doing an awful lot of assuming here,' said Gregory again. 'We need more evidence. We need to know if that's who your father thought was the spy. Some of this information doesn't look complete. We need the other newspapers.'

'Robert gave me his new address yesterday,' said Hana. 'It's in my bag.'

The drive from Newton Longville to Bletchley village seemed to take forever, but five minutes later they were outside a little terraced cottage. There was no sign of Robert's car, for which Hana was grateful. She didn't really want a showdown between Robert and Gregory. Not that she thought Gregory would do anything like that, but she didn't want Robert saying anything to Gregory to humiliate him. She hadn't liked his spiteful, not to mention unnecessary, comments about Gregory's injury.

There was no answer when she knocked on the front door and when she tried the handle, it was locked. 'I'll go around the back,' she said, leaving Gregory sitting in the car. She returned a few minutes later. 'I need your help. The kitchen window is open, but I need a leg up.'

Gregory raised his eyebrows. 'A leg up?'

Hana inwardly winced. 'I mean a hop up.'

Gregory's smiled. 'I'm joking,' he said, getting out of the car. 'I'll go as far as saying I was pulling your leg.'

Hana looked at him from the corner of her eye. Gregory had never made jokes about his leg. All right, these weren't particularly funny jokes, but it was an attempt at humour. Something he had been very good at when she'd first met him, but also something that had fallen by the wayside in recent years.

They made their way around to the back of the cottage, using the footpath that ran across the back of the row of terraced properties, entering through the end of the garden.

Hana had pulled the window wide open. All she needed to do was get hold of the ledge and pull herself in. Gregory pressed his back against the house, bending his good knee and keeping his injured leg stretched out in front of him. He pushed hard on the walking stick to help keep himself in position, while he cupped his free hand into a foothold for Hana. The first attempt had them slipping down in a heap, but undeterred, they tried again. This time Hana managed to keep a hold of the window frame and propel herself halfway through the window with a boost from Gregory.

'This sink is in rather an inconvenient place,' she gasped, trying to wriggle her body through the opening.

'Hold on. I'll give you a push,' said Gregory, now standing up and, rather unceremoniously, pushing her further into the cottage.

Hana managed hook one leg up and in a rather unladylike fashion, half-crawl and half-climb, through the window, swung her legs around to clamber into the kitchen, knocking an empty saucepan as she did so. 'I'm fine!' she called back. 'I'll be out in a minute. Wait in the car.'

After pulling the window closed, Hana went through to the front room, which was empty. The front door opened straight into the living room and in the corner was a narrow flight of stairs.

'Robert!' Hana called out, just in case he was there. She went upstairs, reaching a small landing. She poked her head into the room at the back which had a single bed and a desk. The main bedroom was at the front of the cottage. She could see Robert's kitbag on the floor.

Hana called his name again before stepping into the room, breathing a sigh of relief that it was empty.

She quickly searched both bedrooms looking for the missing newspapers, even lifting the mattresses and raking around in the depths of the wardrobe, but she couldn't see them anywhere.

She went back downstairs and scanned the living room. She almost missed it, but as she peered over the side of the sofa, there they were. Three copies of *The Daily Telegraph*, next to a small brown suitcase. She picked them up and was about to leave when something familiar sitting on the coffee table, next to an empty cup, caught her eye. She took a step closer.

There was no kidding herself anymore and her heart began a slow descent to the pit of her stomach as she picked up the paper. It was the crossword that had gone missing from her bag. The one her father had given her the morning of his accident. It was only then she saw another sheet of paper underneath. On it was written other Japanese symbols and below that the translations. She recognised the handwriting. It was of course Robert's.

Hana's pulse pumped faster as she looked back at the small brown suitcase at the side of the sofa. She wanted to turn and run; to pretend she hadn't seen it, but she couldn't. She knelt and unclipped the locks. Her hands shook as she opened the case.

'Oh, Robert,' she whispered as she stared at the radio transmitter set before her.

A voice behind her, startled Hana. 'I was hoping you wouldn't see that.'

Hana spun around to see Robert standing in the doorway of the kitchen. She slowly got to her feet. Her heart now at the bottom of her stomach. Devastation flooded through her body, swamping her emotions. She had been so stupid. So very stupid. A hundred different questions hurtled through her brain. How had she been so gullible? How had she not even considered this scenario?

'Tell me it's not true,' she said, finally finding her voice. 'Actually, don't. Why would I believe anything you tell me now?'

'I'm sorry, Hana. I really am,' said Robert. He took a step towards her, and she matched it with a step backwards, nearly tripping over the open suitcase.

'Did I mean anything to you?' she asked.

Robert let out a sigh. 'Does that matter? You had already changed your mind about me.'

'It does matter. I need to know how much you lied to me.' She was angry now.

'Everything between you and me was the truth.' He ran a hand along his jawline. 'I didn't ever lie to you where we were concerned.'

'But everything else? That was a lie?'

'Not everything, but there were things I couldn't tell you.'

'Did you get close to me just to get the name of the spy or was that just a ruse? A cover story for you being there, because really you were gathering information for Germany or . . .' She paused as suddenly things began to fall into place. 'You were gathering intelligence and relaying it back to

Japan.' She looked down at the radio transmitter and back to Robert. 'That's why you were in our hut.'

'Don't. I can't tell you anything.'

'You don't need to. It's obvious now. The Americans put you in to find the spy, but all along you were spying for the Japanese.' She put her hands to her mouth, as she took a moment to get her breath. 'You were feeding back information to them about British intelligence capabilities. How well we were tracking their naval movements, if we were breaking their diplomatic and military codes, what we knew.'

'I wish you hadn't worked all this out,' said Robert.

Hana shook her head. 'Am I going to end up like Audrey? Is that why she was killed?'

'Don't,' Robert snapped the word out. 'I would never want to hurt you.'

She noted the caveat in his reply.

'Whatever my motives were originally, I couldn't help falling in love with you, Hana.' He took another step further into the room. 'But you weren't going to come with me, were you? You got cold feet. That's why you went to your mom's. You still love him.'

Hana looked up to the ceiling, swallowing hard and trying not to cry. 'No. I wasn't going to come with you,' she said softly.

Robert made a grunting noise. 'You deserve better than him.'

She shook her head. 'No. You're wrong. It's Gregory I don't deserve, but that's something I will have to live with.'

'Never underestimate yourself, sweetheart.'

Hana's gaze shifted to the crossword on the coffee table. 'Why didn't you just wait for me to work out who the spy was? MI5 would have taken them out. Why did you need to know?'

'Because MI5 is denying there's a spy. They aren't sharing the intel with us – the Americans. We wanted to know ourselves.'

'You say "we" like you're a proud, loyal American. But your loyalty is with the enemy.'

'Don't forget, I have American and Japanese heritage. I'm hedging my bets,' he said.

'So, have you worked out who the spy is yet?'

'Not yet. But maybe you can help me?'

Hana scoffed at the suggestion. 'I don't think so.'

'You know I'll work it out sooner or later, so why don't you save me the trouble?' He moved his hand to his side.

Hana's eyes widened at the sight of the pistol tucked into the waistband of his trousers. His hand rested on the grip of the firearm. She made a scoffing sound. 'Do you think I'm going to help you, only for you to kill me? I mean, let's be honest here, I know what you've been doing. I'm a threat to you.'

'I told you, I would never want to hurt you,' said Robert. He drew the gun from his waistband, pointing it at her. 'You can still change your mind, Hana. You could work with me. We could have that future in America. I could make you happy.'

Hana slowly shook her head. 'I can't.'

'You can.'

'You're not listening to her.'

Hana startled as she looked up to see Gregory coming into the living room from the kitchen. Robert spun around and the two men faced each other.

Robert gave a chuckle. 'Well, well, well. Look who we have here. The cavalry.' He looked down at Gregory's leg. 'Kind of, anyway.'

Robert had his back to Hana, and she took a step closer to the fireplace, her eye on the poker resting against the brick fire surround. But before she could reach it, Robert had backed further into the room, his gun trained on Gregory. 'Hana, come here,' he said.

'Don't,' said Gregory, not taking his eyes off the American.

'Hana, do what I say, otherwise I'll shoot him.' Robert, too, kept his stare fixed on the other man.

'Don't shoot him,' said Hana, panic in her voice. As she stepped in front of the fireplace, she managed to grab the poker. Robert was still looking at Gregory. She held the poker behind her back and moved to Robert's side.

Robert grabbed her arm with his free hand. 'That's it, sweetheart. Nice and close.'

'Let her go,' said Gregory.

'*Let her go*,' mimicked Robert. 'Why would I do that? She's coming with me. And you're not.' Robert raised the gun higher, the barrel in line with Gregory's forehead.

Hana watched in horror as if it was all happening at half the speed. She could see Robert's finger squeezing the trigger, and he momentarily let go of her arm. Hana didn't miss her chance. She swung the poker from behind her back, grabbing it so she had both hands on it. She swung it in an upward movement with all her might. She could hear a scream. It was her. The poker connected with Robert's wrist, and she launched herself at him, trying to take him down. Then there was a gun shot.

She felt a searing pain above her heart. A white-hot heat. She couldn't work out what it was. She heard herself scream again. A shout. Someone shouted her name. Then another gunshot. Her vision blurred. She was looking down a black tunnel that was closing in on her. Her legs gave way and she hit the floor. A thud of another body landing next to her. The whisper of her name was the last thing she remembered.

Chapter 28

'Hana? Hana? Can you hear me?'

The voice sounded distant and far away, as if it was calling to her through a closed window.

Hana turned her head towards the sound. She couldn't make out who was talking. She tried to open her eyelids, but they were heavy. Her throat was dry, and she swallowed hard.

'Have some water,' came the muffled voice. There was a hand at the back of her head, tilting it slightly, and then she felt the cool glass at her mouth and the water touch her lips. She swallowed several times, relishing the relief to her parched throat.

She put her head back against the pillow, trying to drag herself from the deep sleep she was in. Gradually, the grogginess began to lift. The first thing she became aware of was a pain in her shoulder. She went to move her arm but couldn't without wincing sharply.

'Don't try to move,' came the voice again. This time it was clearer.

Hana took a moment to take stock of her body and where she was.

She didn't hurt anywhere else. Just her shoulder when she tried to move her arm, which felt constricted somehow. She knew she was in a bed. Judging by the faint smell of disinfectant and the starchy feel of the sheets over her, she was in hospital. Why? And then she remembered, with a clarity so forceful that she let out a cry and her whole body flinched.

'It's all right, Hana. Everything's all right.'

Now she knew the voice. Her eyes pinged open and there he was, leaning towards her, his hand brushing the hair back from her face.

She went to speak, but no sound came out. Hana cleared her throat and tried a second time. 'Gregory.'

'Nice to see you awake,' he said with a smile. He picked up the glass again and helped her take another sip.

Hana looked down at her left shoulder. 'I was shot?' She was pretty sure that's what had happened but needed Gregory to confirm it.

He nodded. 'By accident.'

'Who . . .?'

'Robert.'

Hana remembered struggling with Robert, whacking him with the poker. She remembered the gun firing and the pain that tore through her shoulder. She had been lucky. A few inches lower and it would have been her heart. Then she remembered the gun going off again. She looked up at Gregory. 'There was a second shot.'

'That was my gun.'

Hana studied Gregory's face but could not read his expression at all. 'What happened to him?' She felt her body tense as she waited for the answer.

'He's alive, if that's what you want to know.'

Relief was her initial emotion. Whatever she felt about Robert, she hadn't wanted him dead, even if he was a spy and had fooled her. She did believe that he had developed feelings for her, but whether it was love, she wasn't so sure.

She tried to examine her own feelings beyond the relief but struggled to find anything.

'I'm glad you didn't kill him,' she said eventually.

'That's something we can agree to disagree on,' said Gregory. 'As you took him down with the poker, it was just enough to push him out of the trajectory of my aim. The bullet went through his upper arm. Missing all main arteries and bone. A flesh wound.'

'And he didn't try to shoot you?'

'No. It all happened quickly after that. MI5 turned up and he was arrested. You were rushed here to the hospital. He was treated for a flesh wound and is now in military custody.'

Hana was sure Gregory was being minimal with the details, but her head was hurting, so she was content with just a summary for today. She closed her eyes. She didn't try to fight the overwhelming sense of tiredness that washed over her.

*

When she next woke up, it must have been much later in the day. The light was fading as dusk began to settle. A nurse was putting up the blackout blinds. She turned to Hana. 'Oh, nice to see you're awake. I'll just finish these and then I'll let your mum know. She's outside in the visitor's room having a cup of tea.'

A few minutes later, Pamela bustled in. 'Hello, darling. How are you feeling?'

Hana smiled at her. No matter how old she was, there was something reassuring and comforting having her mother there. 'Better for seeing you, Mum.'

The nurse was now checking Hana's pulse. Her left arm was in a sling and her shoulder had been bandaged.

'It looks worse than it is,' said the nurse. 'Tissue damage. You'll soon be back to fighting fit.'

That was something, at least. Hana looked to the other side of the bed. 'Where's Gregory?'

'He had to go,' said Pamela. 'But he'll be back before visiting time is over.'

The nurse wrote something on the chart and then left the room after telling them that afternoon tea would be doing the rounds soon.

'Is Gregory all right?' Hana tried to move into a more upright position.

'He has barely left your bedside the past twenty-four hours,' said Pamela, helping Hana to sit up better.

'Is that how long I've been here?' Time had no meaning at all to her.

'You hit your head when you went down and had concussion. You were very lucky. Or foolish.' Pamela gave her a reproachful look. 'Jumping in front of someone with a gun. Honestly, Hana.' She shook her head.

'He was going to shoot Gregory.'

'Even so.' Pamela clearly wasn't going to forgive her that easily. 'Gwen sends her love and says to hurry up and come home.'

'Home.' Hana sighed. 'I'm not sure where home is anymore.'

'It can be wherever you want it to be,' said Pamela. 'Preferably where your heart is, if you want my advice.'

'I think I might have burned my bridges there,' said Hana. Home. That was back at Tall Trees where she'd lived with Gregory for the past five years. Where they had moved into when they'd first got married. Where they had dreamed and planned for a future. Where some of those dreams had been extinguished. Where they had drifted apart and where she had betrayed him. She pressed her lips together trying to control her emotions. She didn't deserve to call it home anymore.

'You must never assume anything,' said Pamela. 'And the worst thing you can do is to keep quiet. Talking. Communication is everything. Hasn't your father drummed that into you. There are many languages in life, and the language of love is just as broad. Speak it, show it, feel it.'

It was probably the most sentimental thing Pamela had ever said to Hana.

A movement in her peripheral vision had Hana looking towards the door. Gregory stepped into the room. She wondered how much of the conversation he had overheard.

'Nice to see you awake,' he said coming in the room with a vase of flowers in one hand. He placed them on the bedside table. 'Thought these might cheer the place up a bit.'

'They're beautiful,' said Hana, noting the yellow roses. Her favourites. She'd had them in her wedding bouquet. She wondered if that was intentional on Gregory's part. 'Speaking of Dad. How is he?' she asked her mother.

'Well, more good news,' said Pamela. 'He's very slowly coming around. He hasn't been able to communicate properly, but he has had moments of wakefulness. Today it was several minutes.'

'Is that good?' asked Hana. 'It is, isn't it?'

'It's a good sign,' said Gregory gently.

Hana noted the cautionary undertone in his answer, and she changed the subject, not wanting to discuss the negatives of her father's progress. 'Hopefully, they'll let me go home tomorrow,' she said.

Pamela and Gregory exchanged a look across the bed. Pamela got to her feet. 'I should be getting off now,' she said, leaning over and giving Hana a kiss on the cheek. 'I'll see you tomorrow. I feel like I should ask for a room here. What with your father in one ward and you in another.' She gave a small laugh.

Hana said goodbye to her mum, genuinely disappointed to see her go, but also relieved. 'She looks so tired,' Hana said to Gregory when it was just the two of them in the room.

'She deserves a rest, once you and your father are better,' said Gregory. He sat down in the chair next to the bed.

Hana twiddled the sheet around her finger. There were so many questions she had for Gregory. She'd had time to think everything over. 'I'm surprised someone from MI5 hasn't been in to quiz me.'

'About that,' said Gregory. 'Hopkins is actually outside waiting to come and speak to you. I can put him off until tomorrow, if you're not up to it.'

'He's here? Now?' Hana whispered the words.

'Shall I tell him to come back tomorrow?'

'No! Don't send him away. I need to know everything.'

Gregory grinned. 'I'll get him in, then.' He went outside and returned almost straightaway with the MI5 agent.

'Ah, Hana. Good to see you,' said Hopkins. 'How's the old shoulder?'

'Sore, but I should make a full recovery according to the nurse.'

'Absolutely,' said Hopkins. 'Once you're out of here, perhaps you can come down to the Park for a full debrief.'

'Yes. Of course,' replied Hana.

'Firstly, congratulations on finding the intelligence your father had gathered. You did an excellent job there.'

'Thank you.'

'But that seems to be the tip of the iceberg.' Hopkins smiled at her. 'You brought us the spy. Lottie Rawlins. I knew you'd do it. And because of her, we also got Crosslands.'

'I'm just sorry I didn't work it out sooner,' said Hana. 'Audrey might still be alive today.'

'Now, now. Don't be taking that on. That was not your fault. Do not carry someone else's burden.'

Hana nodded. It was, of course, easier said than done.

'You also gave us Becker. An added bonus that none of us knew about,' continued Hopkins. 'Left egg on the faces of the Americans.'

Hana couldn't celebrate or pat herself on the back. She'd been taken in by Robert, played by him. He was on the verge of finding out the information before she did.

'You should be proud of yourself, Hana,' said Gregory.

'You certainly should,' said Hopkins. 'You did all the hard work there. Without your unique understanding of your father's coding, we might never have found out. We certainly wouldn't have thought to go looking through old newspapers.'

Hana couldn't help feeling a small swell of pride at the praise. 'Thank you.' She seemed to be saying that a lot.

'So, codenames. The Eagle was Captain Robert Becker. The Cuckoo was Bill Crosslands. Flamingo, Captain Phillips. Nightingale was Audrey. And Sparrow, well that was our spy, Lottie Rawlins,' said Hopkins. 'She was smuggling out messages and handing them over to Crosslands. He in turn was passing them on to the Russians.'

Hana's eyes widened. 'The Russians?'

'Yes. It was important for them to know what was happening in the East, especially where Japan was concerned,' explained Hopkins.

There was a small silence as they all considered the situation.

'Did Lottie kill Audrey?' asked Hana after a time.

'She did, I'm afraid. She confessed under questioning,' said Hopkins. 'She managed to overpower Audrey who was sleeping soundly, having taken a sleeping tablet. Lottie crushed a cyanide pill between Audrey's teeth. I assume she held her nose, making Audrey swallow. Poor girl was as good as dead by the time she realised what was happening. The empty sleeping pill pot was left to throw us off the scent.'

'Where did she get the cyanide pill from?'

'From Crosslands.'

'And the note?'

'She made a good attempt at copying Audrey's handwriting, but not that good.'

'That's why it was such a short note, I suppose.'

'I imagine so.'

Hana looked down at the sling cradling her left arm. 'Audrey had worked it out, hadn't she?'

Hopkins nodded. 'She was gathering intelligence off her own back. The day before she was killed, she had put in a request for a meeting with the commander.'

'Poor Audrey,' whispered Hana, wiping a tear from her eye. 'Where does Robert fit into all this?'

'Ah, that's a little more complicated,' said Hopkins. 'MI5 suspected a spy in the hut, but we didn't want to share the information with the Americans until we had proof. We're not in the habit of speculating. The Americans must have got wind of it somehow and sent Becker in to find out what he could. A very loose remit.'

'But he wasn't just working for the Americans,' said Hana.

'Sadly, not. His personal links with Japan appear to run deeper than he let on. He managed to fool everyone, it seems,' admitted Hopkins. 'The Americans sent him in, believing him to be on their side. They had no reason to doubt him. But somewhere along the line, probably before he even came to the Park, he had started colluding with the Japanese.'

'I had no idea until yesterday morning,' said Hana.

'That's all right,' said Gregory. 'You don't have to defend yourself.'

'Your husband is right,' agreed Hopkins. 'No. Becker was gathering intel for the Japanese. It was imperative to their efforts to know just how much we knew about them. Whether their messages, both diplomatic and military, were being decoded. It helped with their military planning, understanding allied capabilities, the extent of our intelligence sharing and just what was going back to the Yanks. All that sort of thing.'

'I don't understand why he would do it,' said Hana.

'Only Becker can answer that,' said Hopkins. 'And he's not talking just now.'

Hana was aware of the emphasis on the last two words. She didn't want to know how they proposed to get Robert to talk. 'What's happened to Crosslands and Lottie?' she asked.

'Arrested. And still being questioned. Lottie is clearly madly in love with Crosslands. He persuaded her to help him. He was working on Audrey, but she wasn't quite so easy to turn, although she was pretending somewhat. She was trying to get close to him, to find out more,' said Hopkins. 'Sadly, she was on her own. We had no idea so we couldn't protect her, and she paid the ultimate price. Her efforts will be acknowledged.'

'Why did Crosslands do it?' asked Hana. She wanted to understand their motives. What made people turn against their countries? To lie and to kill?

'Communist beliefs,' said Hopkins. 'Crosslands was turned at Cambridge. He was ideologically committed to Communism and believed that supporting the Soviet Union would help defeat Nazi Germany. He thought sharing intelligence would bring that about quicker.'

'So he was trying to help,' said Hana.

'You could say that, if you're being generous, but he was essentially a spy,' said Hopkins.

He looked at Hana and then at Gregory. 'Well, I think that's about it for tonight. I'll see you tomorrow. Goodnight, Hana. And thank you again. Sterling work.'

Once he'd left the room, Hana met Gregory's gaze. 'I'm so sorry,' she said.

'No more talking tonight,' said Gregory. 'You need to rest. Get some sleep and we'll talk tomorrow.'

There was a lot to talk about tomorrow, that was for sure.

Chapter 29

Hana spent a further two days in hospital before the doctors finally agreed to let her leave, but under the proviso she was not to be left on her own and wasn't to use her arm for another week. Gregory had been to visit her every day, as had her mother.

'All ready?' asked Gregory as Hana got up from where she was perched on the edge of the hospital bed.

'Try and stop me. I can't wait to get out of this place.' As Hana looked up at Gregory, she realised he had a very smug look on his face. 'You look pleased with yourself.'

'I have some good news,' he replied. 'You may not want to get out of this place quite so quick.'

'I can't imagine that I want to stay any longer than necessary,' said Hana. 'But go on, spill the beans.'

'Follow me.' Gregory picked up her bag and set off out of thc room, leaving Hana with no option but to do as he said and follow.

A few minutes later they were standing outside the door to Alfred's room. 'Why are we here? It's not visiting time?' asked Hana in a whisper, glancing up and down the corridor. She hadn't been allowed to see her father all the time she was a patient herself, but Pamela had given her daily updates. He was staying awake for longer periods of time and had been able to answer some questions with nods and shakes of his head.

'I asked the nurse. She's given you special permission,' replied Gregory. 'In other words, she's turning a blind eye, so you have to be quick.'

Hana paused with her hand on the door. 'You said good news, didn't you?'

'Yes. Very much so. Now go on in.'

Hana didn't need telling twice. She slipped quietly into the room with Gregory behind her. She was expecting her father to be asleep and nearly jumped with shock to see him sitting up in bed, wide awake and looking at her. A smile spread across his face, and he held out a hand. 'Hana.' His voice was raspy and weak but the love and joy in his eyes was immense. '*Kon'nichiwa, Hana-chan*.'

Hana rushed across the room, somehow managing to hug her father with her good arm. 'Oh, Dad. *Kon'nichiwa*,' she said, but couldn't form any more words as tears of joy and relief streaked down her face. It was like a release of all the emotion she had been keeping under wraps the past few weeks. Emotion that she hadn't dared poke or prod for fear of being overwhelmed by the enormity of it.

'There. There. Nothing to cry about,' her father whispered in her ear, as he wrapped both arms around her and gently patted her back. 'Everything is all right.'

Finally, Hana was able to pull herself away. 'I've been so worried about you.' She studied her father's face. He had lost weight, and his cheeks were a little more hollowed – and there were dark circles under his eyes – but his eyes themselves looked just like they always had. Pale green, flecked with gold, generating and radiating the same love and affection that she had known all her life.

'You don't have to worry about me anymore,' said Alfred. 'Everything is going to be all right.'

The door opened and the nurse who had let them sneak in popped her head around the door. 'Sorry, but Matron will be round soon. She'll have my guts for garters if she finds you here.'

'One minute,' said Hana, as the nurse retreated back to her desk in the corridor. She turned to her father. 'I'll come back and see you later, Dad.'

He patted her hand. 'Come tomorrow. You need your rest, too.' He eyed her shoulder. 'I've heard all about your antics.'

With one last gentle hug, Hana reluctantly left him, after he made her promise to go home and rest.

'Thank you, so much,' Hana said to Gregory as he got into the driver's seat next to her.

'My pleasure.' Gregory started the engine and accelerated out of the car park and onto the main road. 'He was as keen to see you as you were to see him. Your mum had a job persuading him not to come and find you last night.'

Hana smiled at the thought. 'How much does he know?'

'Probably just the bare bones at the moment,' said Gregory. 'Hopkins is going to see him today and will debrief him.'

'I'm glad most of this nightmare is over,' said Hana, looking out of the window at the passing street.

'Most of it?' asked Gregory.

'It doesn't matter,' said Hana, not turning to look at him. There was so much she wanted to say to Gregory, but now wasn't the right time. She was grateful when he didn't pursue the conversation further. She didn't want to talk about Robert to him, it wasn't fair. She had such mixed feelings about the American, but what she was certain of was that she hadn't loved him. She might have been in love with the escapism and excitement of the moment, but not the man.

She hadn't considered it fully, not beyond making her feel wanted and making her feel like a person in her own right again. Now, it seemed shallow and self-indulgent. She had been blinded by all the glitter, as Gwen had told her. Her pride was also a little dented, but it was no more than she deserved. Robert may have fallen in love with her, probably in the same way she had with him, but his affection had been born out of the desire for information, not her. She realised that now.

Soon enough they were in Newton Longville and just about to turn into the road where Pamela lived. 'I'll drop you home and then I need to get to work,' said Gregory.

'Home?'

'Bramble House. I assume that's where you want to go.' There was an uncertainty in Gregory's voice.

'I suppose so,' said Hana. She hadn't really thought of it in those terms. Home had always been where she lived with Gregory. The house in which they'd created their home. Her dad always said that home is where the heart is. Hana didn't know if that was possible now.

*

As it happened, Gregory hadn't been able to call back in to see Hana for the rest of the week. She had found herself first looking forward to seeing him and then missing him and wishing he was there. She had been to visit her father several times and there were muted suggestions that he could return home the following week. Hana had also visited the hospital to have her shoulder redressed. She still had to use the sling but was allowed to take it off three or four times a day for gentle exercise.

Her debrief with Hopkins had gone well but had taken longer than anticipated as he and another chap from MI5, Mr Dobbs, had gone into great detail about what she'd found out, how she'd found out things, checking, double-checking and triple-checking her account of events.

'We just have to make sure we haven't missed anything,' Hopkins had reassured her.

It had been embarrassing to have to talk about her relationship with Robert and only made her feel more guilt than she did already for betraying Gregory in such a way. She was not proud of herself in the slightest.

'So, let me just go over this last part,' said Hopkins. 'By the time Captain Robert Becker was arrested, you had already decided you were not going to cohabit with him, and, in fact, you were contemplating whether a future together was what you wanted?'

Hana nodded. 'I realised I didn't love Robert. He was just filling an emotional void.'

'Mmm.' Hopkins seemed satisfied with her response. 'Well, I think that's all. Make yourself available for any further questions, but unless you hear from us again, you can consider the matter closed.'

'Thank you.' Hana got up to leave.

'I'll see you out,' said Hopkins, standing and then proceeding to follow her out of the room and down the wood-panelled hallways of Bletchley mansion house. As they stepped out into the fresh air. He took a cigarette from his case. 'Cigarette?'

'No. Thank you. I don't smoke.'

'That's right. I remember you said that before. Nasty habit, anyway, but you know, I could have worse vices.' He lit the cigarette, blowing smoke into the damp autumn air.

'Do you have anything you'd like to ask me, off the record, that is?'

Hana was surprised by the question but had no intention of missing an opportunity like this. 'I do, actually,' she said. 'When I first came to work here, I was getting some fresh air around the back of the house, where the trees are. Anyway, I heard two men talking. They didn't know I was there. They were talking about Gregory, saying he was in London and would be back in a few days. That whatever they were planning, they were going to try again and that they could trust Gregory. I never saw their faces and at the time didn't recognise their voices but now . . .'

'And now you think you know who they are,' concluded Hopkins.

Hana nodded. 'One was you.' She looked at him trying to gauge his reaction.

'Yes. That's right. One was me. Rather careless that I should have been overheard,' he mused. 'I was talking to Mr Dobbs. We had asked your husband to gather some intelligence for us. It was rather delicate and involved another woman.'

'Another woman?' A shockwave of surprise shot through Hana, swiftly followed by one of jealousy. 'How much involvement?'

Hopkins waved a hand dismissively. 'Nothing like that, it was just some groundwork while we tried to work out who the spy was in the hut. Your husband was asked to find out what he could from Lottie Rawlins. Things like her political persuasions, thoughts on Communism, and the like. He was tasked with talking to several people.'

Hana was relieved to hear it. Gregory had never explained the photograph she'd found, but it made sense now.

Hopkins finished his cigarette. 'Any other questions?'

'I don't think so,' replied Hana.

'Good,' Hopkins said. 'Oh, and Chatfield is probably going to ask you to stay on,' he called back over his shoulder. 'If you're still about, that is.'

The idea lifted Hana's spirits. She hadn't been sure if they'd still want her, seeing as she was only there because of her knowledge of her father's ciphers. The thought of leaving had been playing on her mind. She liked going to work and she liked the sense of doing something tangible, even if it was a little boring most of the time. But after the events of the past few weeks, she could put up with boring.

Hana made her way down the path, towards the gate to catch the bus back home. Funny how just a few weeks ago she thought her life was without love, without excitement. She had been so wrong. Her life had been full of love, from all directions, she had just chosen not to see it. She'd thought the grass was greener on the other side. She'd been wrong about that, too. Was there a way back? She wasn't sure she deserved forgiveness, but she had to at least try.

*

It felt strange and somewhat absurd knocking on her own front door, but there she was, having just walked from her parents' house, ten minutes away. It was five-thirty and, of course, already dark. Hana shivered as a gust of wind swirled around her ankles.

Gregory opened the door. 'You don't have to knock,' he said, as if tuning into her thoughts. 'This is still your house.'

She noted he didn't say home, and she couldn't deny the small pang to her heart. 'I didn't bring my key.' It was easier to explain away her actions than launch straight into a discussion about the nuances between house and home. She had telephoned Gregory an hour ago, to ask if she could come over. She hadn't said why as she didn't want him to say no. The smell of cooked vegetables drifted down from the back of the house.

'I've just made some supper,' said Gregory as Hana stepped into the hallway. 'Would you like to join me?'

'Thank you. That would be nice.'

They ate supper, vegetable soup, and they talked about Alfred and how he would be home the following week, and how her shoulder was healing. All the time Hana couldn't help thinking this was how it used to be between them: informal and easy conversation about their lives and the people in their lives. As the meal ended, so did the light conversation. There was no more avoiding the proverbial elephant in the room.

'So,' began Gregory, after insisting he clear the table. He leaned back against the worktop. 'We've established your father is doing well. Your shoulder is healing nicely. That you'd like to go back to work at the Park. That the hens are back to laying eggs and Freddie is now potty-trained. I rather feel that leaves the subject of us. I take it that's why you wanted to call in tonight?'

Hana swallowed. It was now or never. Well, actually, another five minutes and a drink might help first. 'Could I have a sherry?'

Gregory chuckled. 'Oh dear. Is it that bad? No, don't answer. Come on.'

Hana followed him down the hall to the sitting room and perched on the edge of the sofa while Gregory poured two drinks, handing one to her. He sat down on the other end of the sofa and took a sip of the whisky he'd made for himself.

Hana took several sips of her drink, before she plucked up enough courage to speak. 'I want to say sorry,' she said, looking up at Gregory.

'You don't have to,' said Gregory, softly.

'I do. I want to.' Another sip of her sherry. She'd need a top up at this rate. She put the glass down on the coffee table. 'I'm so sorry. More sorry than I can explain. I wish there was a word that meant more.'

'What are you sorry for?'

'For everything. For . . . the relationship with Robert. For not being the wife you deserve.' She could feel the tears forming in her eyes, but she didn't want to cry in case Gregory interpreted her tears for self-pity, when in actual fact they were for regret, deep and profound regret. For hurting him, when he didn't deserve it.

Gregory didn't speak for a few moments. He swirled the golden-brown liquid around in his glass several times. 'Do you love him? Or did you love him before all this spy business came to light?'

'No. I thought I did, but it wasn't love. I loved the idea of being someone different, doing something exciting, or what I thought was exciting. I thought I would be happy. I was wrong. Happiness has to come from the heart, not the external things around a person.'

Gregory was silent for a moment before he spoke. 'After my accident, I hated myself. I hated my stupid leg and most of all, these god-awful scars. Still do, but I'm coming to terms with it all.' He moved a little closer to her on the sofa, resting his glass on the table. 'I couldn't imagine why you wanted to stay with me. I pushed you away on purpose. I mean, you deserved better than me. I didn't want you staying out of some sort of duty. I couldn't be the man you married. I wasn't him anymore.'

Hana's heart contracted at the torturous thoughts Gregory must have been having. 'I . . .' She went to speak but didn't know what to say.

'I thought you'd thank me one day for letting you go,' continued Gregory. 'That was the only way I thought you'd ever have any kind of liking for me – because I had let you go.'

Hana shook her head slowly, as a tear trickled down her face. 'I loved you with all my heart,' she said earnestly.

'Past tense, I note.' He gave a wry smile.

'Stop. I still love you, but I didn't think you'd want to hear me say that. I have no right to tell you how much I love you, not after what I did,' said Hana. 'I thought you didn't love me anymore but now . . . now I know that's not true. You were just scared, that's all.' How had she been so blind to this before now? It was all making sense. A strange, crazy sort of sense that she probably needed a psychology degree to fully dissect and understand, but here, for the first time, he was showing her his vulnerable side. By opening up to her, he was laying his heart and mind bare for her to see.

He was looking at her with his head tipped to one side. 'Say that again.'

Hana blinked. 'Erm . . . I thought you didn't love me anymore.'

'Not that bit. The first bit.'

'I still love you?'

A smile lifted the corners of his mouth. 'Say it again.'

Hana reached for his hand – his scarred hand and for the first time, he didn't recoil from her touch. He allowed her fingers to rest on his damaged skin and she felt him exhale slowly. In that touch lay every tomorrow they'd almost lost and every chance they had in the future. 'I still love you,' she repeated with a smile.

'I thought that's what you said.' He drew her towards him. 'I still love you, too. I have never stopped loving you. I was a self-absorbed self-pitying fool, and I pushed you away.'

Hana could barely breathe. 'You don't have to push me away anymore.'

'I know I haven't dealt with things well, but I'm getting help from the doctor to come to terms with what's happened. I'm trying to accept myself as I am now. Trying to banish the monster I'd let take me over.'

'I'm so proud of you for getting help,' said Hana.

Gregory leaned forward, his lips touching hers. A light, gentle kiss. He pulled away a fraction. 'Come home, Hana. Say you'll come home.'

Hana threw her good arm around her husband. 'I'm home,' she sobbed into his shoulder. 'I'm already home.'

Acknowledgements

As always, much gratitude to the whole of the Embla team who have been involved in getting this book to publication. Your feedback and enthusiasm are very much appreciated.

Many thanks to my agent Hattie Grunewald and The Blair Partnership Team.

Special thanks to my mum for being my research assistant on our trip to Bletchley Park.

Bletchley Park is a fascinating place, and I highly recommend visiting to learn about the remarkable men and women who worked tirelessly breaking codes during World War II. While the events in this book are entirely fictional, the historical resources available at the Park provided invaluable inspiration throughout my writing process.

About the Author

Suzanne Fortin writes historical fiction, predominantly told through dual timeline and largely set in France. Her books feature courageous women in extraordinary circumstances with love and family at the heart of all the stories.

About Embla Books

Embla Books is a digital-first publisher of standout commercial adult fiction. Passionate about storytelling, the team at Embla believe our lives are built on stories – and publish books that will make you 'laugh, love, look over your shoulder and lose sleep'. Launched by Bonnier Books UK in 2021, the imprint is named after the first woman from the creation myth in Norse mythology. Embla was carved by the gods from a tree trunk found on the seashore; an image of the kind of creative work and crafting that writers do, and a symbol of how stories shape our lives.

Find out about some of our other books and stay in touch:

X, Facebook, Instagram: @emblabooks
Newsletter: https://bit.ly/emblanewsletter